THE PILGRIM'S SOUL

Sam Kane

Edited By: Kathleen Bradshaw

Sage's Tower Publishing

2021 Sage's Tower Publishing

Copyright © 2021 by Samuel Kane

Cover Design © Tess Kane

Published in the United States by Sage's Tower Publishing.

Sage's Tower Publishing is a registered trademark.

Hardcover ISBN 978-1-63706-009-4

Softcover ISBN 978-1-63706-010-0

EPUB ISBN 978-1-63706-011-7

Mobi ISBN 978-1-63706-012-4

Printed in the United States of America

www.sagestowerpublishing.com

DEDICATION

This book is dedicated to Brian Adee and my loving family. May we all find the seam in the darkness that leads us into light.

This book is also dedicated to Amy Reeves and Sage's Tower Publishing. Thank you for giving me the chance to tell a story to the world.

WHEN YOU ARE OLD

When you are old and grey and full of sleep,

And nodding by the fire, take down this book,

And slowly read, and dream of the soft look

Your eyes had once, and of their shadows deep;

How many loved your moments of glad grace,

And loved your beauty with love false or true,

But one man loved the pilgrim soul in you,

And loved the sorrows of your changing face;

And bending down beside the glowing bars,

Murmur, a little sadly, how Love fled

And paced upon the mountains overhead

And hid his face amid a crowd of stars.

- BY WILLIAM BUTLER YEATS, 1893

TABLE OF CONTENTS

CHAPTER 1-FULL OF SLEEP

Simon was dying. There was no power in this knowledge, no shining light of epiphany cascading down from some high spiritual plane. A part of him had believed that certain death would make him more centered, more at peace, but instead it left him feeling ... pragmatic. Death was a simple fact, a simple statement, with everlasting repercussions. Nothing to be done anymore. Just sit and play the worst kind of waiting game, the only game left.

Cancer, stage ... some fucking thing. It was the last stage; that was for sure. The doctors had tried all they could, but the Emperor of all Maladies had decided to claim Simon Floyd for his own, and it intended to collect. Lying on a bed, attached to machines meant to keep his frail, strangely grey body functioning for a little bit longer, Simon let his mind wander. *Can't do much else,* he thought as his life danced in his head. Memories, distant and evergreen, repeated over and over in his mind. *At least I still have my mind. Thank God the cancer didn't take that.*

The chemo had failed, the prayers had remained unanswered, and his life was over. The tumor inside Simon's wasted frame seemed to pulse (though the doctors said this was impossible), and the frail man grunted as he tried to roll to his side.

Traditionally, there are four stages of cancer, depending on how big the tumor was when it was found, but Simon knew he and the rampant cell growth inside him were well past the traditional fourth stage. People don't like thinking about death, so they often stop naming things when there is still hope. But Simon knew that there weren't four stages of cancer, but five. It's almost as if society believes that if death is not defined, it might just pass them by. *After Stage Four? That's it, you're done. Don't think about it. No need to worry!* Simon laughed, a raspy sound that had replaced joy with gravel, and pushed the button that sent morphine into his bloodstream through one of the many tubes that ran from his dying body to various clicking and whirring gadgets. *Thank God for that, at least.*

He sighed and lay back into the off-white pillow. *In fact, the only person who even mentions Stage Five, the only one who has to contemplate it, is the person who is afflicted. Just another way of proving that I'm on my own for this last stretch. At least the drugs are good.* Simon's eyelids drooped, and his mind wandered, strangely, to moments when he arrested people for trying to feel exactly as he did now. *Should have gotten cancer first, you junkies.* Simon laughed again and coughed up some strange pea-green fluid. He left it on his chin. *Not exactly getting ready for a photo shoot.*

Simon had named his tumor Nero, and even had a tattoo of a violin pricked into his chest one drunken night between hospital stays. His ex-wife Anna had hated tattoos, had crinkled her tiny nose and said that they made him look like a criminal. *Good riddance to that bitch, anyway. Couldn't even come visit me before I die. Decades of our lives spent together, and she can't even come to say goodbye.* Simon's mind flitted back to an unhappy marriage, to kids who never visited, grandkids he barely knew. He grimaced and rubbed his nose, as if the past was an unpleasant odor that he couldn't quite get rid of. *Ah well, at least I never got fat.* Simon coughed again.

Never one to contemplate the hereafter, Simon found himself thinking about the afterlife almost continuously. Ever since he was forced into the hospital bed and basically told he would never leave his room alive, the old man's mind had danced between all-consuming fear and begrudging acceptance of his own mortality. He had even started becoming angry when he woke up each day. *Another Goddamn day,* he would think to himself as the medical staff slowly swirled around him each morning. Once he had tried to escape, but found his body so useless he might as well have tried to pull a boat ashore with his eyelids. Since then, he had requested his dose of mind numbing medication to be increased, and had lived in a boring but not unpleasant fog.

"Hey Mr. Floyd good morning. How'd you sleep?" A male attendant had walked into Simon's room and was checking the glowing screens that surrounded his bed. Buttons were pushed and notes were written, but Simon had no idea why.

"Oh you know, just stretching and getting ready for the marathon tomorrow. Not sure if I should wear the little yellow shorts or the little green shorts. Yellow feels more, aerodynamic." Simon weakly pumped his arms to simulate jogging. The attendant laughed. *Johnny? Johnny's his name.*

"You got me on that one Mr. Floyd." The man laughed again, squinting his eyes and absently pushing his curly dark hair back out of his eyes. *He's got a kind face* Simon thought. *I wonder if the hospital picked him to work here so people feel calm about dying.* Simon shook his head quickly, *damn that was morbid.*

"Johnny? Your name is Johnny right?"

"That's me Mr. Floyd."

"Alright Johnny. Had a friend named Johnny. Johnny Stevens. Good man. Well, Johnny, let me ask you a question: why are you spending your days with the dying?" Johnny's pen stopped moving on his clipboard, and his hands dropped to his sides as he turned to look at the old man in the hospital bed. His look softened as he took a step forward.

"Man, just coming out with the heavy questions today huh Mr. Floyd?"

"Son, I'm dying. Time isn't on my side. It's easier to just come out with it."

3

Johnny nodded. "Fair enough. I, well, I think that people all deserve dignity Mr. Floyd, even at the end. I want to do my part to ensure that."

Simon smiled. *Good man.* He looked at the young man, thinking of his own youth and the life he had led. *Glad there's people like him, out there. Kind of reminds me of Tim. Wish he was here.* Images of his son and daughter danced in his head. A strange video played of his twin children, a boy and a girl, both as babies and adults. *I wish they were here with me* Simon sighed. *But maybe I don't want them to see me like this. Got to go out alone anyway. No reason to make other people suffer.* He forced his thought to the present.

"Well, as an old dying man, I got to tell you, it's good to have you here," Simon coughed again, "but God bless it you are ugly." Johnny laughed again, shaking his head and returning to his clipboard, finishing whatever he was writing about. "Don't worry Mr. Floyd, the other nurse will be along in a moment. Yeah yeah," Johnny held up his hand before Simon could talk, "save the male nurse jokes alright? I'll see ya later Mr. Floyd." Johnny smiled again and disappeared out the door.

The old man had joked—to anyone who would listen—that he could use a pretty young thing to keep him warm if the lights were really going out for good. Simon knew it made the doctors and nurses uncomfortable, but he didn't care. The only thing the doctors saw was his disease, and the man, Simon, and his memories and experiences, were just ancillary details. Because of this, Simon relished their discomfort, as it made him feel like his words still mattered, even a little bit. *What are they going to do, kick me out?* Simon relaxed into the soft pillow behind him and stared at the ceiling.

He had already counted all the tiles that made a checkered pattern above him. There were 52, but no one cared when he told them. No one spoke to him, not really, except Johnny and one pretty nurse. The other doctors and hospital staff would just smile sadly or remain expressionless and check the various clicking and whirring devices around him. Once,

4

Simon had said that the screens attached to his life giving automaton army were touched more than he ever would be, and the nurse, a young man named Bryce, blurted, "Well we need to make sure that they work for the next guy, after ..." Color flooded his face, and without another word, Bryce left the room. Simon had laughed for days about that. He never saw him again, but if Simon had, he would have thanked Bryce for being honest with him. *They forget that us old timers have lived a full life. We aren't pets or babies. We can handle it.*

The routine of the day dragged slowly on, with Simon largely alone in his bland hospital room. Sleep, eat, bedpan, drugs, sleep again. With no schedule to adhere to, being awake at night or the day was largely the same. He barely ate, and when he did it often came back up in the worst possible way. Shifts changed, people moved around him, but Simon remained alone. The only thing that kept him consistent company were the nagging, world-ending questions.

Should he accept that the darkness sending large, finger-like tendrils toward him was the end of his existence, or should he cling to the notion that there was, in fact, something, some life, after death? Would he ever walk again, talk again, hold a woman again? Looking down, watching the tubes shoved up his nose and stuck into his frail arms pump oxygen and chemicals into him, Simon glanced at his legs and tried to wiggle his toes. He couldn't remember the last time he managed to fully feel his feet. They looked odd and alien down there, attached to him yet somehow separate, two tiny hillocks pushing the fuzzy blanket landscape toward the tiled ceiling. Simon attempted to wiggle his left big toe and received a bowel disruption for his efforts. Simon groaned and hit the nurse button. *I'm not even embarrassed about it anymore. How crazy is that?* The door to his room quickly opened.

"Mr. Floyd, is everything okay?" A young, pretty nurse with cherry-red lipstick and curly black hair peeked her head through the entrance of Simon's room. "Do you need anything?" Her voice was lyrical and honey sweet. Simon felt life follow her into the room. "Not unless you have some extra time hidden in those scrubs, though they look pretty full to me." Simon's voice cracked, which annoyed him.

Simon caught the dark eyes of his nurse and smiled his most winning smile. How he hoped against hope, with the madness of an old man, that the nurse would want to do more than simply clean him. His mind, still able to conjure up vivid images, played out a plethora of scenarios between him and the beautiful woman, though it was not with the husk of a body that he found himself in. Even when dying, even with the last glimpses of life becoming less and less frequent, like sun rays in the evening, one would be surprised how often thoughts led to sex, how strong was the desire for physical contact.

Anger flooded Simon's thoughts. *Boy, you think for one second that she wants you? All you are doing is making her uncomfortable. I mean come on, she's changing your bed pan for Christ's sake.* Simon grunted. *But God bless it, she is a good looking gal.*

"Oh, Mr. Floyd, you know I'm married, and the way you're talking makes it sound like I am fat." The nurse's smile was patient. "You sure I can't get you a juice or another pillow?" The nurse's warm hand touched Simon's own, and it felt like springtime.

"I never thought I would end up dying in front of a beautiful woman without some sort of story to tell the angels. Perhaps you can give me a little rousing tale to tell St. Peter as I cross the Pearly Gates? Not a bad dying wish, if I do say so myself." Simon continued to smile at the nurse: *Jackie? Judy?* "Now, if that isn't the best pick-up line you've ever heard, I don't know what is."

"That's pretty good, Mr. Floyd, I'll admit." *But you didn't laugh.* "Maybe tell it to me again when we both meet the angels. See what happens."

"That's a date?"

"It's a date."

The nurse finished cleaning and replacing Simon's bed pan, tucked him tightly into the fuzzy blanket, and touched his frail fingers once more. *Might as well kiss me on the forehead and tell me a story,* Simon thought, but he didn't feel upset by the idea.

Smiling, the nurse slid out of the doorway, and Simon caught a brief whiff of flower petals. *Lavender? Rose water?* He couldn't quite put his finger on it. He sighed, letting his eyes slide around the various machines that monitored his vital signs and managed to keep him alive with cold calculation and robotic efficiency. *Jesus Christ, why is everything white and beige? I'm dying, can't I have just a little bit of color somewhere?* Simon's gaze fell to a single balloon and a small teddy bear holding a heart with a "Get Well Soon" message stitched into it, placed next to the armchair by his room's single window. A single splash of red among a sea of muted colors and vaguely unpleasant smells. Simon smiled ruefully, thinking that the person who gave him that bear—one of the only people to visit him at all—had not understood the irony of the plush animal's statement. There was no getting better. He would never be well again. *You would think that these damn little hoses jammed up my nose would shut out that stench. At least I got to smell the nurse's perfume.*

Simon shook himself, feeling self-loathing rise unannounced from inside him. *Jesus Christ, Floyd, why do you have to make such a fool out of yourself? There's no way in hell that pretty nurse would ever touch you. I know you are dying, but hell, have you seen your face in a mirror lately?* The liver spots on his hands and arms made a strange tapestry as they danced underneath faded tattoos. The blotches made Simon think of dark red lakes nestled in a skin-toned landscape, though he never would have phrased it that way. He knew how he must look, with the tubes shoved deep inside his nostrils and his emaciated frame covered by a scratchy beige blanket. *Jesus Christ, I am the very picture of pathetic.* He coughed. *I hope that nurse comes back.*

Simon always thought of himself as a pretty good-looking guy. When he was young, he had thick sandy hair, grey eyes that various gals in smoky bars had called piercing—or, if they knew him and were trying to make a joke, "arresting." He kept himself in relatively good shape before his diagnosis, and his love of whiskey rather than beer had kept his stomach fairly flat for most of his life. Now, he knew that, with his hair gone and the chemotherapy wracking his body, he looked the very definition of pathetic. *I wonder where my old uniform is. Shouldn't have cut all those guys out of my life. The force would have been there for me if I had been there for them. I bet that nurse would have liked me in my blues.* Every time he saw a pretty woman, every time some sweet-smelling somebody came into his room, he still straightened his posture, looked into her eyes, and shamelessly flirted. *Simon Floyd is dying, but he isn't dead. Not yet anyway.* He stared at the wall, letting his mind dance with the ghosts of his past. Soon the world became fuzzy, and he slipped into sleep.

Simon woke with an alarming amount of clarity. He looked to the small window to his left, and saw inky darkness creeping in. A single light cast long shadows in the quiet room. Simon blinked, reveling in the clarity of his vision. *Jesus Christ, when was the last time I felt this awake?* A flutter of hope bloomed in his chest, and energy crackled under his skin. *Am I getting better?* A broad smile threatened to crack aged lips. Simon started to push himself up.

Without warning, seemingly falling from the ceiling, a cold hand settled on Simon, freezing his muscles and organs. Sweat bloomed out of his forehead, and he tried to cry out, only managing a withered rattle. His body seemed to be attacking itself, struggling to maintain function. He felt himself fighting to breathe, fighting to move, fighting to keep muscles functioning. A fear so overwhelming that it electrified his entire body overtook him. *I do not want to die. Please don't let me die. I* can't *die!* It was too soon; he needed more time. He tried crying out to God, to any entity that might give him a chance to continue, but all that came out was a garbled croak. Fire and ice swirled into a destructive yin and yang within him, fighting to keep him alive or to pull him into the final cessation of all movement.

Steadily, the ice began to gain ground. His extremities grew cold, then disappeared from his senses. The emptiness crept ever inward, pushing its way up into his chest. Within his head, Simon felt like a trapped animal scurrying in an ever-shrinking box, terrified and squealing for a way to escape, yet only finding itself spinning in a maddeningly small space. His mind flashed to a moment in his childhood when he caught a chipmunk in a small metal trap, how the little creature flew from one end of the cage to the other until it collapsed from exhaustion. Simon screamed in his head, tried to reach for the button to call the nurse, but his body had lost the battle long before his mind.

He felt his lungs stop and his heart cease the rhythm that had guided him for every moment of his life. His brain pushed all its energy into his eyes, and they frantically darted about, searching for an escape, for a way out, for anything that could be used as a respite from the inevitable. Dimly, he was aware of people darting in and out of his vision, of a flat, luminescent line on a screen to his left. He tried to scream to the people in the room, to beg them for help, but no words came, no sound burst from his mouth.

He looked at the foot of his bed, at those fleshy mounds that carried him around ever since he toddled about, placing his first steps on the soft soil in front of his old family house. He could not feel them, couldn't feel anything from his feet but an icy cold. In fact, he couldn't associate with any of his appendages at all. Feverishly, furiously, Simon tried to move the big toe of his left foot. To his dismay, his mind couldn't reach it, could not touch any of his body at all. His mind became wrapped in the cold chill of the inevitable. Simon attempted to look up, to plead with heaven, and realized that his eyes had stopped moving, that he could not force his windows to the world to close their shutters or adjust at all. Horrified, terrified, utterly alone, Simon looked at his feet in shock, until walls of black slowly closed in, and all things ceased.

What was left of Simon Floyd—his consciousness, his memories— retreated inward, a representation of his body floating on the top of a dark, cosmic sea. The body was a Self, but not in any way that made sense. It was somehow separate, yet a part of the flowing pool of time that surrounded it. As the Self moved away from the physical form it left behind, shedding the limits of the mortal world, it flipped a strange switch in the pineal gland of the brain right before it left. The Self felt, if a bodiless mind can feel, that its entire existence had become a river, a slideshow that brought forth a torrent of images. The disembodied form found itself looking at its oldest memory: riding on a fire-engine-red tricycle, slowly wheeling through a kitchen with yellow wallpaper, and watching a woman—his mother—talking to a friend across the table. She wore a red dress and had perfectly curled blonde hair, and the boy who watched her had a heart that was bursting with love.

From there, the Self was sent to a memory where it experienced its first physical injury: falling from a pecan tree and breaking an arm. The consciousness saw George Jenkins, the boy next door, running away as if the fractured bone was contagious. More moments emerged: a first kiss, the first fist fight, and the first time with a woman. The sea of Firsts marched by and through the Self, bleeding into the fabric of the universe. Each image, each moment, was of great importance to the man that had lain in a hospital bed, yet as each memory flowed passed, the Self knew, with the definitive gravity of the grave, that it would never see that image again. Each moment, as it passed on, also took a piece of the Self with it, separating and dropping into the ocean of cosmic eternity. Image after image, moment after moment sped by, and each disappeared into the ether, slowly draining the consciousness of its selfhood, until the last moment passed, taking the lights of perception with it. What was once Simon was being pulled into the river of memory, to ride the current until it disappeared forever. *This is true death,* the Self thought, but it felt peace.

Suddenly, one memory bubbled to the forefront and became sticky, and refused to join the current pulling the rest of Simon's life away. Stubborn and headstrong, this singular moment solidified itself and became a dam, simply refusing to slide away into the abyss. It was a strong memory to be sure, but not the strongest when compared to the life the Self had lived, yet it coiled and writhed, wrapping around what was left of Simon Floyd, forcing its way up the dark river of eternity and pushing itself somewhere just past the back of Simon's mind. There are no words to describe such a sensation, but to Simon, it felt as though the writhing, churning memory was searching for something deep within, until it slipped into something like a key into a lock. Something, somewhere within the recesses of what was left of the mind opened, and an entity, a force, stirred within the Self. The memory slid into the seam of reality that had opened, and disappeared from the cosmic sea.

The rest of the memories—from the mundane to moments held most dear—continued moving onward, the river of Simon's memory joining the force that held the universe together. All of Simon's life passed through and disappeared, dying like the disease-ridden body in the hospital room. The vision of the Self became foggy and dull as each memory coursed through it to join its brethren, and it thought vaguely of how a human body, if returned to the earth, can feed life with its death.

The Self's perception became more and more dim, the edges of its mental vision fogging over. A memory of Rex, the family dog that Anna had left behind when she moved to Florida, took on a grainy quality, as if doused in sand. Simon had hated that dog, its bark high-pitched and annoying. The Self, feeling more transparent and less and less like Simon Floyd, hated how the dog could move and jump, young and fresh, while it was stuck in an old, breaking body. It remembered being confined to

11

an armchair, the kitchen, and the bed, as the disease ate Simon from the inside out. Even the hatred flowed out and disappeared.

The memories continued, but Simon slowly became less and less aware of them. A deep dark blackness enveloped what was left, a shell drained of life, as the depths of the ocean envelops a pebble. Everything was washed away, and what was Simon—the amalgamation of physical response and memory that is the human experience—finally, completely, utterly, winked out.

To exist without form, without a body, is to not truly exist. Almost everything that defines a person, a human being, is linked in some way to the tissues, organs, and bones that comprise its structure. Morality, self-preservation, sex, truth, love-all are linked to the physical self. To not have a self, to not exist within the physical plane, causes whatever is left over to slide about in the cavernous region between science and faith. The Memory, the last piece of what was once Simon, moved through this place. *Moved* is the wrong word, for movement requires some form of locomotion. It would be more accurate to say the Memory dispersed, that it blanketed and filled the space around it. There was so much gone, so much of what was once a man, but this one thing, this remembrance, refused to disappear.

If the Memory had eyes, had the will to perceive in the way that humanity understands, it would see a flowing current of twilight, of forms comprised of prismatic substances that refracted light around inky darkness. The place that the Memory found itself was the point between light and matter, form and space. It was a place where the universe kept its sketchbook. Yet the Memory could not see any of these things nor be awed by the presence of light flirting with darkness. The Memory simply was.

The Memory, the aura of what once was a person, had no body, no senses, but it was aware. It was aware like the wind is aware of a rock and bends its way around it—as a seed is aware it is in soil. The

Memory knew where to go, was pulled in the direction of its purpose, as water knows to flow downstream. There is no decision to be made between the river and gravity; the water simply flows where it must. Like water hitting a dam, the Memory pooled and began to take shape.

Chapter II: Take Down This Book

When someone wakes after a long sleep, there is a moment when the body moves as the brain slumbers. Limbs unfold, and motion is generated. It is in these moments when true mindfulness exists. Everything has its place, all things are right because no thought has pushed its way into the clear pond of experience, muddying the image. Sharp senses react to outside stimuli and translate it into response and reaction by the body. Eyes adjust to light absorbed, and the small hairs of the arms and legs send information up the spinal column, alerting the brain to a cool breeze.

Slowly, consciousness and cognizance invaded the body, crashing into it like a wall of flame.

"My Name is Simon."

The thought sprung from nowhere and leapt out of the man's mouth, and it sent a lightning current through the youthful form, awakening limbs and organs with an electric pulse. Simon became hyper aware of his arms and legs, of his fingers and feet as they flexed in the light of a warm summer sun. Simon rolled his shoulders forward and back, flexing taut, lean muscle. He was standing upright, yet he had no memory of rising. Grass, about thigh-high, danced to the rhythm of a dancing breeze. Blinking his eyes into focus, Simon turned his vision outward, and felt a dizzying awe overwhelm his senses as an incredibly foreign, strikingly beautiful world stretched out before him.

A mountain range encircled the horizon, but something was wrong. They seemed to grow from the clouds toward the ground, a realization that made Simon dizzy. *Must be a trick of the light, but Jesus Christ, those things are upside down! Not all of them it looks like, but some of them are definitely growing the wrong way. Do mountains grow?* Simon's eyes quickly darted away from the upside down range, searching for something more normal to hold on to. He was quickly disappointed.

A huge ocean flowed from the cloudy sky to a beautiful valley down below, complete with white crested waves and circling seagulls, or what looked like seagulls. Rivers and creeks glistened in the sunshine as they cut through the giant valley, making their way from the giant wall of water to disappear beyond Simon's vision. *Wait, the water isn't flowing away from the ocean. It's flowing toward it!* What would have been a completely normal, if gigantic, waterfall was flippantly defying gravity and logic by flowing into the blue sky above, crashing somewhere past the clouds.

"That's not clouds, that's mist." Simon said to himself. *Where the hell am I? Why is everything backwards, or upside down?* Simon was not allowed to process such a thought, because his attention was once again drawn to a new wonder of the strange, alien world.

To the left of the vertical ocean, sprawled over hills and valleys, vegetation blanketed the landscape. Trees of all shapes and sizes butted up against each other in one giant ecological amalgamation, with pine trees dropping their cones on palms, and weeping willows growing out of the sides of redwoods. Flowers exploded everywhere. Blooms of all varieties, hailing from different climates, nestled against each other, and created a kaleidoscopic explosion of color not seen in the organic, natural world. Yet the vegetation, the forest, the water, even the mountains growing from the sky like the incisors of a giant, gaping mouth, could not compare to the vast quantities of living things running, crawling, and flying through the lush valley below the plain where Simon stood.

15

Huge herds of African elephants meandered about with giant tortoises, and a pride of lions stalked after a lumbering grizzly bear. Salmon leaped out and up from inside the vertical ocean, to be caught by a giant flying lizard with a strange combination of feathers and scales. Gigantic herds of odd, four-legged behemoths ambled next to six-foot-long bugs of a shape that reminded Simon of cockroaches, causing a visceral shudder to snake its way up his spine. *Hey, that felt pretty good. I feel, I feel amazing!* Simon looked from the madness of the new world around him and looked down. *Dear God. Now we are talking!* He let out a whoop that he immediately regretted, in case one of the strange creatures decided he would be a tasty snack, but he could barely contain his glee as he crouched down and brought his hands up for a closer look.

What had once been an old, faded memory of a body was replaced by a young and fluid organic machine. Eyes once dim now took in with sharp clarity the physical specimen Simon had not seen for many decades. He had sturdy, wide hands; strong arms; legs that did not wobble every time movement was required. Young fingers touched the top of his head, to discover that his bald, liver-spotted dome was once again full of thick, sandy hair that stuck out through his fingers. Familiar old blue jeans covered his young legs, and a long sleeved flannel shirt stuck to his chest. The jeans were soaked through, and the shirt and pants were covered in mud. Everything was the same as the moment of his memory, even the blood…

Jerking himself to the present, Simon used his revitalized grey eyes to search his surroundings for somewhere to hide. The pragmatic side of him that had served him so well for all his years as an officer was screaming for him to find shelter and warmth immediately. Simon raised his head to just above the waving grass and looked around for any form of shelter. *What is this place? Was Father Michael right after all? Is this heaven? I sure hope it isn't the alternative.*

This world, whatever it was, seemed shockingly familiar and simultaneously the most foreign concept ever perceived by a human mind. It was as if thoughts and images had been flung onto a canvas by a child, with little regard for form, structure, or the concept of gravity. The world had become a museum come to life, an art exhibit hit by a tornado, a lunatic's ramblings. Simon could not help but disappear into its weirdness.

He was so engrossed in the scenery, in the different forms of life that butted up against each other in this new world, that Simon did not realize that one of the more aggressive creatures of this world had taken an interest in *him*. Gazing about, drinking in his new surroundings, he did not see the swishing tail, the powerful muscles and bundles of sinew gliding through the high grass behind him. Had Simon turned, he would have seen powerful haunches, taut and ready to spring, with golden eyes locked on a piece of pink flesh unprotected by claws or teeth. The high grass swayed, and a powerful form slid through it, ever closer to its prey, deadly purpose set on its features. Fur and claws and teeth almost seemed to swim in the swaying steppe, so liquid was its movements. It drew its back legs to the ground and tightened its corded muscles, ready to spring.

Simon stood, attempting to look further into the valley in the hopes of finding some kind of civilization or shelter, and as he did he felt what could only be a sharp vise driven by a truck collide into his shoulder. White-hot pain shot through his entire body, and he screamed as he was thrown to the ground. Quickly he turned to face the creator of such pain, and grey-green eyes locked onto golden ones. Simon threw his one functioning arm in front of his face just in time for it to be crushed by a giant vise-like jaw. Pain as he had never felt erupted from his forearm as the bone within made a sickening crunch. With a growl, the giant lioness sunk large teeth into Simon's forearm and began jerking him about.

Kicking, fighting for breath, for space, Simon slid his bare feet under the chest of the giant cat and heaved. Timing and a shred of luck sent the predator spinning away from him, giving the man time to turn and wildly glance about for a weapon, a rock, anything. Both of his arms flapped uselessly at his sides, as he desperately looked for a defense of some kind. Finding none, Simon felt nearly overwhelming terror shoot a blazing dart through his brain as he tried to scurry away from the deadly feline. Not to be dissuaded from her prey, the lioness collected herself and ran toward Simon with breath taking speed. Looking over his shoulder, hands flopping at his sides, Air was punched out of Simon's lungs as giant paws forced him to the ground, driving his head into the dirt. Simon screamed into the earth.

Thunk!

The crushing weight of the lioness was suddenly lifted from Simon's back, and he rolled to his side to see the fierce feline thrashing and biting at what appeared to a new appendage sticking out of its side. Snapping at this new pain, the lioness attempted to attack the wooden arm protruding out of its golden fur. Mewing and bellowing, Simon completely forgotten, the giant predator fought this new adversary, never quite able to reach the shaft. Simon watched, transfixed, as the thrashing slowed to small spasms, and the fight bleed out from the animal's side. The lioness laid down slowly, panting with its tongue out, utterly spent. It locked eyes with Simon as its lifeblood stained the ground, and with another giant shudder, the giant cat lay still.

Adrenaline rushed out of Simon like an uncorked barrel, matching the pace of the red fluid slipping out of the large cat in front of him. Dizziness made the world swim, and he flopped onto the dusty earth, laying numbly on the rustling grass. Breathing heavily, eyes slipping in and out of focus, he peered at his ruined shoulder and useless arms. Somewhere deep inside his mind, a voice in Simon's head was screaming in agony, but the only sound that slipped past bloody lips was a pitiful grunt. He closed his eyes.

"You are dying and cannot be saved. Do you wish to remain or shall I end it?"

Confusion crossing his face, Simon opened one eye and craned his neck toward the sound. A man stood over the carcass of the lioness, the spear hanging loosely from his right hand. Dark, curly hair coated almost his entire body, jutting out of corded muscles. To his dim surprise, Simon noticed the hairy man was completely nude. His voice sounded like whisky over gravel as he stepped forward and repeated his question.

"Can you, not put that in my face?" Simon's words were choked and ragged. The hairy man looked down at Simon's broken body with an unreadable expression. Simon forced himself to make eye contact, to try to make sense of those eyes, dark brown and caring, but firmly set to a purpose.

"I got bit ... by a lion. Please..."

"Your clothes are foreign stranger, and they are a style that I have never seen. This must mean that you have just recently come to our land." The man crouched so that his deep brown eyes, sunken into his large face, were level with Simon's. He smelled of musk and blood. Simon cringed slightly as the naked man bent closer. "I know this is strange, and, judging from your wounds, painful, but I can assure you what I do next is for your own good. You will come back, strong and healthy. I bid you safe Return."

The man's arm twitched, and the spear lashed out. Simon felt the searing light of pain blooming from his chest and looked down to see the dark, blood-coated tip slide out of his rib cage. Disbelieving, Simon stared up at his murderer, head cocked quizzically to one side.

"You stabbed me."

The man simply looked at him, dark eyes locked onto green, refusing to look away. "You will be back soon, my new friend. A new life awaits, one without your organs residing on the grass."

"Why would you?" Simon managed to mumble, but the world seemed suddenly very far away. *I'm really sleepy.* Simon's head lolled on his rubbery neck and darkness, held at bay briefly in the corners of his vision, came rushing in like a flood, and Simon faded away.

Chapter III–Nodding by the Fire

The moment of birth is not often remembered by the new life being squeezed out of a woman and into the world. The brain has not developed enough, and the newborn does not have previous experience and understanding to draw on in order to understand what is happening to it. It is simply born. The traumatic experience of being pushed onto the planet would be terrifying to remember and would more than likely be the cause for quite a few psychotic episodes. With luck, human babies do not *understand* that they are being born, they simply are—or else humans would look at the beginning of life quite differently.

Simon did not possess the luxury of ignorance.

He awoke (a term used lightly, as babies being born are not exactly stretching their legs and putting on their slippers) to a pair of earth-shattering realizations: that he was being pushed, organically, inevitably, in some direction, and that he no longer had the ability to see. All around him, he felt a pressure, a pushing, yet when he tried to look about, his eyes did not react. When he tried to open his mouth to scream, he could not breathe. Panicked, Simon thrashed about, only to find that the motor functions he had taken for granted—his ability to move his limbs and digits at will—had all but disappeared. Those who believe that birth is a magical miracle to be celebrated and enjoyed have never been privy to leaving a woman's body with the recollection of a grown man. This was by far the most terrifying experience for Simon, a man who had died twice within a short span of time. The sheer *inevitability* of being born was enough for Simon to become walleyed, if that was an option. Screaming in his soft-skulled head, Simon continued to be pressed forward.

He felt as if his entire body was being pushed through the head of a needle after he had been dipped in jelly. An enormous pressure on Simon's skull made him terrified that his brain was going to be squeezed out of his ears. He was briefly relieved and immediately terrified again when he felt his skull shift and elongate, molding his head into a rough cone shape. Soon, crisp air completely enveloped his malleable skull, and the frigid sensation continued down to his shoulders, his torso, and his lower half as he was pushed into the world. The air became a cold blast, and Simon realized that he was naked, and the sticky goo that covered his body seemed to become slightly more solid as it came in contact with the air. *Don't think about where the jelly comes from. Don't think about it.* Simon barely had time to register the fact that he had escaped whatever prison he had been held when the sensation of being lifted by giant appendages overwhelmed him. He felt himself moved toward a destination he did not know, and that hopelessness sent a cold shiver through Simon's spine. Something shifted inside him, his lungs opened like two small wings in his chest, and he took his first, raggedy breath as a newborn, reborn babe. Tears erupted from his eyes, and his tiny cries racked the world. *I can't see! I can't move! Why won't my mouth work right?* Questions shot through his mind like bullets, overwhelming Simon and making him thrash about. His cries became more feverish.

"How is it? Is it all right?" A woman's voice, musical and exhausted, broke through the squalling of newborn Simon. "He is perfectly healthy and seems to be without any noticeable deformities. All fingers and toes accounted for. A boy." That sound was definitely male, but with a lilt that seemed to slur the words.

"Thank you for coming. I can do this myself of course, but it is always so much easier with another pair of hands." The woman's voice again. Simon felt inexplicably drawn to it.

Simon was lifted again, and those giant crane things wrapped his small body snugly into some sort of blanket. *Hands. Those have to be hands. Jesus Christ I am so tiny!* Trying to glance about, Simon realized that his neck lacked the strength to lift his cone-shaped head. He tried to escape the tight confines of the blanket, but again his body rebelled. His hands, arms, and legs were only capable of the most basic function—a jerking motion that only seemed to worsen his predicament. With a hint of embarrassment and an overwhelming feeling of helplessness, Simon began to cry again. *Get it together Floyd. You're alright. Just take everything in. You are... You are a baby now. Jesus Christ I'm a baby.* Simon tried to move his arms with more control and regularity, but they just would not agree to do what they were told.

"He's hungry. You should feed him."

"I know what he needs. I have done this a few times."

The male voice coughed. "Of course. I'm sorry. Can't seem to shake the doctor's habit of telling everyone what to do." A small laugh emanated from the woman, which caused a deep feeling of warmth to blossom in Simon's stomach.

Simon felt himself lifted again, passed from one enormous entity to another, and cradled in arms twice as big as his entire body. His neck was supported by what he thought was the crook of an elbow, and his head was guided toward something that possessed a smell so intoxicating the feeling of desire overwhelmed all other feelings of fear and reticence. As he was brought closer to the sweet-smelling entity, Simon's barely functioning eyes worked to focus on a dark, fleshy mound. An unbelievable, overwhelming desire overtook his tiny body. He wanted to put his little mouth on the source of that delicious smell. Nothing else mattered. His death, his previous life, his rebirth all paled in comparison to his desire. With all the strength that resided in his tiny frame, Simon pushed himself to that fleshy mound, latched onto it with his mouth, and experienced one of the greatest pleasures of his entire existence.

Liquid flooded into Simon's mouth, enveloped his entire body, with a feeling of supreme ecstasy and warmth. *This is like if a steak dinner and a bottle of bourbon had a baby with a chocolate milkshake.* Simon drank deep.

If he wasn't so obsessed with sucking every ounce that his tiny body could handle, Simon might have laughed. That is, if he could have laughed. He wasn't sure. Chortling and cooing, he continued to suck. Once his tiny vessel was completely filled, he withdrew himself from the nipple, deep satisfaction sliding from his mushy head to his inoperative toes.

Damn it, I think I drank too much. My stomach is not happy. Why did I drink so much? Hold it in Simon, hold it! Shit, I can't. No, no, no, no!

With a burp and a hic, Simon unloaded some of his stomach's liquid contents onto the surface in which he found himself. Wobbling his bobblehead down, he perceived a blurred angle and relatively firm surface. His best guess: He vomited on a giant shoulder or knee. Mortified, he attempted to give some form of apology to the knee/shoulder, and was rewarded with a sound that could only be described as "Bahbeblllrrrr."

Furrowing his tiny brow, Simon tried again. He focused on his mouth, on his tongue, working to form words. Struggling to speak, he was completely blindsided by the bottom half of his body rebelling against him and evacuating whatever was to be found in a newborn's stomach. Having puked and soiled himself, Simon simply gave up on speaking and was relieved to find sleep coming to take him away from such nonsense.

Simon awoke, warm and comfortable, still wrapped in the cloth he had been placed in. His bottom had been cleaned of whatever had escaped it, and his face had been wiped of all excess vomit. Embarrassed but clean, Simon glanced about him with his barely focusing eyes. Wherever he was, it was dimly lit, with illumination coming at an odd angle to his right. Movement captured his attention, and he shifted his little rubber neck to glance at a vaguely human-shaped blob. The section of the blur where the head should be shifted, moving down to come close to baby Simon. *Is this what I looked like to my own kids? Everything feels so damn enormous!* Simon attempted to speak to the giant head, but the only sound he could make was a confused coo.

"Hello little one. Welcome back. You have Returned to Mary, who lives just outside of Valoren. Move your right hand if you know where that is, and your left if you do not."

A voice, deep and immense to Simon's new ears, seemed to drown out every other sound in the room. *Seems a little weird for an adult to be talking to a baby like this.* Simon tried squinting at the human blob, but that did nothing. *But, I did see dinosaurs and upside down mountains and I'm pretty sure I was murdered by a naked monkey man, so what do I know?* Simon crinkled his eyebrows, eyes glancing up toward the blob as he concentrated on moving his hand.

A thought bloomed in Simon's chest as he worked, filling his tiny chest with warmth: he was alive! He had died twice, in a matter of minutes, hours, or days—he could not be sure—but he was gloriously, irrefutably alive. He felt his mouth form a toothless grin. *And they think babies only smile when they fart.*

"Strange. It seems like you are taking a lot longer than normal to move." There was a pause. "Maybe, hmm. Alright, try very hard this time. Move your right hand if you have Returned before," the voice intoned, sending sound waves through Simon's body. "Move your left arm if this is your first time remembering your own birth." There was a slight change in the booming voice. *It's like he's more eager, or something. I can't place it.* Simon concentrated.

Baby Simon, unsure of everything except the fact that he had been fully cognizant of his own birth and that death had spit him out twice, managed to make a slight gesture with his small, pudgy pink digits from his left hand. He pushed his tiny arm into the sky, which, after being held aloft for no more than a few seconds, began to jerk about without rhyme or reason. Simon felt the need to apologize to the loud voice about his lack of motor skills and wanted to say as much, but instead, he simply made a bubble of spit with his mouth.

"First time? Hmm. Been a while since we had one of those." The blob turned and spoke to someone Simon could not see. "Looks like you were right."

Another voice, musical and rhythmic, said something that Simon could not quite catch. His body reacted quickly to it, however, sending a lightning bolt of love and a desire to be held right into the center of Simon's brain. *That must be Mary.*

"I understand, " the human blob said to the voice before turning back to Simon. The blob's voice was much softer now. "All right, now I have no idea how old you were when you first died, but I can assure you that you are indeed a baby once again. You may be wondering how you are a newborn, how you have found yourself in this unique predicament, and I understand just how shocking an experience this must be. But fear not, for this is one of the wonders of this world. For, just as your Moment of Ascension allowed you to cross over from the old world to this one, so, too, does your ability to transcend humanity grant you the ability to come back—to Return, as we say here." The voice coughed and muttered something about "confusing wording" before continuing once more.

"Your Moment of Ascension is how your consciousness managed to transfer to this place, and who you were in that moment appeared here the second your consciousness was released from your body back on Earth. However, once you died here, that form disappeared, which is why a new body was needed. Hence, why you are a baby once more." There was a brief silence before the voice continued. "I don't know how long you survived on Dara, this place, before being killed, but since I didn't hear of a newcomer it couldn't have been too long. I hope it was relatively painless the first time you died." The blob coughed "For me, I was so terrified when I arrived here that I ran right into a dark cave. I don't know what happened next, only that I was born in Valoren a few moments later. Not to Mary of course, I am much older than she is. I have happily made this place my home ever since."

The words that were spoken fell onto Simon's ears, then promptly evaporated. *That didn't make an ounce of sense. Moment of Ascension? Return? He sounds worse than that homeless man who was convinced that he was Moses before attacking me with scissors. Jesus Christ.* Simon's arms flailed about, seemingly of their own volition. He felt tears well up in his eyes again.

"All right. Welcome to Dara, the Plane After Death. I'm sure you have a myriad of questions, and they all will be answered in time. For now, rest assured that you will be cared for during your infancy and will be nurtured throughout your young life. Miss Mary"

"Mary is fine, thank you." The musical voice in the corner of the room seemed to bring Simon a subconscious peace.

"Mary. Thank you. Your carrier, Mary, has elected to care for you herself, rather than place you with the Nurturers, something that we often do in Valoren. She will be your caretaker until such time as you can take care of yourself."

Simon's head spun as he tried to grab at any word that made sense. *Focus, you idiot. Figure this out.* He felt his head grow hot.

"Count yourself lucky that you were born here, where there are those who wish to care for you and see you grow. There are places in this world where young ones are not so lucky." A tinge of sadness tainted the booming voice, and it fell silent. Mary, the other vague shape, had come closer to stand by the booming voice. They whispered quietly, and Simon could only make out one word: Journey. He made a point of holding onto that word as best he could.

Simon looked at the two vaguely human-shaped blobs above him. Questions invaded his head, but with no way to express them, they simply planted themselves firmly within his skull and refused to budge until they were answered. *Carrier? Nurturer? Returned?* What could these words mean? Simon wondered why the doctor was speaking to him like he was an adult. *Who the hell is Mary? I'm pretty sure I'm dead but...*

With a start, Simon realized that Mary was probably the woman who had given birth to him. Was she his ... mother? Images of a smiling woman with red-gold hair flashed into his mind, along with memories of larger-than-life moments, like the time he first rode his bike as the woman watched; the moment she caught him smoking pot behind their small, white house on Queen Street. Finally his mind rested on the night with the rain, the flashing lights, and dark blood reflected off a flashlight's beam. Simon quickly pushed the last memory away, but her face, her smiling face, remained. *That* woman, that was his mother. This Mary person—she had simply pushed him out again. At best, she was an organic bus system, and his stop had been called. Simon felt poorly for being so angry at this woman, but he just couldn't help it. No one can replace a man's mother.

Painful memories flooded over Simon. Deaths, births, love—a myriad of moments fluttered through him. He felt overwhelmed by the sheer weight of his experiences, and, with a deep intake of breath, he tightened his eyes shut and began to wail. He wailed for his losses, wailed for the strangeness of his predicament. He wailed until every last drop of salty sadness was removed from his small frame, and then, utterly exhausted, he descended back into sleep.

The next few days were full of the most simplistic of routines: eat, cry, sleep, and repeat. Simon tried not to think of the fact that he couldn't clean up after himself, but he kept being reminded of the humiliation whenever hands would unceremoniously rip the strange cloth diaper off, efficiently clean his bottom half, and replace his soiled underwear with a fresh pair. *How similar the very young and the old and sick can be,* he thought mirthlessly. *Replace a bedpan with a diaper and lack of motor function with cancer, and it's like I never left the hospital.* Simon did admit that the food was much better however.

He was dimly aware of being moved from one place to another, but, seeing as he had no control over where he went, Simon resigned himself to being carried about and being passed from one set of arms to another. Memories of his old life would shove their way through the inebriation that Mary's milk would give him and send him into fits complemented with uncontrollable torrents of tears. It felt good, being able to cry without repercussions or guilt. Simon hadn't allowed himself to cry for nearly twenty years before his death. Even the passing of his father did not give Simon—in his own mind, at least—an opportunity to express his grief in any way, other than hard drinking and the occasional brawl. He had convinced himself that men didn't cry, but, since he had been Returned as a baby, he figured that he technically wasn't required to uphold the standards of masculinity that he had previously forced on himself. So Simon cried, and often.

Days became weeks, weeks became months, and Simon's eyes began to focus. He found himself able to follow objects, to focus his gaze on specific things. The colors separated around him, much to his fascination, and he was reminded of a certain trip with friends, an abandoned car they found in a field in Illinois, and three hits of LSD. When he was young and dumb, before the force took a lot of his appreciation of drugs away. The colors had blended together and swirled about, and the focusing of his eyes was similar to that sensation, but in reverse. Pigments and shades slid into their appropriate places, and Simon's world came into focus.

Mary, who was once a vague, blurry human shape, became a woman with kind brown eyes and caramel skin, cradling him and gently pushing him up to her breast to feed him. He wondered at her face, her structure, her skin. She looked absolutely nothing like him! Where her hair was dark and kinky, his was sandy and flat. Her eyes were large pools of darky honey, while his were grey and almond-shaped. Their skin tones were nothing alike at all. Did this mean that he no longer looked like himself? He had to know, cried to know, wailed at her, at the world, but all he received was a pat on the back, a nipple, and an inspection to see if he had soiled himself.

As time strolled ever onward, thoughts nagged at Simon, ate at his psyche. Was he himself? Was he invading the body of someone else, like a spirit parasite? What had happened to his old body? When he could walk again, would he be able to visit his grave, dig up his corpse, and look at his own face? What about his family, his genetics, his history? Could he go back and visit? The questions fell into his mind, latched themselves onto the edges, and refused to let go. There was nothing he could do. More weeks slid by, with an adult mind furiously trapped in an infant's form. It was nothing short of maddening.

Stubby little arms and legs slowly came under his control, and he began to reach for things, with varying degrees of success. His depth perception wasn't perfect, which led to him generally falling over himself in his attempt to grab small items that Mary had intentionally left on the ground. Though the falls were either hilarious or incredibly frustrating, Simon was happy to discover that his body was made out of malleable material. He was almost rubbery in fact, and that allowed him to bounce and fall about with little more than a slight dash of discomfort. He began to take stock of his surroundings, to be able to look past Mary's face and body and take in the larger world.

One day, Simon awoke from his small, comfortable bed and realized that he could distinguish shapes and colors with a clarity that he had previously taken for granted. Shades of brown and green flooded the room in which he found himself. Wood, polished and lacquered, made up the walls, and a circular chair built of a polished redwood blossomed out of the ground. The crib that Simon lay in seemed to be woven out of the strong, small limbs of a willow tree, sewn together by vines that looked very much alive. The soft surface that made up the floor was a bed of moss covered by a cream-colored fabric. Light was let in by small, circular windows, and since they did not have glass, a slight breeze blew into the dwelling, bringing with it the scents of the rural outdoors. Simon detected the faint aromas of wildflower and grass as they danced a slow tango into his nostrils.

Green ivy with small purple flowers crept up one of the walls, with other various flowers and plants dotted about the room. The air was clean, and Simon discovered, much to his surprise, that there were no straight lines anywhere in the room. If he didn't know better, he would have thought that he was living in a giant tree, with the furniture *growing* out of the walls and floor.

Maybe I have been born into a crazy tree-hugger's cult, out in the middle of the woods! As soon as I can, I'll waddle my way out of here and find a family member. Who would that be? My granddaughter Cassy should only be a few years older than I, depending on how many years have passed since I … died. Maybe I can convince Tim and Brittany to take me in. My son is a good man. I mean, maybe I just, what's the word, reincarnated somewhere? Maybe I'm still on Earth! Definitely no longer in Pennsylvania, that's for sure. Deep down, Simon knew that what he was saying was ludicrous, but he couldn't help but hope that he could see his family again. He just needed to get outside and see for himself. Maybe the weird upside down mountains and vertical ocean were nothing more than drug side effects. *Can't really explain the lioness, but hey, one step at a time Floyd. One step at a time.*

As his body rapidly grew, thoughts and fears bombarded his waking existence, but Simon's dreams remained strangely quiet. No manifestations of all that he had endured appeared even once in his sleeping psyche. He found it odd but was grateful that he had the opportunity to escape his predicament, if even for brief moments.

One particular morning, Simon, waking from another dreamless night, realized that he could hold his head up more than he was able to previously. With a small smile, he began moving his tiny neck and head about, looking around the room, gazing at the purple flowers growing from the wall to his left and enjoying the warmth of sunlight easing its way through the round window to his right. He laughed, a gummy, pure sound, and as he did, Simon was surprised to find that he had managed to push himself up so much with his small hand that he had toppled over to one side, landing safely and softly on his back. Elation and triumph filled him as Simon thought of how proud he was when his own children had finally rolled over. Carrie was the first, but Tim, seeing his twin learn something new, quickly followed suit. *Now your old man can do it too.*

"It looks as though you can hold your head up enough for your first lesson."

The musical voice of Mary danced over the scent of wildflowers and living things. Turning, Simon triumphantly looked at her, his carrier. He felt an overwhelming pull toward her, a near insatiable need to be picked up by her. *No! She's not your mother. Your mother died in 1967. Her name was Carol.* Simon tried to stop himself from reaching for Mary, but his arms didn't listen and shot skyward. The desire to be near her threatened to overwhelm him. Mary came over and, with strong and practiced grace, picked up Simon and placed him in the crook of her arm as she sat down on one of the chairs that seemed to grow from the wooden floor. She turned his small body to face her on her lap, so that she could look directly into his eyes. Simon struggled to keep his neck upright.

"First, let's get some things out of the way. I am not your mother. Desires and humors are coursing through your new body, screaming that you are connected to me. You are not. My Journey involves the birthing of children, which is why you came through my womb. I will explain Journeys later, when you have formed the ability to speak."

Simon stared, confused and illogically hurt by the statements. Even though he had just feverishly reminded himself that Mary wasn't his mother, to hear his words echoed by her sent a pain deep inside his little pot belly. He felt the need to pout. Tears welled up under his eyes, but he did not let them fall.

"No crying? Good. That shows that you have a generally accepting and curious spirit. That leads me to my second point: You died. Whatever you were after your Memory is gone. This is not reincarnation. This is continuation. Finally, I do not know what role race plays in your time, but it defined my entire existence during the time I was alive. You are white, I am black. Though this may or may not mean something to you, it means very little to me. Consciousness and thought has no skin color unless we make it so. That is the only distinction. It is our experiences that matter. When I died, all I could be was my color. In death, it is what I choose to be. To remember." Mary's eyes became distant and she fell silent.

So he did die. Simon felt a strange degree of relief in that. This wasn't some strange flashback where he dreamt his entire life, only to discover that he had never lived it at all. *You still don't know everything. This could still be some trick. Stay alert.* Simon mumbled, but kept looking up at his giantess caretaker. She had started bouncing Simon on her knee, which he enjoyed very much.

"Continuation is the Life after death. Now, before you start thinking of running off to find lost loved ones, reconnecting with friends who have passed on, let me tell you a simple truth: chances are, no one you ever knew made it to Dara." Mary paused after that, giving Simon time to absorb her words.

I don't think I believe her. Simon thought, with an inward smile. *If I could make it here, then you better believe that my mother is here. I just need to get my legs to work enough to find her. Or, this could be a trick, a way to throw me off from the fact that I came back to the world. I wonder what she gets out of caring for a reincarnated baby? Seems like a lot of work.* Simon babbled

As if she read his thoughts, Mary sighed, and a brief look of sadness shadowed her face. Glancing out the window, she said, "It didn't

32

matter if they deserved to die or not. It didn't matter if they were the best person you ever met. If they didn't manage to have their Moment of Ascension, they aren't here. They dirt. Nothin' to be done about it." A brief twang slithered into Mary's speech, hinting at a life in the American South. Straightening her back, Mary adjusted herself and continued.

"You see, humans are composed almost entirely of instinct. We're animals. We eat, we love, we build, all in accordance with a distinct set of impulses that drive us. Much like every other animal on the Earth you left, we have to answer to our instincts. Nothing unique or interesting about us. We live, we eat, we love, we die. That's it."

Simon cooed, and hated himself for it. Mary kept bouncing him on her knee, and Simon was surprised to find a laugh escaping his lips. Mary smiled back and squeezed his chubby little arm before continuing.

"However, as humans evolved as a species, our consciousness—our self-awareness—was created. We began to live in two places at once. Our physical, instinctive selves still moved and lived within the normal world, while our intellectual, abstract selves began to reside in the mind.

"This abstract self, and that of other humans, unwittingly started the building blocks of this place, this Dara." When Mary said the name, a breeze seemed to blow through the sound, giving it the quality of a stringed instrument.

"Here, look at this." With a gesture, Mary pointed at one of the purple flowers attached to the vines lazily climbing up the wall to Simon's left. "If humans never looked at this flower, which is called a wisteria vine, by the way, would this flower still exist? Of course it would! However, as human consciousness further developed, where we could discover, catalogue, and analyze things within our minds and place an *idea* of a thing within ourselves, then it could grow here, in this world. Wisteria began to grow in this realm as soon as someone was able to place it in their head and carry it with them, long after looking at it." To Simon's amazement, all the buds in the vines burst into vibrant purple flowers at once. He stared open mouthed as the wall became coated in rich lilac. *Did Mary do that?* Simon looked back at Mary, who continued speaking as if nothing happened.

"As people grew and thought and discussed, more and more discoveries took place. People spread around the globe, finding new species, new ideas, new ways to communicate. And as soon as those new, original ideas and discoveries took place, they appeared here." Mary snapped her fingers for emphasis.

"To live in one's mind is to reside on a plane wholly separate from the planet in which we, as a species, found ourselves, and that energy created from those thoughts crafted the world in which you and I now sit. In short, we have created our own heaven and designed our own hell."

As the last words came tumbling out, that far-off look settled on Mary's wide eyes once again. Simon wondered what was behind that stare. Mary mumbled something to herself, and Simon thought he heard the word "moonlight." Shaking herself free of a grasp Simon couldn't see, Mary continued.

"I know this is a lot, and I know that you have questions that you cannot ask, but we have found that exposing people to the facts early on allows them to adjust more fluidly. In the meantime, simply relax and grow. I do not know your name yet, seeing as you can't tell me, so I will refer to you as Sprout. Move your left hand if that is acceptable to you."

Simon gestured briefly with his stubby left appendage.

"Good. Get some sleep, Sprout. We will have lessons throughout the next few years, but for now, focus on growing and learning to talk again."

With a smile, Mary stood, her lively hair bouncing about. As she moved, Simon caught a hint of rose water. The desire to be held became overwhelming. Simon needed to be held by this woman, with the desperation of a dying man. Again, seeming to read him with a mother's intuition, Mary stopped and came over to Simon's willow crib, picked him up, and cradled him in her arms. She shifted his tiny head, opened her shirt, and guided Simon's mouth to her nipple. Simon fed until his eyes glazed over. He spit some of the delicious liquid out and fell deep into slumber.

Time passed. Once one gets over the shock of being reborn, the routine of a baby becomes quite monotonous. Though the constant eating, sleeping, being cleaned, and attempting new sounds can seem quite pleasant to a baby, to a grown man stuck within the body of an infant, it can feel like a prison. Luckily, the body also undergoes the most rapid growth during this time, and soon, Simon became fascinated by the various changes and evolutions his new body underwent. He slowly began to gain—or regain—his body's functions. His vision continued to sharpen, his fingers became capable of grabbing small things, and his feet and legs slowly returned to his control. He cried less and less, though Simon found that a good cry really helped settle his mind. He wondered if he would have had less of a temper as an adult if he had allowed himself to simply cry and release some tension. After a few moments he decided it wasn't worth much more thought.

Though the world was enormous and alien, it was not wholly unnatural to him. He had always loved moving, and he began taking great enjoyment in rolling around on the ground and trying to crawl. It felt like exercise, and Simon hadn't been able to truly exercise since he had gotten sick. It felt good to move again. Simon also began to take great pleasure in belching and relieving himself at whim. He knew it was disgusting, but still he laughed.

When Simon grabbed at objects, he had to constantly fight the overwhelming desire to put whatever was in his little hand into his mouth. He sometimes failed. Once, without thinking, he reached out to grab what he thought was a small piece of chocolate, only to rapidly discover, once he had popped it in his mouth, that it was in fact the feces of a small animal. He had never wished more desperately for mouthwash in his entire life. He didn't even know where the animal could possibly have come from. He hoped it was a squirrel that had darted in from one of the circular windows, but he couldn't be sure. *Why the hell do things still poop in the afterlife?* He wondered as he shouted for Mary to come and clean his tongue.

Before too long, Simon began to sit up on his own. He wondered if he was advancing more rapidly than he had the first time around, but seeing as he couldn't exactly compare it to his previous experience, he focused on growing and moving as quickly as he could. This new ability to sit up allowed Simon to take even greater stock of his surroundings.

The house was, in fact, within a giant tree—or, maybe a better way to put it was the house *was* a giant tree. Windows let in sunlight, and small, circular orbs embedded in the walls would light up at nighttime. They looked like the offspring of a lightbulb that had copulated with a potato, but they gave off a nice warm glow when night arrived.

Plants of various shapes, sizes, and smells littered the home, and Mary slept in a large bed that seemed to have grown from a seed, not been built. When she left home, she would open the circular door that grew out of the wall directly across from Simon's crib and descend what appeared to be a spiral staircase comprised of giant mushrooms. She never took Simon farther than right outside the door, to a deck that seemed grown out of an enormous wood knot. But each time she left, it was never for long, and she always returned before nightfall. He felt enormous relief and gratitude whenever she came back, though he tried not to admit it to himself.

Since that first, monumental discussion, Mary did not speak much to Simon, except for the occasional, one-sided banter:

"Aww, Sprout, are you hungry?"

"Is little baby sleepy?"

"Did my big Sprout make a mess of himself?"

These comments were simultaneously comforting and infuriating to Simon. If he had the ability, he would have angrily reminded her that he had lived his life, had had children, had fought for what he believed in, had cleaned up the streets for thirty years goddamn it! Yes, he was hungry; yes, he had again soiled himself; but Jesus, woman, have a heart! *Don't talk to me that way!* Yet his mouth and tongue still refused to work with him, so he simply babbled, cried, and subjected himself to the will of his giant landlord.

Mary soon started leaving Simon on the strange blanket on the ground for longer and longer, and would leave the tree house for short periods of time, letting Simon sit with his thoughts. The strange covering turned out to be grown from some sort of light colored moss and shaped impossibly into a woven blanket. He could roll around, flip over onto his stomach, and move his head around to take in the tree dwelling. He would roll to his back, gaze at the purple flowers on the wall, and think of his wife.

Anna loved the color purple. When they first moved in together, her entire bedroom suite was painted various shades of lavender, mauve, and plum. Simon didn't mind at all, wouldn't have minded if she had asked him to dye his skin purple. Tears welled up in his eyes as he thought of her smiling face. She would look lovely with those flowers in her hair. If only he could find her...

Maybe it was the thought of his wife, maybe it was the desire to pick a flower, or maybe the time had simply come, but whatever the reason, Simon found himself rolling slowly from his back to his stomach, pushing his hands underneath his chest, and heaving with all his might until he rested on his hands and knees. Euphoria enveloped Simon, and his tiny heart battered his rib cage.

Haltingly, he placed one hand forward and paralleled the movement with his same-side knee. He then did the same with his other hand and knee. He repeated the motion again and again, slowly at first, and then with more speed. He was *moving!* A smile, unabashed and exultant, cracked open upon his little face. He was moving! Simon, laughing like a maniac, sped from his moss rug and scooted his tiny body throughout the house.

The thought of his family forced its way into his mind, stunting his glee. He wondered where they were, how they were doing, how their lives had progressed. Selfishly, he hoped that they had been sufficiently sad at his funeral, then chastised himself for such a thought. They had a right to be as sad—or as happy—as they wished to be. It didn't matter. For them, he was dead.

With a start, Simon realized that, now that he had a form of locomotion, he could possibly find a way to get back to his family, to explain all of this. He paused for a moment, thinking that a baby alone in the world would probably not make it very far, but he pushed such notions from his mind. A normal baby, sure, but he was an old man renewed, not some tot who had no concept of shapes nor directions to places. With eyes fixed determinedly on the door at the other side of the tree house, Simon began his trek to freedom.

From his vantage point, with his eyes so close to the floor, the tree house felt enormous. The main room seemed to stretch on forever, and to reach the door was a trek that could parallel that of the explorers of Everest and other mountains Simon couldn't' remember. He had to stop for breaks on more than one occasion, but the fear of being placed back on the moss rug, of having to start over, would well up within him, and that fear would propel him forward again.

Finally, after what seemed like hours, he reached the arched doorway. He knew from watching Mary exit the house innumerable times that the door could be opened by simply pushing it, so as he reached the tree house exit, he lifted his little paws and pushed.

Nothing. He might as well have been trying to push a concrete wall into place. Confused, Simon tried again. And again. And again. Nothing happened. With all the reserves left within his tiny frame, Simon shoved, then slipped and bumped his tiny head on the solid wood door.

Stars exploded into his eyesight, and, dazed, Simon sat on his backside. The room became a collection of blurring watercolors, and Simon's tiny head felt like it had grown two sizes in two seconds.

Slowly, painfully, the world came back into focus. The contents of the main room snapped back into distinct shapes, and the rules of gravity slid comfortably back into place. Staring at the solid door (*oak, maybe? Pine?*), the little baby body that held Simon's consciousness contemplated its next move. How does one manage to escape, let alone find someone, when they have no idea where they are and the most simplistic of tasks seems unassailable?

Looking down at his potbelly, his near-useless legs, and his stubby arms, Simon had to admit, begrudgingly, that there wasn't a snowflake's chance on Satan's ass crack of his making it ten feet, let alone all the way to his family. Not the way he was then. Muttering to himself, which sounded like adorable baby cooing, Simon began the slow crawl back to the soft green rug where Mary had previously deposited him. The cooing sounds emanating from his tiny mouth only managed to infuriate Simon more, as they were simultaneously adorable and perfectly emasculating, yet he couldn't stop making those noises as he scooted ever closer to his destination.

Having made it back to the moss, the little baby rolled once again onto his back. The stress of the day's exertions had completely exhausted whatever energy stores the little one possessed, and with a small sigh, the young human closed his eyes. *Perhaps it is better to wait; I need my body to strengthen even more.* Impatience and stubbornness began a war against logic and wisdom, and the battle raged within the babe's mind until sleep finally called a halt to the clamor of war.

More time passed, and Simon grew rapidly. Fingers became stronger, legs began to assert their purpose, arms began to push and pull. After the disastrous attempt at escape, Simon contented himself with growing, strengthening his body, and sleeping. Little else occupied his time, and he discovered that the monotony of routine would allow his mind to slip into blissful silence. For if he remained overly stationary, if he allowed his mind to wander, it would always return to moments of blood, to the fear in a dying person's eyes. But if he allowed himself to simply be an infant—to want, to love, to eat, to sleep—such thoughts rarely clouded his mind. His old life, his previous existence, would slide into the back of his thoughts, for which he was exceptionally grateful.

Mary, as caretaker and stand-in mother, was wonderful in her own way. She maintained a certain distance from Simon, holding true to her first lesson, yet she always managed to fill the room with affection and the aroma of peace. Simon's heart would race when he saw her, and then, as if by some magic, his frame would relax and slowly slip into a utopic state of consciousness every time she lifted him into her arms. She would feed him, clothe him, burp him, and change him, all with the infinite patience of a mother. When he finally took his first steps, she was there to cheer him on and catch him. When he bruised himself or cut his tender skin on a sharp edge, she was there to ease his pain. Though he refused to consciously admit it, and fiercely held to the memories of his first mother, Simon developed a deep, loving connection to Mary. Though she looked nothing like him, spoke with a touch of the South, and maintained a degree of emotional aloofness, Simon could not deny that his affection for her had grown. Perhaps those hippies were right: Looks and creeds mean little when love is present.

One particular morning, with sun rays tickling his skin as they danced from the window to the floor, Simon lay on his back, smiling at the ceiling. The roof of the tree house was made of ever-growing circles, which Simon remembered as tree rings, and Simon was counting them. He had remembered that each ring was supposed to symbolize a year of the tree's life, and he wanted to know how many years his habitat had existed. He had counted as far as the ripe old age of 64, when another, terrifying thought forced its way to his mind's eye, pushing his counting to the side like a bully moving up the lunch line of an elementary school. Shaking the image of a cursed doctor and a death sentence out of his head, Simon tried to regain his counting, and realized he had lost his place.

"Shit."

With a start, Simon realized that his first word, his first recognizable utterance, had been spoken. How appropriate that the word, German of origin, was meant to signify human excrement. Moving his tongue around in his mouth, Simon became delightfully aware of the meaty organ that nestled in his mouth and the fact that it had developed enough strength that it could be moved at will to create specific sounds. Concentrating, tiny nose crinkling, Simon moved his jaw and tried again.

"Shit."

Giggling like an idiot, Simon kept his one note band playing.

"Shit. Shit. Shit. Sssssshit. Shiiiiiit."

"Well, isn't that just about right?"

Hands on hips, eyes cast down to look at the little tyke swearing, Mary stood in the doorway to the tree house, the sunbeams forming a halo around her. She looked like a superhero out to bring to justice those who desecrated the beauty of language. Simon's jaw clamped shut, and color rose to his chubby cheeks.

"While I'm glad that you are finally able to speak, I will not allow such language in my house. I don't know where you are from, but where I was raised, children were polite and refrained from speaking that way."

For a brief second, the smallest of moments, Simon considered listening to Mary. One side of him wanted to play the part of the dutiful son, the good soldier. Yet that was immediately tamped down by years of independence and life experience. How dare she tell him what he could or could not say? She had no right! He was a grown man. The fact that he was stuck within the confines of a tiny baby was a mere detail.

Looking Mary square in the eye, face purposefully removed of all emotion, Simon fired: "Shit."

"What did I jus' say? You think just cause you lived before you can throw those awful words around my house? Do not say it again, or so help me, I will teach yo backside to listen if yo ears won't!"

"Shit! Shit shi ...!"

The final consonant of the abhorrent term never had a chance to leave Simon's lips. With a snarl, Simon's caretaker crossed the room in two steps, upended him, spread him across her knee, and delivered three quick slaps to his rump. To an adult viewing this, one would see a young woman disciplining a child, but to Simon, it was as if someone had lifted a shovel out of the ground, still heavy from the soil, and swung it with all his or her might at his tender bottom. Pain and shock rolled through him. Tears welled in his eyes. Turning toward Mary's face, now twisted in anger, he howled:

"Shiiiiiiit!"

The resulting flurry of blows on his backside rivaled the helplessness he felt when he was jumped by three men in a dark alley back in Pittsburgh. He'd had too much to drink, gotten lost in a foreign part of town, and ended up in the wrong place. Yet the blows on his person and pride on that dark street were nothing compared to the sheer helplessness and pain that he felt as Mary struck him. His body didn't work appropriately, he wasn't the right size, he could barely speak at all. The helplessness of his situation overwhelmed him. He felt his consciousness, his personality, bend around the powerless predicament he found himself in. His psyche felt on the edge of breaking.

Finally, after what seemed an eternity, the spanking stopped.

"Are you going to say that filthy word again?"

Silence.

"Good. I'm sorry I had to do that. I would say that it hurt me more than it hurt you, but you and I both know that is a lie, given the circumstances."

Silent tears flowed out of Simon. He had never felt so overwhelmingly powerless. Hatred bloomed in his chest for this woman, this *creature* who had assaulted him. The pain was nothing compared to the blows to his pride, to his belief in his own independence and autonomy. Thoughts of murder, of revenge, flooded his brain, a photographic gallery of destruction erupted in his mind's eye. Somehow, some way, he would have his revenge.

"Come here, little Sprout." Mary picked him up and placed him at her breast. Cradling his head, she undid her blouse and placed his head at her nipple.

There is no goddamn way I am feeding off of this rancid woman. There is no way. I'll die first! Yet even as the thought entered his head, the desire to eat, and, surprisingly, the desire to be held by Mary, overtook his consciousness. Opening his mouth, he began to suck. *Maybe just a little. Goddamn, I know she just hit me, but I want it. I was being an asshole, after all; maybe I deserved it. God only knows what I would do if my own children acted this way. No! I am a child, an infant, and she is an adult! How could she? But I need her.*

Slowly, Simon's anger was replaced with a desire to please this woman, to behave. More than anything, it was the fear of being struck again that pushed his thoughts of vengeance aside. He felt like a coward, like an ant under a soft slipper, but he could not shake the fear and desire to please. Against his better judgment, he finished feeding and nuzzled up against Mary. Her smell filled his nostrils, and her heartbeat drummed through him as he lay against her chest. Never again. He would never again displease this woman. He loved her, right? That made sense, didn't it? Just behave, and the pain wouldn't come back.

Such it was for the next few years. Simon would listen and behave to the best of his ability, occasionally make a mistake, and pay the price. Each time Mary struck him, anger and hatred returned in a torrent, only to be replaced by a desire to please and make Mary happy. Part of him knew that this was wrong, but he couldn't seem to help it. The next few years were simple: eating, learning to talk again, finally walking, and teetering about the house.

As he grew, Simon noticed that Mary no longer allowed him to venture onto the porch with her, and every time she left, he discovered that she would lock the door to the outside. The windows were too high for him to reach, and the furniture, though beautiful, was firmly in place, so escape was out of the question. After a few years, Simon realized that he had accepted his fate. The years passed, and Simon grew.

CHAPTER IV—DREAM OF THE SOFT LOOK

"Sprout, you need to get up for your next lesson. Wake up, Sprout. It's time."

With eyes foggy from sleep, still adjusting to the early morning light, Simon roused himself from his tiny bed and sat up. Stretching his arms luxuriously, he kicked his blankets, woven out of the same moss he used to roll on as a baby, off his feet and swung his legs down onto the wooden floor of his bedroom.

"Simon," he said.

"What's that?"

"Simon. My name is Simon."

"I like Sprout."

"Okay."

This had happened too often to count, and Mary still refused to call him anything but the nickname she had given him. Simon had accepted it, but it didn't stop him from trying to remind Mary of his name every morning.

"Get up. Get dressed. It's finally time for you to come to town with me and see the world you have been reborn into."

With a start, Simon's grey-green eyes widened. He was finally going to be able to see more of the world than just the tree house and the glen that surrounded it. *I finally get to leave this strange prison! I can finally see what this world looks like, or, maybe, escape whatever lab they have grown me in.* Simon wasn't much of a science fiction reader, but he had seen movies of people that had been cloned and placed in weird areas to grow

45

up. Maybe Mary was the scientist he had been given? Ideas swirled in his head, threatening to overwhelm him.

He had prayed of this moment, wished for it, had thoughts of making a dash for the door almost daily, but the memory of Mary's discipline, along with a securely locked door, had always stayed his little feet.

Yet today, after all this time, he could finally leave! He could finally put to rest his nagging doubts and see for himself whether the stories Mary told him were true. *I can't wait to take in everything with my own eyes! Seven years, give or take, is much too long to be stuck in one place.*

Jumping out of bed, Simon hurriedly dressed, putting on the blue shirt that Mary had provided for him, and shoved his skinny, pale legs into the animal-hide pants he had seen her sew. They were quite large, so he had to roll them up a few times at the bottom and use a rope to hold them up at the waist. Mary said he would grow into them and that there was no point in creating anything that was only useful for a short time. "You'll be making your own clothes soon anyway," she had said, so matter-of-fact, though Simon hadn't sewn a stitch a day in his life. Images of children wearing overly large pants and jumping onto trains jumped into his mind, a garbled picture from an old television show, then quickly disappeared. He knew he looked ridiculous but didn't care. Tucking his oversized sky-blue shirt into his giant leggings, he quickly tied the rope that served as a belt around his waist. Fully clothed, he looked at Mary, his small features rippling with anticipation.

"Before we leave, there are some things we need to discuss. Let's eat and talk," Mary said.

Nodding, Simon rushed out of the tiny alcove that was his bedroom to the main room, where fresh fruit and juice waited for him in wooden bowls on top of a flat, circular table. The table was a solid piece of wood, grown out of the floor and mushrooming at the top. He had asked Mary about how the furniture had sprouted out of the floor, how the bowls and cups he ate out of showed no cuts or signs of being shaped. She had told him, with a straight face, that she had grown them, had altered the shape of seedlings to suit her needs. Silently adding her explanation to a long list of responses that made her seem insane, Simon dropped the subject.

Wanting to be fueled for his exodus, he dug in to the sweet melons and oranges and gulped down fresh water that held a hint of herbs. As he ate, Simon thought of all the times he had tried to see what was outside the ring of trees outside his home, what secrets of his predicament Mary hid from him. As he dug in to his breakfast, Mary took a seat next to him, her white blouse without wrinkles, a rich brown skirt flowing to her ankles. Her dark hair seemed larger today, making a halo around her heart shaped face. Simon pushed aside the desire to touch those curly ringlets.

Simon's mind flitted to previous conversations he had had with Mary where he pleaded to see the outside world. *She always says, "It's too dangerous" or "You'll get eaten." I see right through that. Just wait until I get a chance to get out of here. Just wait.* Simon kept eating and tried to hide the small smile that threatened to invade his mouth.

Looking at him, face unreadable, brown eyes like deep pools in a shady forest, Mary began to speak. "As you know, Dara is where consciousness manifests. It is the place where discovery and unique thought reside. Where you and I originally came from, the Earth was comprised of the building blocks of life: atoms, molecules, particles that would bond together according to natural laws that govern the world."

Taking a deep breath and smoothing an invisible wrinkle from her blouse, Mary straightened and continued.

"The world that you find yourself in now does not abide by these natural laws. In fact, the building materials are completely different. On Earth, everything has a place and natural laws to cater to. It's just like that here, only the rules are different."

47

"I know all this stuff," Simon blurted out, the words dancing around a bite of cantaloupe to escape his mouth. "When can we go outside?" Excitement bubbled inside him, made him dance on the edge of becoming manic.

"Sprout, don't interrupt me! If I so decide, I can lock you in this room and keep you here until you calm down. Do you hear me?" Simon bit down a retort and turned his gaze downward. Mary clucked in approval.

"Good. As I was saying, the world you find yourself in now was not built by atoms and bonds. It is the byproduct of consciousness. As a result, the rules of nature have been bent, and sometimes, even broken entirely."

Opening his mouth to reply and receiving a glare from Mary, Simon bit off the question that had formed in his mind. Perhaps Mary would answer it anyway. The feelings of dependence, affection, and hatred all warred within Simon as he forced himself to choke down the words trying to fight their way out of his mouth.

"Good, Sprout. Thank you for not interrupting. Now, what you will see has little to do with the laws of nature. Things show up in Dara when they are discovered and analyzed on Earth. The more detail discovered, the more it appears here. Think back: Can you remember the moment you first came to Dara? The lioness and the naked man?"

Flashes of red teeth and vicious claws erupted in Simon's mind. The pain of jaws clamping down, of wild eyes and the slash of a spear— dozens of images competed for his attention. Wiping the sweat that had blossomed from his palms, Simon nodded.

"Well, I know that you told me he made you Return."

"He stabbed me in the chest with a spear."

"It was for your own good. No use in you sitting and suffering when you can simply Return to try again. Now, if I recall correctly, you said you were looking at some upside-down mountains and a vertical ocean?" Simon nodded again.

"Physics denying mountains sprouting out of the sky, water flowing upward, animals being nothing but skeletons, and strips of flesh, all live and thrive here in Dara. No one truly knows why these things happen, only that they do. A few people believe that there is an actual correlation between where the discovery took place on Earth and the location of where they end up in Dara, but I think they are barking up the wrong tree. But hey, how would I know? I worked on a farm before I Ascended." Simon desperately wanted to ask about Mary's past for what felt like the hundredth time, but his caretaker simply barreled forward.

"What you are going to see when you walk out that door is going to be both incredibly familiar and wholly foreign to you. Stay close to me, do not wander off, and do not get hurt. Here in Dara, people are much more likely to kill you rather than heal you, seeing as we are all destined to Return anyway." Mary paused, looking Simon dead in the eye, waiting for her words to truly sink in.

Well, that part makes sense. Can't have a bunch of people nearly dead wandering around eternity. Doesn't seem like they invest a lot in doctors and health care, probably for this reason. I wonder if people of faith paid less for medical care when I was still alive. I bet they banked on something like this being around. Simon shook himself slightly. *But keep your head on straight Floyd, this could all be a trick. Know the facts. Goddamn it, but if I run, Mary is going to tan my hide so much my backside will look like a leather purse.*

Simon tried to shake the fear of Mary's punishment and couldn't do it. *Damn that woman!* Nodding, Simon turned to face the doorway to the tree house. With a quick jerk of her slender neck, Mary nodded.

"Now, finish your breakfast, Sprout. We're going to be walking all day, and you'll need to keep those little legs moving."

Mary stood, smoothed her skirts, and walked to the door. Simon quickly finished his fruity repast, rose, and joined her. Pausing for a moment for what Simon swore seemed to be dramatic effect, Mary turned and opened the door to a world that seemed to have been swirled around God's mouth and spat out.

The door of the tree house opened to the knotted deck, with the mushroom staircase spiraling down the trunk of a huge oak. Giant, reaching branches slid down to the ground before rising many feet above Simon's head, their green leaves sprouting everywhere, bursting with life. Though he had seen the porch before, Simon was still taken aback by the fact that it seemed to have grown from the tree itself, without any human intervention. In fact, life seemed to burst from every corner of Simon's vision.

Just outside the tree house door lay a world that hit Simon full in the face with its vibrancy and extravagance every time he saw it. The tree house grew in the center of a glade encircled by trees that exploded into a kaleidoscope of shapes and colors. Reds and yellows collided with purples and greens, all fighting for Simon's attention. The sounds of animals cooing, cawing, and rustling filled Simon's ears. Flowers spouted haphazardly from every nook and cranny, some even growing right out of tree trunks at odd angles, and their sweet aromas tickled Simon's nostrils. The sun, a blasting ball of pleasant heat, lazily rested directly above Simon's head, beaming down bright rays onto the vivid landscape.

From his vantage on the porch, Simon could make out a wall of water, far in the distance, cascading from the sky and disappearing beneath the tree line. Surrounding the vertical ocean far off to his right, dark grey clouds were forming, partially obscuring the wall of water and the looming mountain range poking through the clouds, some reaching their jagged mountaintops toward the ground, and others climbing into the fog as mountains should grow. Both the vertical ocean and upside-down mountains were visible just above the tops of trees. They must have been very far away, as they took on the blurred outline and slightly blue color that objects possess when seen from a great distance.

Beautiful, whatever and wherever I am. It's beautiful. A roar echoed off the trees in the distance. *Beautiful, and Goddamn terrifying. That sounded like a lion and a thunderclap. Definitely need to stick close to Mary for this expedition. Jesus Christ I wish I had my gun. Hell, I wish I wasn't seven Goddamn years old or however old I am. I'm so small!*

Simon's thoughts whirled through his head, his assumptions roughly pushed out by his observations. His belief in and his hope for being able to escape to find his family were being shaken out of his head. Even though he had played in the leaf covered earth at the base of the tree house, he had always assumed, somehow, that if he were to leave the small circle of trees that the normal world would rise up to meet him. With Mary inviting him to walk into the forest for the first time, Simon realized that he no longer felt sure. His heart began to race in his small chest, and sweat sprang up from his forehead. His breathing became ragged. His eyes couldn't seem to focus on anything in particular. Knees shaking, he grabbed at the smooth railing of the tree house deck and forced himself to remain upright.

"I remember the first time I chose to leave the safety of my own first home. I threw up on the ground and fainted. I remember not believing my first carrier, thinking that she was tricking me somehow. Imagine my surprise when I saw all of *this*." Mary gestured at the cacophony of colors and sounds that overwhelmed the landscape. She placed her hand on Simon's shoulder, and he closed his eyes, thankful for the hand's warmth and pressure. He consciously worked to slow his breathing.

Hands gripping the railing so hard his knuckles whitened, Simon finally looked back at Mary, his eyes betraying his longing to return to the safety of the tree house, to escape the harsh realities that were forcing their way into his mind. He was not on Earth; he would never see his family again. Secretly, he had been clinging to his old life, believing somehow that he could return to who he was. He thought of his old house on Wharton Street, of small children playing in the small backyard. *I'll never see them again.* Tears welled up in his eyes, and he angrily fought them down. *You don't know that!* He thought angrily. *Let's get into this town and see what we see. You don't know what's on the other side of the trees.* Yet, though he tried to convince himself that this could be plausible, deep inside his mind Simon knew it was a lie.

"I know this must be hard, the *truth* of it. The fact that I wasn't just telling you a simple story. The only way to get past it is to move through it." The Southern twang that slipped into Mary's speech whenever she was sad or angry glazed over her words like thick syrup. "Best we get moving." She muttered

Taking her eyes from Simon, Mary descended the fungi steps and picked something up that was leaning against the giant trunk of the tree. Sunlight glinted off a metal tip, and Mary gripped the wooden shaft with a high degree of familiarity. A giant owl hooted above Mary's head as she turned to face Simon.

"Come on down. There are things you need to see and a lot to learn."

Taking a deep breath, Simon released his grip on the railing. His knees wobbled slightly, but he willed them to straighten, to support his small frame. Thoughts still careened in his head, screaming at him, and he tried to force them back into the dark recesses of his mind. Images of his wife, his children, his work, invaded Simon's inner world, threatening to drown him in a never-ending cascade of hopelessness. Tears and sweat poured from him. Yet somehow, he managed to keep a grip on his sanity, to not devolve into a heap of weeping bones and skin. He forced himself to focus on small things, like taking a step toward Mary, or getting his breathing under control.

Small steps to manage stress was a trick he'd learned at the Academy, and as his thoughts and sweat glands were brought to bear, Simon silently thanked Frankie Johnson, his first partner, who trained him all those years ago. *I never really thanked the old bastard.* Images of

52

an old squad car swirled with memories of bitter coffee and cigarette smoke, and Johnson's voice cascaded over it all:

"Don't think too big. Focus on the small things when you're in a bad place. Are you hurt? Can you escape? Where are you? Can you breathe? Keeping it small and simple keeps you calm. Can save your life one day. You remember that." Simon did, and was thankful for it, *but I bet Johnson would have crapped a turkey if he saw where I am now!* Simon took another step downward.

Descending the soft, spongy steps helped Simon regain his composure, and by the time his feet landed on thick green grass and warm soil, dotted with falling leaves from his giant arboreal abode, he felt as though his body was his once again. It is amazing how simple movement and motion can calm the mind. It is standing still, laying stagnant, that allows the brain to truly devour itself. A human being is a species meant to move, and the mind always seems to right itself with a certain amount of locomotion.

Mary smiled briefly when Simon finished his descent, seemingly happy he had managed to overcome yet another overwhelming experience. She shouldered the hefty walking stick that was leaning against a tree trunk and motioned with it toward a well-worn path etched into the ground by thousands of boots—a path that curved around the tree house and meandered into a forest dense with growth. The walking stick glinted dully in the sun, and Simon quickly realized that it was actually a spear with a thin, leaf shaped tip at the top. Shadows played with the wind as Simon's vision turned from the spear to gaze down the beaten trail. How many times Simon had thought about running down that path, how many times he had almost sprinted down the packed earth, he could not count, but now that he was actually going to walk it, he felt as though he was unprepared.

"We'll be heading into the town now. Shouldn't be any problems, but just in case..." Reaching into the folds of her skirt, Mary withdrew a small knife, the handle worn with use. The blade was tucked into a scabbard made out of dark, hardboiled leather. Reaching out, Simon grasped the handle and tucked the knife into the rope that served as his belt. It felt good, having something to protect himself. *But a knife? Why a goddamn knife? I am small as hell. I need something with some more punch.*

"I need a gun."

Mary looked at Simon, face unreadable. Simon forced himself to meet her eyes.

"I am three feet tall and made out of bird bones. A knife is nice, don't get me wrong, and thank you, but I need something better. You said this place is human thought, right? Well, I thought about guns a lot when I was alive. Where are they?"

Mary didn't say anything for quite a while; she simply stared at Simon. *Why is she just staring at me? She just gave a child a knife, and now she is looking like I slapped her with a dead fish.* Simon met her gaze. Moments passed. Finally, Mary spoke.

"There are so many ways to end human life here, Sprout. You can light their clothes on fire simply by speeding up the molecules that hold the fabric together. You can hurl sharp wind through someone's eye by compressing a vortex down to the size of a needle. Yes, there are guns here, but those who wish to kill simply find them to be primitive. That knife is really to make *you* feel safe. Do not forget where you are." Simon looked down, feeling strangely ashamed, *like a damn chastised child. Wait, what about the wind thing again?*

"Can you teach me to shoot a wind bullet into someone's eye then?"

Mary ignored his question. "Remember what I said. If you get hurt, people will be just as likely to kill you as help you. Sometimes it's just easier to let you Return than to try and heal a poisonous bite or serious injury. Got it?"

Simon nodded.

"Good. Another thing: There hasn't been a newly Returned in a long time, at least not here. I will try to keep that a secret for as long as I can, but as soon as it gets out that you are new, you will be overrun with people, and not all of them will have your best interest at heart. Stay with me and stay silent."

Her leather moccasins gliding across the dirt, Mary set off, spear over her shoulder and back straight as a bar of iron. Simon, after pausing to contemplate what Mary had just said, scurried after her, his own homemade slippers barely making a sound as he trotted up next to the woman. Mary glided through her steps, her motions fluid and easy. As she walked, she began speaking, looking straight ahead, assuming Simon would listen without even bothering to check and make sure that he was there. Simon had to quicken his pace, and he found himself missing the long strides of his previous body.

"The town we are about to enter has been around for a very, very long time. Almost since the beginning of this place. The people keep the more dangerous creatures away, though a lion or mammoth has been known to slip through and wreak havoc before it's put down. You should be safe, Sprout, but be on your guard just in case."

Simon's eyes darted to the undergrowth, and his pulse quickened. They had walked into the dense forest, where the sunlight flitted among the trees, giving the place a mystical, fantastical air. Simon stifled a laugh. *Everything was fantastical. Why would the forest be any different?* Yet his chuckle caught in his throat when Simon remembered what Mary had said about lions and mammoths. Almost without realizing, he inched closer to Mary's brown skirt.

"Now, the people you are going to meet, they are going to be a *surprise* at first. Some have lived in this village for millennia, others only a century, so you can imagine the differences in opinion. Stay away from the Greek. His view on ... *relationships* would come as quite a shock to you."

Confusion danced over Simon's face, but he said nothing. He had a friend, Nick Stephanopoulos, who was Greek. Kind of loud and prone to sticking to his opinions, sure, but never shocking. Maybe Mary didn't like Greek people for some reason. As he looked up at her, Simon's face became quizzical. He never thought much about race personally, but judging from her accent, she must have lived her life where people still held on to certain beliefs about skin color. *I bet she knew some racist Greek people.* Settling on the belief that she had a strange prejudice against Greek culture or attitudes, Simon turned his eyes back on the road and kept pace with his caretaker's long strides. As he was thinking about Mary's prejudices, the woman had continued speaking. Simon snapped his focus back to her voice.

"People of different periods of time have different opinions on things. Some opinions have changed as the people have progressed through their Journeys, and some have not." Mary stopped in the middle of the path and turned so quickly to face Simon that her curly hair bounced and swayed. Her brown eyes looked as though they could chip a diamond.

"You listen here, now. If you make it here, if you make it to Dara, it doesn't mean you're *good*. It doesn't mean you were a *good person*. All it means is that you managed to step outside of your own instincts and base impulses, creating a part of yourself separate from your physical body, which kept you from completely dying." She extended a slender brown finger and jabbed it into his chest. "You can eat a pie by baking it or stealing it. Either way, you get to taste something sweet. Keep your head on a swivel, don't be afraid to use that knife, and don't find yourself alone with the Greek!"

Satisfied, at least for the moment, Mary turned and began striding down the road once more, curly hair bouncing with each step. Simon, for seemingly the thousandth time that day, had been struck speechless. After the events of the morning, of finding his world turned sideways and upside down, the boy had begun to feel as though he was gaining at least a semblance of understanding regarding his current predicament. However, the new information that Mary had just force-fed his mind had again cast all of his rudimentary understanding aside, like a gust of wind blowing down a house of cards.

A sudden idea stopped Simon. He grabbed the sleeve of Mary's blouse, and his caretaker, a flash of annoyance on her face, turned and looked down.

"Is, is God here?"

Annoyance bled into a soft smile on Mary's face. "That, Sprout, is a question I am not meant to answer. It is a question I do not want to know the answer to. Maybe you will discover such a truth one day, but for now, be silent and listen."

Lost in thought, Simon walked with Mary through the trees. Though she continued to speak, Simon barely heard her. He was preoccupied with the idea of God, which inevitably led him to thoughts of his family—how he hoped they were here, or somewhere.

The sunlight was warming, and the light dancing through the leaves gave the morning a cheery, relaxing atmosphere—a sharp contrast to his current mood. He fought down the childish urge to hold Mary's hand as they walked on the path of packed earth.

After a time, Simon saw the forest thin and the shade of the trees recede and be replaced by the sun sending its warm rays cascading down onto open ground. The path sloped upward slightly and gave way to high grass and open fields. As Simon ascended the sloping path with tall, swaying green blades on either side, a memory of claws and teeth again flashed through his head. He gripped the worn leather hilt of the knife Mary had given him and darted his eyes back and forth, worried that at any moment something would spring up to end his newly begun life.

As Simon and Mary walked, the tall grass became shorter, and in the distance, Simon could make out buildings jutting out of the horizon. As the pair approached, the structures came into focus, and the town began to take shape. Simon could see buildings butting up against each other in the distance, and his heart began to race at the thought of meeting the people of this strange world. Both sides of the well-worn road were lined with trees and shrubbery, well-manicured and tended, with foliage pruned to resemble animals and people. As he walked closer, Simon could make out the shapes of the buildings, and his mind immediately jumped to pictures of ancient European towns that he had read about in a world history class.

Jesus Christ, what does this remind me of? What are those festivals where people dress like they lived in the middle ages? It's on the tip of my tongue. Damn. What a weird world.

Soon, Simon's feet led to a bridge that stretched over a murmuring creek, crafted from a muted beige material that had the appearance of cement with exposed stones, growing from one bank and cascading down to the other. Simon could make out the shapes of people milling about, unhurried but purposeful.

As they strode to the bridge, Simon glanced down into the crystal-clear water of the small stream that meandered along the outskirts of the village, and his breath caught in his throat. Salmon danced out of the water, silver scales glistening, and alligators caught them in their mouths as they descended. *Never see that in the real world,* Simon thought as the alligator munched happily on its shining treat, scaring a school of multi-hued fish and creating a rainbow of scales flashing in the sunlight.

As Mary and Simon approached the opposite side of the bridge, Simon saw that the cobblestones and cement that made up the bridge were not what they had appeared to be. The cement was sand from the riverbank, and the cobblestones were, in fact, river-smoothed rocks. The bridge looked as though it had sprouted from the riverbed and leaped across the clear waters of the river to take root on the opposite shore. Beauty surrounded him, engulfed his senses, flirting with his nose, his ears, and his eyes.

Walking across the bridge and into the town proper, Simon looked up at the squat, single-story buildings, made of a dark wood and carved with intricate designs. Signs with various symbols stuck out from just above open doors, signaling that these buildings had wares to sell. The open doors allowed the sweet-and-sour scents of industry to dance on the road. With his eyes whirling about, Simon was nearly giddy with the overwhelming magic of the small town.

At first glance, the place could have been a small village in England or Scotland, quiet and well-maintained. Yet the façade of normalcy quickly slipped off its mask when given a closer look. As his eyes danced about, trying to look everywhere at once, Simon knew that this wasn't going to be like any place he had ever visited in his first life.

Two dancers, hewn into shrub, looked at first to be blowing in the breeze but were, in fact swaying to a rhythm wholly different and distinct from the soft wind. It took the female dancer's second pirouette for Simon to realize that the shrubs were dancing. Simon's eyes darted among the other shapes carved into the local flora. Animals moved as best they could with roots attached to the ground, birds extended large green wings to expose a plethora of multihued flowers underneath. Everywhere, the plants seemed to dance and sway in accordance with the way in which they were cut.

As Simon continued to take in his surroundings, his apprehension and wonder grew, and his pulse quickened. Nothing seemed to work the way it was supposed to. The people, for instance, wore clothes from a plethora of time periods. The first person he could make out as he entered the village proper was an older man with striking blue eyes and cotton-white hair, sporting a fur cloak of animal skins and a kilt of patchwork cloth that hung to his knees. *Some kind of Viking, maybe?* Chatting amicably with the white-haired man was another resident, seemingly in his middle years as well, with a woolen suit, sharp eyebrows, and a downturned mouth with wrinkles on the sides that spoke of continuous concentration. Other people milled about, sporting tunics, cloaks, leggings, dresses of all cuts and fabrics, and clothing that Simon did not quite have a name for. *This place looks like a strange comic book convention that took a wrong turn and ended up invading a village in the English countryside.*

The homes and buildings of the town also became stranger and stranger upon a slightly greater degree of inspection. Simple one-story homes had the appearance of houses that had grown out of trees and bushes, with green leafy canopies for roofs and interlacing branches for windows. Like Mary's tree house, the buildings seemed to have been *grown,* not built. Looking down the various side paths that feathered out from the main road, Simon saw similar dwellings, with some made out of solid rock. This was no longer a simple, rustic village, and Simon felt like he had fallen into a fantasy author's rough draft.

So entranced was he with the village and its inhabitants, that Simon did not notice the small rock protruding haphazardly from the well-worn road. He barely had time to yelp in pain before he fell flat on his face. He heard Mary attempt to hide a chuckle by coughing, and his face reddened. White-hot anger and shame exploded from Simon as he picked himself up, dusted off his now-soiled blue shirt, and kicked the rocky culprit. He hated being seen as weak, hated being seen as clumsy, and he hated crowds. He directed all that hatred toward the rock that had caused him such embarrassment, wishing for it to turn into dust.

As soon as his small foot, encased in his moccasin, connected, the rock exploded into tiny particles that burst into the air. Bewildered, Simon leapt back with a yelp, and fell right back down onto his backside.

"Careful, Sprout! You aren't ready to Change things yet."

Mary's voice cut through Simon's disbelief and wonder as he stared at the empty space where the rock had been. Simon locked eyes with Mary, confusion all over his little face. The townspeople, hearing the commotion, looked briefly at Simon, then returned to their business. With a sigh, Mary continued.

"Right. You have no idea what I'm talking about. Well, you see, Sprout, this whole place is built from human consciousness. It only stands to reason that human consciousness can manipulate it. You were angry and embarrassed that you fell, and you directed your energy toward that thing that was the cause of your anger. See those houses that seemed to have grown from the ground without any help from a person? Those are trees that have been Changed. Plants and rocks are the easiest to work with, but the animals are extremely difficult and often just snap back to what they were. We don't really know why. People cannot be Changed at all, so don't even try."

Giving him a meaningful look, Mary lazily hefted the spear on her shoulder and stared at Simon, waiting for any questions he might have.

"Why doesn't it…" Simon cleared his throat. He was still surprised to hear the high, juvenile voice coming from his mouth. It always took him aback, which might be why he hardly ever spoke.

"Why doesn't it work on people and animals?

"No one really knows," Mary responded, "but some believe it has something to do with humanity being separate from Dara. Perhaps it is consciousness that allows us to remain unmalleable. That would make sense with animals, too. The more self-aware the creature, the less likely it can be manipulated. Funny how that made just as much sense in my old life."

Mary chuckled, and Simon just looked at her, wondering whether or not Mary was completely out of her mind. *I mean, if she is what she says she is, she must be really, really old. That has to do something to the mind, doesn't it?*

Seeing that Simon did not appreciate, or even understand, her joke, Mary continued. "There are things that you can do here, Sprout, that you couldn't even dream of before. This world is much more malleable, more open, than the place that you left. Try it. Make that stick over there move."

Mary gestured over to the left-hand side of the walking trail, pointing with her spear at a gnarled stick crowned with dead leaves lying on the ground.

"How do I ..." *damn childish voice!* "How do I do it?"

"Think of what a stick's natural purpose is. What does it do?"

Simon stared at Mary for a moment, wondering if it was a trick question. "It's a stick. It doesn't *do* anything."

"Right, but what was it *before* it became a stick? What was it attached to?" Mary smiled slightly.

"A tree? Or a bush maybe. It was a branch."

"Excellent! Well done Sprout." Simon felt a surge of pride. He couldn't help it.

"So you must Change the stick according to what it already does naturally. You can alter the shape, the pace of the item, but it must be according to its nature. So, what does it do?" Mary looked at Simon expectantly.

The boy was quiet for a moment, thinking furiously. *I can't help it; this feels like a trick. What does a stick do? What do trees do? What does a branch do?* Simon had a thought, but it felt silly. He hesitated, but finally spoke:

"It, it grows?"

"Wonderful Sprout! Well done. Yes, it grows. So, reach into the stick with your mind, and make it grow until it reaches your hand. You can do it." Mary looked at Simon, waiting.

Looking from Mary to the stick and back again, Simon briefly wondered if he was being made fun of, if his caretaker would wait for him to focus completely on the stick and then laugh at his expense. Trust never came easy for him. Yet Mary just stood there, neither overly interested nor disinterested, her spear over one shoulder and the opposite hand on her hip. Not sure if it was a trick or not but willing to give it a try, Simon turned to face the piece of wood hanging haphazardly to the side of the path.

Alright stick, it's you and me now. Jesus Christ I feel like a lunatic. Okay okay Floyd, focus. Make the stick grow, somehow. I feel foolish. Just, stretch my brain or something. Here goes.

Looking at the stick, pushing his tiny features into one mass in the center of his face, Simon tried to get the stick to grow toward him. In his mind, he placed the image of the stick growing like a tree, of it shooting toward him like a vine. He outstretched his hand..

Nothing happened. The stick, gnarled and twisted, remained firmly stagnant. Frustrated, Simon looked to Mary. The same impassive expression that haunted Simon's new childhood graced her small features. She looked him in the eye, raising her eyebrows. The expression of bored expectation caused embarrassment to flood Simon's tiny face. Blushing, he scowled and returned to staring at the gnarled wood. He stared at it and felt beads of sweat cause his sandy hair to stick to his scalp.

Come on stick, MOVE. Move, damn you. Just a little. Is she still staring at me? Why do I want her approval so much? Goddamn it, move, you stupid sack of garbage. Move, or I'll light you on fire—I swear to whatever rules this upside-down place! Simon's mind jumped to the inside of the stick, but rather than growth, his mind danced to images of destruction. His mind flexed.

With a yelp, Simon jumped back. The blazing stick, inches from his outstretched hand, put off an astounding amount of heat. Within moments, the gnarled wood and the leaves surrounding it were reduced to ash. The hungry flames had set upon the branch with the fury of a small sun, leaving a circle of ash and scorched earth where the stick once stood.

Looking to Mary, confused and not a little scared, Simon was surprised to find a smiling face and a chuckle bubbling out of that delicate face. Fear turned to hurt, which turned to confusion and anger. Why was she laughing? What had he done? Simon felt a sting in his hand and looked down to see red blooming from his palm. The heat of the burn fueled the fire of his indignation. He scowled at his mentor, which just caused the woman to laugh harder.

Mary, after her brief lapse into laughter, wiped her hands on her skirt and pointed at the circle of ash.

"You see? You probably got angry at the stick for not moving, thought of it being on fire, and *poof!* You've got a burning bush." Humor disappeared and was replaced with seriousness and Mary's voice dropped.

"So, why did the stick burn but not grow? What is the difference?"

Simon thought hard, trying to see why it did one thing but not the other. *I've always hated tests, ever since elementary school. Wasn't the best at making connections.* He sat quietly for a few more moments, then mumbled that he didn't know.

"Because Sprout, it is always easier to destroy than to grow. It takes months for a flower to bloom, and a second to crush it underfoot. Remember that."

Mary paused, and squeezed Simon's shoulder. "You are picking this up quickly. Remind me to introduce you to a friend of mine today."

Simon, taking his eyes from his handiwork, looked up at Mary and nodded. He felt a strange pulsing in his head, and rubbed his temples. Mary saw it and patted his back. The gesture was reassuring and kind.

"I think that's enough on Changing for the time being, Sprout. When you are a little older and have more control, we will try again. The more control you have, the less headaches you feel." As if in response to Mary's voice, Simon's head began to pound.

"For now, just try to listen and learn. We were given two ears and one mouth for a reason."

Without another word, Mary turned and strode down the path. Giving one last glance at the pile of ash that was once a stick, Simon ran to keep up. *I can't even imagine what the rest of the day is going to bring in this town, if the first thing is spontaneous combustion and warnings about damn lions!* Mentally shuddering, Simon moved even closer to Mary and once again found himself fighting the urge to hold her hand.

The street led the pair toward the center of the small, fantastical village, and Simon began trying to find out what the signs above each door meant. The doors were painted their own unique, bright colors, and Simon surmised that had some significance as well. Here was a red door with a golden anvil for a sign. There stood a small building with a bright blue door—*the blue of my daughter's eyes,* he thought—with a multicolored pot on its sign. Across the street, a green-doored shop was adorned with a little plant in a pot, painted on some sort of silver wood above it.

Abruptly, Simon's curly-haired caretaker stopped in front of a bronze, circular entrance with what could only be a loaf of bread on its gold-bordered sign. Looking down and smiling at her flaxen-haired charge, Mary winked and walked in. Simon, having never seen Mary wink and reeling from all of the overwhelming, unique, and decidedly *foreign* sights and sounds that surrounded him, was overjoyed to find his nostrils filled with the familiar smell of bread baking.

It was like his mind was grasping for anything that could be familiar, any shred of normalcy from his past life, and the smell of freshly baking pastries was exactly that. He thought of the small bakery near the station where he had worked, about how he was greeted with the smell of sweet, sticky loaves rising in heat as he walked into that grey, utilitarian building every morning. He thought of those early-morning strolls, of the sun creeping through the buildings, of the little bell that rang above his head whenever he walked in to buy a loaf of bread or something sweet. He smiled, and for a brief moment, felt at peace—felt as though there was a small chance for a semblance of something being normal. *Perhaps food can bridge the gap between worlds, help me remember the man I was.* He followed Mary inside.

Simon sought out the scent inside the small building and smiled as the warmth of a stove caressed his face. The smell of bread was more powerful indoors, and his stomach began to rumble. The store was well-kept, with polished wooden countertops that shone with reflected sunlight from the circular windows to Simon's right. A countertop with a bulbous glass case sat atop one of the counters, with various pastries, coated and filled with frostings and jams, ornately displayed within. To the right of the confectioner's dream sat various bread loaves, arranged in intricate pyramids and towers. Sourdough made a fair replication of the pyramids of Giza, next to a pumpernickel-and-rye clock tower, complete with breadsticks for the hour- and minute-hands. *The bread smells fresh. Whoever runs this place must change this crazy clock-tower thing every day!*

As Simon was staring at the impressive clock tower, made even larger by his tiny frame and height vantage, a man stepped through a curtained doorway behind the polished wooden countertops. Turning to face the creator of such delicious treats and edible art, Simon was instead fixated upon one of the largest noses he had ever seen. The sharp features surrounding the nose, as well as the hardened quality of the eyes, gave the face from which the giant proboscis grew, a frame not dissimilar to an ancient battle-axe. The large, sharp, expressionless gaze seemed to take in the whole room at once, to assess its value and uncover its worth. However, when the eyes fell on Mary, the skin surrounding those eyes crinkled, and a giant, genuine smile cracked the sharp steel, replacing it with a warmth and readiness to bring comfort. His face, when smiling, seemed to better suit his sizable girth. *This guy must make the bread. Never trust a thin chef, and no one likes an angry fat man. Two phrases that hold true both in the past life and this one I bet.*

"Mary, how wonderful to see you! It seems an eternity since I saw you last!"

"*Bonjour,* Taillevent. It's good to see you as well. How are things?"

"Ahh, things are beautiful! When one has all the time in the world to cook, wonders cannot help but be created. Ha, all the time in the world!"

A deep, booming laugh erupted from Taillevent's mouth, and that sizable stomach shook with mirth. Mary's musical laughter, like the tinkling of silver bells, joined the chef's bellow, creating an orchestra of merriment in the bakery. The bellow became a rumble, and Taillevent wiped his hands on a spotless apron that hung from his waist.

"What can I make for you this beautiful day of days? Something sweet, a little savory? Perhaps something with a bite?" The twinkle in the big man's eye suggested more than a simple spicy dish.

"Oh, just a few loaves of bread, some of that delicious lemon meringue pie, and those little crackers I love so much."

"Of course, of course. Anything for the little Master?"

"Oh, my goodness, where are my manners?" Mary answered. "This is Sprout. It is his first time to town. As a matter of fact, it is his first time for just about everything. He's newly Returned."

"Ah! *C'est merveilleux!* I always love new people. Sprout, it is a pleasure to meet you. My name is Guillaume Tirel, and I was the chef of kings and lords in my native France"

Then why did Mary call you Taillevent? Must be a nickname, Simon thought.

"How did I end up here, you ask? Well, you know the way to a man's heart is through his stomach, yes? Well, it appears as though he keeps his soul there, too!"

Another laugh blossomed from his chest. This time, both Mary and Simon joined in. The sound was infectious and seemed to pull merriment out of Simon's small lungs. Both the man and the boy liked Guillaume immediately.

"When you have settled in, you must tell me all about my home. Are we still the best chefs, lovers, writers, and musicians? Have we conquered the entire world? Do not answer yet; I want to really have time to listen."

Simon, mouth open, immediately closed it as the large chef smiled and extended his hand.

"Come here, Sprout, come here." Gesturing with large hams that looked like sausages sewn onto a catcher's mitt, Guillaume led Simon to the bulbous glass enclosure. With a smile, the chef pointed at one section of the glass case and said, "Pick any one of these that you like. My special cookies never disappoint!"

Looking in, Simon saw cookies baked to represent various animals and plants, nestled in tiny wicker baskets. Frosting coated the tops of the delicious pieces of edible art with vibrant colors of all hues. Simon's mouth watered. Peering through the various shapes lying in their enclosures, Simon pointed to a blue-frosted elephant. He always liked elephants. Chuckling, Guillaume reached in, grabbed the cookie, and gently placed it in a small basket. As he handed it to Simon, his tone took on a sound of mock severity.

"You remember your mama saying, 'Don't play with your food!'? Well, in Taillevent's bakery, you must! There is magic here, and it is to be enjoyed!"

Looking down, Simon's mouth went dry, and shock rolled over him. The tiny elephant cookie was no longer lying on its side. It was standing, walking about its little enclosure, and letting out tiny bellows from its small sugary trunk. Shock turned into delight as Simon touched the tiny creature and it pranced about its cage. Simon was surprised to find a pure, childish laugh escape his mouth. The elephant bellowed again, and some of the frosting fell off its round bottom.

"Oh Taillevent, you really can't help yourself, can you? Change it back," Mary said.

"Of course, Miss Mary. Of course."

Simon's eye, briefly taken away from his tiny friend by Mary and Guillaume, turned back to see a simple cookie lying on its side. He was surprised to find himself relieved. He liked elephants and he loved cookies, but he wasn't overly fond of the idea of eating a cookie that seemed alive. Suddenly, a memory of golden fur and razor teeth bubbled in his mind. As the chef was preparing Mary's order and speaking to her in low, confidential tones, Simon walked up, cookie in hand, and placed it on the counter.

"Does the young Master not want the cookie? I assure you they are quite delicious."

Looking Guillaume in the eye, Simon extended his tray to him.

"Do you have any lions?"

Confusion and a little amusement crossed the big chef's face.

"*Bien sur.* Of course!"

Placing the blue-frosted elephant behind the glass again, Guillaume reached in and plucked a yellow-frosted, four-legged feline from a different basket. As he placed it in the little wicker enclosure, where the elephant had found itself, and handed it to Simon, the boy could see a little sugary tail swishing about. Looking in, Simon gazed at the edible lioness, and a smile that could only be described as wicked grew on his face.

It was the best cookie he had ever eaten.

CHAPTER V: YOUR EYES HAD ONCE

Walking out of the shop, frosting still on his lips, Simon could not help but feel elated. A sense of happiness and peace had been born in the bakery, and it followed him out as he and Mary strolled back onto the well-worn road that split the town in two. Simon glanced about, drinking in the various colors and cuts of clothing. He was so enthralled with the sights and sounds of this historical nexus that he did not realize that he had wandered into a strange, white-clothed forest until his head collided with what, at first, appeared to be a white sheet.

Looking up, Simon's eyes widened, and the color drained from his face. Without paying attention, he had wandered into a circle of bearded men, resplendent with white togas and severe faces. They had been talking animatedly among themselves, but all conversation ceased when they realized that someone new had entered their midst. Mary's warning began careening around inside Simon's skull, and sweat instantly broke out all over his body. He was surrounded and terrified and small.

"Well, what do we have here? I do not think I have met you before. Where and when do you come from, young sir?" An overwhelmingly tall gentleman with hair the color of coffee and eyes to match bent at the waist to look right into Simon's eyes as he spoke. Simon could smell olives and garlic on his breath.

"It has been quite a while since a traveler has graced our town. Even in death, it appears as though people like to stay put. What is your name? From whence do you hail? I am Thales of Greece."

As the word "Greece" fell from the tall man's lips, Simon's back stiffened. *Is this the Greek? Wait, these men are all wearing togas. Are they* all

Greek? Mary should have warned me! Where is that woman? Simon stared directly into the man's coffee-colored eyes and said nothing.

"He looks like he could be of some use to me. I haven't had someone like him in a long time. I like the color of his eyes," someone said.

The face attached to the new voice had no warmth in it. Simon turned to place human features to the sound and looked up into a sharp-faced man with a knife for a nose and chipped flint for eyes. Cold calculation lived where warmth and empathy should be, and what could only be described as a ravenous hunger writhed just beneath the stony flecks as they looked Simon up and down. *This, this is the Greek. I put away men like him by the dozen in my old life. Damn, what I wouldn't give for a gun right now.* Simon stepped back, ready to run if need be, and slid his hand to the knife at his waist.

"Step back, sir. He is much too young to be your *eromenos.*" The dark, bearded companion of the Greek placed his arm on the flint-eyed man's shoulder. "Besides, we do not even know where he is from. His people may not support the idea of pederasty."

"When are you going to learn, Thales? The rules and traditions of the past must be kept in the past. This is Dara, a place where we build our own heaven." The thin man smiled, a predatory, invasive smile. His eyes remained on Simon as he spoke, and his words sent cold daggers into Simon's chest. "Mine just happens to look considerably *younger* than yours does."

What the hell is eromenos, *and why does Hawk-Face want me as one? What's a pederast?* Simon again found himself confused, but this time he also felt a strong determination, a rigidity of purpose, form in his chest. There was absolutely no way, in this world or worlds previous, where he would be caught dead with the hawk-faced man. *This is definitely the Greek.*

Keeping those flint-flecked eyes locked on the youth, the speaker walked toward Simon with predatory grace, like a tiger stalking a baby water buffalo separated from its herd. The tiger does not rush when prey is so easily acquired. It savors the inevitability of capture. Simon's right hand stayed on his knife, and his left came up, palm up, just like he had been taught in the Academy.

"Stay back," he shouted, trying to make himself sound authoritative and in control, but his small frame and falsetto voice only made him feel the fool. *Jesus Christ, I am small. Makes me hate predators even more. I bet if I cut his nuts, he'd stop moving.* Undeterred, the hawk-faced man kept walking toward Simon.

"Why don't you and I take a walk, young one? I have many things to show you," the Greek said. Walking toward Simon, looming over him, he extended a large hand with thin fingers and brought it to rest upon Simon's shoulder. The touch felt cold. Taking a deep breath, Simon bent his knees and dropped his weight onto the balls of his feet, ready to spring forward with the strongest slash he could muster. He knew that if he could pierce an eyeball or slice between his legs, the hawk-faced man would not be able to chase him far. He just prayed his little legs could get him to safety and away from the other bearded men. He pushed the man's hand away, and the blade sighed as it scraped free of its leather sheath.

"There you are, Sprout! I swear, I turn my back for one minute… Gentlemen, I am so sorry if he was bothering you. It's his first time here in town, and he hasn't learned all the rules, no matter how often I teach them." The familiar voice of Mary caused Simon to halt his movement, and the sight of her sent relief coursing through his body. As Mary spoke, she came and placed a hand on Simon's shoulder and meaningfully stepped between him and the gentleman with the flint-flecked eyes. She gave Simon a purposeful glance.

The sharp nose looked down at Simon as the Greek addressed his caregiver. "That's quite all right, Miss Mary. Sprout is welcome to … bump into me at any time. In fact, I hope to see him again real soon."

Turning to face those emotionless, rock-flake eyes, Mary slid the spear shaft she carried from her shoulder and began slowly picking dirt from under her fingernails with the sharp, gleaming tip. With an amazing degree of nonchalance, she looked up from her task and smiled, but no merriment touched her eyes.

"I think the only thing bumping into you, if I see you near Sprout again, will be my blade tickling your insides. Time for you to continue your Journey somewhere else."

What seemed like an eternity passed, with neither Mary nor the hawk-faced man refusing to break eye contact. Simon, keeping a firm grip on his knife, tried to make himself as small as possible. He hated how weak he felt, how vulnerable, almost as much as he hated the feeling of relief seeing that Mary had stepped in to protect him. Without thinking, he stepped back and toward Mary, away from the stone-eyed man.

The Greek broke eye contact first, looking down at Simon with a malicious smile.

"Very well. I do not feel like being Returned any time soon, and I don't think my brethren will step in on my behalf. Perhaps we will meet at another time." The last was for Simon. The boy felt those eyes slide onto him, holding him, looking for weaknesses to exploit, to manipulate. Simon returned the gaze with as gruff a glare as he could muster, but he knew that he must look foolish.

"I am glad to hear it. May your Journey end quickly. Now, if you will excuse me, Sprout and I have some shopping to do. Thales, I hope to see you soon; we have much to discuss. Sprout, let's not keep the attention of these gentlemen for any longer than we already have. Come along."

Hand outstretched, Mary smiled down at Simon. He hated himself, but only a little, for being relieved to place his tiny palm in hers. Taking one last look at the hawk-faced man, Simon trundled off behind Mary.

Goddamn it, but that was scary, he thought. *I haven't been hit on that severely since I broke up that meth ring at the Screw Box—that weird bar under the overpass.* Glancing behind him, Simon saw the hawk-faced man, eyes like chipped stones, boring a hole into him. Emotions fluttered over his face: anger, jealousy, but the emotion he saw the most of was painful, aggressive, amorous intent. Simon clenched Mary's hand a little tighter and continued walking.

Strolling next to the comfortable presence of Mary, Simon slowly felt his heart rate rhythm return to its relaxed pace and felt his hands drying in the heat of the early afternoon. The village once again cloaked itself in charm, the green trees and perfectly manicured plants lending a mystical air. Mary walked, hips swaying, and Simon followed. They entered more shops, or homes—Simon couldn't tell—with Mary introducing Simon as Sprout, Simon gazing at the wonders each establishment possessed, and Mary acquiring things from each vendor. Simon never saw money exchanged, but the oddity of not paying for goods barely made a ripple in the weird waters he had so recently found himself, so he didn't ask and simply followed Mary from one odd fever dream to another.

Simon felt his senses might shut down from overstimulation as he walked into a little silver-signed store that was a place to acquire plants that had been grown to suit every need, from food to furniture. Beautiful chairs woven out of a single tree stood next to tiny apple trees that, according to the merry man who tended them, produced fruit every three hours. Simon wondered why there weren't piles of fruit in every corner of the store, and Mary simply said, "It's a trick Mendel did. Something to do with Changing genetic structure. He absolutely loves beans, by the way. Talk to him about it sometime, when you have a month or two to spare." Not interested in hearing about what the strange man in the corner with the stranger haircut had to say about hanging fruit, Simon simply shook his head and followed Mary out the door.

If it weren't for that lunatic wearing a sheet, this would be a pretty amazing day, Simon thought as the sun warmed his shoulders and head.

It felt good to walk a greater distance than the length and width of the tree house. Mary continued to chat with different people and pop her head into different doorways, each with a myriad of delights and wonders that boggled Simon's mind, and as the day stretched onward, a feeling of peace and tranquility flooded through him, and with it, a kind of acceptance. The human mind can acclimate and adapt to anything, given the appropriate amount of time, and Simon felt himself—the old self—unwind just a little and flow into the new body and begin to accept this new world. With a small smile, he let himself drift, walking through shops and alleys, in and out of the shade of giant trees Changed to look like nymphs, dryads, and dragons. The day was going quite well, all things considered.

"I knew I would find you alone. I just didn't know it would be so soon."

With a start, Simon's attention jerked from a wall that had flowers growing from it in the shape of a ship sailing on leaves and spun to face the noise. The hawk-faced man, voice calm and eyes like cold granite, stood between Simon and the main road, a long, wicked blade held easily in his right hand. Simon realized to his dismay that he had wandered into a small, dark alley between two buildings, and Hawk-Face stood between him and the rest of the world. Whipping his knife out of its sheath, Simon dropped into a crouch. *This fucker doesn't know who he's dealing with. Goddamn it, he's huge. It's all right; stay calm. All I have to do is get out of this alley. Let your guard down for two seconds, I swear!*

Simon had one moment to take a breath, and faster than he thought possible, the Greek was towering over him. He tried to swing with the knife at the man's midsection, but his hand was gripped by the impossibly strong fingers, huge by contrast to his own, and a bloom of pain blossomed from his head as the back of a gigantic hand slammed into the side of it. The world suddenly became less solid, less tangible.

Simon began to fall to the ground, but found himself caught by the Greek's large hands. He was spun about as if he weighed less than an ounce, and his eyes turned in time to lock with the flint-flecked, emotionless orbs that protruded from the hawk-faced man's face— except now, behind those eyes, something dark smoldered.

"Scream, and I'll pop an eye out. I'll keep you alive and in agony. This is the world of second chances, of second choices, but we only reset when we die. I won't let you do that if you scream."

The knife flickered dangerously close to Simon's eye, the Greek's last statement driven home by the sharp blade. Simon tried to fight, to move his arms and legs, to strike out at the thin man holding him, but he might as well have been trying to punch a mountain to uproot it. The knife Mary had given him was lying useless on the ground to his left. Roughly, the Greek pushed him up against the side of a building and turned him so his face was dragged against rough stone, his right cheek rubbed so hard he felt a trickle of blood. Desperately, he tried to turn, to fight, but to no avail. The Greek had him pinned.

"You are mine, little one, and I will never let you forget it. Even when you age and I cast you aside, you will still be mine. It is easier, little Sprout, to submit to me now. Less painful."

The Greek's breath was hot and rancid against his ear. Simon smelled garlic this time. The man's breathing became ragged as it cascaded down Simon's neck. Simon tried to push off the wall, to turn and face his attacker, but the Greek had arms like iron. A palm enveloped the back of his head and violently bounced his cranium against the rough stone wall he was pushed against.

The world became fuzzy and slow, and Simon's legs and arms went limp. He was screaming in fear and pain inside his head, but the voice seemed to be very far away. Dimly, he was aware of big hands pulling the rope off his waist, of his pants coming down. He was terrified and hopeless.

Strangely, as his small legs were pushed apart, Simon's mind tried to escape. Part of him felt, if he just went limp, just let the Greek do what he was going to, it would be over quickly. He hated himself, despised himself, was disgusted with the thought, but the hopelessness of his plight overwhelmed everything else. With his face pushed against stone, pushed into a hopeless position, Simon closed his eyes and swore to himself that, when he could, he would cut the Greek's balls off and feed them to him.

Suddenly, the pressure on his head was released, and a warm liquid sprayed onto his back. *Nasty fucker couldn't even hold it in. Good. Now I can find a way to kill him.* Turning, ready to run, Simon locked his green eyes onto the flint ones in front of him, but instead of the dark intent of assault, fear and disbelief crossed those sharp features. Looking down, Simon saw that the liquid that showered him was actually a font of blood gushing from the Greek's throat. Red stained the white toga, blood slipping between fingers as the Greek desperately tried to hold his opened throat together.

"I bid you safe Return, though you do not deserve it," a voice intoned, the owner hidden behind the bloody mess that was the Greek. With eyes still wide, the bleeding man turned to find Thales, the knife with the well-worn handle glistening red in his left hand, looking at him. Gurgling, the Greek took a step toward his attacker, hand outstretched, and the knife snapped out, piercing one of those cold eyes. The Greek became very still and fell into a lifeless pile of red and white.

"Are you all right, Sprout?"

Concern replaced malice, kindness washed away violent intent, as Thales knelt to look Simon in the eye. Pulling his oversized pants up quickly and tying his rope belt around his waist, Simon paused, then hugged Thales for all he was worth. He knew there was no way to express his appreciation for what the man had done for him, how he had pulled him from the brink of a fate he could not bring himself to even think about, so he hugged him. He hugged him and let the fear wash out of him. He was not surprised to find himself crying.

"It's over now. No need to worry. He is gone. It will be quite some time before he ages enough to be a problem." Thales spoke in a soothing murmur and stroked Simon's hair. The blood on his toga gave off a faint hint of copper. "In the meantime, let's get out of this alley and get you some clean clothes."

Looking down, Simon realized that his clean sky-blue shirt was soaked in blood, and he became painfully aware of a sticky liquid on the back of his neck and head. Looking up at Thales, Simon couldn't help but ask, "Why ... why did you help me?"

"Never liked him. Have to spend an eternity with him. However, I do get to kill him from time to time. Sometimes that man will spend an entire lifetime without incident, and other times, well, he has to be reset. I'm just glad I found you when I did. You aren't the first boy who was broken by him. The damage can be ... long-reaching."

"Thank you. Thank you so much." Tears again trickled out of his eyes, but for the first time in many, many years, Simon felt no shame in shedding them.

"It was my pleasure. Now, again, let's get out of here. We need to see you cleaned up and back with Mary." Reaching down, Thales cleaned the knife blade on the Greek's toga. "Here, this is yours. Keep it safe."

Simon nodded and quickly tucked the blade back into its sheath of boiled leather and then into the rope around his waist. Thales smiled and turned to leave. Simon followed him out of the alleyway. He took one last look at the heap on the ground that had once been his attacker, then turned and walked into the main road, sunlight, and safety.

"Sweet jumping Jesus, what happened to you? I swear, Sprout, I turn my back to speak to Par for one second ... Are you alright?" Mary's tone went from surprised and annoyed to concerned and caring within an instant. She looked Simon up and down, taking in the blood spatter and ruined shirt. Thales, standing with his hand on Simon's shoulder, was the next to be looked up and down.

"What happened?"

"Little Sprout here had an uninvited admirer. I found him in the alley next to Mendel's. Do not worry; I bid the man safe Return and brought Sprout back to you."

A flash of anger slashed across Mary's pretty features, like a cloud darting in front of morning sunshine.

"Well, I'm glad you were there when you were, Thales. I suppose it was only a matter of time before Sprout realized that living here with our heads in the clouds will often lead to death, or worse." She glared at Simon, hands folded beneath her breasts. "Now, if you will excuse me, Master Thales, Sprout and I should be headed back home. Come on, Sprout, help me with these bags."

"Actually, if you wouldn't mind, Miss Mary, I would be honored if you would allow me to become Sprout's guide." A far-off look entered the eyes of Thales, but when he noticed Simon watching him, the philosopher's face quickly reverted back to its pleasant disposition. "It has been ... quite a long time ... since I had a pupil, and since Sprout and I are already acquainted—" He looked down at the young boy and smiled. "Since our paths seemed to have been crossed for a purpose, I think this would be quite a good fit."

"How do you know that Sprout needs a guide?" Mary asked, wariness in her voice.

"It is quite obvious that he is new to this plane. Do not worry; I will not tell anyone. I know how ... *insistent* ... some of our residents can be when a new soul arrives." Thales' smile deepened and he winked at Simon. *What does that mean? Why is everyone so calm? Didn't Thales just kill someone?* Simon's heart banged in his chest, trying to escape, but the young boy kept his mouth closed as Mary spoke to his rescuer.

"I will think on it. Thank you again, Master Thales. I will see you at the festival I am sure. Come along, Sprout." With a nod to Thales, Mary clasped Simon's hand and began to march out of the road.

Simon looked at Thales, eyes and wrinkled face smiling down at him. "Thank you" was all Simon managed to say, before he was pulled away by his caretaker.

They walked in silence for a while, the blood drying on Simon's skin and shirt to a thick crust. His body ached, and a small purple egg was forming under the skin on his forehead. Simon's eyes still had trouble focusing occasionally as he walked, but his mind had never felt sharper. The weather was warm, the sun dipping slowly overhead to give the trees and path an even more mystical air. It is amazing how beautiful the world around one becomes when death and destruction are avoided. The air smelled sweeter, the sun rays a gentle caress on Simon's skin. The water he drank tasted of life itself.

Simon could recall from his past life a time when he cornered a man, who was drugged out of his mind and flailing a snub-nosed pistol in all directions, in a small apartment. The man was yelling about the need to purify his mind, to purify the evils in his blood. Apparently, the only way to do that was through large quantities of methamphetamine. Simon was young, his knees shaking and arms trembling as he held his firearm with both hands at the man, telling him to drop the weapon. Wild-eyed, the man turned, sweat pouring from every pore, soaking his white underwear, the only stitch of clothing he had on him. He looked Simon dead in the eye and said something that death itself couldn't erase from Simon's memory.

"Time to see the white prince, motherfucker."

Two shots were fired. One from Simon's weapon, the other from the snub-nosed pistol. One bullet found its target, the other grazed past an ear, the wind of the bullet sliding near an eardrum. One man died, the other walked away and vomited on the ground outside a seedy apartment building.

That night, Simon had the best food he had ever tasted. It was his wife's meatloaf, with mashed potatoes and green beans, a meal that

Simon had eaten a thousand times if he had eaten it once. Yet that night, every spice popped, every texture cascaded around his tongue and taste buds. The beer he drank, unassuming in its aluminum can, seemed to have been brewed by a friar who had fermented the stars. Life was exploding all around him, and his mind, his spirit, had been honed to a razor's edge to discern it. When he made love to Anna, her skin was electric, her mouth a flower. Her nails digging in his back sent sweet fire cascading through him, and when he was finished, he disappeared into her soft skin and slept the sleep of the righteous man. The brush of death brings all the vivid colors out onto the canvas of life.

Simon's senses were that raw once again, his perception honed and sharpened to perceive all the beauty that was Dara. Even Mary, the woman whom he loved and hated with equal measure, seemed to be clothed in light and glazed with beauty. Sending a silent thanks to Thales once more, Simon continued his walk back to the safety of the tree house.

As they walked, a question came out of nowhere. As is the case with most questions, it had no rhyme nor reason, it simply came to be, bubbling forth from the recesses of Simon's mind and jumping front and center to Simon's mental stage. Confusion spreading through him, Simon turned his face to Mary, looking up as he spoke.

"Why does Taillevent speak French, but Thales speaks English?"

Mary, a smile playing on her full lips, continued walking as she replied. "What makes you think that *we* are speaking English right now?"

"Because ... because it is the only language I know. I couldn't speak in any other language."

"It is a good question, Sprout, it's true, but the answer is simple. We are communicating in the universal language of consciousness, in the language that all of humanity shares once it has transcended its base impulses and embraces what it means to be more than human. We speak in a language we all know and can't define."

Simon, confused, reached up and began twirling his hair, a habit he had formed when he still had hair in his past life. *Goddamn it, I love having my hair back,* Simon thought, and he smiled as he played with his short tresses. Sandy hair twirled around his fingers as Simon tried to understand what Mary meant.

Mary continued, "In fact, the name of this place, Dara, is a word only for you. What I call this place is something entirely different because this world is so directly attached to who we are."

"Then, why does Taillevent speak French? And why … why does your accent change sometimes?"

Mary stopped, her shoulders sagging as if a weight had been unceremoniously dropped upon them. She turned and faced her young ward, and when she did, there was a deep sadness in those dark eyes.

"It is because … it is because our language is tied tightly to who we *are,* to the people we were before we ascended. For Guillaume, his cooking is his soul, and French cuisine can sometimes only be paired perfectly with the French language. For me …"

Mary's eyes became distant, focusing on a misty memory that was reserved only for her eyes "For me, the twang of my accent is tied tightly to the world I once lived in, and when I forget myself, my spirit dashes back to that place, to a time…" Mary trailed off, staring at nothing.

Simon stood, watching his surrogate mother grapple with a pain he could not see. Soon, she shook herself, looked to Simon, and smiled briefly.

"Let's keep walking. You have had an eventful day, and I'm sure you're tired. We're almost home."

Without another word, Mary turned and once again began strolling down the road. Simon, his question answered, was somehow more confused, he hurried to catch up. *This world makes no sense at all. I just hope I can get out of here somehow.* Quickening his steps, Simon strode with Mary, the day bouncing in his head, the event reflected by his surrogate mother's sad eyes. Simon was relieved beyond measure to see the familiar sight of the tree house and quickly scurried up the winding steps and pushed open the door, happy to see the familiarity of the purple flowers and beautiful wooden furniture.

Once again safe inside the arbor dwelling, Simon was surprised to find just how much like a home the tree house had become. He rushed to his room, an audible sigh of relief escaped his lips, and the day melted out of his body and into the twilight when he turned and walked toward his bed.

His "room" was actually a small nook, an arch in the trunk of the tree, which had been hidden by the wall of purple flowers. Simon pushed aside the sweet-smelling petals and bright green vines and flopped onto his small bed with a sigh.

He loved his room as a child, in the tiny house where he had grown up. To those from the outside looking in, his home had appeared small and humble, and his room, little more than an oversized closet. But to him, his room had been an oasis. Model airplanes lined the shelves, and toy soldiers launched an assault on his father's feet when he came to wake him in the morning for school. It was a place where he had felt truly safe, even when the world was upside down, as it so often was with a father like his. He was surprised to discover those same feelings of safety and peace emanating from him as soon as he stepped into the room designated for him in Mary's house.

Small children, even those with adult minds, need a sacred space all their own to sometimes shut out the gigantic and often terrifying world that surrounds them. Stretched out on his small bed, with the pain in his head reduced to a dull ache, Simon closed his eyes and drifted seamlessly into a deep sleep.

CHAPTER VI: THEIR SHADOWS DEEP

For the next two days, Simon was in excruciating pain. He lay in his bed and refused to leave it. Mary came in occasionally, either to check on him or feed him, but otherwise she left him alone. Once, when his head ached to a particularly severe degree, and the contents of his breakfast had been vomited onto the floor, Mary appeared in his field of blurry vision.

Looking at the pile of vomit, then at the pale form of tiny Simon, Mary suggested that "maybe this is too much to bear, Sprout. Maybe we can have you Return again, and you won't have such a headache." Keeping her eyes on the small child who was once a man, Mary stroked the handle of her belt knife. Simon shook his head vigorously, though it made the room spin, and stated that he was feeling much better and would be out of bed in no time. Mary, the ghost of a smile on her lips, simply stared at Simon and walked out of the door. *Please be joking, oh please, be joking! I don't know if I'll ever be able to sleep again if you're not joking!* The last thought sent a piercing pain through Simon's skull.

Though Mary did not return for the rest of the day, Simon had an incredibly hard time falling asleep that night and kept catching himself staring at the wall of flowering vines that was the door to his bedroom. He prayed that Mary just had a sick sense of humor and wouldn't come murder him when he slept. It was well into the dark night when Simon finally slipped into sleep, and the smallest noise or creak would send him flying awake, hands flailing to defend an imaginary knife attack. It was nearly dawn when sleep actually came and held Simon, finally dragging him down into a deep, calm abyss, and the young boy sent a silent prayer of thanks as he was led down into darkness.

Simon awoke to sunshine warming his cheeks, and, with the exception of a small ache in his head, a refreshed state of being. *Being young again isn't all bad,* he thought. *I forgot how quickly I healed as a young boy.* With a smile, Simon stretched luxuriously, slipped out of bed, pulled on an overly large white cotton shirt, and strolled out to meet Mary at the table for breakfast, or lunch, or whatever meal was available. Yet, rather than domestic tranquility, Simon found himself thrown into a world engulfed in chaos.

The purple flowers were in disarray, with a thick liquid resembling dark red paint coating purple petals and green leaves. Bowls and cups, once beautifully formed and seamless, lay broken or overturned all around the small arbor abode. An air of disorder seemed to flood the tiny space. Even the sunshine seemed jagged, piercing the air through torn leafy curtains.

Frantic, Simon's eyes darted about, looking for some sign of life. Nothing seemed to move but the slight breeze sliding through the room like a whisper full of dark news. Simon hurried about, looking under the table, darting behind a chair, searching for something, anything— some sign that would help him find Mary. He was briefly surprised by how worried he was for his caretaker, but he quickly pushed that aside. Loving or not, overbearing or not, Mary had taken care of him, *was* taking care of him, and without her ... With a shudder, Simon pushed down the bubble of fear rising from his middle. *You are a cop, goddamn it; act like one. Find out what's going on.* Setting his tiny jaw, Simon continued searching for his caretaker.

So intent was he on looking that he barely registered a sound coming from the outside deck—a kind of muffled gurgling. The noise sounded human, but also, somehow, not quite right. Instinctively, Simon dropped into a crouch, hand darting to where his belt knife should be, and silently cursed when he realized that he was still in his underwear. The gurgling continued, followed by what must have been a barely suppressed giggle. Simon's hackles rose; something deep inside of him knew that a dark and twisted thing was the source of that barely contained laugh. Dropping even further, now onto his belly, Simon crawled toward the window and the sound.

Slowly, he made it to the window. The suppressed giggle came and went, followed almost immediately by the gurgle, and as he inched closer, a new sound—like fingers sliding, slashing over paper—filled his ears. Slash, gurgle, giggle. Slash, gurgle, giggle. Simon's heart beat faster as he pressed his hands onto the ground, lifted himself off his belly, and gazed out of the tiny window and onto the outside porch.

A large tree branch, beautiful and green, provided a natural canopy over the deck, with leafy offshoots that were as thick as Simon's waist. The landing itself seemed to have grown out of the tree trunk, and when Simon looked down, he could see individual tree rings that looked remarkably similar to the roof of the house inside the tree. Generally a place of peace, with shade from the sun and a view that stretched to the upside-down mountain range and vertical ocean, the deck had turned into something from a nightmare.

Mary was there, stark naked and bound by a thick rope that descended from one of the powerful branches, the chorded twine knotted around her hands and pulled taut, so that her toes barely touched the deck's smooth wooden surface. Another, smaller rope twisted around her neck, constricting her breathing. Looking up along the rope, Simon saw that Mary's bonds had been thrown over a thick branch and tied off to a small knot that jutted out of the tree-house wall. The smaller rope was tied there as well, so tight that if Mary were to fall forward even a little, the rope would bite into her throat.

As his gaze slid from the rope back to the naked woman, what he saw made his stomach do backflips. His caregiver's kinky hair was matted with blood, and her entire body—from her small shoulders down to her slender ankles—was covered in tiny, barely seen slashes, with blood trickling down from each one. As he watched, Simon saw something metallic reflect light as it sliced into his field of vision, making that sound of fingers sliding over paper. A new thin cut appeared just above Mary's left nipple, the red blood sliding down and coating her dark areola. Simon was horrified to hear Mary's gurgling cry of pain, but he was even more terrified to hear the giggle that emanated from her captor. Turning slowly, careful not to make a sound, Simon turned to look upon Mary's tormentor.

A small, average looking man crouched, shining eyes intent on Mary. A wicked smile adorned a face that had seen the abominations of hell and enjoyed the view. A blade, bright red with the blood of his captive, was comfortably resting in the palm of his hand, and by the crouching form lay a small bag with the drawstrings hanging open. Pushing his thin fingers through his hair, the man reached into the bag, walked over to Mary with his hands full of something white, and began caressing her. White flakes covered Mary as they showered through the fingers of the man. Every time the white flakes touched an open wound, Mary would jerk and attempt to cry out, but no sound came. Each time she jerked, the man's eyes shone a little brighter, the smile a little wider, until it seemed as though his grin would split his wicked face in half.

The bastard is literally rubbing salt into her wounds! How can I stop him? What do I do? Mind racing, Simon slowly formed an idea in his mind. Mary's eyes were beginning to glaze over, her jerking body seemed to stop responding to the salt being poured into her cuts. *She's going into shock. I have to do something! What the hell is a kid supposed to do?*

The man began to slow his rubbing, the smile disappearing from his face. His pleasure seemed to drain with Mary's consciousness. Sighing, he stepped back and took in the full view of Mary's naked body. Glancing at the knife, he seemed to come to a decision. Stepping forward, he placed his hand on Mary's shoulder, clenched the knife handle, and placed the tip of the blade right above Mary's heart.

"Fun's over," he whispered.

With a scream that bubbled from somewhere deep inside of him, Simon jumped through the open window and slammed his entire body into the man, his shoulder colliding with his hip. Getting his feet under him, Simon kept pushing forward, fighting to keep the man off balance. With a yelp, the man stumbled and tried to collect his footing. His hands flailed for something to grip, and the knife slashed out. Simon felt a bloom of fire erupt from his arm as blade bit skin, but he kept pushing, tucking his chin and churning his legs.

Suddenly, he stopped, and the man continued his forward momentum, hands and arms flapping wildly in an attempt to stop himself. The man turned and locked eyes with Simon as arms and legs made frantic motions in an attempt to stop gravity's inevitable pull.

What should have been fear lighting his eyes as two dark orbs turned to lock with Simon's green ones, was instead an entirely different emotion. If all of his life experience didn't allow him to know better, Simon would have sworn that the man's face was full of anticipation and a little fear, but that of all things, pleasure was the most prominent. With an almost rapturous smile, the man lost his balance and toppled headfirst toward the hard ground. The crack of bones and splatter of fluids announced that the descent had not been pleasant.

Simon peered briefly over the edge and immediately regretted it. It appeared as though the stranger had decided to dive headfirst to the ground, not even bringing his hands up to break his fall, which caused brain matter to come oozing out of his skull like an egg cracked over a skillet. Simon shuddered, silently thankful that he hadn't had a chance to eat breakfast yet, and ran over to Mary.

Mary's face was a perfect encapsulation of a woman in shock, with her body trying to slide away from consciousness, but the tight rope around her neck kept jerking her back to the land of the focused, of the alert. Simon dashed inside, rushed into his bedroom, and retrieved the knife with the well-worn handle from beneath his small pillow. Running back to the porch, he rushed to the knot where both ropes were tied and began hacking at a feverish pace. The ropes, pulled taut by Mary and her unknown assailant, gave way easily under the sharp blade of Simon's knife, and before long, Mary was quickly freed of her bondage.

Simon ran to her, hands delicately fingering the rope still around her neck. The tightness of the knot had bit into her soft skin, and as Simon tried to pull it, hot tears sprouted out of the woman's eyes. As carefully as he could, Simon brought his knife up and gingerly cut the rope from Mary's neck. She gasped for air, eyes rolling. She coughed, pushed her hands down to the wooden platform, and cried out in pain. Looking at her hands, eyes widening, Simon saw an unbelievable number of small cuts crisscrossing Mary's palms. Trying to sit back down, Mary cried out again as the cuts on her back were given the additional pressure of her weight.

Everywhere she turned seemed to drive salt into her wounds, or her weight would open up a previously unseen cut, causing blood to run over her brown skin. It was a mercy when her eyes rolled in the back of her head, and consciousness slipped from her.

Relieved that Mary was, at least for the moment, given respite from her injuries, Simon reached his arms under her shoulders and, as gently as he could, dragged her inside. Slick blood left a trail of red on the porch, and Mary's loose neck caused her head to bob about as Simon dragged her limp frame into the tree house. He cursed silently at the weakness of his small body, and what seemed like hours passed before he finally had Mary inside.

As soon as her small feet slid past the frame to the entrance of the tree house, Simon slammed the door and ran to Mary's bedroom. He ripped a blanket from her immaculately made bed and snatched a pillow, tucking it under his arm. He darted back to the main room and, kneeling beside his caretaker, gently placed her head onto the pillow. His heart hammered in his chest as he looked down at Mary's naked body.

Knife slashes crisscrossed almost every inch of her, and tiny white flakes of salt lay in most of them. *Fucking bastard. Bastard! Why would he do this? Why would anyone do this? What could Mary possibly have done to deserve such treatment? No. There's nothing that would give an excuse for this.*

Rushing to the kitchen, Simon found a small white cloth with the likeness of a purple flower stitched into its corners, dampened it with some water from the wooden pitcher, and slowly began to dab at Mary's wounds. Mary winced as he worked but did not wake up. Simon said a silent word of thanks and continued working.

It took almost five linen cloths and nearly an hour, but Simon removed the salt from Mary's wounds. He even managed to cleanse some of the deeper cuts in her back. Throughout the entirety of his attempts to clean her, Mary remained unconscious. Some of the smaller cuts had stopped bleeding, but the others still ran with sticky red blood. Simon knew that if he didn't stop the bleeding, Mary might never wake up.

Tearing bits of cloth from the sheet he had brought, he made the best bandages he could and bound Mary's wounds on her arms and legs. For the cuts on the chest, he took a longer piece of sheet and wrapped it around her ribs and back. After she was covered in bandages, Simon sat down, staring at her, scared for her—terrified. He sat down and brought his knees to his chest, desperately willing Mary to wake.

As he watched, Mary began to move, ever so slightly. Her eyelids fluttered, and her forehead creased in pain. Pupils slid out from under eyelids, the whites being replaced by golden brown. Eyes wrinkled, first in confusion, then in pain as Mary tried to rise. Red bloomed from the white linens covering her wounds, and, with a gasp, she lay as still as she could. Simon knelt at her side, concern on his face. Every inch was agony for Mary, and her face was pale and drawn tight. Locking eyes with Simon, a whisper escaped her lips that seemed to fill the room:

"Kill me. Sprout, kill me."

Confusion crossed Simon's face. How could she possibly expect him to kill her? More importantly, *why* should he kill her? Chin down, Simon shook his head.

"Sprout, this is agony. Every move is like fire bursting out of the cuts in my skin. The pain ..." As if to demonstrate, Mary adjusted her shoulders, and fresh blood oozed from under the bandages on her side. Tears sprang to her eyes, but she kept them locked on Simon.

"Mengele, the man you killed, did his work well. He cut tendons just right, sliced just deep enough for maximum pain, but never deep enough to let me bleed out. This body is ruined, and I can't bear the burden of such pain. Kill me, Sprout. There is no reason not to. I will Return, fresh and new. Sure, it will take a while to look like the woman you see before you, but anythin's better than wut I feel naw. Bid me safe Return, Sprout, and end this, please."

Again, the American South had seeped into her voice, meaning she was barely in control. A passing thought made Simon wonder why she hated her native dialect, but that thought was overwhelmed immediately by the magnitude of Mary's request.

"I ... I *can't!*" Old memories raced through his mind as tears threatened to fall down Simon's face. Flashes of light in pouring rain filled his mind's eye. He hurriedly pushed them away and focused on his caretaker.

He loved and cared for the woman; he knew that now. It is flabbergasting, overwhelming, how many people require the certainty of death to realize the depths of their love. He loved Mary, and now she wanted him to kill her. Choking back a sob, he tried to stand, but a brown bloodied hand stopped him. Mary turned, and groaned from her weight being shifted onto new cuts, but still she held on.

"Kill me, Sprout! Lemme go. I will Return, and we will be able to see each other once more. Please stop the pain. Please!"

91

Simon, ashamed of his cowardice, looked down at the knife with the well-worn handle next to his knee, where he dropped it after cutting the sheet for Mary's bandage. Slowly, he reached down, gripping the hardened leather, feeling the wood underneath. The blade shimmered as it caught the sunlight sliding in through an open window.

"Yes, yes." Mary breathed, relief evident in her tone and on her face. "Stab hard and true righ' here." With shaking fingers, she pointed just above her left breast. "Make it fast. Bid me safe Return. Safe Return." The last was almost a whisper, and with those last words spoken, Mary closed her eyes, a small smile drifting onto her lips.

Gripping the knife in his small hands, Simon felt his sweat slide from his palms and soak the leather handle. Shifting his weight forward, he raised up onto both knees, looking down at his bandaged caretaker, at his friend, at his proxy mother. Knife pointed down, he readied it about her chest, watching the breasts that fed him rise and fall. His hand that gripped the knife began to shake, and he brought the other over the top of the handle. Tears dropped from his eyes, freely falling.

"I bid you safe Return."

For what felt like days, weeks, though it must have only been hours, Simon sat with Mary's head lying on his lap. He looked down at her now peaceful face, stroked that curly hair that framed her delicate features. Blood that had seeped out of her wounds lay in a pool beneath her, and her bandages were soaked with red, but Simon only saw her beautiful face in his arms. It was a face that looked strikingly young—a contrast to the face that he conjured in his mind when he envisioned her alive, scolding him or teaching him. Simon looked at Mary and cried.

After a time that he could not quantify, the depths of his sadness, of his anger, his denial, had hollowed him out, leaving an empty, consuming void inside of him. Numbness overtook the entirety of his selfhood, and with nearly lifeless eyes, he stared at his caretaker, his teacher, his prison guard, his landlord. Without even realizing it, Mary had taken up residence within Simon, filling his days with her presence, his head with her lessons, and his heart with affection. It's amazing how the human mind can effortlessly switch from near hatred and fear to affection and love when a simple thing like death becomes a part of one's relationship to another being. *I would love to see ol' Daryl at my funeral. That son of a bitch and I sat next to each other for decades at work. Hated him. Never learned how to chew with his mouth closed in the twenty years I knew him. I bet he cried over my casket, saying what a nice guy I was, if he came.* The thought of his own death broke Simon of his numbness, his reverie, and with a sigh and a grunt, he gently placed Mary's head on the wooden floor and pushed himself onto his feet.

Mary's blood had covered his white shirt, and the sticky red liquid had dried on his face and hands. He thought about changing but decided that if he had to move Mary, there was no sense in changing clothes just to get fresh ones bloodied. *How on earth am I supposed to get her out of the tree house?* Simon thought with dismay. *Should I have a funeral for her? Bury her? Do they even have funerals here? What am I supposed to do?* Feeling helpless and alone, Simon instinctively looked to Mary, almost as if he believed she would have the answers. All he received for a response was a lifeless form, eyes closed, without the remotest care for Simon's predicament. Needing to clear his head, to step out from the horrible situation in which he found himself, Simon walked outside onto the porch.

Stepping through the entryway, Simon was immediately greeted by red staining the porch floor and pieces of rope still hanging from the knots jutting out of the tree trunk. Images of a flashing blade, murderous eyes, and Mary's face fixed in pain invaded his mind, overwhelming him. Seeing that he would have no peace where he was, Simon left the porch and descended from the heights of the tree house to the forest floor below. He was dimly aware that he was barefoot, that his pants were still in his room, but he did not care. He descended the mushroom steps, a shadow of a child barely touching the fungus.

Stepping off the spiraling stairs and onto the soft ground, Simon tried to take a deep breath and gagged. The stench of death and human refuse invaded his nostrils and choked the breath out of his lungs, giving him a coughing fit. Near his feet, brain matter and blood splattered the ground, originating from a twisted form lying among dead leaves and whispering grass. The man, Mary's tormentor, had soiled himself upon death, which added a rancid quality to the already ripe smell surrounding the body.

Simon gagged again and, using a piece of his shirt, covered his nose and mouth. The iron tang of blood helped cover up the stench of the man Simon had sent careening to his death, but just barely. Simon was surprised to see that he still held the knife with the well-worn handle in a white-knuckle grip. Coughing again, Simon continued walking, knife at his side and bloody shirt covering his face. It was as if the world had conspired to push him away from the tree house, giving him no peace until he was moving away from the murderous scene.

Stepping onto the path, a safe distance away from the murder scene in the tree house and the gruesome faceplant at the base of the tree, Simon dropped his blood-soaked shirt from his face and continued walking. The movement began to clear his mind, to allow him to begin planning what to do next. Taking a deep breath, he strode toward town, ideas solidifying in his mind.

The forest barely registered in his peripheral vision as he marched on. Trees swayed and danced to the music of the wind, and birds from all climes lent their voices to the breathy song. Sounds slipped in and out of Simon's ears as he continued his march. He knew that he had to keep walking, to find someone to help him, someone who knew this world better than he. Someone *big*. Simon walked until the forest gave way to fields, and the bridge that seemed to grow out of the banks of the small river came into view. The dancing shrubs and small trees altered their dance as he approached, their movements taking on a hurried grace. He barely gave them a second glance as he entered the town.

Signs that advertised the wares of the square buildings swayed lazily in the breeze, and people milled about in the clothes that depicted the era from which they had first lived. The pain in Simon's heart and the freshness of the wounds were violently contrasted by the normalcy and rhythm of everyday life that could be found in the village. Simon felt anger rise up—anger at the people who could manage to maintain a normal existence when his own world had descended into madness, spiraled into chaos. Frowning and squaring his shoulders, Simon marched on.

Some people noticed his face, his bloodstained shirt, but none stopped to ask him what was wrong. He might as well have stained his shirt with juice, for all the reaction it received. *Jesus Christ, this place is nuts. Do death and violence really have no meaning to these people? I almost wish someone would ask me if I'm all right.*

Simon kept trudging until his steps brought him to the shop of Taillevent, the man who had been friendly to him and one of the few people he knew in this world. Pushing the door open, he stepped inside.

The smell of fresh bread and pastries filled his nose, a pleasant aroma that made Simon want to cry. He thought of Mary again, of a version of her that was bathed in light and pleasant recollection. She had become angelic in his memory, and he missed her. Taillevent, his back turned to the door, his eyes fixed on something out of Simon's vision, called behind him, "I will be with you in a moment. Not to worry."

"Mary's dead, Taillevent. Someone tortured and killed her on our porch."

Taillevent stiffened and stood up. Taking a deep breath, he sighed and turned around. When he looked at Simon, his eyes, peeking around his giant nose, were filled with sadness.

"*Je suis désolé,* Sprout. I am sorry for you. I bid her safe Return. What happened?"

"Simon. My name is Simon." Simon squared his shoulders and stood as tall as he could. He didn't know why, but for some reason, he needed to be called Simon. Sprout was a name given by Mary, and Mary was gone. The kind eyes regarded Simon, seeming to read his thoughts.

"Very well, Simon it shall be. What happened?"

Tears welling in his eyes, Simon forced them down and told of the gruesome end of his caretaker. Taillevent listened quietly, occasionally muttering a curse under his breath or shaking his head despondently.

"Why would anyone do this to her? Why ... why would they be so, so *evil* to Mary? Why would this lunatic want to torture someone like that? What am I missing?" The familiarity of interrogation made Simon feel better. His mind flashed back to windowless rooms with harsh overhead light, with him and a partner pumping the witness or suspect for information. That's what he needed more than anything else; he needed to *know,* both because of the man he was and for his own sanity.

"*C'est affreux.* It's awful, but it doesn't sound as if Mary was targeted for any other reason than that she was alone, and she was a woman. Sit down, Simon. There are things about Dara that you do not know, dark things that we usually do not speak of until a new arrival such as yourself has lived here longer. We try to save you the pain until you are more capable, but it seems as though pain has found its way to you."

"It's all right. I can take it," Simon responded. *Before coming here, let's just say that I had seen my fair share of the evils humanity is able to commit.* "Please, tell me. I need to know."

"Very well. The man you threw off your deck, the man who was torturing Mary, he was not alone. He is a part of a group of people who have taken everything good about Dara and twisted it to fit their most devilish desires. So much of human morality, for the majority of people, is based on fear. What greater fear than the fear of death was there in our previous lives?" Taillevent coughed.

"But, when people came here, they realized that death is no longer permanent, that we always Return. For some, this meant a reevaluation of all that is important, of all that is *real,* of all that matters. For all of us, the removal of the fear of death meant that we were free. We were free to be exactly who we wished to be. This freedom proved to be wonderful for many people. Art, music, food ..." Taillevent's face cracked into a small, sad smile. "All these things we were free to truly understand. We fell into our passions with a vigor that could never be matched in our old lives."

Simon nodded. It made sense. Once the fear of death, the ultimate punishment, is removed from humanity, all people are free to do anything they wish. "I think I understand, but this still does not explain why someone would ... would ... do what they did." Tears sprang to his eyes again, and Simon let them fall. *It's too much. It's too much!* Images of Mary danced in his head.

"Oh, my dear Simon, but it does. While the freedom of Dara helped most of us aspire to create a better world, to embrace our passions and proclivities, for others, it was a doorway in which to step into the darkest corners of their souls." The chef's eyes turned down and away from Simon, his shoulders sagging.

"Without death to stop us, without fear, some gave in to their darker desires. It started as humanist debauchery, of people testing the boundaries of sex and pleasure. Dionysus would have been proud. But, after a time, the pursuit of pleasure began to take a darker turn. People began to capture and torture others, to push the boundary further. Before long, not even children were safe from such things, which is why we try to protect the newly Returned—to not let them fall into the hands of these people."

Images of a dark alley and a rough stone wall burst into Simon's mind. The copper taste of blood crept into his mouth.

"It was one of those people, one of those vile creatures, who tortured Mary. I hate to think of what this man would have done if you had not been there, or worse, if he had found you and not Mary. There are things so much worse than death here in Dara, Simon. It is best that you remember that."

"I understand just how evil humanity can be. In my past life, I was a cop, a police officer."

"You were a watchman. A hard man." Taillevent nodded.

"Sure. I know just how evil people can be, but it was usually for a reason: for drugs, or sex, or insanity, or just plain evil. But here, isn't this place supposed to have a *purpose?*"

"I do not have answers to that question. I have heard some people say that those who have embraced this darkness believe that the exploration of all facets of humanity must be experienced before they can leave Dara and move on to the next plane. Some say that these people had their Moment of Ascension, their entrance to this plane, by committing an act so vile that it transcended human nature. Their belief is that, since the shadowy side of humanity ensured their continuation, that same evil will help to complete their Journey. I do not know and do not wish to know. I just understand that these people exist and must be avoided at all costs."

Simon looked at the large man, and as he did, images of the worst people he ever put behind bars began dancing in his mind. *How could this be? How can the good people truly die while these monsters continue? If there is a God, he is a prick.* Worse, a dark memory of his own bubbled forth, forcing him to recall that night, all those years ago. He furiously fought it, forced it down. He was not like these people! He was a good man, a good person. And damn anyone who made him think otherwise! His anger for the people who had committed such an atrocious act for the sake of their own pleasure burned white-hot, and he felt sweat begin to bead on his forehead.

"Where can I find these people? They must pay for what they did."

"I agree, Simon, I do, but what can be done? If we kill them, they simply Return, and it is hard to know who is of their ranks until they reach adulthood, and often that is too late. Those who live in this town capture many of these people and confine them to prison, but they just slit their wrists or crack their skulls to Return again."

"There must be something we can do! These people cannot simply be allowed to run free." Simon's knuckles became white as he flexed his small fists at his sides. Hot tears threatened to spring from his face.

"*Je suis d'accord.* I agree, but it is not something that you can do now. You have the mind of a man, but you are still a child. If you wish to fight, to stand against the darkness, there is much you need to learn. You must grow."

Moving from behind the polished counter to face Simon, Taillevent dropped to one knee to be at eye level with the boy. His hand moved to his shoulder, and his tone became soft.

"You must grow, Simon. Learn to Change, how to use the powers of this world, if you wish to stand against these people. The one who attacked Mary, his absence will arouse suspicion with the others. You need protection and cannot return to your home, at least not yet. Is there somewhere you can stay?"

Simon thought, and the image of a man with a beard and bloodied knife came to mind.

"Do you know of a man named Thales?'

"*Oui.* Yes, he is a good man, one who can teach you much. How do you know him?"

"He saved my life. He told Mary that he wanted to become my guide. I think I can trust him."

"This is good. Wait here, and he will come by soon. Everyone in this village visits me at some point during the day." A hint of what could have been pride garnished the chef's words, adding a depth to the tone.

"Thank you, Taillevent. I cannot thank you enough."

"*De rien.* It is nothing. Here, have a cookie, and I will go grab you one of my shirts." Taillevent patted his belly and smiled again. "I am sure it will be much too large, but it is clean and dry. Stay as long as is needed. Thales will be along shortly."

With a final kind smile, the chef slid his large frame through the back door and disappeared. Simon stared down at the treat handed to him and thought of Mary's presence. The ghost of rose water touched his nose, a memory of a scent as vague as an embrace written about but never felt. Tears fell down, and he let them. Drops fell on yellow icing, forming little craters. Loneliness crept in, and Simon waited.

CHAPTER VII–HOW MANY LOVED

Ten Years Later

Simon's eyes, fighting the sun rays tickling his lashes, squeezed shut, trying to hide from the morning. He turned away from the light, throwing his quilted blanket over his head, trying to block out the day. Yet the progression of time would not be derailed, and with a sigh, Simon's eyes opened, and he kicked his thin blanket off with a grunt. Looking down, Simon grunted again. *Every day, it's like this, I knew it would happen, but every day? Jesus Christ, I hate being a teenager. I hated it the first time, and I hate it now.* Simon waited, thought of trees and baseball, until everything finally relaxed and fell back into its resting place, then sat up.

Shaking his head and running his hands over the top of his head, Simon couldn't resist tugging at the thick hair hanging down past his shoulders. A small smile danced across his mouth. *Well, it's not all bad, I suppose. I sure hated being bald.* Rolling out of bed, bare feet touching cold stone, Simon shuffled out of the nook that held his bed and stepped into sunlight.

The smell of olives and baked bread filled his nostrils, and the sound of an ancient tune being hummed with familiarity touched his ears. Simon's room, if it could even be called that, opened directly into a square courtyard, with olive and palm trees lining the outside and a fountain bubbling happily in its center.

Thales was already moving about, his lips humming that ancient song he always did, though Simon could never remember the name. His long brown fingers moved deftly, placing wine goblets, fresh bread, and those strange pancakes he called *teganites* on the small table on which he and Simon always ate. The familiarity of the scene was pleasant to Simon, and he smiled as he walked up to greet the man preparing the morning meal.

"Good morning, Master Thales. I hope you slept well."

"And good morning to you, young Simon. I see you have decided to rise too late to help me prepare the meal, but just in time to eat it." Thales did not look up from his preparations.

"You know how teenagers are. We need our sleep. Growing bodies and all that. I tell you, Thales, I did not realize how much I missed my bones not aching every morning, and all of my ... *parts* working just right."

"Yes, yes, I'm so happy for you and your 'parts.' Pass me some bread, please." As Simon tried to reach over to grab the loaf, Thales cleared his throat. "Today, I would like you to visit a friend of mine. Out of everyone I know, he has the best grasp of Journeys and how they work, and it is time for you to understand your own Journey."

Simon plopped down, adjusting his leggings as he did. He always slept in his pants, but could not bear to sleep in his shirt, as it kept bunching in the night. Thales claimed to sleep in the nude and was confused that Simon did not, and the youth was thankful that his eccentric guide did not sleep walk.

Simon reached to grab a loaf of bread, passed it to Thales, then began plowing into his own breakfast. He ate with the vigor and life of a young man in the throes of vitality and youth.

Simon's eyes came up to look at his teacher, as what Thales said finally registered in his mind. He pushed a piece of the strange pancake-like pastry that Thales enjoyed so much to the side of his mouth, freeing his tongue. "I know what Journeys are, Master Thales. You told me of them already, almost every day for the last ten years that I have been here. Miss Mary mentioned them before you. They are the reason we are here, the reason we keep Returning to Dara."

"And why is that, young Simon? Why do we keep Returning to Dara?"

"Because, though we managed to step outside of the human experience, to become something more than human during our Moment of Ascension, who we are as people never fully evolved. Something happened to us in our lives that stunted us, arrested our development, kept us from fully developing our souls, or spirits, or whatever."

Thales nodded and gave his curly beard a quick scratch. "But why this particular moment, my young pupil? Can you remember? All of our lives are centered around experiences that shape us, mold us into who we are. What makes this moment so different?"

Simon's eyes looked down at the floor, his mind trying to concentrate on what Thales taught him. There was so much that he and the philosopher had talked about, so much that he learned since Mary had passed, that it made his head spin. Information swirled through the caverns of his mind: thoughts about Changing, Returning, the Moment of Ascension, Journeys … But for some reason, he could not grasp the answer to his mentor's question. *Goddamn it. I hate forgetting things.* Looking up, meeting those expectant eyes, Simon said he could not recall.

Thwack!

Seemingly out of nowhere, Thales had withdrawn a small cylindrical stick and had rapped Simon's knuckles with it, causing him to yelp in pain and drop his pastry. Before he could curse or insult, Thales shouted

"Moment of Definition!"

Simon stopped, confusion sticking to his face. The philosopher shouted the phrase again, then immediately continued in a calm voice as if nothing happened.

"Use the pain to remember the phrase. That is the name of the moment that defines us here. The seed of our Journey." The philosopher had sat back down and was slowly stroking his curly facial hair once again.

103

Thales stopped scratching his beard after a few moments, and turned to look at the bewildered Simon. He nodded. "You spoke true about Journeys, but you do not know *why* Journeys exist, nor, more importantly, *how* they exist. As a result, you will be very confused when your own Journey starts pulling at you. It is around your age that Journeys start to guide a soul in a specific direction, and Paracelsus can help you prepare for just such a moment."

"What do you mean, my Journey will start pulling at me? How am I supposed to know when that happens?"

"Oh, trust me, my young Simon, you will know. It will feel like fate has thrown you into its fast currents, and there is nothing to hold on to. It seems we have a purpose, a course, even after death, and it is best that you are prepared for it. Now, get dressed and meet me near the olive trees."

"Yes, Master Thales." The words slid out of Simon's mouth automatically. His teacher and mentor was a good man and had been kind to the youth, but he demanded respect, and when a command was given, it was carried out, or uncomfortable results ensued. Grabbing one more slice of warm bread, Simon drained his cup and returned to the enclave that held his bed.

The house of Thales the philosopher had been constructed in the ancient Greek style, with stone walls, a square courtyard, and a red roof. Apparently, the walls had been a solid piece of rock, Changed by Thales to suit his needs. The result was what looked like the inside of a strange cave, naturally eroded and shaped to make rooms and a stone floor.

Touching the smooth stone as he passed, Simon stooped down, picked up a shirt he had tossed on the floor, and threw it over his head. It was a simple piece of clothing, tan and unadorned, but Simon was proud of it. It was the first piece of clothing he had sewn on his own, and it did not look half bad. Turning cotton into cloth using nothing but his mind was something that Thales had to do, but once the philosopher had completed the transformation, Simon had stitched the pieces together using a needle and thread. It took days to complete, with Thales constantly instructing him and remarking on how slow he was. Yet the shirt was made, and Simon's chest swelled just a little bit each time the soft fabric touched his skin.

Reaching down, Simon grabbed his sewn moccasins from the ground, hurriedly shoving his feet into the shoes. Thales did not understand why he wouldn't adopt the toga, saying it was much easier and more comfortable than pants and a shirt. Yet Simon could not bring himself to wear the garment, as it felt like he had just decided to take his sheet with him after getting out of bed. He needed to feel some connection to his old self, to who he was, and part of that connection could be found with his clothes. *God, if I could have a pair of blue jeans again. My Levi's and a sturdy pair of hiking boots would be just right.*

Having stuffed his skinny teenage arms and awkward feet into their respective proper places, Simon fastened a leather belt around his waist and reached under his pillow to retrieve his knife. As always, a murmur of pain floated in as he grasped the smooth wooden hilt wrapped in dark leather, and on the heels of the murmur, an image of a woman drenched in blood stabbed into his thoughts. Shaking it out, Simon tightened the belt and straightened.

Fully clothed, he jumped out of his small enclave and hurried outside of the walled courtyard, where Thales had his olive grove. He smiled as he moved quickly. It *feels good to have everything work again.* Simon picked up the pace to meet the philosopher, grinning as he ran.

The smell of olives greeted him as he stepped into the rows of trees—bushy explosions of green covering the flat plane just outside of Thales's home. Simon had spent many an hour in this grove, tending the trees, harvesting the olives, clearing the soil. He enjoyed the olive grove more than the vine-covered hill on the other side of the compound, where Thales grew his grapes for wine. The earthy, slightly tart smell brought him peace, gave him a relaxed view of the world. The vines, they just smacked of a hard day's work and a sore back.

Thales was there, white toga sliding across the ground, surveying his trees. Seeing Simon walk up to him, he turned and smiled, then immediately let the smile drop to be replaced with a more serious expression. On the ground was a small barrel, plugged and smelling of fermentation.

"Time to start moving. Paracelsus is a man of routine, to a fault. He found his way here through his abilities to analyze. Very structured man. We better hurry, or he will be gone, and we won't find him until tomorrow. You will need to carry this with you. It will come in handy, as I am sure Paracelsus has already forgotten we are coming. He is very structured in his analysis of the world, of his interests, but in everything else, he lives in a constant state of near-chaos. This should help smooth things along."

Without another word, Thales set off, toga flapping in the wind caused by his motion, his beard and chin pointing down the road. Simon reached down, hefted the small barrel onto his shoulder, the contents splashing inside their wooden enclosure. Having secured his bundle, Simon shuffled to match the pace of his learned companion, his gangly legs sometimes arguing with his mind, causing him to stumble. *Was I really this awkward as a teenager? It feels as though my body and brain are having a war to see who can embarrass me more.* Focusing on his movement, Simon matched the ancient philosopher's stride, and together they strode down the path, heading west toward town.

Trees swayed in a quiet breeze, and grass danced to either side of the well-worn path. Green was occasionally mottled by the splash of yellow and blue, of purple and red, as flowers of various climes shot up through the grass or out of the sides of trees. In the distance, the broken teeth of the upside-down mountains could be seen, with a giant splash of streaking clouds gracing the sky even farther away. The oddity of the topography, even after years, amazed Simon. Birds gave their song to the world, and insects buzzed contentedly. Enchantment reigned, and Simon allowed his mind to be swallowed by the world's mysteries.

"Now, why don't you see anything but the occasional herbivore on the path, Simon?" Thales's voice broke through the young man's daydream. "Where are they? Where are the dangerous creatures, the dinosaur skeletons, the mastodons, the tigers?"

"The village ensures that all dangerous creatures are either pushed back or killed, so that we may walk in peace," Simon intoned, the words automatic and rehearsed. A feeling of annoyance spiked inside him. Why must Thales *always* be teaching? Can't he have just a moment to be himself, to be a part of the world? *Shut up, idiot! You sound like your daughters at 13. I don't need the angst. Thales is just trying to help.*

"Very good, Simon, very good. We make sure that young ones are protected and that people can have a semblance of normalcy and peace in a world that is, for all intents and purposes, completely without said peace and normalcy—at least not in the way we used to view it. Now, what is this village called, and what are the other 15 to be found on this plane?"

"Do we have to do this? I really was hoping we could just walk— enjoy the morning."

Thales stopped and turned with a speed Simon never expected. His eyes locked onto Simon's, and all of the lightness of his tone hardened to stone. Simon nearly dropped the wooden barrel as he skidded his feet to avoid hitting his mentor.

"Simon, I know there are chemicals rushing through you right now that cause your mood to waiver, but I need you to focus. Dara can be cruel, as you well know, and you may wake up with nothing and no one by your side, simply because someone else decided it was a good idea to murder your loved ones. How old were you when you died?"

"I was 67 years old."

"Very good. Remember who you were at that age, and not the age you are now. Be objective and do not let youthfulness cloud your judgement."

"I'm sorry, Master Thales, you are right. I will try harder."

Simon looked down at the ground for a moment, trying to focus on the experiences he had, the life he had led, the children he had raised. He had to make sure to not let the foul essence of puberty cloud his judgment. Part of him thought, *Jesus, it was just town names. Why does Thales have to be such a hard-ass?* Yet that thought was quickly tamped down by the simple truth of Thales's words. He had to know all that he could learn, or else he would be fodder for the animals and the blood cults.

"Very good, Simon. Now, what are the names of the 15 villages of Dara? The 15 we know of, anyway. Some people believe there are more. I cannot say whether that is true or not. Let's start with what we know."

Walking through the grassy fields and past small, flowering trees, Simon began to recite the names of the towns he remembered. There was Elysium, Shangris Las, and Tuatha, all bordering the village in which Simon had ascended: Valoren. There was Paradisio, Eden Town, Valhalla, and Xibalba to the south, and the town of Hope in the plains.

"Now, what is the significance of Hope, Simon? Was it always called Hope? What makes that town of particular interest?"

Simon stopped rattling off names and turned to his bearded companion. "The town of Hope, if I recall correctly, used to be called Mesis, from the Greek for *middle*. However, a few decades ago, the village of Mesis endured a catastrophe so severe that its name was changed."

"Very good. What was the catastrophe?"

"The moon landing."

"Excellent! As you know by now, everything that was discovered, everything that has been added to the human consciousness, ends up here, sometimes without rhyme nor reason. Now, humans have been looking at the moon ..." Thales sent one bony digit to point at the sky, where the moon hung suspended, next to the fiery sun. "...for thousands of years. However, as soon as someone set foot on that floating orb, as soon as they managed to add it to human consciousness, *BAM!*"

The philosopher made a fist and slammed it into his palm, making a cracking sound. His eyes sparkled as he became enraptured in his tale. "A giant ball of space rock crashed into the middle of our home, mere meters away from the outskirts of Mesis. As a result, the people, having recovered from such a shock, changed the name of the town from Mesis to Hope and watched the sky a little more warily."

"I would hate to see what happens when humans discover another planet. Could it destroy this place?" Simon asked, and he felt nervousness stab through him. He had already died once, well, twice now, if being the lunch of a lioness counted, and both times were terrible. He would hate to have the life that he was just beginning to understand be taken from him, all because the civilization on Earth had become advanced enough to find somewhere new.

"I do not know," his teacher responded, "but, I find it to be unlikely. I do not think that space, distance, and time work the same here as they do on the plane we have left. I think that Dara stretches to accommodate new discoveries, new leaps in human consciousness. The moon probably made this place bigger by its presence. Now, where were we? Yes, what are the towns of the south? Keep going. We have a way to go yet."

Sighing, resigning himself to being lectured and tested, Simon kept rattling off the names of the various towns he could remember. Time passed, and he and his philosopher guardian walked on, through the plains and into town. They stopped briefly to pick up a loaf of bread from Taillevent, and, as usual, the big chef was happy to see Simon, laughing and slapping his back as he commented on how much he had grown. After bidding farewell to his friend, Simon followed Thales out of the small shop door and continued walking through the village.

Thales stopped briefly to speak to some of his fellow Greeks, and as he did, Simon sat back and watched the village move through its peaceful, lazy machinations. Having completed his brief exchange with his colleagues, Thales continued walking, and Simon followed. Soon, they were out of the village, heading west.

The plains that surrounded the village, dotted with tree houses like the one that Simon had been raised in, were bordered by a giant pine and redwood forest. Grass and the occasional tree were replaced with boulders and large oaks, with giant redwoods reaching into the sky and pine trees that gave off the scent of freshness and ancient holidays.

After a few minutes of walking deeper and deeper into the shady wood, Thales suddenly turned left, onto a small path that looked like it was used more by deer and other wildlife than humanity. Moccasins and sandaled feet slid over crackling pine needles and cones, and prickly branches grazed Simon's arms and pants. As the trail narrowed more, Simon had to transfer the barrel from his shoulder to his arms, and he awkwardly shuffled behind Thales, who seemed to walk without the slightest hindrance. *I bet this wine makes you hallucinate or something.*

Simon stopped dead in his tracks. "Master Thales?"

"Yes, young Simon?"

"Are there ... are there drugs here? What happens if you hallucinate? Do you create things?"

The middle-aged philosopher stopped, and for a moment, there was nothing but the ever-present breeze dancing on the path. Finally, Thales turned to Simon, and a sad smile played upon his lips as he spoke.

"Yes, there are drugs here, but if it is relief you seek, you can simply learn to Change the number of endorphins in your brain. Oh, you should have seen this world when brain-mapping was discovered!" Thales laughed, and its sound danced among the trees. *Never thought of that. Maybe I should try that. Never could say no to a good time.*

Thales's laugh stopped, a biting change that made Simon snap his head toward the philosopher. As if reading his thoughts, Thales grabbed the youth's shoulders, looking straight into his eyes.

110

"Do not try it yet, young Simon. You may accidentally make yourself an imbecile, which will leave me without a companion, and you without your lessons until you Return."

Simon nodded. "What about hallucinogens? They were pretty intense when I was alive. Do they exist here?"

Thales's head bobbed in ascent. "I spent a few lifetimes among the Vision Seekers in Gardenia, the mountain village north and west of here. Many people lose themselves in that place because it allows them to see those who have passed on, never to Return."

Simon cocked his head but remained silent. He had found that if he kept his mouth shut, Thales would eventually answer his questions. However, Thales became silent, lost in thought, and then, without another word, the bearded man returned to walking. Simon decided to not press the issue further and, instead, hurried to catch up to his guide, but not before he made a mental note to visit this Gardenia. *It would be good to see Anna and the kids and grandkids again. I wonder if she's still around? I wish I could talk to her.* Simon walked behind his guide and mentor, his mind swirling with the memories of family and friends.

Chapter VIII– Your Moments

The vibrant trees gave way to a circular clearing, ringed by giant redwoods and oaks, and in the center of the glen sat a grey stone, hewn in the middle to give a flat surface like a table. Birds chirped, insects hummed, and small rodents flitted through the grass and up the giant trunks of trees. A white flash bounced by Simon's feet, and he looked down to see the white, fluffy tail of a rabbit disappear from view. The place felt both wild and safe simultaneously, as if the caretaker of the glen was part human, part bear or badger.

Simon loved the place immediately, as it catered to the youthful need for adventure and danger that many young men find in their hearts, while also giving an air of the mystical. A smile came across his face, and his shoulders relaxed. Gently, he dropped the barrel of wine onto the grassy earth and drank in the tranquility of the clearing.

In the middle of the glade, on the stone table, a figure was hunched over, intent on an object obscured by his body, his hands moving quickly. One hand held a stick with one end burned to a black charcoal, which provided a rudimentary writing utensil for the hunched-over figure, and he used it to furiously write on the stone slab. The other hand was hurriedly stuffing items into a bag, its sides made of wicker, and its lid, pulled up, made of animal skin. The straps were worn with use. The figure kept packing and writing, showing absolutely no interest in the two men who had walked into his glen. Simon looked to Thales and was surprised to see a fond smile raking across the man's face.

"I am glad we caught you, Master Paracelsus. It looks like if we had arrived a few minutes later, we would have had to wait until tomorrow to see you again. I see that you have forgotten you were to meet my young pupil Simon today, but no matter. We are here now, and that is what is important."

Surprised by the sound of a human voice, the figure stiffened, his work momentarily forgotten. He turned, a look of frustration at being interrupted sliding across his features, only to be replaced by recognition of Thales and then sliding right back into a look of frustration. Simon guessed that he must wear that expression a lot, as it did not leave his face for a moment as he and Thales approached.

He was not a tall man, and his round features made him look as though he carried extra fat in odd places, causing his body to seem lumpy and unbalanced. Broad shoulders slumped downward in a dirty linen shirt, its laces undone at the neck and with wrinkles that showed it had been slept in the night before. A pot belly hung over belted, tight leggings, and soft, dark-leather boots graced his feet. A traveling cloak of dark forest green, well used and as wrinkled as his shirt, draped over his shoulders. He did not look young, and he did not look old; he looked perpetually upset, like his tongue continuously produced saliva that tasted of lemons and salt. Light red hair fell to his shoulders, thinning at the top of his large bulbous head. Yet the eyes were bright and intelligent and took in both Thales and Simon in an instant. His right hand fell to touch the hilt of a sword hanging from his hip, its handle worn from sweat and constant use. *This is a dangerous man,* Simon thought, *though you could never guess from looking at him. Better watch my back.*

"What do you want, Thales? I have much to do and don't intend on staying here chatting all day. Who is this? Simon? I don't know the name. Get out of here. There's only so much light in the day, and I want to be nearly halfway to Tuatha by nightfall."

Paracelsus let his hand fall from his sword and turned his back to Thales and Simon, returning to packing strange items into his wicker pack and taking notes with his charcoal stick.

Unperturbed, Thales walked up to Paracelsus and placed his hand on the strange man's shoulder. Paracelsus stiffened at the contact and continued packing.

"Simon here, as I told you before, is new to Dara. He does not know of Journeys or how they work, and you are the best at explaining such things, at helping people discover their Journeys. You always said that you enjoyed teaching people the truth. Is that not so?"

The strange man stopped and turned to look Thales dead in the eyes, then looked past the philosopher to stare at Simon. The eyes, beady and too close together, seemed to regard Simon with the look of a scientist dissecting a frog, not caring about the creature itself, just what secrets it held. The man hesitated and returned to regard Thales.

"It is true, I enjoy speaking truth to those who will listen, unlike those damn fools of my time, calling me a witch and screaming for my head. That is how I came to be here, boy—through my unflinching search for truth. Did you know that people of my day used to try to cure wounds by coating them in cow dung? Bah! Cover it in shit, and then you're surprised when it festers? Bah! Yet when I healed them, pointed out their lunacy, they would try to *kill* me! Damn fools."

The man seemed to regard them a second time. "Now, Thales, I don't recall agreeing to teach your boy here, and as much as I love the telling of truths, I must be going. Perhaps some other time, when I don't have so much to do."

Paracelsus shouldered his pack and made to leave the clearing. Without a word, Thales retrieved the small barrel Simon had set down and popped the bung out of it. Paracelsus, having walked toward Thales and the barrel, stopped abruptly as the smell of fermented grapes filled the air. The red-haired man appeared to be frozen, as if by the magic of Bacchus himself.

"It would be such a shame not to toast your travels before you left, especially since young Simon here had to carry this barrel all the way from my home to yours. Would you mind sharing a cup of wine with us before your travels?" Thales looked at Paracelsus expectantly, the barrel of wine held in his hands.

Paracelsus, transfixed by the smell of fermented grape and the size of the barrel, straightened slightly as he spoke. "I am a hunter of truth, Thales, a seeker of knowledge, both in this life and the ones to follow. In the hunt for truth, I must be honest with myself as well, and my body is telling me that the road to Tuatha will be there tomorrow, but that wine might not."

With that, Paracelsus unceremoniously dropped his wicker backpack, opened the animal-skin lid, and produced three small wooden drinking cups, shining dully in the sun. Walking back to the center of the clearing, he set them on the stone slab and looked at Thales eagerly. Thales immediately lifted the barrel, walked over to the stone slab, and filled Paracelsus's cup to the brim, then filled his own cup and Simon's to about half full. Snatching the wine, Paracelsus raised his cup in salute.

"To your health. May you live forever." With a chortle, Paracelsus tipped his glass and drained the whole of its contents in a single gulp. He sighed contentedly as he set the cup back down.

Thales refilled it immediately. The beady eyes seemed to lose some of their sharpness.

"Now, what is it you wanted of me? What can Paracelsus, the hunter of truth, assist you travelers with?" The man's small chest puffed in mock boasting as he spoke, and he drained another glass. As he filled the cup again, Thales spoke.

"Well, this is Simon's first time in Dara. He has been learning from me for the ten years, ever since his carrier, Mary, was murdered by one of ... those people."

Both Thales and Paracelsus looked down and murmured, "I bid her safe Return," and took a sip from their glasses. Eyes going distant for a moment, Thales shook himself, squared his shoulders back, and continued.

"He knows a little of Changing, what it means to Return, and the Moment of Ascension and Definition. What he needs to learn about is Journeys and how to handle it when the pull begins. One's Journey is such a large part of life here in Dara that I decided it was best that Simon learned from the most skilled historian on the topic. Hence, why we are drinking my wine, and why you will be drunk shortly."

With a small raising of his cup in salute, Thales nodded to Paracelsus and drained his cup. After refilling it from the barrel, he sat down, leaned against the stone slab, and looked at Paracelsus, waiting for something. Simon shifted his gaze between his learned tutor and the strange portly man in the dark green traveler's cloak. Paracelsus leaned against the stone slab on the opposite side of Thales, and Simon sat down cross-legged in the grass, looking between the bulbous traveler and the well-kempt philosopher. After a moment, Paracelsus spoke.

"Well, I am glad you have come, if nothing else, to enjoy wine with me. However, boy, your caretaker speaks truth; I am one of the most learned people on this plane about Journeys. Some say it is because I wandered my entire first life, first as a war medic and then as a doctor, trying to keep the idiots of the world from killing themselves by believing snake venom could cure headaches and horse piss could staunch the flow of a spear thrust. Both true beliefs, by the way!"

Paracelsus's voice, having raised in pitch and fervor as he spoke, filled the glade, and, with face red from fury, he angrily drained another glass. *This guy really does not like ignorance,* Simon thought, *if he still gets this mad at people who probably died a long time ago.* Not knowing exactly how to respond, Simon nodded and took a sip of his wine. It tasted rich and earthy, with a little hint of blackberries. He sat and sipped as Paracelsus went to fill his cup for the fourth time in as many minutes.

Having replenished his supply of liquid cheer and settled back down to a seated position in the grass, Paracelsus looked at Simon and continued. "The truth is, I know about Journeys because I have spent the last five centuries, give or take a couple decades, researching them. Each person has one, and each person must complete their Journey if they are to have any peace at all."

Simon looked at Paracelsus, confusion criss crossing his face. "But why? What really are Journeys, Mr. Paracelsus? What is their purpose? What is the point of having them?"

Rather than answer right away, Paracelsus leaned his head back and laughed, a giant guffaw that caused tears to stream down his portly cheeks. "Why do we have Journeys? Why do we breathe air instead of water? Why do we have to die? Why do we communicate as a species? Why? *Why!* Foolish child, such questions are not the path to learning. You must first learn the *what* before you can begin to even imagine the *how,* let alone the *why.* So, tell me, boy, *what* is a Journey? What is yours?"

Simon stopped, more than a little off-put that this fat little man found his questions so funny, and he was equally perturbed by his answer. *Calm down Floyd, this is just the way of the world here. People are not supposed to live this long, so of course the older ones are a bit nutty. Doesn't explain Thales though. Glad he's my guide instead of this paunchy loon.*

Paracelsus, staring at Simon, drank his wine and watched the youth impatiently. Snapping back to reality and banking on the fact that this Paracelsus was as wise as Thales claimed, Simon dug deep into his lessons with Thales over the last decade and began to recite as much as he could remember.

"Journeys are the actions we must take in order to evolve into our true selves. At some point in our first, original lives, we had two important moments: the Moment of Ascension, which allowed us to step outside of our animalistic, base impulses and become something more than human, which got us here in the first place, and the Moment of Definition," Simon's knuckles smarted from a phantom blow. He quickly rubbed them as he continued. "Is what most people call the Memory. It is the moment in our lives that led to defining us as human beings and stunted us from progressing any further than we did. Our Journey is to evolve past that particular moment, to discover the truth of ourselves and ascend further."

Paracelsus nodded, but poked a singular, small fat finger into the air. "That's very close, Master Steven"

"My name is Simon."

"Whatever, it is close, Simpson. However, the Moment of Ascension is our Memory. It is the moment that we return to when we first enter Dara. The Moment of Definition is the often cataclysmic event that anchors us to this place, and does not let us move forward. Not that some of us want to." Paracelsus made an exaggerated toast toward Thales. The philosopher's face became a singular frown, and Simon made a mental note to inquire into that further. Paracelsus continued

"And what, pray tell, is the difference between the moment that defines our Journey and any other moment that helped us grow and progress as human beings? What is the difference?"

Here, Simon faltered. He looked at Thales for answers, but the bearded man kept sipping his wine, eyes moving lazily from Paracelsus to Simon, simultaneously interested and disinterested in the conversation. *Fantastic. Thanks for the help.* "In all honesty, Mr. Paracelsus, I do not know."

"Ahh! That is why you are here, boy. That is why you are here. Not here in Dara, of course, but here in my home. Do you like my home? I surely do. Thales here always used to ask me why I chose to live rough."

Paracelsus, face becoming red from drink, apparently had a personality like a river rock; with enough liquid, it became smooth and easy. He smiled at Simon, all warmth and jovial disposition.

"Truth is, I haven't ever trusted villages or the people in them. When I was alive, in the … other place …" Here, he waved his hand behind him, which was an apparent indication of where the old Earth was. "Almost every village I went to, after having given medical aid and care to the people, healing wounds and easing the suffering of the sick, almost every damn one of them would try to hang me or burn me at the stake. Called me a witch!"

The man giggled and drank again. "Never could get the fear of being hanged or burned like a pig on a spit out of my mind. So, when I Ascended, I found this place and have hung my hat here ever since."

Paracelsus turned his attention back to Simon. "Tell me this then: what is your Moment of Ascension? Leave no detail removed."

Thales chuckled slightly, and Simon became a little red faced.

"It, was stupid really."

"Then I cannot wait to hear every single second of it." To solidify his point, Paracelsus adjusted himself to a more comfortable seated position, exaggerating his rump digging into the earth.

Simon took a deep breath, then plunged right in.

"I was with my friend, Tommy Keane, and we were floating in a river at night on this rickety boat we had made ourselves." Images of Tommy's ruddy, smiling face floated in Simon's memory. "We had been drinking, and had decided that we weren't going to check the water's height beforehand. Tommy left his truck near this shallow place, at a bend in the river, and I drove us to the top, so we could float down, drink some beer, and maybe fish a little."

"Why would you fish at night? This does not make sense to me." Paracelsus breathed heavily then belched as he spoke.

"Well, we weren't really going to fish. We were just wanting a place to be alone so we could have some drinks, smoke some things, and stare at the stars." Paracelsus nodded, as if he completely understood the sentiment. Simon continued.

"I was wearing this flannel shirt and blue jeans, no life jacket because I was a strong swimmer, and Tommy wasn't either because he thought that life jackets were for pu- for weak people." Seeing a look of confusion, Simon quickly explained that life jackets were flotation devices to prevent people from drowning. Paracelsus and Thales nodded sagely.

"Well, as luck would have it, the water had risen because we had torrential rain for a week straight, so instead of a lazy river we had crashing rapids and brutal switch backs. We didn't see a rock jutting out of the water until it was too late. I remember Tommy screaming for us to row to shore, but that just turned our boat so we hit the damn rock broadside. We smacked it, went flying when the boat flipped, and I saw Tommy crack his head on a rock before I got a mouthful and a lungful of water. I thought that was it for me."

Flashes of cold black water flooded Simon's mind now. He saw the fear in Tommy Keane's face as he went sailing through the air, heard the crack of bone on rock. Felt the flash of pain in his arm where he had been dragged across a sharp rock. He remembered the burning sensation as the stone bit deep.

"It was a bad situation. It was cold, and dark, and we hadn't brought anything for emergencies. Somehow Tommy and I ended up on this rock, the water ripping around us, both of us clinging for dear life. I remember seeing Tommy's eyes roll around like marbles in his skull, and thinking 'if I don't get this guy to a hospital soon, it's over.' I tried to grab him, but saw that my left arm was just, hanging there like a limp noodle. But, Tommy's grip was slipping, and I knew I had to make a choice." Simon took another deep breath, letting that strange moment of acceptance fill him once again.

"I just knew that, if I could get him to his truck, then he would be alright. So, I grabbed him with my good hand, turned my head downstream, and made myself into a raft for old Tommy Keane. Couldn't tell you the amount of times that I was knocked, stabbed, and jolted around during that ride, but still I held onto my friend. It was weird; as I was floating downwards, my body slowly giving out, I remember making peace with my own death. I remember something just, clicking in my head. I remember the water slowing down, and seeing the bridge near where Tommy parked come into view, and I knew I made it. The last thing I remember was pushing Tommy, with the last of my strength, onto that sandy shore, then my body gave out completely and everything went black."

"Luckily for both of us, Tommy told his girlfriend what we were doing, so she was waiting for him by his truck with another friend of hers, a girl named Anna." Simon's throat caught as his ex-wife, young and beautiful, danced before his mind's eye. "When they got Tommy in the truck, he managed to mumble my name or something, because they went back and found me, face up, in a pile of reeds. They dragged me out too. And would you believe it, I married that girl Anna five years later."

Silence filled the grove for a moment, each man thinking of various moments of their lives that defined them. Finally Paracelsus spoke, his voice thick. "Your willingness to disregard your own life for the well-being of your friend, without provocation or mental manipulation, caused you to become more than simply the manifestation of your instinct. Well done." Simon coughed.

"But, why aren't there more soldiers, more warriors here? I remember hearing dozens of stories of people risking their lives for others." Simon's heart raced. *Anna would definitely be here then. She must be.*

Paracelsus shook his head. "No, no no. Wrong again. We all have the instinct to preserve our tribe, to keep a clan going. How do you think we survived so long without claws and sharp teeth and fur for all those thousands of years? No, your Moment must be completely intentional and conscious. I love the human spirit, love its desire to preserve, but that is not how we made it here." Paracelsus raised his glass. "But, there are more soldiers here than philosophers, I can tell you that!" He roared with laughter and looked at Thales, who was intentionally and deliberately ignoring him, looking for any smudge of dirt on his hands and sipping his wine absently.

The man in the toga, having satisfactorily examined his nails for any dirt and the surrounding area for anything more interesting than a drunk man telling stories to a boy, turned to Paracelsus. "That is all well and good, but you were telling young Simon here about Journeys. That is why we came, remember?"

"What? Oh yes, of course, of course. I apologize, old friend. The tongue begins to wag when it's given a treat. In this case, a very nice treat. What is this delightful wine?" Paracelsus smiled and waved his cup toward the philosopher, causing a dark red liquid to spill on his hand. The liquid slid down his thick arm, and a red stain bloomed on his shirt sleeve.

"It's a grape I discovered near the home of Spandaramet. It seems as though she found *vitis vinifera* near the southern mountains and decided to make her home there. I keep forgetting to thank her. Next time I'm down south, I should stop by her vineyards." The cheeks of Thales, under his curly chestnut beard, had also begun to sport the slight rouge of a man who was beginning the descent into his cups.

"Who is Spandaramet? What kind of name is that? Is it Greek?" Simon blurted out.

"Armenian, as a matter of fact, and don't change the subject. We have a purpose here, young Simon. Now, pay attention. This is serious." Thales giggled slightly at the last, waving his cup about his face. "Well, as serious as a barrel of wine and three dead men chatting in a field can be. Right, Paracelsus?" Simon laughed at that.

"Quite right, my friend. Now, where was I? Oh, yes. Journeys. The difference between moments that shape us and *the* moment. The truth is, we need moments to define us, to mold us, into the people we are to become. Our lives go from the very malleable and fluid to the concrete and solid very quickly."

"This sounds like fate."

"Don't interrupt me!" Paracelsus's face became purple with rage, causing Simon to flinch and spill some of his own wine on the ground. As quickly as the anger erupted, it drained from Paracelsus's face, and he continued as if nothing happened.

"We stride on to our enlightenment, our ascension of self. The moment that stops our enlightenment, that moment …" Paracelsus stuck his fleshy hand out and snapped his fingers, albeit poorly. "… that moment is the impetus for our Journey in Dara. Have you felt it yet? Felt the desire to fix something from your past life?"

Simon paused, trying to think. The only moment he wanted to alter since he came here was the death of his caretaker, Mary. He wanted to help her, to save her, but he had been too late, too young, too small. *But what about my past life? What is my moment? There are a million things I would like to change. What is the moment that altered who I am?*

"I do not know, Mr. Paracelsus. I do not know. I have many regrets in my life, if I am being honest. I could have been a better man."

"You will know, young one, you will." The eyes of the traveler went distant, disappeared into the depths of a swirling past. "It will come to you, and some days, many days, you will wish that it hadn't. There are moments loaded to the brim with pain, and all you want to do is push them down, remove them from your memory. But if it is your moment, it will never go away. You will have to face it, relive it for almost every second that you manage to draw breath. From the instant you wake until the moment you sleep, it stays with you. Death does not stop it, drink does not stop it, sex does not stop it. You must face it; there is no other way. No other way." The last was spoken barely above a whisper.

Simon felt sympathy for the man, this poor creature who had seemed to be living a solitary life for a few hundred years. The drooping shoulders and slack red hair seemed to slide toward the ground, and the bulbous head hung down. *I can't even imagine what it would be like to live like him for this long. I wonder what his moment was? Why does he say that word so much?* Simon shook himself. He was getting quite drunk.

With a violent shudder and a deep inhalation, Paracelsus straightened himself, belched, and drained his cup. "Well, that is neither here nor there. When your moment arises, when it bubbles up, you will know. It will be your constant companion, and you will have to begin your Journey to overcome it."

Shuffling to his feet, Paracelsus moved over to the barrel and filled his cup, then filled the cup of Thales, and grabbed Simon's and filled it to the brim. Simon sipped again. Sweet heat cascaded down his throat and into his chest. He looked at Paracelsus, a question on his lips.

"But how? How do I overcome my Moment of Ascension? And what happens if I do? I am already dead. What else is there? This is the afterlife, right?"

"That, my good boy, is an *excellent* question. As I'm sure you have already figured out, we don't exactly die here, at least not in the way that we did on the plane in which we were first born. You had someone that you knew die here already, correct? Mary?"

Simon nodded. He was grateful for the wine's numbing effects, as the image of a tortured woman did not come so readily to his mind.

"Well, not to worry. They have probably already Returned, brought through a woman whose Journey involves children. That's the other thing: Journeys will shape your experience here in Dara. You will begin to notice your life taking a distinct shape. If you have to experience childbirth, you will suddenly become pregnant, over and over again. If you have to overcome the death of a loved one, people will surround you, care about you, and then die in front of you so many times that you will feel your soul being ripped apart. There is no escape."

Paracelsus's eyes filled with tears, and Simon felt embarrassment for him and looked away.

"Do not feel shame for tears boy. They are a gift from whatever god you believe in." When Paracelsus looked up, Simon saw the beady eyes of the drunk wanderer staring at him, his face wet with tears. "The sooner you can experience the truth of who you are, of what you feel, the happier you will be." Simon nodded.

"As I was saying, if you manage to overcome, to fulfill your Journey, to evolve into the person you were meant to be, to achieve enlightenment, then, my boy, you will die a true death."

Simon choked on the wine he was sipping, causing a coughing fit that made his eyes water. "Die? Then I can die? What do you mean?"

"I mean exactly what I said, boy! Do you not listen?"

Paracelsus's voice raised into a roar, and he stood, gesturing fiercely with a long, bony finger. Just as quickly, the portly man sat back down, though his tone remained sour.

"Few have managed to complete their Journey, to fight against their natures, and become enlightened, and when they do, their eyes roll back into their heads, and they fall to the ground, dead as this rock." The man patted the stone slab he leaned against. "They disappear, becoming air. And they never, ever, Return. They are gone."

Thales spoke, and his words swayed just like his body. "Now, Paracelsus, that does not mean that they are dead. They could go somewhere else. To another Dara, another plane."

The red-haired man nodded, glassy eyes turning to Thales as he gave him a salute with his cup. "Aye, that's the theory some have. It would make sense that, if we made it here after death, then maybe we simply move on to another plane of existence. Yet I do not believe that to be true."

"And why, pray tell, is that?" Thales hiccuped as he spoke.

"Well, it stands to reason, does it not? Only a few of humanity's population managed to make it here, many completely by accident. Why would the next plane be any different? Also, this place was created by discovery and the expansion of human consciousness. What would the next place even be made of? How could it possibly have been created? No, Master Thales, the fact is, even after making it through to the next plane, death still wishes to claim us as its own. The universe wishes to right its wrong, and it has found a way."

Simon stopped, staring at the portly man with the red stain blooming on his shirt. Wine had painted his small teeth, and they were smiling at him, though the grin never made it to the small eyes that were set too close together. *Jesus, this guy is a barrel of laughs if I ever saw one.*

"With respect, Mr. Paracelsus, I do not believe that. I do not believe that we could make it here, to defeat death, just to be forced to take part in these Journeys, and then die. It isn't fair. It doesn't make sense."

"Make sense? *Make sense?* Thales, is this boy soft in the head? What about where you are standing makes sense? You are speaking to someone who has lived here for five centuries, and the man you live with has been here for millennia! What about this makes sense? No, sense has nothing to do with it, boy."

Paracelsus began to gesticulate wildly, causing wine to stain his shirt and slosh onto the ground.

"Human consciousness doesn't make sense. It is an evolutionary mistake, and now, some of us can't even *die* correctly! No, no, after this, there is nothing. It must be nothing!" Shaking himself, wrestling his emotions under control until his anger only simmered, the strange man in the glade continued.

"There are only two things to do: Resist your Journey and Return, again and again, or complete the task set to you by fate and join your loved ones in death. There is no other way."

The man's voice had taken on a distinct slur, like he had decided to stuff his cheeks with cotton. His eyes, glassy with wine, peered into Simon's soul and did not like what they saw. He had stood to emphasize his point, but his body disagreed with his attempt, and he swayed and gripped the stone table to keep from falling. With a grunt, Paracelsus refilled his cup and sat down.

Simon felt a chill, and nausea swept up from the ground, threatening to send his stomach through his mouth. *Is that it? Is that all there is, truly? When will my time come? When will my Journey begin? I will not allow it; I cannot! I do not wish to die, not again. Why did you bring me here, Thales? Why am I here?*

Thales, seeming to sense what Simon was thinking, cleared his throat. His eyes had also become slightly glassy, and he must have been filling his cup with the frequency of Paracelsus, as the slight rouge on his cheeks had invaded the rest of his face as well.

"Now, Paracelsus, you are scaring the lad. We do not know for certain what happens when our Journeys end. Besides, only a few people have actually managed to complete their Journeys, as you yourself pointed out. There is still time left, either way. We have time, if nothing else." With that, Thales refreshed his drink.

Jesus Christ, these guys drink more than ol' Daryl did, at the end. Guy used to come to work reeking of Clan M. scotch and stale cigarettes. He was a choir boy compared to these two.

"Either way, that is the Journey. Chances are, you have already begun yours and don't even know it. Have people died around you, without you being able to save them? Have you been overwhelmed with the desire to have children? Have you wished to serve other people as you meet them? Does guilt plague you yet? Tell me, young one: What has happened in Dara that seems to be shaping your path?"

Kinky hair and kind eyes flashed in Simon's mind. Blood-stained flowers and slashed skin, the gurgling sound of someone choking that filled his dreams. As soon as he tried to force that image away from the forefront, another jumped in its place. A giant man, breath reeking, with a knife pointed at his eye. Feelings of helplessness as he was pushed against a wall. Thales saving him. The stone-flecked eyes of his attacker were replaced by the death-filled eyes sunk into an almost-too-normal face, the mouth twisted into a smile as his blade slashed back and forth with practiced expertise into Mary's flesh. He shuddered. Apparently, the wine wasn't as effective at numbing his feelings as he first thought. He went and refilled his own glass and sat down.

"Well? What has happened since you came here that has shaped your view of this world? Tell me."

127

With a start, Simon came back to the present, and with his breath shaking out of his throat, he told the tale of the man with the unremarkable features who attacked Mary, of the Greek who wished to have more than his company, of Thales saving him, agreeing to be his guide. His eyes glistened with tears as he spoke of Mary, and he quickly downed his fresh cup of wine to suppress the sadness forming a knot in his throat.

Paracelsus and Thales looked at him, sipping their wine and not speaking, listening to his tale. With his story finished, Simon felt tired. He realized that this was the most he had spoken since coming to Dara. His throat felt dry, and his tongue hurt. He must have spoken for quite some time, as the sun, no longer in the center of the sky, was dipping down into the west, sending long shadows through the glade.

Silence reigned for a while after Simon finished his story. Thales stroked his beard, and Paracelsus looked off into the distance at something only he could see. Minutes passed, and then, without a word, Paracelsus stood and went behind the slab of stone, retrieving some logs. He placed them about equidistant from Simon, Thales, and himself, making them stand against each other like a miniature teepee. The beady eyes of the traveler focused on the logs, seeming to look into them, through them, discovering their hidden depths. Suddenly, with a pop and a crackle, the logs burst into flame, and Paracelsus stumbled back over to the wine barrel. Filling his cup, he returned to his spot on the ground, lounging lazily and gazing at the flames licking the logs with their fiery tongues. For a while, all three companions simply stared at the fire, letting its fiery dance invade their minds. It was Thales who spoke first.

"What do you think, Paracelsus? This is your area of expertise. What is the boy's Journey?"

"It seems to me, the boy failed in protecting those he loves and never recovered. He couldn't protect himself against the Greek, he couldn't protect Mary, and when the time comes, he won't be able to protect you."

Paracelsus gave the bearded philosopher a meaningful glance. "That's right. Since he cares for you, and you for him, it is more than likely that you will be killed because of the boy's Journey. Be forewarned. I know what your Journey requires you to do, Thales, so be ready."

Thales stared into the fire, a look of sadness coming onto his face. "I thank you for that, Paracelsus. I do."

Simon looked at his caretaker, confusion and shock rolling through his body as the words of Paracelsus struck home. "What do you mean, Thales will be killed because of me? Can't I leave? I do not want someone to die because of me. I won't allow it. *I won't!*" The raised voice of Simon surprised even him. *Damn it, I think I'm drunk. But so, what? Thales can't die because of me!*

"It is already too late. Once you began to care for Thales, and he for you, you became wrapped in the other's Journey. For Thales, he must protect his pupils in order to complete his own Journey. He chose to be your guide because he knew, one day, you would be in danger. If he wishes to complete his Journey, he must save you from death."

Simon looked at Thales, aghast. "You knew?"

"Do not judge me too harshly, Simon. The fact is, we all must die, and Return, and die again. For millennia, I have lived here, and for millennia, I resisted the urge to have a pupil, as I knew that, if I saved them, I may not Return, and if I did not, then they would suffer. Yet, after resisting for thousands of years, I feel as though I am ready. I feel as though I am ready to die, to move on."

The philosopher, though he looked to be in his middle years, seemed to have aged exponentially in moments. His shoulders sagged, and his eyes looked at the grassy floor. Simon did not know what emotion to latch onto. Hate, disbelief, pain, affection all swirled inside of him, forcing his eyes to swim and his head to dance. Not sure why, he stood up, tried to leap to his feet. His long hair flew into his face, and he angrily, sloppily pushed it aside, and he pointed at his guide, anger criss crossing his face.

129

"You listen to me, you son of a bitch. I have already seen enough death, both in my past life and this one. I will not have you die on my account. I will not allow it!" Simon's head swam, and his knees buckled. *Jesus Christ, I am really, really drunk.* With a thump, Simon landed hard on his bottom. Embarrassed and angry, he simply pointed at Thales again, muttered, "son of a bitch," and promptly threw up. Wiping his mouth, uttering expletives over and over, Simon fell backwards, descended unceremoniously into a sea of grass and the deep darkness of sleep.

CHAPTER IX– OF GLAD GRACE

Simon awoke to a foggy landscape and a splitting headache. Rolling to a seated position, he clutched his head in his hands, trying to make the broken shards of his consciousness fuse back together. His eyes felt like they had been rubbed violently with a handful of sand, and his mouth tasted of bile. Eyes blurry, he managed to make out a shape, cloaked in white, moving about the edges of a dying fire. Pushing his hair back and rubbing his eyes with his palms, Simon blinked rapidly as his world came into focus.

Thales was there, sitting next to the dying flames of the previous night's fire. In his hands, he held a cup and a chunk of the bread Simon had picked up from Taillevent. He was looking at Simon, and when he saw his eyes coming into focus, he said, "You need to eat something and drink this. Unfortunately, the only way to cure the illness you have given yourself is more of the poison that hurt you in the first place."

Simon took the bread and cup from Thales, and the smell of wine made his stomach lurch. Grimacing, he took a sip, then another, and finally gulped the red liquid down. He nibbled on the bread and prayed to whatever deity held sway in this place that his head would cease its incessant thrumming and his stomach wouldn't empty its contents at the smallest provocation.

Thales watched him, face unreadable, dark eyes watching his every move. Groggily, Simon began to recall the events of the night before, of Thales and Paracelsus, of Journeys, of Thales choosing to be his guide. He snapped up, headache and stomach acrobatics momentarily forgotten, and looked at his companion.

"Is it true? Will you die and not Return because of me? Did you choose me to be your pupil so you could complete your Journey, and die? Is it true, Thales?"

"As I said last night, it is true."

"But why? Why me?"

"Because you needed a guide. When I saw you with Mary, newly arrived to Dara, I saw my opportunity. I have lived here for thousands of years, traveled throughout this world, avoided my Journey as best I could, but the truth is, the undeniable truth is, there are certain things beyond my control. Sit down, Simon, you look like you are about to sick up."

Simon, having realized that the memories from the previous night were not drunken dreams and were real, stood. Immediately, the world spun, his face turned grey, and he sat back down. *Jesus Christ, I don't remember being this hungover since my buddy's bachelor party. Jesus Christ, my head.* Simon sat back down and tried to finish the bread he had been given. He was embarrassed to look down and see what could only be the remnants of vomit staining his shirt.

Having sat back down, Thales continued. "My Journey involves the rescuing of a pupil, of saving him or her from a dark and twisted fate. Yet each time I have tried, each time I have attempted to be a guide to someone, they inevitably suffer—many die, or worse." Simon arched an eyebrow at that. "Now, before you get too upset at me, remember that I did save your life, and I saved you from a worse fate than a simple death. I did not have to walk down that alley. In fact, I wasn't even supposed to be walking that direction at all. My colleagues and I were going to continue our debate at my home, but for some reason, some *purpose*, I was drawn away. Drawn toward you."

Thales took a breath and adjusted his tunic. Simon took the pause in conversation to attempt to clean the sick out of his shirt with leaves

132

and blades of grass. After a moment, Thales continued. "And so, when I saved you and saw you did not yet have a guide, I decided to try to complete my Journey once more. I felt the pull toward you, and this time, I did not resist."

Simon, wiping his mouth and taking another bite of the hard bread, stopped to consider Thales. He did save his life, that was true, and from what he said, it didn't seem as though fate had left him much of a choice when it came to being Simon's guide. *Well, at least he is trying to help. It's more than I can say for many people I've known. Just, why does he have to die?*

"So, what now? What happens next? Do you just teach me, guide me, until someone comes along and tries to kill me, and you prevent that? What am I supposed to do? Do we just carry on with our lives and wait for something to kill me?" Simon was only a little upset at the bitterness that had crept into his voice.

Thales rose, dusting off imaginary bits of dirt from his still unblemished toga. How he managed to keep his clothing so clean, even on the road, Simon had no idea. "No, what we must do now, young Simon, is begin your Journey. I will help when and where I can, and, hopefully, it will be enough for my own Journey to end. "

"But what is my Journey? What am I supposed to do while I'm here?"

"Isn't it obvious? You must find the blood cults, as I am almost certain one of their number killed Miss Mary. It appears as though, in your past life, you failed in protecting loved ones as well, or failed when someone needed you the most. Your Journey seems to be about overcoming helplessness."

Suddenly, Simon's mind swept to flashes of red, a bloodstained t-shirt, lights dancing in the rain, and an overwhelming fear seeping into every ounce of his body. Pain in his legs as he ran, tears streaming down his cheeks.

Angrily, he shoved it down, shut it away into the room of the mind where people hide their dark truths. The fear still remained, like an echo of a memory he wished to forget. Frustrated at himself and the world around him, Simon wiped sweaty palms on his dusty pants. His head swam again, and it took a moment for him to regain his composure. When he finally had his head under control, Thales returned with another cup of wine. Simon downed it and was relieved when his head's throbbing became a distant ache. One step closer to normalcy, Simon returned to questioning Thales.

"Why the blood cults? They have nothing to do with me, besides killing someone who cared for me when I was small. How do you know that I am supposed to fight them?"

"I do not know for certain, but it appears as though your life here has been shaped by your interaction with them. Do you not realize the man who followed you into the dark alley all those years ago had been one of their number? True, he said he did not wish to be among them anymore, but we all knew the truth. Your Journey, for better or worse, seems to revolve around these people. You must face them, investigate them, fight them, maybe. But your Journey lies with them."

Simon shuddered at the thought of interacting with those people—the people who relish violence and destruction, who find joy in death and torture. He hoped and pleaded in his heart that he would not become one of their number. He recalled how sick to the stomach he was when Thales first told him about the strange group of people who believed that Dara was a place to experience all of what humanity had been forbidden when they walked in the original world. The torture and destruction that Thales had described had made Simon's stomach do backflips.

Simon shook himself and forced his mind back to the present. "What if I refuse? What if I simply return to the villa and plant grapes and olive trees? Can't I choose that?"

"Of course you can. There is nothing stopping you from simply walking away, back to safety. You can even return to the tree house where you and Mary lived and try to create a new life there. However, I must warn you that Journeys are powerful things. If you become close to anyone, chances are they will meet a terrible fate just like Mary, and like you almost did all those years ago. If you do not complete your Journey, you must stay alone, avoid everyone, for as soon as you get close to someone, your fate will come to test you, to draw you back onto the path that destiny has set out for you."

Simon continued eating his bread, and Thales poured himself a cup of wine, having to tilt the barrel to access the last dregs from the wooden container. They sat in silence for a while, Simon eating and trying to think, and Thales sitting against the stone slab, a statue of patience. Simon looked around the field, half expecting to see a portly red-haired man lying face-down in the grass. He was surprised to find that the strange man and his wicker backpack had disappeared. The man had drunk enough for three, and was gone with the morning. Looking about him once more, Simon asked his guide where Paracelsus had gone.

"Oh, he is a man of routine and cannot be derailed for long. The only reason we managed to convince him to stay is that his love of fine wine is greater than his need for structure, though not by much. I suspect Paracelsus is well on his way to Tuatha by now, traveling the road and continuing his search."

"What is he searching for? Is that his Journey?"

"Yes, sadly. Paracelsus would be considered the father of psychology, and in many ways, modern medicine, but he made mistakes. As a seeker of knowledge and a hunter for truth, he never managed to recover from the lives lost because of his ignorance—his inability to understand the injuries and ailments of certain patients. His Journey pulls him around the whole of Dara, searching for some way to repay the debt of lost lives he is responsible for."

"How is he supposed to do that?"

135

"In truth, I do not believe even he knows. Perhaps if he found a patient who died and made it here, he could apologize, beg for forgiveness, and find peace. Perhaps he needs to fully understand the world in which we live now, to never be ignorant of what ails us, which is why he is obsessed with Journeys. It was his idea to have us search out the blood cults for you, because he 'doesn't believe in fucking coincidence.' His words. No, Paracelsus is doomed to wander this plane for some time yet." Thales seemed sad at his last statement, the weight of millennia sinking the tone of his words. "Well, young Simon, what are we to do? Off to search for your truth, or to return home? Safety or death? Which to choose?" Thales spread his palms wide.

Simon thought, his mind scrambling for time. How much like life on Earth this place was. Years of inactivity followed by a single day that changes everything. He remembered hearing once that life was like a storm building on the horizon: Little happens for the majority of the time, but when it does, it comes in a torrent, then is gone, to be replaced by waiting for the next storm to hit. Sighing, he stood again, slowly this time.

"I will follow your advice, Mr. Thales. I do not know the first thing about what to do next, so I should defer to my older, wiser counterparts, right? I just hope you are right about this."

"I cannot promise that I am. I cannot promise anything, but I know my Journey is intertwined with yours, at least for the time being. Let's be off. We need to pack for the journey ahead, and I do not think an empty barrel of wine will suffice."

Without another word, Thales strode out of the clearing, leaving Simon to grab the empty barrel and scurry after him.

CHAPTER X–WITH LOVE FALSE OR TRUE

The walk back to Thales's home was uneventful. The two companions spoke little, and when they did speak, it was only about practical matters: how far they had to travel, what provisions to bring on their trip, and where they were headed. The two would only stop at the home of Thales long enough to resupply their food and water, and then their feet would quickly find the road again. As the two travelers neared Thales's abode, the philosopher began to explain where they were headed. Simon listened intently and said little, hoping to learn as much as possible.

The dark and twisted people Thales spoke of resided near the upside-down mountains and vertical ocean, because they "celebrated the perverse, the upside down, the reverse," the philosopher had said as he and Simon returned to the outskirts of the village of Valoren. They were to take the main road from the village north and west to Elysium, a small village that drew people who passionately looked for community and togetherness as part of their Journeys.

Thales looked at Simon meaningfully at this description and laughed when Simon appeared confused. "You will see, young Simon, you will see. They will welcome us in every way, and you will witness how Dara is decidedly different from the world you left."

Simon did not know what to make of that and said as much, which caused Thales to laugh again and continue walking. Thinking his guide must still be drunk from the night before, Simon shrugged his shoulders and walked on.

As Simon and Thales neared the small town, they began to see more and more men and women walking about in the clothing of different periods and areas. Simon could not help but stare as a beauty with raven hair, completely naked except for a reed skirt, smiled at him with dark laughing eyes and continued walking past in a graceful near-dance on bare feet. The young man tripped on a rock as he attempted to stretch his neck's ability to turn and fell face-first in the dirt. Thales laughed again and helped him up.

As Simon brushed himself off, Thales smiled and said, "If that is enough for you to trip over your own feet, I shall have to get you a wagon to sit in when we reach Elysium." Simon's face reddened so much that it burned, but he found himself laughing with his companion at his own voyeurism as they continued walking down the road.

The rest of the walk was pleasant and largely uneventful, with Simon casually asking questions of Journeys and the world he saw, and Thales answering and speaking briefly to passersby. Simon loved just how peaceful and right it felt to walk with Thales, even with his splitting headache.

Once back at the villa, Simon quickly separated himself from Thales and retired to his own small room. The smell of olives helped him feel a sense of familiarity and peace, and he breathed deeply. He felt contentment and safety, a connection to the place. *Just like the tree house,* he thought with a touch of bitterness, *and now I am leaving home again. Is Dara designed to only bring peace in small doses? Perhaps my Journey is built around losing my home.* Almost as quickly, Simon chided himself, believing that his teenage body had allowed its angst to slip into his mind. Emotions once again under control, he gathered his meager belongings.

He had a hand-stitched thin blue blanket; a traveling cloak; needle and thread; his knife with the familiar, well-worn handle; a traveling stick; and a perfectly cylindrical wooden bottle for water, with a cap that looked like the small rings of a tree, which fit perfectly over the opening. Simon smiled. It was the first thing he had ever Changed on his own, under the guidance of Thales, turning a large branch into a perfectly concave drinking vessel, complete with an air-tight lid. Thales had appeared proud, smiling and nodding in approval, and a sense of accomplishment filled the youth to the brim every time he touched his simple creation.

He placed his belongings, all neatly arranged, on his blanket, and then he wrapped and tied the blanket into a nice bundle. Taking an extra piece of leather cord, Simon secured it to his traveling stick, creating a bindle like he had seen used by train-hoppers in his past life. With a quick thought, Simon took out his knife and cut a bit of cord and used it to tie his hair behind his head. Tying his traveling cloak over his shoulders and hoisting his gear, Simon walked outside, where he saw Thales, still in his toga, with a similar bundle over his shoulder. But, rather than a walking stick, at the end of his staff was a wicked sharp point stuck out at an angle—a good six inches of dark steel forged for one deadly purpose. *Note to self: Don't walk behind Thales today. He is too often prone to simply stopping, and I would hate to have made it this far to have it all end with my guide's spear accidentally in my eye.*

"Ready to go? Do you have everything you need? We will be on the road for a few days and will be sleeping on the ground, so make sure that you have everything to make the trip as pleasant as possible."

"You know what I could really use—what would make me feel absolutely fantastic? A gun. I know, I know." Simon held up his hand before Thales could speak. "I know that Changing is better, and a gun isn't as effective when you can literally alter reality, but still." Simon placed his hand on his simple belt, right where his holster used to rest for all those years. *It would definitely make me feel better. That's for sure.*

For a moment, Thales just looked at his ward, processing something behind his coffee-colored eyes. Eventually, he smiled, and, to Simon's surprise, he nodded.

"Very well. If it makes you feel better, makes you feel safer, then I will try to find you a gun, but I must warn you: A person who understands Changing will use your weapon against you."

Simon nodded, adjusting his belongings on his right shoulder, and prepared to walk out the western gate. Thales, smiling to himself, quickly strode next to Simon, careful to keep the spear point away from him. Together, they looked down the road, preparing in silence for the trials that lay ahead.

***

There is something about youth and adventure, a calling from deep within the subconscious, that screams in victory when a young person begins traveling into a world full of the unknown. The soul shines brighter, the step is lighter, the air sweeter. Simon felt that calling of the road and found himself smiling. He hadn't felt this way in decades, hadn't felt the joy of an untouched trail, an uncharted territory.

As Thales strode, his long legs causing the fabric of the tunic to swirl in the breeze, Simon felt his muscles awaken, and his heart open to the sunshine. *All I need now is a pretty young thing with me—someone to hold—and I will feel truly and completely young again. I wonder if there will be girls in this town, this Elysium, we are heading toward.*

A quick flash of his wife appeared in his mind's eye. *Ex-wife. She didn't even come visit me as I was dying, not even after two kids and almost a lifetime together.* Clearing his throat, matching his stride with that of his companion, Simon asked Thales to remind him what kind of place Elysium was.

"Elysium, young Simon, is a place of community, in every sense of the word. People whose Journeys involve connectedness, the desire to be a part of something bigger than one's self, find themselves Returning to Elysium. It is a place where the people attempt to connect with everyone, to find a depth of purpose in collaboration."

"So, it's what? Some kind of hippie commune?"

"Remind me again what a hippie is, young Simon."

140

"You know, someone who is a ... a free thinker. Someone who believes in free love, living off of the land, and just ... not judging anyone for their life choices."

"Free love? What does this mean?"

Simon blushed briefly "Well, it's like ... it's when ... it's when someone is willing to *show* their love to anyone who needs it."

Thales's mustachioed lips twitched upward, a hidden smile that spoke volumes.

"You could say the people of Elysium are something like that. Yes, I remember a musician friend who told me of hippies and their places of free expression. A fascinating group of people, these hippies. Yes, young Simon, Elysium is somewhat like a hippie commune. Though I think you will find that even the hippies of your time might find Elysium to be, shall we say, *devoted* to their idea of community." Thales continued smiling, and the heat on Simon's face deepened. Still, he pressed on.

"Will there ... will there be ... will there be girls at this place? Girls my age?"

No sooner did the question leave his lips than Thales burst out laughing—a fit of mirth so intense that tears came to his eyes. *Jesus Christ, it's like he's about to roll on the ground, he's laughing so hard.* Simon warily watched the spear point as it bounced about, due to the shaking shoulders of his laughing guide. Simultaneously, his cheeks began to burn, and he became afraid that he had made some error, embarrassed himself in some way, that he had not intended to. As is so often the case with young men, embarrassment turned to anger, and Simon stomped off, walking west down the path as quickly as he could, until the sound of Thales's wheezing laughs was safely behind him.

Grumbling to himself, Simon marched onward. His mood, sour as it was, could not remain so—not when his vision was filled with a landscape that made his breath catch in his throat. The road rose upward, and as Simon crested the rise, the world around him shifted so suddenly that his heart leapt, and everything around him transformed.

The upside-down mountains—snow-covered peaks touching the earth like jagged teeth—butted up against the vertical ocean to the west. Simon could hear the crashing of waves in the distance. In front of him, the hill gave way to a flat plain, with green grass that danced in a breeze he did not feel. The grass seemed to move, to mimic an ocean, rising and falling in waves, with iron storm clouds near the mountain range causing the greens of the blades to pop out into a fantastical explosion of nature's favorite color. Yet what made his breath catch were the trees and the bubbles.

Suspended in midair, turning lazily in that same breeze, mammoth trees of every possible variety floated slowly in the ever-present wind, their roots and branches mimicking each other in size and scope. Within the forest of floating flora, birds of every sort roosted in the trees, as did small animals and primates. Simon locked eyes with a small monkey, its ears tufted almost to the point of looking like small feathers. It chirped merrily as it stared at Simon and ate a strange fruit that Simon did not recognize.

Contrasting the greens and browns of the trees, giant water bubbles floated lazily about, with fish seeming to dance inside of them, lending their beautiful hues of blue and yellow, of red and purple, to the already fantastic scene. Simon was dumbstruck. As he gazed at the suspended trees and tiny, spherical oceans, Simon's eyes sent rapid, confused signals to his brain, fearing somehow that something was terribly wrong, that he had somehow managed to descend completely into madness. Trying to process this, Simon froze and remained rooted for some time.

"Welcome to the Floating Forest, the beginning of the Apicem Terra Range—those upside-down mountains over there."

Simon jerked at the noise, shocked out of his awe-struck state. He had seen much since coming to Dara—had his senses pushed to their limit. Yet the magic of the place, the almost inexplicable *strangeness* of the floating forest, had pushed his mind past what he thought was possible—even after death.

"Why ... why are there bubbles of water with fish in them?" seemed to be the only words that Simon could utter, the only collection of sounds his tongue could wrap around. He turned, his face a mask of confusion, and repeated himself: "Why are there giant bubbles of water in a forest with fish in them?"

"Well, no one knows for certain, but the idea is that these fish were discovered while diving in the ocean. When you dive, you aren't exactly fully immersed in the environment you dove into; that would be impossible. Instead, you are viewing the world through a bubble. That is why you see these bubbles of fish. They are in the world, but in a world of their own. You would have to ask Da Vinci about that. His love of invention led him here, and the diving bell, as he called it, started humanity's ability to move underwater at will. What's really fascinating are the trees. Did you know ..."

Simon stood very still, only half listening, as Thales continued to talk about the water bubbles, Da Vinci, and other things that were of interest in the floating forest—at least, from a seemingly intellectual standpoint. He was too amazed by his surroundings to fully hear what his guide was saying. Simon's attention, however, was ripped from the words of Thales toward a monster of horrific size and shape, ambling through the floating forest straight toward the young boy and the chatty academic. For the second time in several minutes, Simon felt his feet fuse with the ground.

The creature was huge—unbelievably gargantuan—and it was not completely covered by skin. Muscle and bone stuck out at odd places, and its giant skull, with teeth as large as bananas, was mostly exposed bone. Simon was somehow more terrified to realize that its eye sockets were empty. *Is that ... is that a dinosaur? Where did its skin go?* "Thales? *Thales!* What the fuck is that?"

"Now, young Simon, there is no reason to curse. As I was saying …" Thales trailed off, having finally turned to look to where Simon was pointing. Thales became very still, a human statue whose only movement could be found in his eyes, tracking the monstrous creature. Bone and pieces of flesh sauntered toward Simon and Thales, huge clawed feet meandering in a casual manner. Simon kept completely still, but his mind was flying around the forest and ascending to the sky.

"What do we do? What do we do? Can we kill this thing?" Simon whispered, trying to move as little of his mouth as possible. The creature, neither hurried nor slow, continued its steady pace toward the two travelers. Simon's heart began trying to jump out of his chest and make a run for the cover of the floating trees.

Thales lips barely moved, and the sound that came up was hardly above a whisper. "What we do, young Simon, is not move at all. This poor creature has not yet been fully understood by humanity, which is why it is the piecemeal version of itself you see lumbering toward us. Luckily, it does not appear to have eyes and, I would guess, probably not much of a nose either. As long as we stay still and don't disturb it, it should pass us by. Now, be quiet, and *don't move.*"

Simon attempted to grant his guide's wish by willing all of his biological functions to cease. He tried to stop breathing, stop blinking, to stop the trapped animal in his ribcage from hammering at his chest. Sweat bloomed from his skin, dampening his clothes and dripping into his eyes, briefly blurring his vision. Frozen in place, terrified, he watched as the giant lizard, missing so many vital pieces of its body, wandered toward them. *How is this thing moving? How is it alive? I don't understand. Shouldn't it just die immediately after... Jesus Christ, is this thing born?*

The giant lizard, king of reptiles from a long-ago era, was now moving up the hill, mere feet away from Simon and Thales's frozen forms, like a low-budget horror movie of museum monsters come to life or a lab experiment gone awry. As it walked, pieces of its flesh bounced back and forth, held precariously to the bone. Simon felt his stomach lurch as it came within inches of them, with the smell of open wounds and the iron tang of blood filling Simon's nostrils. The beast, whether due to its lack of senses or a disinterest in the tiny creatures by its feet, or simply by pure chance, walked on, sliding past Simon and Thales like a nightmare through a mind's eye.

As the large tail, with the white of bone sticking through the end, slid by, Simon felt his shoulders relax slightly. The giant monstrosity kept walking, past the pair of humans and toward an unknown destination. Staring at the monster, Simon felt as if his mind had retreated into the dark recesses of his skull. The madness of the landscape, the improbability of what had just passed before his eyes, seemed to have formed a bubble in his stomach.

All he could think about was the idiocy of what he had just seen, of all he knew turned upside down. "Upside down," he murmured, turning his eyes to the mountain range, "upside down. The world is literally upside down."

The bubble, as if queued by his words, climbed up through his stomach, past his lungs, and out of his mouth in a maniacal, nearly uncontrollable laugh. It was the laugh of a madman, coming from a mind whose grip on reality had slipped. Forcibly, Simon reclaimed his senses, choking off the laughter still rising from his chest. Yet even before he turned to look, he knew it was too late.

Not twenty feet away, eyeless sockets turned toward the sound, followed by the rest of the monstrous body. Simon could see muscles in the powerful neck tensing, the tail moving back and forth dangerously, like a cat who had found a mouse to play the most dangerous game with. He heard Thales curse silently and ease the spear from over his shoulder to point it at the giant lizard. The size of his weapon compared to the beast made Simon want to laugh again. *It's like throwing a toothpick at a tank.*

"Now, listen," Thales muttered, perfectly still except for the slight movement of his bearded lips. "The beast still cannot see us, but it seems as though it can hear us. It will charge, and when it does, wait until I say, then jump with all your might to your left, and run through the floating forest. Don't run in a straight line, and don't stop moving!" Looking over at Simon through the corner of his eye, Thales smiled. *Jesus, is he actually enjoying this? The man must be out of his mind!* "Do you hear me, young Simon?"

Simon managed to let out a sound, not much more than a broken squeak, but Thales nodded. "Good. Now, wait."

Simon waited and stared at the beast. It seemed to have centered its attention on Thales. Simon watched as it lowered on its haunches, tail snapping, and then sprang forward, moving at a speed that nearly caused Simon to soil himself and fall on his backside. As the creature exploded toward its potential prey, it let out a terrible roar, filling Simon's ears. Simon's eyes widened so far that they felt as though they might pop out of his head, and his vision fixated on the open mouth careening toward him. He looked into and through the gaping maw, seeing exposed vertebrae as the giant monster's huge teeth came hurtling toward him.

"Now!" With a shove, Thales threw Simon to the side and launched himself away from the beast. The young man could feel the wind as the giant incisors snapped shut, inches from his hand that had flayed out to catch himself. Without thinking, without any consciousness left— moving on the purity of instinct, the truth of terror—Simon found his legs and began to run. He ran with all he had—every muscle fiber, every drop of strength. With all the power in his possession, he hurtled down the hill and into the floating forest.

He could hear the sound of the giant predator turning, of undergrowth and trees snapping as the half-creature, half-skeleton changed direction and came crashing toward him. As he ran, Simon could feel the earth shake, sense the vibrations in the ground with each enormous footstep. He pushed harder, running between floating trees and around the bubbles full of fish. He ran until his lungs burned, dancing around obstacles and sliding under suspended roots. He could hear the beast moving, could feel the tremors through his feet, and still he ran. As he propelled himself through the forest, he chanced a look behind him and immediately wished that he had not.

Having no eyes, the monster, rather than moving around the suspended trees and aquatic ecosystems, was simply rushing through them. It caused marine life to explode into tree branches and trees to spin upside down, their roots to the sun, or to continue in the monster's momentum, ripping more pieces of flesh from its piecemeal hide. It did not seem to feel even the slightest hindrance, besides occasionally snapping its jaws to break a wooden limb or rip open a fish that was unfortunate enough to find its fate inside those large incisors. Simon turned his back to the creature and ran, a scream of futility escaping his lips.

The lizard closed in, as was inevitable. It was too large and too fast, and before long, Simon saw a shadow fall on him. He dove to the side just as the jaws came down, rolling painfully onto a sharp rock protruding from the ground. He felt a sharp pain in his shoulder but managed to roll onto his feet. Clutching his shoulder, Simon felt that his shirt had ripped, and when he brought his hand back, he saw the familiar red of fresh blood. However, as he was staring numbly at his bloody fingers, the pain in his shoulder caused by the rock tugged at his memory, and he was briefly transported to another trail, to a time when he made another rock turn to dust. An idea began to form in his mind—a thought that just might provide him a chance. He looked at the large predator—looked at the powerful, muscular legs turning its frame of torn flesh toward him, preparing themselves for a new assault. Shoulder aching, lungs burning, Simon forced himself to concentrate.

The giant beast, mouth open and covered with the gore of aquatic life, began its charge, a bellow exploding from its throat. It then stopped, seemingly transfixed. One of the giant trees, its roots jutting out at an odd angle, had stabbed its way through the monstrous creature and buried itself into the ground. The monster, bony tail thrashing and throat screaming, began trying to bite the tree trunk that seemed to have grown out of it, but to no avail. The sharp teeth and small claws simply could not reach the giant tree.

Then, turning its empty eye sockets back in the direction of Simon, the monster, to the youth's unfortunate surprise, returned to its deadly purpose. Its jaws snapped, its tail thrashed, its legs churned, until it finally moved a step. It moved another, dragging itself through the tree. Simon felt nausea as the beast ripped flesh off of its bones and continued forward, leaving behind a mass of organ and tissue on the brown, leafy branches. The creature, now more skeleton than beast, continued toward Simon, teeth snapping at him. Simon was horrified, transfixed. He could not move. The jaws snapped closer, closer. Simon just stood there, dumbfounded. *So, after all this, I'm going to be killed by a museum exhibit. Goddamn it.*

Crack! The giant mouth seemed to have frozen in mid-bite. The mammoth head fell straight downwards, jaws to bite no more, and the body fell almost lazily to the side. Somehow, the head had simply slipped from the body and now lay at Simon's feet.

"Now, young Simon, you were doing wonderfully until the end. I thought you had him. The idea to skewer him with a tree was brilliant, but one thing about these kinds of creatures: You have to remove the head from the body, or they will keep coming. Something to do with our knowledge of brains and vertebrates, I guess." Thales stood a few feet to Simon's left, calmly cleaning the iron spear tip of a dark fluid. "A good slice or thrust to the spine usually does the trick."

Simon stood, shock rolling through him in waves, eyes attempting to seize complete control of his face. "You … you knew how to kill it, and you let it *chase* me? You let it almost *kill* me? Are you out of your fucking mind?"

"Now, young Simon, there is no need for such language. I knew how to stop the beast, yes, but I am also your guide, and an essential part of any tutelage is teaching pupils that they can handle themselves and can stand on their own, without the teacher. You thought of Changing on your own and almost stopped the creature single-handed. Well done. I merely stepped in to finish the job. Now, take a moment to gather your things, then we will set off again."

Without another word, Thales shouldered his spear, brushed imaginary dirt from his toga, and continued walking. Simon watched him go, while the feelings of disbelief, anger, and relief warred inside of him. He put his head in his hands, shaking back and forth, then lifted his eyes to the heavens, opened his mouth, and screamed.

It did not take long for Simon to retrace his steps and find his walking stick and belongings; he simply had to follow the carnage of broken trees and dead fish. Surprisingly, the bubbles of ocean seemed to have reformed and collected the creatures that had not been trampled or chewed. The trees had righted themselves and returned to their peaceful, suspended state, albeit with significantly less branches and foliage. It was as though the world around him had been reset, the pieces of a giant game replaced to their positions, with the figures of the game only a little worse for wear. Shouldering his stick, Simon turned to look down the path of destruction he had just walked.

He did not remember throwing his belongings or how he ended up near the rock, but he vividly remembered Changing the tree, turning it into a projectile weapon and hurling it through his adversary. He remembered how it felt: like growing roots and driving them into the soil, becoming part of the world. As he retrieved his wooden water bottle, the first item he had ever Changed on his own, he thought of how little of Changing he actually knew. Thales had taught him very little, and as he stared at the corpse of the monster that almost claimed his life, Simon's lack of understanding became a glaring scar in his mind.

As he had grown up with his philosopher caretaker, Simon had to completely relearn almost everything about existence, and Changing was only one of many lessons that Thales had tried to teach him. Yet now, as he gazed back on the terrible scene, it was all he could think about, all he could grasp. He stared at the skeletal corpse and the tree that still had its flesh wrapped around its trunk. The tree had begun to float again and was dripping viscous fluid to the ground. It looked as though an ancient pagan priest had made an offering to the floating forest—a gift of blood and violence. Simon looked at the scene, and the desire to learn, to *know,* filled him.

Simon had never been particularly fond of academics as a young boy, preferring instead to be outdoors with his friends. He cared for them even less as a young man, finding that he would much rather spend his time in the company of young ladies or things he could manipulate with his hands. He was smart, true, but not in the way that led people to a university—not in the sense that could be easily quantified on a test—so he lost interest in school. Yet as he stood staring at the bloody scene, his shoulder aching, he could not help but wish to learn everything there was to know about this miracle called Changing. He was fascinated, and the desire to learn also fascinated him. *If only I had this much desire in school, I could have changed the world!* he thought. Shouldering his bindle and swearing to learn everything that could be learned about Changing, he rushed to catch up with Thales, who was already walking through the floating forest, strolling west toward the Apicem Terra Range.

CHAPTER XI-SOUL IN YOU

For a while, they walked in silence, Thales with his eyes straight ahead, humming a wordless tune, and Simon walking alongside him, unsuccessfully trying to lift and throw sticks and stones with his mind. He would try to make a stick skid across the path, try to make a rock float, and all he would receive in return was frustration and a headache. Yet he kept trying, stopping to pick up branches or stones, spending hours staring at them, willing them to move. And the entire time, Thales walked on, humming his tune. The sound, coupled with his frustration, became maddening to Simon, and he began picking up and hurling stones and sticks into the trees as he stomped down the road, furious at his failure and ignorance.

"Why were there only parts of the dinosaurs visible? Was that some kind of zombie dinosaur, or what?" Simon blurted out his question as soon as he thought it, and regretted it for reasons he could not readily identify. *You were sulking, remember?* Such a ridiculous notion made Simon laugh to himself and shake his head. *Goddamn I hated being a teenager.* "Thales? Where is the rest of the dinosaur?"

His guide continued walking in his unhurried, casual gait, and when he spoke, his words were as rolling as his stride.

"Young Simon, this world is the space of consciousness and discovery. Some claim to have unlocked secrets of the ancient past, and you can see those creations wander as well, but what we came across is what the collective human consciousness *knows* about that great beast. There are creatures of conjecture and fantasy here, but they are rarely tangible or noteworthy, having found refuge only in a few of humanities' minds. The thing you slew today, it was as close as our species has come to recreating the dead species of the ancient world." Without another word Thales strode on, leaving Simon to grapple with what he was told. He could already feel his head begin to ache.

The floating forest gave way to rolling hills and valleys, where a collection of life from all over the world grazed, ran, and flew. Simon kept his eyes out for predators and caught sight of a few creatures that seemed more than capable of killing him and his companion. But after one glance in their direction, the predators moved on, more interested in hunting the herbivores grazing in the lush grass.

Thales kept walking, seemingly unperturbed by the wildlife. He and Simon kept to the road, him humming without any perceivable care, and Simon alternating between being furious and terrified. They walked until Thales suddenly turned right, off the road and into the tall grass, walking until he reached a single tree on top of a particularly tall hill. Simon was surprised to find himself relieved to see that this tree had its roots firmly in the ground. As they crested the hill, Simon saw a small stream meandering on the opposite side, its waters fresh and clear.

With a sigh, Simon slid his bindle off his shoulder and placed it against the tree. His shoulder, though it ached, was not really damaged, the blood being from a small scratch just above his clavicle. Simon sat on the ground and took off his shirt. Without thinking, he went about the business of mending his clothing, pulling a needle and thread from his small bindle. He was happy that Thales had taught him this simple skill, as there weren't many tailors in Dara. Thales came and stood over Simon and his work, leaning his spear against the tall tree and knuckling his back.

"It is best we get a fire going. There are things that might find us tasty in the night, and fire is a great deterrent. You start work on that young Simon, and I will get us something to eat."

Looking up from his work, Simon saw Thales's smiling face glancing down at him, then without another word, the philosopher retrieved his spear and walked into the tall grass. Grumbling about old philosophers and their damn smiling faces, Simon stood up and began walking around the tree, finding dead branches and twigs scattered around the ground. He circled and circled until he had acquired quite a few armfuls, and, satisfied that he would have enough for the fire to last the night, Simon went down to the creek to fill his bottle with water.

Not realizing how thirsty he was until he came near the small bank, Simon forgot his water bottle and stuck his face into the cold water, ingesting the refreshing liquid in giant gulps. The cold water tasted of springtime, of frost melting in sunlight. He then submerged his head, the cold shocking his system and invigorating his senses. Once he drank his fill, Simon filled his bottle and headed back to the campsite. Looking at his perfectly shaped bottle, he decided to renew his efforts, to return to trying to Change. This time, he would focus on the fire.

As soon as he returned to the campsite, Simon got to work. He began by clearing a patch of ground and creating a teepee of sticks, with a small nest of kindling in the bottom. *All right, now focus! You can do this.* Staring at the small bundle of flammable twigs, Simon concentrated and waited. He tried thinking of images of fire, of the sticks bursting into flames. He tried thinking of what heat felt like and how it would feel once his fire had taken hold. He thought, he concentrated, and he waited.

What seemed like hours passed, and the bundle of twigs and branches remained infuriatingly unburnt. The brown hues seemed to mock Simon as he stared, willing them to ignite, praying for them to ignite, screaming at them to ignite. Yet try as he might, all that Simon managed to do was to make himself break into a sweat and to worsen his headache. *I will not give up. I will not! I just moved an entire tree, goddammit. I can light a stick on fire!* Eyes squinting, head throbbing, Simon kept staring at the inert fireplace, wishing for a sign.

"What, pray tell, are you doing?" Thales asked as he came wandering up the hill to their campsite. Two rabbits were suspended across his shoulder, and the spear was held comfortably in his other hand, point pointed down. He looked at Simon, head cocked to one side, and that knowing smile slipped across his lips for an instant, then was gone, replaced by a look of ambivalence.

"I am trying to start the fire." Simon regretted to hear a hint of whining in his voice. "But, no matter what I do, it remains unlit. Why? Why doesn't it work? I managed to push a tree through a dinosaur's side, yet I can't start a fire? Why?"

"For much the same reason that you couldn't move the sticks and rocks you were experimenting with on the road." Thales replied.

Simon stiffened. *Of course he knew what I was doing. Why didn't he help me? This son of a bitch likes watching me suffer.* But Simon held his tongue, wanting more to learn something of Changing than to tell his guide what he really thought of him. The desire to learn burned in his chest.

Thales looked at him, face unreadable, obviously waiting for him to respond. When the young man didn't, Thales continued. "Well, I am starving. Let's eat, then talk some more. I can see that you wish to learn, which is always a pleasant expression for an old teacher to see, but first things first."

Without another word, Thales glanced at the bundle of branches and twigs, and it burst into flame, creating a merry fire. Watching the flames dance, hearing the familiar crackle and pop of burning wood, Simon felt embarrassment wash over him. Thales began humming that maddening wordless tune, handed Simon a rabbit to skin, and set to work on his own. Before long, they had created a spit, and two stripped hares adorned it, slowly turning over the open flame. Dripping fat made the flames crackle, and Simon's mouth watered.

When the food was cooked, Thales produced a loaf of hard bread and two polished wooden plates from his sack. Ripping the loaf in half and handing a share to Simon, Thales then proceeded to remove the spit from the flame and slide the two hares off, one for Simon and one for himself. The dripping fat congealed on the plates, and after the hares had sufficiently cooled, Simon ate with the ravenous appetite of a man who had just escaped death. The food, like his wife's cooking all those years ago, was delicious. *At least near-death makes food delicious,* Simon thought as he tore off a leg and chewed, using the bread to soak up the cooling fat at the bottom of his wooden plate and stuffing it in his mouth. As he looked up, mouth dripping with grease, he was surprised to find Thales not eating but staring at him, that small smile again on his lips.

"Brushing with death does make food delicious, does it not?" Thales asked.

"Mph" was all Simon could say, without enough space in his mouth for words to maneuver out. Yet he nodded his head vigorously, and Thales smiled again.

"Very good, young Simon, very good. We will talk after we have eaten." And with that, the philosopher joined the boy in devouring his hare, nearly matching the young man's zeal and joy in the simple repast. The fire crackled merrily, snapping and popping, sending sparks into the approaching dark. The world seemed to right itself, allowing the horror of the day to slip away and to be replaced with the normalcy of everyday life. Somewhere in the distance, an owl hooted, and crickets chirped merrily in the grass.

Having finished their meal, the two travelers sat back, Thales leaning against the tree and Simon lying on his back, staring up at the tree's branches, adorned with broad leaves that came to three points. As the trees danced in the breeze, Simon tried to cause a leaf to fall, to move on its own—to do anything that the wind did not intend. He was frustrated to find the leaves, uncaring of his attempts, simply swaying along to the breeze's song, not even realizing that a young man was trying to make them dance to his tune. Simon snorted and rolled onto his side, propping himself up on his elbow and turning to Thales. The man seemed on the verge of sleep.

"Thales, I need you to teach me more about Changing. You said you would teach me after we ate."

The philosopher, without opening his eyes, murmured something incomprehensible. The only word that Simon managed to hear was the final word: "tomorrow."

"Thales, I need to know *now*. Here, in this world, on the road, Changing might save my life, and there is a very real possibility that one of us might die tomorrow, if today was any indication of how our travels will go. Please, Thales, I need to know." Simon was proud that he managed to keep his voice from sounding too close to whining.

Lazily, slowly, the philosopher lifted one eyelid. He gazed at Simon, seemed to weigh and measure him, and, with a sigh, opened the other eye and straightened, sitting upright against the tree.

"Frustrating, wasn't it?" Thales asked as he tried to make himself more alert. "Trying to Change something, to alter it, without knowing how. Tell me something: What were you trying to make those sticks and stones *do?*"

"I was … I was trying to make them float over to my hand. Yet every time I tried, nothing happened. They just lay there like, well, like rocks and sticks. What am I doing wrong?"

"Tell me, do you remember the time you first Changed?"

Simon thought back, and an image of an exploding rock and a burning stick burst into view.

"I changed a rock and a stick with Mary! Strange, I didn't think about that before. Maybe I try to repress memories more than I think."

"Maybe, the human mind does amazing things to preserve itself. I also had a small part to play in that, though I do not like to admit it. I placed a small block on your memory by Changing your mind, but only a little. I have lifted it."

Thales picked up a small stick lying on the ground. "You see, young Simon, though the rules are different here than where you came from, there are rules. Each part of this world has its nature, and it must be catered to in order for Changing to work properly. For example, look at this stick." He gestured toward Simon with the small branch, twirling it in his fingers. "Is there anything about this small piece of wood, any instinct or impetus, that tells it to float? It's not a floating tree. It's not a bird. It is a twig. No, there is very little about this twig's nature that tells it to float. However ..."

Thales turned the stick so that it was directly in front of Simon. Simon looked at it, then back at his guide, confusion on his face. Yet confusion changed to wonder, as a small bud began to grow, bloom, and form into one of the giant three-pronged leaves that adorned the tree branches above the campsite. Simon watched in amazement as more leaves sprang from the lifeless stick, until green covered every inch of the tiny wand, with the only exception being where Thales held the branch between his fingers.

"Changing works best when you cater to the object's nature. Within this object, this twig, is the desire to grow the leaves you see above you. All I did was help it along." Thales, stretching out his hand, offered the twig to Simon.

That is incredible! I can't wait to try this. Wait... did Thales just say he messed with my brain? *How could he?* Simon felt his face grow hot, and his hands clench into fists.

"You, *Changed* my memories?! How could you? That is an incredible breach of privacy! I can't, I can't believe you did that. And speaking of that, how did I manage to Change my bottle at all, if I had been doing it wrong this entire time?"

"Truth be told, I helped with that. You were trying, and I think if I would have told you how, you would have been more successful, but you were so angry then—so angry at the man who killed Mary, so full of hate

157

toward those who shared his beliefs. I feared if you knew how to Change, you would try to avenge her too soon. That, young Simon, would have ended in complete disaster. I am sorry for the fiction, but it was with the best of intentions, I can assure you."

Anger boiled up within Simon—anger at the lie and anger at the underlying truth, of the necessity for that lie. Many nights he had stayed awake, thinking of ways in which to destroy those who had murdered his carrier, the woman who had become so much more. Many nights he had wanted to leave under the cover of darkness and find a way to hurt those who had hurt him. Yet he could only Change around Thales and was still small for those first few years, so he had bided his time and waited. But the lie still stung. With anger in his heart, Simon turned to his guide.

"Jesus Christ, Thales, I thought I made that myself! I was proud of it. And all this time, you had made it all along. And you changed my Goddamn memories! How can I trust that anything I remembered is real? How can I trust *you?*"

"You would not have survived long enough to learn of my treachery if I hadn't. I saw the hatred in your heart, and knew what you would do. If I was to save you, I had to lie to you. Of that I am truly sorry, but I am not sorry for saving your life." Thales's voice was sad but firm.

Simon, the part that was still him—the man that had lived a long life—understood that Thales was right, understood that he was too young, too small, to have done anything but get himself killed. Yet the other part of him—the young, rejuvenated part of him—wanted to lash out, to strike his guide full in the face with the bottle that he thought he had made himself.

He rose and prepared to stalk off into the night, away from this man, this liar. His mind felt like a tempest, and the storm became all the more violent as he looked on Thales's ever-calm face.

"I would not leave, if I were you. You are upset, not thinking clearly, and there are things that would love nothing more than to have you as an evening meal. Sit, and let us talk some more."

"I'm done talking! I can't believe this. I'm done."

Simon secretly hated himself for sounding just like his teenage daughter when he wouldn't let her leave the house wearing a shirt that showed way too much midriff. But he couldn't stop the feelings of anger building inside of him. He felt as though Thales had betrayed a sacred trust and couldn't fully understand why. *Bet if I walked out in the dark, he would feed me to another animal, just so he could save me at the last minute again. Where does this guy get off?* Frustrated and more than a little afraid of whatever it was that lurked in the dark, Simon angrily covered himself in his blanket, turning his back to the fire and Thales, and pretended to go to sleep.

"Turning your back and faking slumber will not help you learn what you want to know. I am sorry for lying to you, but it was for your own safety. Surely the man you were can understand that: having to alter the truth to keep loved ones safe."

Sure, when it was me that did the protecting, Simon thought. He rolled back over and looked at his guide's face. The philosopher's bushy eyebrows cast shadows in the firelight, hiding his eyes, but the downturned mouth and posture at least hinted at concern. The hope to acquire as much wisdom as possible, the need to *know*, outweighed Simon's feelings of betrayal and hatred. In his mind, he felt the burning desire to learn quickly eclipse any misgivings his heart could conjure, and he sat up.

"Fine. Fine, I get it. Doesn't make it any better, but I get it. Now, how do I use something's nature to help it Change? What do I have to do?"

Rather than answering outright, Thales went and picked up another stick and handed it to Simon. As the young man grasped the twig, he felt its shape, its rough texture. "Well? How am I supposed to make this Change? I don't know what you want me to do with this. All the other times we practiced was a lie apparently." Thales simply sat back down and started talking as if Simon hadn't asked a question at all.

"When I was young, I believed I was invincible. I thought that nothing could hurt me and that I would live forever, just as many young men do. I told my family and friends that I was too young to be married and, many years later, that I was too old. Yet as age came to claim me, I realized that I had missed out on one of the most important aspects of life: having children. I adopted my nephew as a way to cope, but that did not turn out too well."

Thales stopped, lost in thought, transported to a time thousands of years ago. He stared off in the distance, forgetting Simon and the world around him. It was only after Simon began twirling the stick in his hands that Thales snapped back to the present.

"Yes, yes, all those years ago, I was not true to myself, trying to put things off for a later date, until my dates became numbered," he continued. "I did not listen to my nature, and when you tried to make those rocks and sticks float, young Simon, you were not listening to their nature. Look at the stick and tell me exactly what it is."

"It's a stick."

"Yes, that's true, but what *kind* of stick? Where does it come from? Why is it in your hand?"

"It came from the tree above us, and you handed it to me."

"Think, Simon. How did the tree come to be? How did any of this …" Thales swept his leaf-covered baton in a wide arc, "… come to be? Why is it here at all?"

"Because … because someone began to think about it on Earth? Because we discovered it in our world, which caused it to come alive here?"

"Exactly!" Thales clapped his hands together, causing some leaves to fall off his wand. "Through discovery, human consciousness, and human *thought,* this place was created. When I lived on Earth, I believed that all things were connected by a single entity that brought them together. In the old world, I thought it was water—that all of the universe began with water. Here, it is the human mind, the universal consciousness, that binds all things."

"So, all I need to do is to use my mind to make things Change? But I have been trying that, and it doesn't work." Simon hated how his voice, once again, acquired a little bit of a whining quality.

"Not to worry. You simply need to change your thought process. The tool still works; you just need to change the way you use it. Focus on the stick and conjure all the images you can of trees growing their leaves. Imagine springtime."

Closing his eyes, Simon focused. He remembered the sweet smell of flowers whenever his mother would place fresh buds in the windowsill in their small home. He remembered his wife, with her wide-brimmed hat, tilling the earth in front of their home as children played in the sprinkler. He thought of trees, blooming with pink flowers, just outside the window where his desk used to sit at work. He smiled.

"Good. Now, look at the tree above us. See the leaves? Notice how they move in the wind, their shape, their size? Imagine their texture. Next, focus on the stick and send all of those feelings associated with spring into it, while imagining those leaves sprouting from the stick. Combine the emotions associated with spring with the images of those leaves growing on what you hold. Focus."

Simon focused. He focused on the feelings that spring brought to him—of how the sun warmed his skin and made flowers grow. He thought of how the rains of April would cause new growth in May. *How does it make me feel? What feelings do I have that are connected with spring?* Simon thought about this and faltered for a moment. *Well, it makes me feel young. It makes me feel invigorated. I think of spring and desire my wife again.* Simon blushed slightly, but he held onto those feelings and focused on the leaves above them growing on the stick he held, fixing images of sprouting blossoms in his mind's eye. He focused and waited.

Moments passed; seconds that felt like hours slid by, and the stick did nothing. Simon, about to lose hope, gave the experiment one final push, thinking of his wife and him laying together as newlyweds. He felt her touch, smelled her hair, touched her soft skin. He thought of what it felt like to lay with her, of how his passion for her never diminished, even after she left him. Just to hold her again, kiss her again. He thought of making love to her on a bed of those three-fingered leaves above his head, laying her down on the soft earth as showers of green life rained down on their bodies.

"Well done, Simon, well done!"

Simon snapped back to the present and was amazed and delighted to discover a single leaf growing from the end of the stick. He almost dropped it, then clung to the branch with all his might, as if it was the only thing keeping him from drowning in the moment. Surprise was quickly replaced by elation, and, like a child, he brandished the stick and thrust it into Thales's face.

"I did it! I did it! I Changed! I made the leaf grow!"

"Well done, young Simon, well done. It seems as if you have tapped into the *primitive* view of spring, but well done. Now sit down and take a moment to *ease* your tension."

Simon blushed furiously as he looked down and sat down so sharply that his backside stung. *Jesus Christ, I almost forgot that I am a teenager. Easy, Simon, easy. Think about baseball. Just think about baseball.* Thankfully, the tightness in his breeches eased as quickly as it came. Thales continued talking, unperturbed.

"As you have just discovered, Changing requires an emotional as well as mental connection to work, as well as needing to cater to the object's nature that you are going to Change. This is why you managed to move the tree so quickly. You feared as though you were going to die, so your mind reacted. Lucky for you, we were in the floating forest, or else that would not have worked, because you could not have lifted the tree if it was rooted to the earth."

Simon, taking deep breaths, felt his cheeks cool and his tension lessen. He looked down at his branch, at the little leaf he had grown. He felt a sense of possession over it—felt as though, since he Changed the branch to fit his needs, that it somehow belonged to him. He wanted to carry that stick for the rest of his life—to hold it with him forever, as a reminder of his triumph.

"Now, try again. This time, without the physical reaction."

Laughter touched the edges of Thales's words, and Simon blushed again. Placing the stick in both hands, he again tried to hold the feeling of spring and the image of the leaf in his mind.

For the rest of the evening and for the next two days on the road to Elysium, Thales taught Simon about Changing, and Simon listened and practiced. Thales told him of how growing things is easiest, as so much of the world wants to grow and reproduce. He explained how taking things away is harder, that the object will resist more. He explained how animals are hardest to Change because they know something is different—something is happening that is unnatural—and they resist.

Simon grew more leaves, flattened a stone into an oval, and caused a tree to shrink to the size of his knee. He struggled when Thales tried to teach him how to separate metals from rock, but Thales simply smiled and assured him that he would have to learn about blacksmithing before such a form of Change would become easier. Days passed, and the sting of Thales's lie faded away as the pair continued west.

Chapter XII - Sorrows of Your Changing Face

Simon awoke, washed his hands in a small creek where he and Thales had made camp, and was splashing water in his face when a sound made him jerk his head over to one side, and nearly topple into the cold water at his feet. The noise was distant, and faint, but decidedly human. It sounded like laughter, and not just laughter, but the laughter of a young woman, the sound light and full of gleeful mischief. Simon, still untrusting of people, but curious, found his feet turning in the direction of the sound. Using the tall grass and reeds that grew by the bank as cover, he slowly made his way down the small bank of the creek, creeping forward on his hands and feet like an animal stalking its prey. Peals of laughter mingled with the sound of splashing, and as he rounded a bend in the creek, the waterway widened and slid down a slight incline into a cool dark pool, and as Simon looked upon the open view, a scene unfolded before his eyes that seemed to have come straight out of a pastoral fantasy.

To the right and left of the pool, huge rows of corn reached toward the blue sky, providing a sense of seclusion from the road off to the right. Giant corn stalks waved in rows, their tops standing tall and green. In the distance, the upside down mountains cast a long shadow, but it did not quite reach these crops and pastures. Creeks and rivers sent their fingers along the flat fertile land, and cows, pigs, and chickens moved about in small clusters, neither hurried or stagnant, simply reaping the bounty the land provided. In the distance, the road snaked through the green landscape, toward a collection of buildings that bore a striking resemblance to ancient farmhouses, and red barns dotted the landscape like bursts of rose petals jumping out of an emerald green quilt. The entire scene teemed with life and bounty. Yet, it was what was in the pool that took Simon's breath away.

Men and women darted and slid through the deep, dark water, laughing and splashing in the cool liquid, their sun browned bodies breaking the clear pool's surface with practiced grace. Simon was surprised more than a little to see that all of them, from the youngest youth to the oldest grandmother, were completely naked, their clothes tossed haphazardly amongst the corn stalks. *Is this some weird nudist colony? I heard about these when I was still alive. Wrinkly old people who were just looking for an excuse to disrobe in public.* As soon as the thought had formed in his mind, Simon watched with amazement as a young lady and a man, having bumped into each other, had begun a bout of vigorous lovemaking that nearly made Simon's eyes pop out of his head. The rest of the group, uncaring of the lascivious act that was taking place in their midst, simply kept swimming and laughing. *Definitely some hippie nudist colony.* He felt ashamed that he couldn't look away from the happy couple.

The man and the woman, after a few minutes of pleasurable exercise, smiled lovingly at each other and left the pool to lay in between the corn stalks, the man using his clothes as a sort of blanket for the two of them. Legs intertwined and eyes closed, the couple appeared to be completely unselfconscious about their nakedness, and appeared to drift off to sleep. As Simon turned back to the group of swimming lunatics, his heart nearly stopped when he saw Thales stride out from between two corn stalks. *Well, maybe he will talk some sense into them,* Simon thought as the swimmers turned to offer salutations. Thales smiled, and waved, and then to Simon's complete and utter shock, *removed his toga* and jumped in to join the merriment, as naked as the day he was born. Before he knew it, Simon was running, away from the pool, and away from whatever madness he had just seen. He didn't care if anyone heard him crashing about from above the swimming hole, he only knew that he needed to get away from the weirdness he had just witnessed as quickly as possible.

He reached the campsite, a small clearing again adorned with a single tree, and sat down, his heart racing and his mind doing confused somersaults. *What the hell was that? What just happened back there? Has Thales lost his mind?* Simon's thoughts rattled around in his head, and he found it nearly impossible to focus. Leaning against the tree trunk, Simon took a deep breath, and tried to calm himself. *Okay, okay. Not the weirdest thing you have ever seen. Get it together bud, everything is okay. Just relax, maybe this is a dream.*

"Are you all right?"

Simon's eyes snapped open, his hand instinctually closed on the knife with the well-worn handle, and he pulled it out of his belt as he turned, moving into a crouch. A young lady stood before him, clothed in a flowing white dress that hugged the curves of her frame. She was beautiful, with dark hair that curled into ringlets, and brown eyes that reminded Simon of the feeling of the first cup of coffee in the morning. Her skin was brown like toffee. *Keep it together Simon. Just because she is beautiful doesn't mean she's not a member of the blood cults. Keep your wits about you.* Eyes furrowed, Simon growled, "What do you want?", and was surprised to hear the young woman laugh, a musical sound that caused his heart, if not to completely melt, then to at least thaw a great deal.

"My name is Julia Maesa, and you have nothing to fear from me. Put the knife away."

Simon stepped back. "How do I know I can trust you? I don't know you at all."

"Well, I'm guessing you are Simon, or 'Young Simon' as Thales called you. He asked me to find you, to tell you that he had gone for a swim, and for you not to worry."

"I know where he is. I, I saw him." Simon blushed again. *Jesus Christ, I've been blushing more than a 12-year-old in a whorehouse. Get it together!* Julia's laughter came again, the musical tinkling ringing in his head. "Who were all of those people? Where is this place?"

"This is Elysium, and our arms are always open. Where you saw Thales was where many of us enjoy swimming. There is nothing odd about swimming, is there?" Julia's face was the picture of innocence. "Ah, you are referring instead to the nudity and sex. You see, *Young* Simon," the emphasis on the word made Simon blush again, and he cursed inwardly. "Here at Elysium we embrace community in all its forms, and anything that brings us closer is enjoyed and celebrated. Tell me, is this your first time to Elysium?"

Simon nodded, and was shocked to find Julia's face, a perfect oval, turn from the portrait of innocence to that of a cat who had just realized the mouse she was playing with could also be eaten. Her eyes twinkled, licked her full lips, and bit her bottom lip slightly. Simon, thoroughly confused by her reaction, crouched again, waiting for an attack.

"I must admit, Young Simon, that I do enjoy *introducing* people to our ways when they first come to us. It makes me feel, invigorated."

"What do you mean, 'introduce me to your ways'? I don't understand. Hey, don't move! I'm not sure if I trust you yet. I said..." The words died in his throat, his tongue tied into knots, as Simon watched Julia, without a care or touch of self-consciousness, remove her white gown and let it fall to the grass at her feet. Her eyes, dark pools of tantric hypnosis, locked on Simon. Her breasts were perfect tear drops, and the sun rays seemed to dance as they touched her tanned skin. His tongue felt dry as she slid down, eyes penetrating into Simon. His heart began to hammer, and his clothes suddenly felt too tight. Julia leaned in, her breath smelling of apples and springtime, the scent of her body sweet and sharp. Her bosom pressed into Simon's chest, and her mouth, full and seemingly stuck in an eternal pout, kissed Simon. Her lips were incredibly soft. Simon felt as though he was drowning in her, in this woman, and that he never, ever wanted to be rescued. For a time, all of life disappeared, except for pure existence in a single moment. Everything above, below, from the past to the future, simply faded into the background, slid into nothing but props for the scene to properly unfold. Simon lost himself in the moment, and was consumed by it.

When Simon opened his eyes, he was alone, laying underneath the tree where he and Thales had made camp. He had awoken with a feeling of refreshment and strength, and for a time, all he did was gaze up into the leafy branches of his arboretum, watching the sunshine flit through the leaves as they swayed in the invisible breeze. Simon, judging from the angle of the sunbeams, guessed that it would be dark in a few hours. With a sigh, he stretched luxuriously, and slowly began to rise.

"I am glad you are awake. I am hoping to spend the night in a nice bed, and would really love to enjoy some of Elysium's famous apple cider. Get dressed, and let's be off. Or don't, if that is your desire now, but wear shoes. Rocks still sting, even here. I will be by the road when you are ready"

Without another word, Thales strode off, his spear bindle over his shoulder. The knowing smile that seemed to have become a staple of Simon's new life remained on his face, even as he left the camp. With a start, Simon looked down, and realized that he did not have a stitch of clothing on him. Even as a grown man, in his own house, he did not like people seeing him nude, and his cheeks grew hot as he rushed to shove his skinny legs into the pants that lay crumpled where he had discarded them a few hours ago.

Jerking the shirt over his head, Simon's embarrassment grew as he wondered how long he had lay there, and worse, how long Thales had watched him. *These damn Greeks are not what I learned about in school! Perverts, every last one of them! I swear, if Thales hadn't saved my life all those years ago, I would think the guy was some kind of degenerate.* Simon's embarrassment grew to anger as he stuffed his feet into his soft moccasins, angrily tied his belt around his waist, and secured his trusty knife onto it, grumbling as he did. *Where does he get off, looking at me like that? That is unacceptable! I'm not taking this one second longer. I'm going to knock that smug look right off of his face!* Features set in a determined scowl, Simon gathered his belongings, wrapped them into his bindle, and strode toward the road, fully intending to show Thales just what he thought of him looking at a teenager as he lay in a state of undress.

Thales stood on the road, spear and bundle resting easily on his shoulder. When Simon saw him, everything about the man enraged him, from the way his beard covered his mouth to his strong, straight posture. Calm, with his head turned slightly away from Simon's approach, the philosopher seemed to exude smugness. Simon strode up to him, fists balled up. Thales barely managed to turn his head, and Simon's fist slammed into his bearded chin, knocking him back.

"What makes you think you can just stare at me like that and get away with it? You can't just look at me while I'm, I'm, *indisposed*! It's perverted! I..." Simon's words were unceremoniously cut off, because Thales, in one fluid motion, had unholstered the spear from his shoulder and slid the shaft between Simon's legs, and with a quick yank, caused his teenage feet to leave the earth. The air in his lungs was pushed out by the impact with the hard road, and as his head smacked against the packed earth, the world swam. Shaking his head, trying to clear it of sudden cobwebs, Simon tried to rise, and found the sharp tip of Thales's spear resting on his Adam's apple, pushing slightly inward. A thin trickle of blood slid down his neck where the sharp point had bit into him.

"Now, listen to me very carefully. What you just did was wrong. I did not harm you in any way, nor did I intend to. Nudity does not mean vulnerability, especially here in Elysium. Did you think that I had taken advantage of you as you slept? Wouldn't you feel such a thing?" Thales tone seemed, *amused* as he spoke. Simon looked up, and saw a slight swelling under his Guide's brown beard. Looking down, spear unmoving, Thales continued. As he spoke, his voice dropped to just above a whisper, and dripped with menace. "I understand the time when you died was different than mine in many regards, and I have taken that into account during your instruction, but if you strike me again, I will end your life and hope to not see you when you Return. Do you understand?"

Simon felt the cold hand of fear seize his heart, and realized, with a sickening clarity, that Thales would make good on his promise if pressed. He had seen the man commit murder before. Swallowing made the spear bob on his throat.

"Yes. I understand."

"Good Young Simon, good." With a smooth, fluid motion, Thales withdrew the sharp barb, and easily placed his spear back on his shoulder. Simon, rubbing his neck, saw that the blood had already stopped its flow. Thales held out his hand. "Now, shall we continue? We have a little less than an hour's walk, and I do so enjoy walking the Elysium countryside, seeing all the farms and homes along its outskirts. It is truly one of my favorite places to visit. Let's get moving."

Simon took the hand offered to him, and, once he had regained his feet and his belongings, strode off with Thales toward the buildings and farms he had seen in the distance. Simon, decidedly humbled and quiet, made sure to stay a few feet behind his Guide as they walked.

As the pair strode down the road, Simon was again struck by how the world around him seemed to be more the product of a painter's brush than actual, physical reality. The richness of the colors, the fertility of the soil as shown by bountiful trees and fields of grain, seemed to border on the surreal. Simon felt as if his own colors, from his skin to his clothes, had somehow become muted when he walked by the bright array of growing things and colorful structures. Homesteads painted vibrant blues, yellows, and greens overlooked massive fields of wheat and corn, so large in fact that they appeared to be a veritable ocean of green and amber, forming waves as the stalks blew in the ever present breeze. Orchards of apples and oranges, of pears and lemons, covered the remaining visible landscape. As Simon walked, wheat and corn gave way to large berry bushes that lined the road, sporting fruits of red, blue, and deep purple. Simon plucked a raspberry from a bush to his left, and popped the little red morsel in his mouth. The sweet juices of the tiny fruit, both tart and sweet, reminded him of peanut butter and jelly sandwiches eaten on summer afternoons. The lushness of the landscape, the sweetness of the berry, and the bursting of life helped Simon forget why he was mad at Thales, made him forget the terrors of his adventure to this place. It was as if the world around him had cast a spell, spread a blanket of peace and plenty.

After the road had meandered its way through the rich fields and trees heavy with fruit, past the beautiful homes and large brightly colored barns, it made a stop at the idyllic town of Elysium. Beauty barely began to describe the place Simon's feet had led him. Crossing into the village proper from the countryside, it seemed that every time he turned his head, he was engrossed in a new wonder to behold. Truth be told, Simon felt overwhelmed by the beauty of the place. His mouth hung open as he stepped into the shadow of the buildings.

Walking into the quaint town, the first thing to draw the eye were the flowers. Hibiscus and hydrangea mingled with geranium and rose, colors bursting out of every windowsill and climbing to the heavens from the border of the road. Jasmine vines climbed up the side of houses, and the sweet smell of their flowers filled Simon's nostrils. The buildings were of wood, grown out of what seemed to be giant redwood trees, their tops reaching past Simon's field of vision. The needle heavy branches of the sequoias interwove above the road, providing a roof like canopy that provided shade when the sun was at its zenith. The road curved around Elysium, and in the center of the village Simon could make out an open green, where little white shapes moved lazily about. As the sun faded directly in line with the road, the trees and flowers were given a mystical air, as the dying day bathed all of the life of Elysium in shades of golden light.

171

Simon was transfixed, and did not notice the town was in fact populated, until his forward momentum came to an abrupt halt when he ran into a white cloak and firm back.

"I am so sorry," he began, but stopped when he realized that the person, an older gentleman in his middle years, with dark hair touched with grey, moved fluidly from getting bumped by Simon's shoulder, and simply wrapped his arms, large and firm from tilling fields, around Simon, and hugged him softly but firmly. Simon subconsciously stiffened as the man's arms enveloped him.

"Thank you for letting us touch. I welcome you to me whenever you desire." Slowly, the man released his embrace of Simon, who remained frozen as his new acquaintance stepped back, but kept his large hands on the youth's shoulders. The dark haired man's eyes, soft green gems slightly downturned, with lines around the corners that spoke of constant laughter, took in Simon's own, and a small smile cracked his weathered face. Simon became even more rigid when the man cupped the back of his neck, and reached to the tips of his toes so he could kiss him on the forehead. His lips were dry like old sandpaper. Smiling once more, the man released the now open mouthed Simon, and without another word, continued to walk down the road. Simon remained very still, afraid to move. *Okay, that guy must be high. What the hell just happened? Better keep my eyes peeled. I bet these hippies grow more than corn in those fields I saw.* The man continued walking until he disappeared behind a large redwood house, snapping Simon back to the present.

Simon turned his attention to the people of the town. At first glance, they appeared to be normal human beings, not dissimilar from the place in which he had first met Thales. Some people even wore the garb of their era. Simon saw togas, breeches, hoop skirts, and leggings, as well as clothing stitched together from animal skins. Yet, though the array of clothing was varied, the amount of white used by the people of Elysium was rampant. Even those who did not wear a fully white tunic or toga had a band of white cloth wrapped around their arm or head. *Just like a cult,* Simon thought, and made a mental note to ask Thales about the people of Elysium's fashion choice when they were alone. Something was odd, something was *different* about these people, that was for sure, and it was not just their love of white. Simon watched them, mingling in front of shops, purchasing items, talking near the beautiful array of plants that dotted the town, and felt as though their interactions with each other seemed, *different.* He couldn't quite put his finger on it, and found himself staring at the people as they moved about their lives.

He watched as a young woman and man stopped in front of a store window, admiring what appeared to be various cakes and pastries. Without really speaking to one another, both looking at a particular dessert, the young people clasped hands, a familiar embrace reserved for lovers or someone held close. Simon looked about him, and saw two men, possibly in their mid-forties, sit down next to one another on a single slab of stone that had been Changed to evoke the image of a park bench. One man, his hair the black of an evening storm cloud, closed his almond shaped eyes and, without a word, leaned into the other resident of the park bench. The other man, facial expression never altering on his dark face, slid his white shirted arm around the resting stranger, and held him close. Tearing his eyes from the scene to once again take in the larger world, Simon realized with a start that *all* the people of this place, whether it be man or woman, young or old, made a point of touching, of embracing in some way, all the people that they encountered. *Okay, this is definitely some weird hippie cult. Why did Thales bring me here? Where is Thales, by the way? Where did that strange old fart run away to?*

Simon looked about him, and realized that, as he had been transfixed by the people of Elysium, his Guide had evaporated. He seemed to have disappeared into the crowd of white, into a population of people who were way too handsy for his taste. He thought briefly of the young lady under the tree, and angrily he forced down the heat trying to rise up

173

to his cheeks. Lost in that awkward, painfully wonderful moment, Simon was jerked back to the reality of the present by the familiar sensation of his hand being clasped. He turned quickly, meaning to pull his hand away, and was immediately thankful he did not.

Standing by him, small hand enveloped by Simon's own, stood a young boy who could not be over the age of seven. He wore denim trousers, *how did these people make denim?,* and straight black hair nearly covered his dark eyes. Simon was surprised and more than a little taken aback by the size of the boy's head in comparison to his body. He looked up at Simon, and smiled, and if Simon didn't know better, it looked to be the kind of smile that someone gives another person to reassure them, to let them know that everything will be alright.

"Are you lost? You look as though someone has left you here, in a foreign place with no friends." The boy spoke in an alliterative manner, focusing hard on consonants and speaking quickly, giving his speech a rhythmic, chant like structure. The accent that had settled on the boy's words seemed to lend itself to music and poetry as well as speaking. Simon looked down at him, wondering where he came from, and couldn't help but marvel at the size of his cranium. *How does a head that big get attached to a body that small?* he wondered. Trying not to stare, he smiled down at the child.

"I'm not lost, thank you, kiddo. I just seem to have misplaced my friend. Have you seen a man in a toga, with a big curly beard, brown hair, and a spear? He was just here, yet he seems to have wandered off." Simon made a show of looking around.

"Oh, you mean Thales? Many know Thales here, and he is welcome to roam where he pleases, as are all people who pass through Elysium. And there is no need to call me 'kiddo.' I do not doubt that I am several centuries your senior, if I had to guess."

Christ, he's right. Just because someone is a child does not mean they are an actual child, *not here anyway.* Simon apologized quickly, hoping that he did not offend his young companion. The boy merely laughed, waving away Simon's apologies with his free hand. Simon wondered why the child was still holding *his* hand, but kept quiet.

"That is quite alright. I believe that I am safe to say you have not Returned before?"

"How could you tell?"

The boy laughed, a musical, reedy sound that made Simon think of a bird chirping. "It's a look that people have, a wideness to the eyes. Don't worry, we love new people here. Too bad we haven't had one come to stay with us for about a century or so."

The boy released Simon's hand, and reached up to clasp his shoulder, locking eyes with Simon in a similar fashion to the man who had bumped into him a few minutes prior. "I am called Ah-Mun, and I welcome you to me. I hope you find all that you need here in Elysium. Come, let us walk together. Two pairs of eyes are better than one to find a friend, and you can tell me of the time you have come from. As I said, it has been awhile since a newly Returned has Ascended, and I would love to know all about the time you spent on the old world." With that, Ah-Mun linked arms with Simon, which he found to be particularly uncomfortable, and began to walk through the crowds of people, occasionally stopping to hug a young man, or kiss a grandmother on the cheek. *Why does he have to touch all of these people? What is wrong with these folks? Just keep walking, that's all you have to do. Just keep walking!* Simon tried to remain nonchalant, but all the stopping was beginning to make him irritated. He just wanted to find Thales and get away from all of the smiling, hugging, kissing, and above all, touching. He tried to keep his eyes in front of him and his hands at his side.

Ah-Mun, seeming to read Simon's thoughts, smiled as he slid his arm through Simon's after kissing a young lady with a purple flower behind her ear.

"You must wonder why we make a point of touching so much. Did no one touch you in your time?"

The young girl that Ah-Mun had kissed must have been no older than eighteen, but she carried herself with a grace and knowledge of a woman well versed in the world. She gave Simon a slow wink. Ah-Mun continued.

"We, as the Returned, are driven to Elysium because of our Journeys. We are either born here by a Carrier, or we find ourselves here soon after."

The girl had smiled, looking up at Simon with expectant eyes, and giggled when he kept his distance from her. Simon smiled awkwardly, enjoying the attention of a young lady but still unsure how to properly react. His hands fidgeted.

"For example, you have people like me who are drawn here, people whose Journeys are surrounded by the creation of community, of the need to be with other people that has proved the impetus for so much of humanities' accomplishments and failures."

The girl, with eyes the color of green sea glass, and hair as red as a maple leaf, slid by Simon, the hint of laughter on her lips. She touched Simon's cheek as she passed, and whispered words that were heated by a force deep in a young person's belly; "I welcome you to me." She turned and walked by, slowly, as if to make sure Simon watched her graceful body move sinuously away from him, her white dress snug against her curves.

"Simon, are you listening to me?"

I bet her name is a flower, Simon thought has he continued to stare.

"Simon? Are you alright?"

Simon, who had stopped dead in his tracks to watch the girl move away, snapped his head back, looking down at his small companion, whose head was cocked to one side, a quizzical look on his face. He was not angry; there was no heat in his question of whether or not Simon had heard what he said. He just looked up at the skinny youth with patience and curiosity.

"Sorry, I got… distracted. Christ, this place really gets to my head."

"Christ? Ahh, so your time still believes in the religion of Jesus and the saints. Interesting. Yes, Elysium has a way of, *distracting*, even those who have lived here for a while. If you can keep your attentions focused, I will try to explain why. Do you think that you can do that?" A hint of a smile played upon the lips of Ah-Mun, slightly mocking, but with no malice behind it. Simon found himself smiling in return.

"I will try, but if that redhead comes back, I make no promises."

"Oh, are you in need of sex? Why didn't you just say so? I always had a problem focusing whenever I needed the companionship of someone myself. Luckily, I am not yet pubescent, so that issue has yet to arise in this lifetime." Ah-Mun chuckled as if he made a joke. "Go, lay with someone. I will wait. I do not wish to lay with you myself, but that is the way of children."

If Simon had been shocked before, he was veritably struck dumb now. Having anyone speak so casually of coitus had always been off putting to him, but to have a *child* inform him that he would wait for Simon to get laid? Such a ridiculous notion nearly caused Simon to want to laugh and run away screaming at the same time. *Goddamn place is absolutely crazy! Maybe this is some strange Elysium joke that I am not aware of.*

Looking to his companion for some sort of confirmation, some indication that he was, in fact, joking, Simon was again surprised to find the boy with the overly large cranium simply staring at him, the very essence of patience. *What the hell is going on? How can this place still surprise me after all I've seen? Jesus Christ, I think there's a chance that I won't ever feel normal again.* Ah-Mun, watching Simon with those impassive, patient eyes, looked for all the world as if waiting for a stranger to go have intimate relationships with someone was simply another element of everyday life.

"I, I think I'm alright. Thank you Ah-Mun. Let's just look for Thales. I need to talk to him about well, everything, and remind him to stop leaving me alone without telling me why."

"Of course, let's continue looking for your friend, Master Simon."

"Simon is fine."

"Ah, such a wonderful name. Great history in that name. Tell me of yourself Simon. Tell me of the world you left behind. What is it like? What country did you come from? How has the world changed? What, what is the *food* like?" At the last question, Ah-Mun's eyes took on a shine that had not been there before. Simon tried to answer the young boy's questions, who listened with interest and patience, smiling and nodding at the appropriate times, occasionally asking a question about the size of cities or the wonders of modern technology. Yet, when Simon began talking about the food of his time, of the convenience of supermarkets and fast food restaurants, Ah-Mun's eyes became as wide as saucers, and he stopped in his tracks, the quest for Thales forgotten.

"So, you are telling me that the people of your time can simply walk into this, *supermarket,* and in exchange for paper money, take whatever they wish? That is amazing! Tell me, Simon, what of maize? Is there still *corn?*" The boy seemed to annunciate the noun with a degree of fervor, filled with an emotion that Simon could not place.

"Is there *corn* in these stores?" When Simon replied that, yes, there was corn everywhere, that it filled the arable land of his old country, and that the corn lobby was one of the most powerful entities in his nation's government, Ah-Mun clapped his hands and nearly jumped for joy. "That is, that is *amazing!* I knew it, Simon, I knew that I would bring the world together. This is good news! I feel like I am one step closer to completing my Journey. Oh thank you Simon, thank you!" and with that, the young boy wrapped his arms around Simon, hugging him tightly. Simon awkwardly returned the embrace, then after a few moments, gently pushed his companion away. As he stepped back, looking up at Simon once more, Ah-Mun's eyes still shone with that feverish light.

"Ah-Mun, I'm glad I made you happy, but I don't understand. What is all this about? Why are you so *obsessed* with corn?"

"Why, isn't it obvious? I created it! Well, I brought it to humanity, and helped my people form part of the modern civilization that you were born into. And it has become such a wonderful place, ho ho! Yes, it has!"

"Wait, you *created* corn? How is that even possible? I'm sorry Ah-Mun, but I just don't understand." *Maybe this place is getting to me after all. I don't even feel that surprised when a young boy claims to have created a staple of agriculture, one of the biggest cash crops in history. Maybe I will find normal in the crazy. Hell, maybe I am already crazy.*

"Ah, now *that* is a story worth telling. Come, let us find a place to rest, and I will tell you my tale. I feel as though I was, *destined,* to speak to you today. The tales of your time have already strengthened my heart. Come, I know just where we can rest. Thales will be found after." Ah-Mun's smile, radiant and open, seemed to illuminate the landscape around him.

Ah-Mun, eyes still shining, clasped Simon's hand, an embrace that still caused the youth to feel uncomfortable, yet this time, he was happy to note the feeling had at least become muted. Ah-Mun led Simon from the canopied road to the open green he had seen when he first entered Elysium. People in white lounged on the green grass and by various bodies of water; eating, drinking, and enjoying the final remnants of the fading daylight. Ah-Mun stopped in front of a small pond, its waters a pale green, bordering on turquoise. In the center, water shot up into the sky, forming a mist that cooled the people lying about the water's shore, and as the spray caught the fading sun rays, rainbows danced amongst the water droplets. The geyser in the middle would shoot up, then turn as if in a breeze, creating various shapes. Simon watched as the fountain formed first a heart, then a tree, then the figure of a woman. The spectators were in various stages of undress, and judging from the movement of some, were engaging in activities that Simon thought were best left to the bedroom. Furiously he tried to focus on Ah-Mun, on the young boy's dark hair, on his large head, as he led him to the far side of the pond.

The child seemed completely impervious to the people around him, walking through the green grass without a touch of self-consciousness or embarrassment. Simon stared stubbornly forward, trying to drown out the sounds of giggling and throaty murmurs of the people of Elysium. Ah-Mun plopped down, produced a water skin from somewhere on his person, took a pull, and passed it to Simon. The water was sweet and refreshing, washing away some of the oddities, and the embarrassments, of the day. Taking the water skin back, Ah-Mun took a long pull, sighed, and laid back. Simon sat down next to him, and tried to not let his eyes wander.

A few moments passed in silence, with Simon staring up at Dara's sky. Clouds raced back and forth, pacing and dancing against the perfect blue backdrop. *Someone is working on their Changing,* he noted as he saw a cloud become a centaur and attack a thin cirrus cloud that had formed into a serpent. *Thales says that working with clouds is easy, because they are not fully solid, liquid, or gas. "They are already Changing" he says, "so they just need a little push", whatever that means.*

"Now, Simon, how familiar are you with the empires of Mesoamerica?" Ah-Mun's reedy voice cut through Simon's reverie. "That is the name of where I come from, at least, according to the person who is closest to your time. I should introduce the two of you! Ah, but that is for later, and he lives far from here. I wish to tell my story; not have you hear another. Are you familiar with the empires of Mesoamerica? The Maya, the Aztecs, the Toltecs?"

Ah-Mun propped himself on his elbow and looked at Simon, waiting for a response. The young man wracked his brain, trying to remember whatever he could about the people of ancient Central America. His mind went to Mr. Thompson, his World History teacher, with his horrible comb over and yellowed fingers from smoking too many unfiltered cigarettes. The man had smelled as though he had just crawled out of a bar and into the classroom, and he recalled his mother saying that his wife had left him for one of his old students. Yet, he did teach on occasion, lecturing from chapters found in a giant tome of a book with waxy paper and a battered green cover. A sudden image of pyramids with what looked like giant steps flashed into Simon's mind, managing to leap off pages that he half remembered thumbing through. "They are the ones with the pyramids right? And, and they worshipped a bird I think?"

"Yes, yes! Those empires did build pyramids, true, and you may be referring to the Thunder Bird, called Quetzalcoatl by some, Kukulkan and Gukumatz by others. Yes, the feathered serpent was worshipped by the Maya and the Aztecs, as well as by more ancient peoples. The Mesoamericans had many gods and goddesses, all of whom dealt with an important aspect of life: love, sex, death, war. However, all of those great gods seem to have disappeared with the empires that built them. But one, one has stood the test of time." The young boy's chest swelled, and he looked up at Simon, brown eyes meeting green. Simon's brow furrowed, and he looked at the boy, feeling as though he missed something important, but didn't know what.

"Well, don't you want to know who survived? Don't you want to know which god managed to transcend death itself?"

"Yes, I think. I am not really sure where this is going, but I think meeting a god would be pretty amazing." Simon's mind flashed to a white beard and lightning flashes as he spoke.

"Well, Simon, you are looking at him. My name, Ah-Mun, means 'green shoot', and I am the god of maize, the symbol of fertility and growing things!" With the last, the boy scrambled up to his feet, and with as much gravity as a small child can muster, gave a bow. As he bent at the waist, he looked up at Simon, black hair nearly covering his eyes, and gave a toothy grin. Simon smiled back, and giggled in spite of himself.

"Okay, so you are a god. Help me out here; how on earth does that work? You seem to be fairly human to me."

"That is exactly correct, my fair haired friend. I am human, but I am also a god. Tell me: do you know of a civilization that existed before the Aztecs? Before the Maya?" Simon shook his head, and confessed that his understanding of the ancient world was extremely limited to say the least. The boy nodded, unperturbed by Simon's ignorance, and continued.

"Well, before the Maya, there was another, older civilization, a more ancient empire: The Xi. These people built pyramids, made scientific advances, and had their own religion. But tell me, my friend: how did they, or any ancient civilization, begin? What made humanity stop hunting and gathering, and decide to plop down and build buildings, create civilization? Huh? Agriculture! Farming! Yes, it was the discovery of farming that shaped humanity. Without it, we would still be running around hunting and gathering, like those folks who insist on doing so in Eden Town." A memory of a bearded man with a spear flashed in Simon's mind, and the phantom pain of a sharp barb touched his chest. Ah-Mun's face showed a brief shift, a slight change in expression lending itself toward disgust, then immediately shifted back to his pleasant smile. The change was so fast, Simon thought that he may have imagined it.

"Now, who do you think brought this agriculture to the ancient Xi? Me, of course!" the young boy's eyes shone, and his posture became even more rigid, causing his chest to thrust forward even more. He almost looked like a proud, black plumed bird, small in stature but fierce in nature.

"I remember discovering how to make plants grow, how to bend nature to my will. I brought it to my clan, and before you knew it, we didn't have to leave one place! We could stay and farm, not worrying about where our next meal came from. True, some of the older people of my group wanted to kill me, saying I was an evil spirit, but once that first harvest became successful, there was no denying that what I did was *good*. My discovery created an empire, and many empires to come! As was the case so often in ancient history, we inventors, we creators, couldn't be fully explained by the minds of the time, so we became part of myth, no longer people, but something more."

"So, you are telling me that you discovered maize, corn, and people turned you into a god?" The boy smiled again, and nodded. "Then what could possibly be your Journey? You helped to create civilization in your society, kick started the world that would later become the place that I was born into. Why are you still here?" As the question fell from his lips, Simon witnessed the young boy, so full of joy and life moments ago, shrink in on himself. His eyes became downcast, and his shoulders slumped. He seemed to have become shorter, somehow frailer, in an instant. "Isn't it obvious my friend? My creation, thought to be so good, was also the epitome of evil. I tell you, it wasn't a few years after my discovery that people began to change. They started competing for the best land, fighting for the areas that would create the best harvest. It wasn't long before someone murdered another for the right to farm on a certain patch of earth, an act unheard of before agriculture! Before farming, we needed each other, we needed every human being to help us survive. With what I invented, we no longer *needed* everyone to hunt, to look for food, to help find shelter. We needed *land* more than *people,* and as a result, we changed forever. I watched as all of this happened, and the weight of those deaths, of that anger, drove into my soul, and has never left." The boy's words were barely a whisper when he finished speaking, and when he ceased his speech, he plopped back down on the ground, head hung low. Simon wanted to comfort him, to help him somehow, but he couldn't think of one way he could possibly comfort a god. Slowly, he placed his hand on Ah-Mun's shoulder. The boy, almost instinctively, reached up and clasped the hand with his own.

"Thank you, Simon. Human touch, community, companionship, sometimes they are the only things that can stand up against the darkness of who and what we are. That is why others like me, why we are pulled to Elysium. We hope, through building a community of peace, companionship, and plenty, we can complete our Journeys, and continue to the next plane. Yes, we believe that there is a next step, another world after this one, and don't believe for a second that the end of a Journey is our true end." Simon's eyes went wide only briefly when Ah-Mun, the god of agriculture and maize, placed his head on Simon's chest, wrapped his small arms around him, and began to cry. He cried without shame, without fear of judgment. He cried, and Simon simply sat there, occasionally patting the boy's back, hoping that he was helping in some way. After a few minutes, the boy slowly released his grip, wiped his eyes, and to Simon's surprise, smiled brightly. Simon's shirt was wet from tears, and he was more than a little off put by the raw emotional expression from Ah-Mun, but he tried to smile back.

"Thank you for telling me of your stores, of your supermarkets and restaurants. It feels good to know that my discovery may help humanity become unified again, that one day we will have enough food for everyone. I am happy you came here, Simon. I hope we will become even greater friends."

Ah-Mun closed his eyes, lifting his face toward the final sun rays as the giant orb in the sky dipped over the horizon. When he spoke, his words possessed a levity that had so recently been absent from his speech.

"I feel lighter. I feel as though we were meant to meet, that our Journeys are intertwined somehow. Tell me; do people still fight? Do we still kill one another for food, for land?" Simon nodded, and the young boy sighed. "Well, I may have started the descent into madness, but as long as I am still cognizant, as long as I am still *aware*, all I can do is try to create a place of peace and plenty, to try and guide people down a different path. I can do no more." The young boy's smile faded, and he appeared to become listless again.

Simon, wanting desperately to comfort his new friend, immediately leapt to agree with Ah-Mun. "That is true. In my time, we have food, shelter, and convenience, yet we still find ways to kill each other. We always seem to want *more.* More money, more power, more land. Hell, I had to witness a man kill another because he didn't have enough *respect* for him. It is sad, but part of our nature seems to drive us toward doing whatever is necessary to get what we want, even if that means destroying the lives of others."

Ah-Mun, his listless face turned to listen to Simon's speech, propped himself up on his elbow.

"Yes, I know people fight for more than just food and land, but I still feel, still believe in my heart, that it can all be traced back to my discovery. The fault still lies with me." Ah-Mun's eyes started to become glassy, tears brimming to the surface. *Goddamn it man stop crying. Or child. Man-child? Just quit crying!*

Simon, still wanting to help, at least in some way, bulled forward. "But you can't hold yourself at fault for all the mistakes of man. Once, I saw a young man stab another with a screwdriver, a sharp metal tool, in the face for a pair of shoes. And besides, if you hadn't found a way to farm, so many people, billions of people, would have never had a chance to live at all. It's true, some people cock up their chance, but without you Ah-Mun, they would have never existed. That's got to be worth something."

The child's dark eyes, still brimming with tears, began to show a whisper of hope in them. Simon pressed on.

"So, not only did you manage to make life possible for billions of people, if you *hadn't* discovered agriculture, people would probably just kill each other over something else. In my time, at least, the good of your discovery far, far outweighs the bad." Ah-Mun listened intently, and when Simon had finished, the light of hope had replaced the tears in Ah-Mun's eyes. Simon smiled again, feeling like he had succeeded in giving his new friend at least a little comfort.

The child, dark hair contrasting green as he lay back on the grass, stared up at the sky. When he spoke again, his words were a rapturous whisper. "For so long, I felt the weight of the world on my shoulders, felt as though all the violence of our species was somehow my fault, and if we could just have enough for everyone, then the violence would cease. Yet, you have shown me that I am wrong. Some of us will always find an excuse to fight, to destroy someone else to get what we want. It has taken me millennia and countless lives to understand this, and I wish someone from your time had come sooner. The weight is lifting, Simon. I do not feel the weight; I do not feel the weight." The boy's eyes shot open, and he stared into the sky, continuously repeating "I do not feel the weight, I do not feel the weight" over and over again. Simon knelt by his friend, concern beginning to creep into his heart.

Suddenly, the boy's repeated phrase died on his lips, and without another sound, Ah-Mun's eyes rolled into the back of his head, his body became limp, and he sank, lifeless, into the soft grass. Simon reached out, and he gently picked up the boy's head, cradling it in his hands, The boy's eyes were open, but the iris and retina were gone, leaving only the whites exposed. "I do not feel the weight" he whispered, and his final breath danced out, the final touch of life withdrawing its fingers, and Ah-Mun lay still. Simon cried out, yelling for help, though he knew that no one could follow the path that Ah-Mun had begun to walk.

CHAPTER XIII–DOWN BESIDE THE GLOWING BARS

People in white rushed over, checking the boy's pulse and his breathing. When they found none, they turned to comfort Simon, murmuring to the body, "I bid you safe Return," before gently straightening the boy's legs and crossing his small arms over his chest. Ah-Mun, so large in life, suddenly appeared unbelievably small to Simon, like a balloon that had lost its air. One older man, his hair grey and his face full of wrinkles, clasped Simon's shoulder.

"Not to worry, my young friend," the man said. "He will Return, and then you can continue your conversation with him. I know it is hard to understand sometimes, and our instinct wars with our knowledge of this place, but Ah-Mun will Return."

"I … I suppose you are right," Simon said, though tears filled his eyes. "Thank you, sir. I am still new to—"

Before he could finish his statement, Simon was interrupted by a collective gasp to his left. Turning, Simon saw everyone staring at the small body of Ah-Mun, and when he followed their gaze down, his breath caught in his throat.

Judging from the placement of two people, one at his head and another at his feet, it looked as though they were preparing to move his body. Briefly, Simon wondered where lifeless bodies were placed in Dara, whether there was a giant graveyard somewhere. But that thought disappeared just as quickly as it arrived, when he looked closer at the motionless form of Ah-Mun—of what remained of his new young friend.

The young boy's body had somehow become less real, less tangible. Somehow, his body had become impossibly light—so light that it could be lifted up into the air by the ever-present breeze of Dara. As the boy who was once a god began to float upwards, his skin seemed to break apart, to flake into glowing confetti that slid into the breeze. Within a few moments, Ah-Mun had become a million pieces of glowing light and was carried away by the soft wind, felt by all living things on this second plane.

Everyone around him was silent—a quiet that became bloated with tension before everyone burst out at once around Simon. A dozen voices danced in the wind, threatening to overwhelm him.

"What ... what *happened?*"

"Where did he go?"

"Has anyone seen anything like this before?"

"What do we do?"

Questions flew about like insects, yet Simon only stared at the space that held his companion, his friend—even though he had known him for only a brief time. He was only dimly aware of the hand that still remained on his shoulder, of someone turning him so that he came face-to-face with the old man who had assured him that Ah-Mun would Return.

"What did he say to you, lad? What were you two talking about? Is this some new kind of Changing that we do not know about? Where did you come from? What *happened?*"

"I ... I do not know. We were talking about ... about food and history and gods." The ridiculousness of his statement nearly made Simon spit out the kind of laugh that can only be produced when it appears as though the world has finally lost all elements of logic and sense, but he pushed it down.

"And then, he started saying, 'I do not feel the weight' over and over again, until he ... until he died. I do not know what happened. I do not know." Simon suddenly felt sick, and, even though he had been staring at the space once filled by Ah-Mun, he couldn't bear the thought of looking at that patch of grass ever again. His knees buckled, and he sat down hard on the grass beneath his feet. *I have seen many people die in my time, have lost so much. But this felt different.* He stared at the turquoise water, at the changing fountain, and whispered, "I do not know. I do not know."

"He has completed his Journey. He has gone on to the next plane, though we know not where," a familiar voice said. Simon turned to see Thales walking up, his immaculate white toga standing out sharply from the green grass. "This is such a rare occurrence that not even I, after living here for thousands of years, have seen it happen, though I have heard of those who complete their Journeys. Whomever young Simon here was speaking to has done just that."

Thales gazed at his young protégé, and his eyes were full of kindness and an emotion that Simon could not quite place. "It is so strange to think that, although you have just arrived, you have seen something that occurs maybe once in a millennium." The philosopher looked at Simon, as if trying to solve a complex puzzle in the back of the young man's skull.

At the mention of the completion of Journeys, of leaving this plane completely, a hush fell over the crowd that had gathered. Simon saw that the numbers had grown since he first called out for help. Thales walked into their midst, his bearded face now wearing an expression that was full of empathy and caring as he looked at his pupil. After a brief moment, he turned and raised his voice, addressing the crowd:

"This, my friends, is not a time of sadness. This is a time of celebration! Some of you may have forgotten, but in the old world, death also helped to bring people together, to help them celebrate the life that still pulsed within them. Let us celebrate the one who left and comfort those who remain."

The crowd began to murmur sounds of approval, and smiles gradually took the place of frowns on the faces of onlookers. People started to clasp hands and to embrace one another again. Thales smiled, looking at the crowd, and spread his hands.

"Spread the word: Tonight, we feast! We will celebrate this momentous event. We will show the world—and each other—that Elysium truly is a place of togetherness and community, and that we can find unity and peace, even in death. Spread the word, my friends, and gather at the Heart."

People cheered, and, laughing, they moved to tell others the news of the upcoming celebration. Many clasped arms again, and as the crowd moved away en masse, smiling and relieved, Simon shook his head.

"Damn cults."

Simon, who had just witnessed the death of his friend—his true death—did not know how to begin to react. He was angry at Thales, and yet he was simultaneously relieved that his guide had come in and helped to turn a time of sadness into a cause for celebration. *Just one more reason why my brain will eventually snap in half.* Thales, after watching the crowd disperse with news of the celebration, turned to his young pupil. His smile was gone, and in its place, concern tinged with curiosity washed over his features.

"Tell me what happened. Tell me everything."

"His name was Ah-Mun. He claimed to be a god of ancient Mesoamerica—the Xi, I think he said."

Haltingly at first, still shocked by what had happened, Simon told Thales all that had transpired, from when he found himself alone to meeting Ah-Mun to his newfound friend's death. Throughout, Thales listened quietly. When Simon was finished, Thales sighed and sat down on the grass. Simon stared outward, watching as a fountain in the pond split into two people dancing an elaborate routine that involved throwing one person in the air, spinning, and catching them again. As the flyer fell into the waiting arms of its partner, both dancers would disappear into the water with a splash.

Thales spoke, but Simon kept watching the fountain. "I knew Ah-Mun. The last I saw of him, he was an old man, dancing with a young gentleman who reminded me of a willow tree. I am glad that his Journey has ended, but I am sad that I will never see him again. It has been a long time since I have experienced true death, young Simon, and the sting does not diminish with age."

Simon sat quietly, thinking of the life of his mentor. *Poor guy. He probably knew Ah-Mun for a thousand years. I only knew him for part of a day. I can't even imagine what that must be like.* Slowly, haltingly, Simon clasped the hand of Thales, in similar fashion to how Ah-Mun had done to him. Thales looked down, and a small smile crossed his face.

"So, it appears as though Elysium has rubbed off on you more quickly than I thought it would. No, no, I do not mean that as a mockery. I am thankful for you trying to comfort me." Simon looked at the vibrant life around him, at the flowers and emerald grass as Thales sighed.

"There is such poetry in this life. When a soul is killed here, set to Return, their body slowly sinks into the earth of Dara, yet when true death occurs, the soul breaks into shimmering shards and disappears, rising into the unknown. Poetry." Thales's eyes suddenly became very serious, and he gripped Simon's hand so strongly that it was almost painful.

"Your Journey, young Simon, has already caused so much death and change," he continued. "It would appear as though it will alter a lot of lives before you are done. This is both fascinating and terrifying, when I look to the future. If nothing else, I am glad that I am your guide, as I will see firsthand just how you will shape the world in which you have found yourself. I do not mean to frighten you; we all affect the world around us to varying degrees. But for you, the changes you have made are decidedly more drastic than the average person." The philosopher shook himself, then smiled. "But that may just be the fact that I have managed to maintain a certain distance from people for the last few thousand years. Maybe being this close to someone makes their actions somehow *larger.*"

Thales smoothed his toga and gestured toward a white mass that had begun churning off in the distance. "Anyway, young Simon, let us join the festivities. I think you will find that Elysium celebrations are unlike anything that you have ever seen before."

Thales slowly released Simon's hand and turned to walk away. Simon, however, remained where he was.

"I don't know if I should go to any celebration right now, Master Thales. It would feel … *weird* to celebrate and enjoy a party right after someone has just passed away in my arms." Simon looked at his guide, hoping that he understood how he felt. *How could I possibly want to party right now? I wouldn't be any fun at all.*

"Tell me, young Simon, how are we supposed to feel when someone dies? What are we supposed to do?"

"We are supposed to feel bad. We should be upset that the person is no longer with us."

"And what does that do? Does it cause the person to come back? Does it make our lives more enriched? Does it help us?"

"Well, no, but you are *supposed* to feel sad when someone dies. You will never see them again. You will never be able to talk to them, ever again."

"Well, that is true, and I do feel sad, but I also am alive. I am painfully aware of that fact, now more than ever. I understand that death—the true death after I complete my Journey—will claim me, and I may never be able to experience anything again. This invigorates me. It makes me realize that I want not only to exist, I want to *live*. That is why we celebrate after a death, young Simon. The dead have given us a gift: the strongest reminder of them all that we are alive, we are aware, we can still experience. Come with me and honor Ah-Mun's gift to us with the people of Elysium."

Jesus Christ, why does that make so much damn sense? Thinking like that would have made all the funerals I went to when I was alive a hell of a lot more fun.

"All right, Master Thales, all right. I will try it your way, but it still feels odd to party after someone has just died."

"Trust me, my young friend, it is the best time of all times to, as you say, *party*." Without another word, Thales strode forward, coming again to the main path that Simon and Ah-Mun had wandered from, what seemed ages ago. Small torches had been lit to push back the coming night, and Simon, not for the first or the last time, hurried after his guide to experience something wholly new—or, at least, something very old from a very new perspective.

As they strode down the curving path, Simon realized that Elysium was designed in a circular fashion, with one road marking the perimeter of the town and two more making a cross that intersected in the center. Flowers and shrubs lined all of the roads, and the smell of growing things was everywhere. *I bet this place looks like a flower from above. I wonder if there are airplanes here. No, of course not. If there were, I wouldn't have been forced to walk to this town and never would have been chased by a giant zombie lizard.*

As Simon and Thales walked forward, they saw an intersection in the distance, which turned out to be a perfectly straight road that shot directly through the center of town. Thales turned at this road, and as Simon turned with him, his eyes fell on a giant lawn, perfectly trimmed, with stone buildings Changed to look like giant tents. Sparkling precious metals reflected dully from the sides of these tents, and the rocks were shaved so thin that Simon was surprised that they didn't flap in the breeze.

Dotted among these unique structures were dancing statues of men and women, depicting various pastoral scenes. One statue, painted to look almost lifelike, depicted a man in overalls climbing a ladder that stood up on its own. The bright red apples that peeked from the burlap bag slung across the statue's shoulder were almost supernaturally red, and seeing them made Simon's stomach rumble. Another statue—this one pale marble and unpainted—showed a woman, hair flowing freely in a breeze that Simon swore he could feel, as she tossed small seeds onto the waiting ground.

Some of the statues, upon closer inspection, were not statues at all, but fountains that burst forth into beautiful scenes, painted by the prismatic effect of light dancing with water. Others were the perfectly carved likenesses of people and animals cut into shrubs and bushes, reminiscent of the first town that Simon had found himself in when he crossed over into Dara. Every square inch of Elysium's perfectly manicured lawn was full of beauty and plenty.

Among the statues, fountains, and shrubs, people had begun to congregate. Some came dancing, arms linked, laughing as they skipped onto the soft green grass. Others came loaded with food, hands full of baskets loaded down with fruit, vegetables, and bread. Simon watched as four burly men came onto the green, carrying a large table seemingly hewn from a single giant tree, and placed it down in the middle of the lawn so that those who brought food could relieve their burden.

A sound behind Simon made him look, then jump out of the way, as huge barrels rolled down the street, pushed by young men and women who guffawed and whooped when Simon leaped out of the barrel's path. They propped up the giant wooden containers near the table, which, by now, had come to be overflowing with food, and helped an older man push a wheelbarrow full of wooden cups near to where the barrels had been turned to sit upward. The smell of sugar, apples, and fermentation filled the air as the barrel was tapped and a wooden spigot shoved into the hole. The whole scene was full of life, joy, and plenty.

Simon heard the familiar sound of hammering and looked to his right to see a stage being erected, with poles lifted to the sky with streamers of every discernable color flapping in the ever-present wind that Simon did not feel. *Why not just Change it into a stage? Why do the work?* Simon thought, but the question was brief and passing, and Simon soon forgot it.

Musicians, with a wide array of instruments that hailed from all corners of the old Earth, began to tune various strings, tighten drums, and take their positions upon the elevated wooden stage. Once all of the performers were satisfied with their instruments and positions, they struck up a merry tune that made Simon, who only danced when he was very, very intoxicated, tap his feet and nod his head.

People, once small splashes of white on a sea of green, had congealed into a large pale mass, flowing toward the food and drink in a merry wave of laughter. They touched and talked, coming together around the tables and barrels, filling cups to the brim with frothy cider and snagging pieces of food from the table.

Some of the crowd had gathered in front of the stage, which held the musicians, and had begun a dance that involved linking arms and moving in circles, occasionally kicking into the air and twirling. Simon watched as one circle formed inside another larger one and began spinning in the opposite direction. The movement was mesmerizing, and the energy of the place was hypnotic.

A man, smiling and sun-dark, with a white shirt and leather breeches, stepped in front of Simon, handed him a mug filled to the brim with a liquid that smelled of rich apples, cinnamon, and fermentation, and danced off with a dark-eyed girl who sang a tune fit for a songbird. As the man and woman stepped away, Simon's eyes widened when he saw the woman's sandalwood-toned hand slide down between the man's legs, and Simon blushed furiously when the man lifted her up and planted a kiss on her that promised that the embrace was only the beginning of his affections. Simon quickly looked away, but soon realized that his eyes could find no true refuge from such revelry.

Everywhere he looked, Simon saw singing, dancing, and coupling in every nature of the word. People would collapse into each other's arms, laughing as they fell, and would not rise for some time, as they had become too intent on the person they had fallen onto. Men and women, young and old, all seemed to be completely incapable of being ashamed of their bodies—or their appetites. *Jesus Christ, this must be where all the babies come from! I wonder if there are STDs here? If so,* everyone *has one in this town.* Simon looked down at his cider, wondering if it was perhaps the cause of the overly joyous celebration. He smelled it and debated whether or not he should throw it away.

"Why are you not engaging in the festivities, young Simon? Did no one dance or make merry where you came from?" Thales had appeared, as he was wont to do when Simon was most uncomfortable. His toga was tied at the waist, leaving his hairy chest exposed, and green leaves poked out haphazardly from the curly hair on top of his head. Judging from his slightly disheveled appearance, Simon guessed that he had already partaken in some of the "festivities" he spoke of.

"Not like this, Mr. Thales. Aren't they worried about getting pregnant? About diseases? Jesus Christ, do they have no *shame?* Where I come from, this sort of thing was generally done behind closed doors."

"Well, for the first two questions, my young pupil, you can set your mind at ease. If one's Journey does not involve the process of childbirth, then there is no possibility of them eventually being with child. As for the diseases that you speak of, though people have discovered them and they exist in Dara, diseases are easily managed. Or did you forget that we can simply Return? When you come back, you do not have the diseases and injuries of the past."

Thales looked at the barrel of cider and down at his cup, which appeared to be empty.

"Young Simon, I am going to leave you to enjoy yourself on your own, but before I do, listen to me. The heart and soul of Elysium is community, yes? It is a place bent on bringing people together. When you remove the taboos and social stigmas around coupling and intimacy, you will find that sex is just another way that we, as people, can come closer together."

The philosopher patted Simon on the back and held his hand there to steady himself. "Now, if you will excuse me, I have cider to drink and a community to help bring together!"

With a loud guffaw and a clap of his hands, the philosopher danced off toward the merrymaking.

Simon stared down at his cider again, sighed, and drained his cup. The liquid was warming and delicious. It numbed his throat as it passed his lips, and Simon felt himself smile. He thought of Ah-Mun, of community, and, as a hand clasped his own and led him toward the music and dancing, Simon nearly felt happy.

"Are you all right?"

A young, warm voice, whispering of a secret promise, danced in Simon's ear. The youth turned to see jet-black hair, almond eyes, and warm, red lips drinking him in.

"I think I need something more than this to help me with this crowd," Simon said as he lifted his mug of cider.

The young woman laughed, a smoky sound that seemed to drown out the din, turning the roar into a murmur.

"Come with me."

Taking his hand, the young woman led Simon away from the crowd and toward a small ring of people just outside of the firelight. They were all sitting or lying around a small fire, contented smiles on their lips.

Confused but intrigued, Simon allowed himself to be led into the strange group and sat cross-legged by the nameless girl.

"Do you like drugs?" a voice asked, smoky and masculine.

"Drugs? What kind of drugs?" Simon mumbled, his eyes pulled to the fire. Animals and spirits made of flame performed acrobatics on the logs. *Of course the fire would do this.*

Suddenly, a man rose, stumbled, and steadied himself. His hair was dark and curly, his skin the color of ancient wood, and a rough crown of branches adorned his head. A large hand went into his trouser pocket and produced a small pouch. As he was fumbling with the string that held the contents inside, Simon repeated his question to his strange host.

"What kind of drugs?"

"All kinds. Elysium is about community, about *feeling*, and there are few things from the old world that shut up our reticence and open up our hearts quite like drugs."

"That is quite a pitch," Simon said, not letting his eyes wander from the pouch.

The young woman who brought him to the fire laughed, and Simon smiled. *God, I always love making a woman laugh.*

The man had finally undone his pouch, and with a triumphant whoop, he threw the contents—some sort of powder—into the fire. Glassy eyes turned to the flames, which hissed and produced a cloud of writhing purple smoke.

As the fumes reached Simon's nostrils, he was instantly transported to a world of deep reverberation, kaleidoscopic light, and amplified touch. His legs gave way, and he fell forward, face-first onto the soft grass. No pain lanced through him, and Simon found himself laughing as he rolled over and stared deeply into the night sky, and he giggled again as he watched the stars dance for him.

"You know, I used to put people in jail for this," he said to no one in particular. "I used to arrest human beings and put them in cages, just because they wanted to feel good. I am an asshole." He laughed again.

"I do not think you are an asshole," a smoky voice said, dangerously close to his ear. Simon continued to look up at the sky, even as it was obscured by dark hair and almond eyes.

"You do not know me."

"I know you are human, and I know you are here. That is enough. Now, disappear with me."

Such a weird thing to say, Simon thought, but it proved to be perfectly apt as his clothes were removed, and the feeling of cloth was replaced by the beauty of human touch. His body relaxed, and with a smile, Simon dove into the darkness of feeling.

Chapter XIV–How Love Fled

Simon awoke, bleary-eyed and dizzy. For a moment, he had no idea where he was, and he had to fight down panic as he sat up quickly, eyes darting around worriedly. *What are you so worried about? You're already dead.* Simon chuckled ruefully, then clutched his head as the world spun. As his eyes took a moment to focus, Simon looked around, taking in the green lawn and sleeping bodies, all in various forms of undress. Simon looked down to discover that he was also unclothed, and, for the first time since before puberty, he did not feel ashamed. Grunting, Simon lay back down and placed his arms around a soft-skinned shoulder that came and nuzzled up to him. Hair that smelled of flowers and a sweet scent he could not place filled his nostrils.

"We must get up soon, my skinny friend. If I recall from what you said last night, you and Thales must be on the road before too much daylight has passed." The words were soft, like a summer breeze dancing in a rose bush, and had a lilt that smacked of Caribbean seas and salt water. Simon turned and smiled at dark eyes, obsidian that seemed to hold laughter in its reflection.

"You are right," he murmured, "but I do not want to go just yet." He bent down to kiss soft lips, forgetting the bees buzzing in his head.

When Simon's companion had bid goodbye, with a kiss and a smile, he began searching for his clothes and belongings. He was surprised to find his pants hanging loosely from a nearby tree, and his comfortable shirt had found a hiding place under the bare belly of a snoring fellow who smiled as he exhaled, still deep in sleep. When Simon managed to finally find his shoes, which were filled with two pieces of hard cheese, of all things, the sun had nearly reached the middle of the sky. The knife with the well-worn handle felt comfortable and familiar on his hip, and his shoes, now freed of their edible tenants, hugged his feet familiarly. His small bindle was nowhere to be seen, so Simon began to search for it, swaying slightly as the remnants of debauchery seeped out of his pores.

To Simon, it felt as though all of life had taken on a certain sweetness, a degree of beauty that had previously been absent. The green grass seemed brighter and richer in color, and the floral odor slipping from various petals around him had become intoxicating. *Why would I ever leave this place? Why should I go somewhere terrible and unknown, when I can just stay here, in paradise?*

As the thought rattled in his head, Simon stopped dead in his tracks, and simply lay back down. The grass was warm and soft, and he stretched out onto his back, propping his head up with his arms. The sky was blue and clear, and the ever-present wind-swept small clouds across his vision. *Why should I leave? Is there any reason why I should go? Goddamn it, I think I deserve a little happiness. Why should I leave?* The shade of the trees that formed the canopy over the road caused shadows to dance over Simon's thin face, and the youth closed his eyes.

"Hello, Sprout."

The familiar voice jerked Simon out of his reverie. His heart jumped into his throat as his head whipped to turn toward the hauntingly familiar sound. Brown eyes met green, and those brown pools were lined by a young face bordered by curly hair that bounced and moved of its own volition. Simon recognized Mary immediately, but seeing her as a child caused his mind to refuse to believe what he was seeing. Mary, his caretaker, his landlord, his friend—all the experiences and memories of her were associated with an adult, someone large. To see her in this diminutive, tiny form, a child not more than nine or ten, made Simon refuse to believe that it was she. *Perhaps she is a relative of Mary, some other child or cousin.*

"Sprout, it's me. Remember that we Return, we do not die. Sprout, do you hear me?" Small hands were placed on hips, and Mary took the defiant, strong stance that Simon had seen so many times before, albeit the taller version.

"Listen here, it's me, an' that's the truth of it." The Southern twang, kept so hidden from Mary's lips unless pulled out by moments of extreme emotion, was all the proof that Simon needed. He stepped forward, haltingly at first, and then rushed, sweeping Mary into his arms and squeezing her tight. She returned the embrace and yelped gleefully, to the surprise of both Simon and herself, when Simon picked her up.

"Put me down, you overgrown bean pole!" Simon, realizing what he had done, felt his cheeks burn as he gently put his former caretaker back onto her feet. Mary calmly adjusted her dress and again placed her hands on her hips to look at her former ward.

"So tell me, my young Sprout, what brings you here to Elysium? Who do you travel with? What has happened since we last … spoke?"

Flashes of steel crossed through Simon's vision, and red tainted the outer fields of his eyesight. Hurriedly, he pushed those images away and instead focused on the joy he felt, the relief, of witnessing first-hand a true conqueror of death in Dara. Looking into Mary's eyes and taking a deep breath, Simon dove headlong into all that had happened since Mary had left him, beginning with his dispatching of Mary's killer, ricocheting around his adventures with Paracelsus, and ending with the bacchanalian events of the night before. He spoke quickly, recounting everything as best as he could, trying to leave nothing out, except the parts that all young men leave out when talking to a caregiver.

Mary listened quietly, occasionally asking for clarification about living with Thales or the discovery of his Journey. She laughed aloud when Simon told her of Paracelsus and the barrel of wine, seemed genuinely concerned when he told her of the destruction of the monster that he and

Thales had encountered on the road, and clapped her hands in delight when Simon told her of his successes with Changing.

Jesus Christ, it is good to hear her laugh again, Simon thought as the musical sound left the child's lips when he told her the embarrassing, naked encounter with Thales under the tree. As he watched her laugh at his discomfort, Simon became overwhelmed with a sense of fondness for this child who was once his mother, in a fashion, and tears threatened to fall down his face. Hurriedly, he wiped them away, while Mary, still laughing, sat down on the soft grass. Simon joined her.

He told of reaching Elysium, of the strange customs he saw when he arrived, and finished with his explanation of the ascension of Ah-Mun, the friend who he made for such a brief moment. Tears nearly fell again as he recounted the terrifying moment when he and the people around him realized that Ah-Mun would not Return, and the words of Paracelsus danced in his head as he told the tale: "*Death still wishes to claim us as its own. The universe wishes to right its wrong, and it has found a way.*"

Mary listened carefully, eyes widening when Simon told her of Ah-Mun never Returning. She whispered something, words under her breath, as Simon spoke. He thought he heard "haven't heard of such a thing in a long time," but he couldn't be sure. Simon decided to leave out his own participation in the previous night's revelry, as it did not seem appropriate to tell this young child. When he finished by telling Mary of how he and Thales were to travel to the place where her killer resided, she nodded gravely.

"Well, Sprout, it appears as though you have kept busy, if nothing else. I am happy that you have decided to follow your Journey and to accept its pull. Some resist such things, and it has proven to be nothing but painful for those who try to fight it."

Simon, with eyes drifting away from Mary and down to the soft grass, nervously began pulling green blades from the ground. "But what if I do not *want* to continue my Journey? I like it here. I feel peaceful and free to do what I want to do. The people are welcoming, and though they are a bit more ... *open* ... than I am used to, I think I can make a home here. Besides, what if I complete my Journey and die—a real death—and I never Return? I do not wish to die, Mary. I do not want to find myself in that darkness ever again. The darkness, the fear, the *helplessness*. I can't do it again. I do not want to die. I won't!"

Simon's voice, almost without his volition, had raised in pitch and sound. His hands were shaking, and when he finished, he ripped the grass in his hands to shreds and threw it on the ground.

"It does not matter, Sprout. You resist all you want, but the pull will claim you, nonetheless. All you really have control over is how painful that pull is."

Mary looked into Simon's eyes, and Simon saw pity there. *She is still trying to be the mom to me. She doesn't have any idea what I've had to go through. She was too busy playing in this paradise. Trying to tell me about my Journey? What does she know about it? All she did was hide in that tree, and now she is hiding again!*

Simon felt his blood boiling, and though he didn't fully understand why, he felt the need to lash out at his former caregiver. Objectively, he knew that Mary could not control how she left him and could not control where she had Returned, but he was not in the mood for objectivity. The words burst from his mouth before he truly understood that they were forming.

"What do you know of it? You seem to have isolated yourself from the world in that old tree house we lived in, hiding from whatever it was that pulled *you!* How can you even understand at all? The friend that I made here, he died, never to Return again, and it's my fault! I never want to see that happen again. You don't know what you're talking about at all!"

"Don't take that tone wit' me, Sprout. I know more than you could hope to imagine, and that's the truth. You know so little, and the little you do know terrifies you, so you run. You cannot possibly understand why I lived the way I lived—what my Journey means."

"You don't know shit! And my name is Simon."

"That language! It wasn't okay then, and it ain't okay now."

Mary took a step toward Simon, a hand raised. Simon, by instinct and conditioning, recoiled instinctively, Mary's tone and her raised hand triggering past memories of an immense giant whipping his backside as he lay helpless. Yet just as quickly, he stopped himself. The person looking at him, fire and violent intention in her eyes, was not the looming ogre of his memories. No, she was a child—a small girl who couldn't possibly do him harm. The motion of her hand, once so terrifying and awe-inspiring, was now *comical.* Simon giggled at the idea of a passerby trying to understand the scene that was unraveling before him. Mary's eyes narrowed, and her face darkened.

"You think it's funny? I'll tan yo' hide until you squeal!"

"Shut up, Mary, just shut up. What are you going to do? Hit me? Go ahead."

Simon spread his hands wide, a smile on his lips. Mary, pushed to a fury that defied logic, flung her small arm in an arc and attempted to slap Simon in the face. As the hand came sailing toward him, Simon, almost casually, grabbed Mary by the wrist and pushed, causing the young girl to fall in a heap on the green ground.

Mary fell but recovered quickly, and when she turned to face Simon again, there was a snarl on her lips and a glint in her eye that could only be described as murderous. Black eyebrows arched downward, Mary stood, fists balled up at her sides. Simon smiled. *That will teach her. She can't hurt me anymore; I'm too big.* Simon crossed his arms and stared at the tiny tyrant, silently mocking her anger. Mary continued to stare, and her body veritably shook with anger.

Behind him, Simon heard a deafening whistle of wind. With a crack, a large branch was ripped off a majestic oak tree, and invisible hands hurled it right toward Simon's thin teenage frame. Simon felt an incredibly focused blast of air. The moss that had been dangling from the branch now snapped back in the wind, making streamers for the wooden lance. Panicking, Simon simply reacted and flung himself onto Mary, pushing the murderous young girl back onto the ground and landing on her with his full weight. He heard a grunt as the wind was knocked out of Mary's lungs. He was relieved to hear a thud as the missile Mary had been controlling simply fell from the sky. But relief was quickly replaced with rage as Simon looked down at the small body of Mary underneath him. *This bitch tried to kill me!* When she tried to rise, Simon pushed her back down and encircled her tiny neck in his hands. He felt the pulse of her heart in his palms.

"If you even *think* of doing that again, I will choke you unconscious!" As the words came out of Simon's mouth, the snarl that had covered Mary's face slipped away, replaced with uncertainty, and, if Simon didn't know better, fear. Pride and elation filled Simon, swelling from the marrow of his bones to the hair follicles on his head. The woman who had controlled him, dominated him, bent him to her will, was now *afraid* of him. Smiling in triumph, Simon looked down again upon his once dictator—the conquered now the conqueror. Yet as he gazed down at Mary's face, victory and triumph quickly turned to shame.

The woman who had made him feel so helpless to her whims was not there. The domineering governess who had beaten him for cursing, who taught him manners again, who forced him to be a child once more, had left without any pomp or circumstance and was replaced with a young girl in a white dress now stained by green grass, with fear and uncertainty in her eyes. All thoughts of enacting any sort of revenge upon her vanished, and Simon, hands still gripping her small neck, now jerked back as if she had been made of hot coals. *What kind of fucking monster am I, scaring her like that? She cared for me, fed me, watched over me, and as soon as she is vulnerable, I attack her? Fucking Christ, I'm an asshole. Even if she did throw a stick at me, I don't have the right to choke her. What is wrong with me?* Simon rubbed his palms on his pants, as if to try to wipe off the taint of his actions.

"I … I'm sorry, Mary. I do not know what came over me."

Rubbing her neck, the young girl sat up, pieces of grass and green leaves stuck to her kinky hair. She looked lost for words, staring off into the distance, not focusing on anything, just simply staring blankly into the void. This scared Simon more. *Jesus Christ, I hurt her. She must have hit her head when she fell. If I hurt her, I'll never forgive myself.*

"It … it is all right, Simon." *Simon?* "I should not have acted as though you were still a child and I could smack your bottom whenever I liked."

Sighing, Mary took a breath and began to stand. Simon tried to help her, but she brushed away his hands as though they were little more than the twigs and leaves clinging to her dress. "Do not be too hard on yourself."

"But I almost *hurt* you. I … I felt as though … as if … as if I *wanted* to. I cannot believe myself," Simon said as he hung his head in shame.

"Why not? Do you not remember growing up the first time? Do you not remember separating yourself from your mother and, later, fighting with your father?"

Simon thought back to his mother, to how wonderfully sweet and kind she was, to her smile. He could not recall a single moment when he had even argued with his mother. *I can't even remember anything negative about her at all!*

"I can't. I honestly can't remember a moment when I fought with my mom. My father was a different story, but never my mom."

"Well, that is probably why you had so many problems with women when you first started dating them. You were trying to replace your mother with them."

"Bullshi—. Sorry."

"Oh, that is quite all right, but thank you for stopping yourself."

"What do you mean that I had problems with women? I don't see how that has anything to do with my mom."

"I mean exactly what I said. You see, Simon, just as you needed to separate yourself from your mother, then your father, in order to become an adult, so, too, must you push against the authority that you find here in Dara. It is the natural progression of the human condition. If you do not do it, then you will remain stuck, stagnant in your development. In fact, some people believe that Journeys are just a continuation of your psychological progression. I can only guess that your inability to connect properly with women in your life traces back to your mother. But what do I know? I've only lived here for almost two centuries, and I am still stuck."

Simon said nothing and instead sat back, wondering about what Mary had said. Perhaps she was right; perhaps there was some validity to the fact that he had never truly separated himself from his mother, that he never managed to fully accept that he was free from his father. Anger, fear, and sadness crept within him. *What does she know? She's still here. If she truly understood what the hell she was talking about, she wouldn't be here anymore.* Raking his hair back with his hand, Simon said as much.

Mary looked down and, for several moments, said nothing. When she finally raised her head, Simon found, to his complete surprise, that her eyes had become glassy. Unshed tears bubbled near the surface, threatening to cascade down her face. She looked at Simon, and he felt the nearly overwhelming desire to hug her, to comfort her somehow.

"You wish to know? You wanna know why I'm still here? I do not speak of it—of the moment that I managed to transcend humanity and, at the same time, damn my soul to eternal suffering. For most folks, it is believed that this is paradise—an escape from death. For me, it is hell—a place for me to relive my sins for all time."

Mary looked down to the soft earth, moving her small bare feet back and forth on the emerald grass. When she turned her gaze back on Simon, her glassy eyes shone with a feverish light.

"I did not want them to have the same fate that I did—to live the same horrors and fears that overtook my every waking moment."

"Who?"

"To not be human, to not be anything more than cattle or a handy tool to suit another's needs. To live in constant fear of another's whims. I could not bear the thought that they might be murdered simply because he was sick from the night before."

Mary's quiet speech suddenly elevated in volume, and her small hands became fists at her sides.

"Or ... or if he thought the *sun* shone too hot. No, I did not want to ever have them live that way."

"Mary, I do not understand."

"I was a slave, Simon—a *thing*, not a person. I was forced to work until my hands bled and to sleep with fifteen other souls in a single room. I never learned my father's name, but I was told my mother was white, and that she made the mistake of falling in love with the wrong man. My father was hanged when I was born." Mary sighed and shook her head.

"As a result of that unmentionable union, I was sold quickly and early, to keep my mother's shame from the public eye. I was sold to a Mr. M., a cotton farmer in Mississippi, where I worked in the Big House until Mrs. M. realized that Mr. M.'s eyes and hands never kept to themselves. I was put in the fields, beaten if I spoke out of turn, and, worst of all, I grew to be beautiful."

Mary, the young girl, clutched her small shoulders with her arms, as if to hug herself. Simon was struck dumb. He sat down, eyes on Mary. He felt glued to the ground, limbs frozen in place. Mary swallowed and, still holding herself tight, continued.

"They were his, all of them: Johnathan, Beth, Lil Tommy, and Hope, the baby. I never lay with another man, and he knew it. Beautiful babies with skin the color of caramel and brown eyes that seemed to soak up the sun, turning sun rays into dark gemstones." Tears rolled down Mary's face freely as she continued, staring into a time only she could see.

"One day, in the heat of summer, everything changed. A man came, asking to buy young slaves from Mr. M.—I still cannot say his name, all these centuries later. His face still haunts my dreams: beady eyes sticking out of a jowly, pale face, with thin tendrils of dark hair slicked back in a desperate attempt to hide his baldness. That face comes to stare at me almost every time I close my eyes."

Mary closed her eyes and took a breath to steady herself, and Simon wondered if she still saw that face looking down at her. He hoped that she didn't.

"Jonathan was old enough to start working the fields, and Beth had begun following me out during the day, helping put the cotton into baskets. When the man came, he looked at Jonathan, then at my Beth, and decided that he wanted to buy them. The Master agreed to sell his own son and daughter, without so much as a glance toward me, and the two men agreed on a price. When the sale was complete, the man and the Master decided to have dinner and then drink late into the night.

"I did not think anyone could sell their *own children* so easily; I did not think it was possible. I cried and screamed and begged for the Master to not take my children—*our* children—away. But he simply stared at me with those unfeeling grey eyes—eyes that I still see to this day—and walked into the house with the man. He left me on the lawn, crying and screaming, and strode into the house as if I was a barking dog on a leash—a creature to be ignored."

Mary's hands had dropped to her sides, but she still stared off into that distant place, into a darkness only she could see.

"Clutching at straws, hoping that maybe the man didn't live far away, that I could find a way to see my babies, I hurried to where the coaches waited. I knew I would find the driver of the white man who had just *bought* my children." Mary bit off the final words through clenched teeth.

"I walked up, saw a tall, broad-shouldered man wiping down two white horses, and rushed to him. Tears in my eyes, I asked him about his Master, where he lived, what kind of man he was."

The scene only she could see suddenly became dark, and her voice dropped almost to a whisper.

"There is an evil that lurks in some men's hearts, a darkness that has poisoned their minds and warped their souls. To have complete power over another human being can pull out the worst in men, and the man who wanted to take my children lived in those inky waters, splashing about gleefully in the depths of wickedness. The driver, he said that he 'like 'em young, and when he done use 'em up, he like to hurt 'em.' He mentioned things that no mother should ever have to hear. As he spoke, his face not unkind, I felt the world close in. The last thing I saw was his concerned face before it all went black."

Simon wanted to comfort Mary, to go to her, hold her close, but felt that he couldn't move.

As the young girl continued, Simon felt his own tears threaten to fall from his face. He thought of his own children, tottering around his home, of his pride at seeing them learn to walk and speak. *What would I do if someone tried to take them? What would I do if I couldn't do anything about it?* Simon quickly rubbed the tears from his eyes as Mary spoke.

"It was dark when I awoke to find myself in my little cot. The other beds in the tiny room had been filled with sweating bodies—by people too exhausted to clean themselves properly or pushed to a place past caring. I felt for Hope and Lil Tommy and found them, nuzzled against me. Hope was like a furnace, and Lil Tommy whimpered in his sleep. Yet I couldn't find Beth or Jonathan. I whispered their names, and then, as I searched to no avail, I yelled. I couldn't find them. I couldn't find them!" Mary had begun to rock slowly back and forth, tears flowing down her cheeks.

"I rushed out of the room, out of that small shack, and was about to run toward the house when I saw them, huddled together on the ground underneath a large oak tree. Jonathan and Beth, my babies, were clinging to each other as if the world would turn upside down at any moment. When I ran to them, wrapped my arms around them, that's when I saw the blood."

Simon's breath caught, but Mary, seemingly on top of a precipice, had decided to plunge forward, and nothing could stop her.

"Jonathan was the worst. His eyes were nearly swollen shut, and his little pants and shirt were ripped to shreds. His lil' belly was out in the moonlight, and cuts was criss crossed across his chest. I saw that it was him that was crying, but Beth, my sweet butterfly, said nothin' at all. She jus' stared, eyes big as saucers, at nothin'— stared at somethin' only she could see. Blood coated her little legs, and the small dress I had stitched for her was cut and soiled.

"When I asked what happened, what happened to my babies, Jonathan looked at me, looked up at his momma through those red puffy eyes. He said, 'He hurt us, Momma. He hurt us! Please don't let him take us. Please! We have to run away, run from the man.' And it was after looking into his pleading face and seeing the dead-eye stare of Beth that I decided to never let this happen, ever again. Not to me and not to my babies. Never again!"

Mary stood with surprising speed, and her distant stare shot past Simon, past the lawn, past the flowers, and past the mountains, toward and through an unseen enemy. If her eyes had been feverish before, they burned now, bright with a light that spoke of horror and a human soul pushed to its breaking point.

"See, to the right of the Big House, there was a little pond, a pretty piece of water that had an old tree that overlooked it. When I was younger, I would hide out there, disappearing into a world that only I could find. That night, I decided to take my babies to a world that only I could touch.

"Grabbing a rope from the barn, I led my little ones out to the middle of the quiet field—to that quiet place. The moon was full, and the rays danced on the shimmering pool. When I brought my children to that liquid mirror, I placed them down behind the tree, so they couldn't see what I was about to do, and I told Lil Tommy to watch Beth and Hope. Grabbing Jonathan by the hand, I led him to the dark shore." Mary continued to stare through the centuries, to a small pond in a dark field.

"One by one, my babies slipped away as I held them under. At first, the pain was more than I thought any human being could bear. As Jonathan fought under the water, I felt my soul break, felt my heart descend to the depths of hell and stay there. Yet I continued. I wanted to save my children from the dark fate that was left for them. When Beth came, she barely struggled at all, simply stared up at me through the water. I felt my shattered soul begin to escape me.

"When I was done with my dark business, I grabbed the rope and climbed the tree. My hands were wet and shaking, and my mouth tasted sour from when I had emptied my stomach. I tied the rope to a giant branch that hung over the pond, then tied it around my neck, and, taking one last look at that pond—one last glance at what I had done—I jumped off."

The light in Mary's eyes died, a candle snuffed out by a passing breeze, yet she kept looking through the centuries at a dark night with moonlight dancing on water.

"That is how I came here. If I had done it simply because I truly felt it would be a better fate for my children, then I wouldn't have ended up here, because it is in the instinct of the mother to protect her children—to save them from an even darker fate. No, Simon, no, on that dark night, in those dark moments, I went *past* my desire to protect my children. I became something more than my instinct, and, in so doing, I damned my soul. Part of me *wanted* to kill my children, for a reason that I can, even now, barely bring myself to say. I was *curious,* and through this inhumane, horrible act, I transcended my humanity. Now, I am doomed to have children, over and over, for the rest of eternity, until I can find a way to evolve. It is the hell that I deserve." Spent, Mary sat back down and stared at the ground, muttering only "the hell that I deserve" under her breath.

The world held its breath as Simon sat open-mouthed, staring at Mary without knowing what to say. He did not know he could feel so many emotions at once, and, gazing at the young girl who had once been his world, he found that no words would come to his lips, as if the moisture in his mouth had left in order to attempt to better lubricate his brain. Of all things, he thought of the small church near his home on Wharton Street, of being baptized by Father Michael, whose hands smelled of Lucky Strike cigarettes and whose kind eyes lined with shadows looked at him reassuringly as he was dunked in the water. He remembered being held under for just a little too long, of the brief panic before being lifted up by his parish priest's strong hands.

"You see, Simon, you cannot run from your Journey any more than I can. When it is time for a soul to Return, it does so, through me or someone like me. I've tried remaining a child, ending it before I could come of age, but you can only do that so many times. Besides, without me and others like me, it is harder for people to Return. No, you cannot stay here. If you did, you would only make those around you suffer, as well as enduring your own suffering as well. You must go on; the only choice you have is how long it will take you to move along your Journey. The pull never goes away."

With the last, Mary hugged her belly and again looked far into the distance, to a place where only she could venture.

Simon wanted to thank her, to scream at her, to hug her, to do *something*—anything—to make his mind stop reeling and his heart cease its racing. Yet for a moment, he simply stood, hands at his sides, and looked at the woman with centuries on her shoulders, at the little girl with memories that pushed her back into and through the earth.

"I love you, Mary."

"I love you too, Sprout. Now, go. Thales will be looking for you, and I need to be heading back toward our old home." Mary straightened and placed a sad smile on her lips. "I feel lighter for having told you, as if the weight of my sins has become just a little less. I still feel its weight, still feel the hurt in my spine, but talking has given me a little reprieve. Thank you, Simon. Thank you, Sprout."

I kind of like Sprout now. Hated it for so many years, but now, it feels better. I want her to call me that. It's almost like I earned it, grew into it. Simon stepped in and enveloped Mary's tiny body in his arms. With only a moment's hesitation, Mary returned the embrace, her small arms circling Simon's abdomen. Tears fell from his cheeks, and Simon did not try to stop them.

The human mind is a selfish thing, and Simon found Mary's story replaced by memories of his own—of children in crack houses, of young and innocent eyes looking out of the windows of the trailers where he and his partner had found all that meth. *What would I do, if I were Mary? What would I do with no hope, nowhere to turn? I hated those women who put their children in those horrible, disgusting houses. Maybe they never had a choice themselves. Damn.* Simon stared straight ahead and watched as his assumptions started to die.

Giving his child mother one more embrace, Simon set off to find his walking stick and belongings to make his bindle. His mind was still full, and his heart was still heavy, but within the confines of such deep emotions, a spark of happiness grew. It was not enough for light or warmth, but enough for him to continue forward. A sad smile crossed his lips, and he began to retrace his steps—back to the meeting place of Ah-Mun and back down the path he was meant to travel.

Chapter XV–Paced Upon Mountains Overhead

"Are you ready to depart, young Simon?" Thales stood at the other end of the road that cut through Elysium, the Apicem Terra mountains looming behind like an open mouth about to bite down. The sky was iron grey, pregnant with rain, and the dark clouds contrasted the immaculate white toga of Thales, making it an almost blinding white.

Though Simon had seen him, albeit briefly, partaking in the raucous affair the night before, it looked as though the philosopher had gone to bed early and had eaten a refreshing breakfast. His beard was perfectly combed, and his eyes looked bright and merry. Simon, slightly annoyed at his companion's ability to never experience a hangover, strode up to meet his fellow traveler.

"Glad you didn't decide to leave me here. I don't think I could live like this for long," Simon grunted as he shuffled up to his teacher. The bindle on his shoulder felt comfortably heavy. He had found it leaning against a tree, filled with apples, soft cheeses, and the delightful cider from the night before. The pain in his head, a dull throb behind his eyes, pulsed with each step.

"How, *how* do you always manage to somehow skip the hangover? It doesn't make any sense." Simon mumbled as the weight of the bag shifted on his shoulder, causing a spike of nausea.

"It's actually quite simple, young Simon," Thales said as he smiled merrily. "I just tell myself that I am not, as you say, hungover. Did you know that the term "hungover" came from a rope that was tied outside of bars and inns? You could pay a small amount to pass out dangling on the rope, thus not having to wake up covered in your own vomit. I can't imagine a rope digging into your waist all night was a welcome feeling to wake up to, but neither is vomit in your beard and horse shit in your nose. I don't remember who told me the origin of that word. Funny, is it not, how some words and phrases linger, and others disappear forever?"

Simon looked into the man's bright eyes and shook his head. Without another word about ropes or drink, Thales turned and began to stride out of the town, the barbed tip of his spear bobbing on his shoulder. Simon fell into step beside him. Almost immediately, their pace began to feel comfortable and familiar as Simon strode westward with his philosopher guide. The road rose up to meet him, and Simon scarcely looked back. He recalled the sea of faces of the inhabitants of Elysium, of their kind smiles and insistence on hugging, and felt a pang of sadness at leaving them. Yet behind some of those smiles, he saw worry and uncertainty and, worst of all, barely hidden relief that he was leaving. For a culture that insisted on community being paramount, on the feelings of self being replaced by the desire to further a group as a whole, Simon felt the relief in those eyes to be exponentially more painful. Shouldering the hurt he felt, he decided to ask his philosopher and guide about it. As he and Thales continued walking toward the mountains, through the rolling fields of golden wheat and corn—a picture of color and agrarian wealth—he asked his companion why people were seemingly happy to see him go.

Thales was silent a moment, walking and staring ahead, his face pulled tight in an expression that Simon recognized. The man was thinking. It was a few minutes before he spoke.

"The truth, young Simon, is that some believe *you* were the cause of Ah-Mun never Returning. Completion of a Journey takes time, and some people, no matter how much they try, cannot handle change. Many of the people you have met, drunk with, coupled with have lived here for centuries and have rarely, if ever, seen someone complete their Journey. So, as you strode into their town, unknown and freshly brought to Dara, and were the last person to speak to Ah-Mun before he passed on, it stands to reason they associate you with the extremely rare and potentially deadly event that took place."

"But I thought Elysium was built around the idea of community. When someone makes a mistake, people simply try to kick them out? Isn't that a little hypocritical?"

"It is, but remember these people did not force you to leave, and not all of them showed relief when you left. Community, like people, is ever-evolving. It is not simply perfected because someone *wants* it to be. It must be worked at, modified, and changed, before it can be truly successful. It is also a composition of individuals, so true homogeneity is nearly impossible, if you think about it."

"Homo what?"

"Homogeneity. Everyone being the same. Having the same culture."

"Oh."

Simon paused to think about what Thales had said. The upside-down mountains had become larger in his eyesight, their white peaks providing a sharp contrast to the deep greens of the plains and the iron-capped clouds floating at the edges of the visible world.

"Well, if homo … homogeneity…" *That word sounds funny.* "… is impossible, then why do so many people try so hard to be together in a community? Why would a place like Elysium even exist?"

Thales chuckled as he walked, his sandals making a crunching sound as they moved over the rocky road. "It is who we are as a species, my young friend. Since the beginning, we have banded together to survive and thrive. If you do not believe me, look at every nation's history, religion, and myths. We are meant to live together, to thrive or fail together. It is in our very nature to call for another human being. Is it perfect? No, of course not. Can there be a perfect community? Not unless it is populated by perfect individuals, and after thousands of years, I still haven't met even *one* of those. However, we are still drawn together, and the people of Elysium even more so, as their Journeys call them to be a part of a tight knit community. Do you understand?"

"I think so. You're saying that nobody is perfect, but if we are to find peace, we need to find it in others as well as ourselves, even if that means it isn't perfect sometimes."

"Exactly, my young pupil. Exactly. You are learning fast, and I am happy to have you as a student."

Thales patted Simon's shoulder and kept walking in the direction of the Apicem Terra range, the end of the spear making a rhythmic crunching sound to match Thales's sandals as the travelers continued walking.

Simon walked with his guide, keeping pace, and they fell into a comfortable silence, both men allowing their minds to wander and the road to swallow them up. Elysium became smaller and smaller until the pair of travelers rounded a bend, and then the town disappeared from vision entirely. Simon smiled, thankful for the experience that Elysium offered and happy that he had taken the advice of Mary to leave it. He sent a quiet prayer to whomever was listening, up into the blue sky. *Let Mary arrive safely home. Make it safe and easy.* Silently, Simon wished for the same for himself.

The farmlands and orchards of Elysium gave way to rolling hills with moss-covered boulders jutting out along their sides, giving the impression of a giant beast with horns or antlers protruding from all over its body at odd angles. The road led right into the midst of these earthly protrusions, and Simon strode behind Thales as the philosopher entered into the hilly landscape.

When night drew near, Thales climbed up one of those rocky mounds and placed his bundle underneath the single tree that grew at the summit. Simon followed, using moss-covered rocks to help him navigate up the hillside. The tree, with giant broad branches and gnarly roots sticking out of the ground, smelled of old age and ancient stories. The ever-present breeze caused the leaves of the tree to dance to an ancient rhythm, and the smell of rosemary tickled Simon's nostrils as he sat down against the old tree trunk.

As night fell, when that dark blanket covered the world, the stars came out to play at the tip of the travelers' noses. While they munched on apples and cheese from Simon's bag, Simon told Thales of meeting Mary again, but kept out the story of her Journey—of how she managed to make it to Dara. *Not my place to say, not my story to tell,* Simon thought as he spoke of his former caretaker, who had now taken the form of a child.

Thales nodded, wished her safe travel, and without another word, leaned against the tree and closed his eyes, his spear within arm's reach of his right hand. Simon found it odd that the man didn't press him further, but then mentally shrugged and thought it was probably because his guide didn't have anything to say on the subject. Simon himself lay down, and sleep came quickly to carry him away. He dreamed of Mary, of a beast with knives for teeth, and a storm that threatened to swallow him whole.

The next morning was quiet as they awoke and headed back onto the road. The trail became narrower the further into the hills they walked and began to ascend at a sharper and sharper angle, until Simon was using his hands almost as much as his feet to move forward. His bindle became more of a walking stick, and his calves began to burn as he and his guide climbed higher and higher. *Wish I had some goddamn hiking boots,* Simon cursed to himself as he scrambled up a steep slope littered with loose pale rocks and slippery moss. As he crested another rocky crag, Simon was relieved to see the road flattening out onto a flat plateau. Looking down the road, forward and upward toward the upside-down mountains, however, Simon found his relief to be short-lived.

The winding road straightened, taking a direct line into a series of plateaus and steep slopes, climbing higher and higher in elevation. It reminded Simon of a giant staircase, leading ever higher toward the base of the upside-down mountains that loomed larger and larger in his vision. The iron-capped clouds, rather than staying high above Simon's head, seemed instead to become closer and closer as he walked. It was almost as though the trail was leading into the clouds. The world began to take on the dense quality of fog and was given a quick coat of grey, covering everything within the young man's field of vision.

Shouldering his bindle, grateful that there were now at least some flat places on the road ahead, Simon continued forward. Thales, ever calm and relaxed, strode with a liquid grace that was infuriating, and the youth had to remind himself almost constantly that there was no actual reason to be angry with the philosopher.

After walking for another hour or so, clambering up steep slopes and strolling on flat plains, the pair reached a narrow plateau overlooking a deep valley to Simon's left, and to his right, tall grass, dry and cracked, swayed in the ever-present breeze. The waves of golden brown cascaded over the flat earth and danced with the wind right up to a sharp cliff edge, and the breeze continued on into nothing but sky. The landscape tickled something in the back of Simon's mind, and almost without thought, he began walking toward the clearing. As Simon walked over to the edge to gaze down into the depths below, Thales set his pack down and knuckled his lower back. The sun, now almost constantly behind those dark clouds, was beginning to disappear completely below the horizon.

Simon, looking down into the valley, felt his heart start to hammer in his chest. Images of sharp claws, impossibly fast movement, and the white light of pain filled his mind. He barely heard Thales behind him.

"I think, young Simon, that it would be best if we camped here for the evening. We still have quite a few days left of traveling, and I would

220

like to rest before we start our descent into the Senka valleys. Did you hear me? Hello? Is everything all right?"

Simon felt frozen to the spot, looking down into the hordes of animals and giant insects that populated the valley below. He watched as a massive creature, resembling a giant cockroach with a hammer head, stalked a young mastodon that had wandered from its herd. With a sickening quickness, the giant insect overcame the small, furry elephant, and, with a crunch that would have been ear-popping if heard up close, used its giant incisors to impale its prey.

Animals from every era seemed to have assembled here, grazing and lounging, hunting and being hunted, but that was not what kept Simon from being able to move even the smallest muscle. Far to his left, near the upside-down mountains, an ocean roared up into the sky, its waters shooting like a geyser into the clouds that hid the root of the mountains.

"Thales, I died here. When I first came to this place, I was a young man. I had on clothes from … from my past life. It was like I just stepped out of space and landed here. There was a creature—a lion attacked me. And a man, he came and finished the job. Jesus Christ, Thales, I *died* here."

Suddenly, a thought gripped Simon, and he rushed about, eyes darting through the tall grass. He racked his brain, trying to remember the exact spot he had fallen.

"I died here. Then, where's my body? Where would my body be? Thales, what happens to our bodies when we die? What happens?"

Simon, talking to Thales but, in reality to no one, continued his frantic search until the philosopher strode over and placed his hand on Simon's shoulder and tried to stop his mad searching. Simon shrugged it off, perhaps a little more violently than he intended, and continued his search.

"My young friend, what you are looking for is not there. As soon as you were killed, what was once the embodiment of you left with your

221

soul. It is different here in Dara. When you die on Earth, the physical aspect of you—the body—remains."

"Not now, Thales. I can't deal with your lecture right now. I died here!"

"Yes, you died here, and chances are, you will die in many more places. We all do."

"Just let me look, okay? I need to look! I need to find where I died. I know you said that our bodies return to Dara, but I still need to look!"

Without another word, Simon continued his mad search. The words spewed by his guide had sounded like a bunch of gibberish, and Simon had only really heard a smattering of them. He continued to dart about, bent at the waist, looking for a splash of denim, a hint of a white t-shirt. Frantically he hoped to find something, anything, from his search. Simon did not even know why he was looking, why he was hunting, but it felt important, so search he did.

Eventually, after what seemed like hours of searching, Simon sat down on a small rock jutting up from the tall grass. He was sweating, and his back hurt from being bent double. Knuckling the base of his spine, he straightened and stared about. *Nothing. Nothing here at all. Where did it go? Why is it gone?*

Simon looked about, at the impassive sea of grass, at the foreign world where nothing made sense and everything was painfully different. Simon felt his sanity slip away, like his mind had been placed in oil and pushed down a slope that led to eternity. He wanted to laugh, wanted to cry, wanted to punch something. The world—with the face of Mary, as both a child and a woman, looking over him with sadness and irritation—closed in on him. He emptied his stomach of its contents and fell into the grass, eyes staring into the impassive sky.

Nothing matters, nothing at all. Who really gives a shit? How can people even manage to care at all here? It's all pointless, all useless. My body just disappears, and I start over? Simon stared upward as an eternal universe continued its endless march toward entropy. He wondered how he hadn't seen the hopelessness of this place before, how nothing mattered here, not really—that death itself didn't even matter. "It doesn't matter. Nothing matters. *I* don't matter. Not even death has meaning."

"That isn't true, my young friend. You matter a great deal. You must see that." Thales had moved to sit near Simon, sitting on the rock that Simon had allowed himself to fall off of.

"How can you say that? Everything that we do, all that we accomplish, simply disappears when we die, and we repeat it over and over again. It feels so ... *empty*. What's the point? Why do we continue walking? Why do we do anything here? Shouldn't we just enjoy this world as much as we can—do whatever we want? There are no real consequences, no rules."

The weight of this truth lay heavily on Simon. He couldn't really understand why, but he had always believed, deep down, that his life had purpose. What if it didn't? What if eternity was simply a purposeless drift? What if nothing truly mattered at all?

Simon looked at the philosopher perched on his stone, watching him stroke his beard. He wished desperately that his guide would give him an answer, and yet he felt as though the man couldn't possibly provide one. The white toga of Thales whipped in rhythm with the golden waves around him, and his curly hair was tousled by the wind as he turned to look at his young ward. For a few moments, he looked as though he were about to speak, then his mouth would clamp shut, and he would stare down at the ground or up at the grey sky, muttering to himself. Finally, he looked at Simon, and when he did, his clear eyes held a heavy purpose.

"It appears as though we are at an impasse finally, Simon. For years, your questions could be answered by me, and I could help you along your path while you faltered. I still want to help you, to see you through this expedition that you and I have begun, but I fear that it might be ending—that our paths are destined to separate."

"What? What do you mean? You can't mean you are going to leave me, can you? I don't know where to go, what to do. Jesus Christ, Thales, I can't even tell you where we are! Are you saying that you are going to leave me here, just because I don't know how people can keep dying and be reborn—how I feel as though there is no meaning in this place? I don't understand." Simon was surprised to find tears in his eyes. *You can't leave me, you son of a bitch, you can't!*

Thales sighed again and turned to face the upside-down mountain range, looking out past the valley of strange flora and even stranger fauna. "I am not leaving you, Simon. Not yet. But in a way, your questions are a signal for our relationship to change, for me to change. Tell me, do you remember learning to walk?"

Simon nodded, and was surprised that his mind generated images of him toddling around Mary's tree house, not his own childhood home back when he was simply a person, living life just like anyone else—back when things made at least some semblance of sense. "I remember."

"Good. Now, did the person who taught you to walk hold your hand for all time, until you found yourself walking into your own grave?" Simon's face crinkled in confusion and he shook his head. "Exactly. Once you learned to walk, your teacher allowed you to take steps on your own. The same is true with the mind; the same is true with the spirit. The truth is, you are beginning to walk, and you do not need me to hold your hand anymore. It is true, you will stumble, and I must be there for a little longer, but I feel as though it won't be long before you are walking and running on your own."

Thales sighed again, and this time, his face cracked into a smile. "I had another pupil once, a nephew. I would not let him grow on his own. I struggled and fought to keep him in my life, to make him need me. When he finally forced himself away, I felt broken. I think, my friend, that you are helping me put the pieces back together, and for that, I thank you." Thales's grin widened, and he slid down against the rock and closed his eyes.

Simon frowned, not sure how to respond. "But what does *any* of what you just said have to do with my question of how people manage to continue living, dying, and Returning? How do they cope with the hopelessness, with the pointlessness?"

"Don't you understand? I cannot answer that question for you. Only you can discover what motivates you to continue, what will drive you to complete your own Journey. I cannot help you. You must walk on your own. Now, be quiet, I am suddenly tired."

Simon's heart began to race as he looked at the closed eyes of his companion. He stared at Thales, desperately hoping that the philosopher hadn't somehow completed his Journey and was going the way of Ah-Mun. He sat on his haunches, staring at his guide, praying silently that his breathing would continue and that he wouldn't just evaporate into the air.

What seemed like hours passed. Thales's breathing became more regular, and his chin slumped to his chest. Satisfied that he was not going to be left alone, Simon settled down into the tall grass, his head nestled in an arm, and stared at the breathtaking night sky. Every astral discovery, every wonder of the human mind as it stared at stars over millennia stood in stark contrast to the dark night. Supernovae in brilliant oranges and purples sent tendrils of color to collide with the spiraling white stars of infinite galaxies. Green and deep red Northern Lights danced with the inky darkness of what Simon could only assume to be a black hole, their colorful fingers making a low humming noise that he found oddly comforting. Simon smiled up at the infinite.

He thought of what Thales said, mulling over the idea of purpose in his head, over and over, like a river running over a rough stone, making it smooth. It felt strange to wonder at his own selfish purpose as he looked into never ending space, but think he did. He continued to wonder and ponder as sleep crept up behind him, laid its silver hair over his eyes, and carried him away on its star-laden black blanket. He thought no more for the night.

Simon awoke in a panic, convinced that Thales had died in the night. Half-forgotten images from grey dreams filled his mind with the overwhelming feeling that he was hopelessly, utterly alone. He frantically scrambled from his resting place on the ground and quickly rubbed his bleary eyes until he could clearly look about the golden fields on which he had laid his head the night before.

He had dreamed of the cliff's edge, but instead of him gazing over the precipice, it had been Thales looking out over the strange, alien landscape. The world was bathed in the colors of near-dusk, a grey filter placed over Simon's eyes. Thales had stood tall at the edge of the world, his sandals dangling halfway off the cliff's edge. Simon had tried to run to him, to pull him away from the sickening drop, but his legs refused to answer his mind's call. He had stood, transfixed, calling to Thales, begging him to step back. Thales turned, those kind eyes locked onto Simon's frantic ones, and his mouth smiled as he spoke. He uttered a sentence Simon could not quite catch, a murmured whisper caught by the wind, and leapt off the cliff face. Simon's heart had dropped like a stone, and he awoke screaming.

"Thales. Thales! Where are you?"

"Why are you yelling at this hour? What is the matter?"

Thales's head stuck up from behind the lichen-covered rock, his head covered by a piece of his white toga. He squinted, looking about him, and scratched his head and beard as he yawned.

"Well? What seems to be the matter? Why are you yelling?" Thales repeated.

"I thought I saw something in the grass. Jesus Christ, Thales, I *died* here, remember? I'm allowed to be a little paranoid."

Simon felt relief to see his friend and companion still alive and, by the look of him, not suicidal. He resisted the urge to hug the man and instead forced a look of indignation.

"I'm allowed to be uneasy here, all right?"

"You're right, you're right. I apologize. You have little to worry about, anyway. Lions don't really come up here unless they are driven up here. Chances are, the man you ran into was either hunting the animal or driving it away from where he lived. But I understand your concern."

Standing and stretching luxuriously, Thales adjusted his toga and grabbed his spear. "Well, since we're up, how about we have ourselves a little something to eat and head onward?"

Simon, surprised at the unnervingly consistent pragmatism of the philosopher, nodded.

They ate largely in silence from their packs, devouring bread and cheese from Elysium, and sipped the cider from Simon's bottle. The bread was crumbly and rich, the white cheese was soft and delicious, and Simon licked his fingers when he had finished, hoping to capture every last morsel. Thales had insisted they save some of their provisions for the days ahead, but Simon looked longingly at his bindle as he and Thales prepared to depart. *I forgot how hungry a teenager can be. It feels like I haven't eaten anything at all!* But even though his stomach rumbled a little, Simon followed the instructions of his guide, shouldered his belongings, and prepared to again return to the road.

The tall grass rustled as they walked, and Simon felt his heart race again as he looked about him, half expecting to see a swishing tail, powerful haunches, and golden eyes. He sighed with relief when his feet touched the rocky road, and he smiled as he and Thales began walking away from the dark, violent memory of his past.

A question popped into Simon's head, and when he tried to answer it, he found himself completely at a loss. Looking back at the

227

golden waves of grass, at the place where he had met death once again, the question became louder in his mind, refusing to be ignored.

"Thales, why is it … why did I come back as a young man when I first came here? Why wasn't I born here first?"

A knowing smile played across the guide's face, and he continued walking, looking across the flat plateau and toward the steep slope that the pair would reach within an hour or so. The sun was just beginning to ascend from its resting place, caressing the world with pale new light.

"There are many theories surrounding how we first come to Dara, but many believe the answer can be found in how the various discoveries of humanity also arrive here. Tell me, how do we have such varied flora and fauna on this plane?"

"When something new is discovered, it appears here, right?"

"Correct. Those discoveries, once found by humanity, live both within the minds of people as well as in the world itself. The same is true with our Moment of Ascension. Once we have transcended our base impulses and have become more than human, that new discovery appears here. When we die, our spirit is released, and it comes to fill our newly discovered aspect of self. Does that make sense?"

Simon's head hurt. "I think so. We discover that we are more than human, make a copy of ourselves, and it waits until we can fill it with our soul or whatever?"

Thales smiled again. "Close enough, my young friend. Close enough. Now, the road is going to get pretty rocky, so let's try to focus on conserving our energy and covering as much ground as possible, shall we?"

Simon nodded, and together they walked across the flat land, Thales calm and collected, and Simon performing painful mental acrobatics as he tried to understand what his guide had just explained to him.

For the remainder of the day, Thales and Simon strode down the road. The winding path led them up rocky hills and down into cool valleys, and each place they walked through held its own wonders. Cherry blossoms from Japan grew near old oaks from the dark forests of Europe, and ancient redwoods grew sideways out of small hills. Birds from every corner of the globe, like bursts of color shooting through evergreen leaves and prickly pine, chirped and fluttered about the branches of every tree ever named and discovered. With the exception of the slight dips in topography, the winding road led the pair ever higher in elevation, providing spectacular views of the world below. The breeze played on Simon's face, and the sun, when it could escape the overcast sky, sent cheery rays down onto the waiting ground. The beauty of the place was overwhelming.

As Simon and Thales rounded a bend in a particular valley, Simon was shocked to discover that a collection of hills were completely transparent, redirecting the sunlight that managed to slip through the dark clouds and converting it into rainbows. The giant prisms bathed the landscape in multicolored light, and Simon's breath caught.

He did not know if he had ever seen anything so beautiful. So transfixed was he that he did not realize that he was standing alone, until he tried to tell Thales how beautiful Dara could be. He must have stood rooted to the spot for longer than he first thought, for he had to run to catch Thales, and even at that pace, many long minutes passed before he caught sight of a white toga.

The prism hills had disappeared behind a bend as he ran, and the sun slipped behind those dark clouds once again, coating the world in dark grey tones. Thales stood at the foot of a sharp slope, holding his spear like a walking stick. The road seemed to have simply stopped in front of the sharp incline, and the bearded man looked as though he was preparing for a climb. Simon came to stand beside him and looked up.

The road seemed to rise upward into eternity, disappearing into a thick fog roughly fifty feet up the slope. The beautiful prismatic effect of the transparent hills had been to fill the world with light and color, yet this hill stood as its distinct opposite, with dark greys and splashes of green jutting out of the hillside from tiny shrubs and trees that grew haphazardly from its sides. The faint sound of a distant roaring tickled the edge of Simon's hearing as he stood by his guide. Following the direction that Thales was gazing, Simon saw, seemingly cut into the hill, stone steps winding their way up the steep slope. *Well, at least it will make the climb easier, thank God.*

"Ah, there you are. What do you say we have a little bread and cheese, and maybe some of those apples, before we make this climb? I could use a little rest."

Simon nodded and retrieved the contents Thales had asked for from his bindle. He and Thales sat, eating their lunch in silence, letting their sore muscles relax and their minds wander. After a few minutes of peaceful silence, Thales spoke.

"You know, my young friend, once we climb this hill, we will be entering into the land of the people who, for all intents and purposes, are completely evil. I must be honest when I tell you that I am not looking forward to interacting with the darker side of humanity. I do not know why you were drawn here—why *I* was drawn here—but I do know that unspeakable horror may await us on the other side of those stairs. All that I can say is that we must be careful."

Simon looked at Thales, not sure how to respond. The philosopher did not seem afraid. *Why would he be afraid? He's probably died a hundred times already.* But he did not seem exactly comfortable, either. If anyone or anything could give this ancient man pause, then Simon felt that *he,* at least, should be worried.

Thales smiled encouragingly to Simon, almost as if he had read his mind. "Do not worry, my young friend, I feel—I *know*—we are on the right path. I haven't felt this sure about much in a thousand years. I feel in my bones that we are moving correctly. You have not lived here long enough to know what it means to really resist your Journey, but when you do, it feels as though a rope has been lassoed around your heart, and every day you must resist its pull. Now, the opposite is taking place. I feel *right,* like a fish swimming happily with the current." Thales smiled, took a big bite out of a bright red apple he was holding, and began munching happily.

How is he still here? If I ever met anyone enlightened in my entire life, it would be this guy. Why hasn't he moved on? Simon looked at his guide, at his dark curly beard, knowing smile, and wrinkles around his eyes, and wondered again how Thales, one of the wisest men he had ever met, could still be stuck in Dara. A half-remembered conversation came to his mind, a story buried in a dark moment between him and a man with flint-flecked eyes. Before he knew it, a question had popped out of Simon's mouth before he could stop himself.

"Thales, what happened between you and your apprentice when you were alive? You just seem so collected, so *knowing.* I don't understand what could have gone wrong."

Thales stopped chewing and swallowed his bite of apple. He looked at Simon, then at the stairs, then back at Simon. "That, my young friend, is exactly my problem. I *need* to be knowing, to be in control. I need to feel as though I am the influence, almost the *only* influence, in my pupils' lives. I still do, even now, after all this time."

Simon looked at his bearded companion, confusion completely masking his features. Thales sighed and seemed to adjust himself, preparing to tell a long tale that would not be comfortable for anyone.

"I never married, when I was alive. I thought at first that I was too young, and then too old, to have a wife. I thought that my theories and contributions to society would be enough to give me peace. Yet as time wore on, I realized that no, it was not enough—not enough for me.

"I began to dream of death, of seeing its shade touch my world, and then I understood, in truth, that I was going to die—that there was nothing I could do about it. I fought against it, railed against it, cried to the gods, but to no avail. I realized that no matter what I was to do, death would inevitably claim me, and that the only way I could live on, to continue in some fashion, was through my legacy." Thales took another bite of the apple, chewed, swallowed, and continued.

"Oh, I had my theories, I had my contributions to mathematics and science, but to me, that wasn't enough. I needed a *person* to continue my legacy, so I decided to have a child, only, to my surprise and humiliation, I had waited too long, and my being a father could not be. So, frantic in my fear, I searched for the next best thing, and adopted my nephew Cybisthus."

Simon had never heard the name before; it meant nothing to him, but uttering the name had caused a change in Thales. His shoulders sagged, and he looked at the ground, his apple forgotten.

"I was completely selfish, my young friend. I loved Cybisthus, but I envied his youth, his young body and mind. In my mad fear, I thought that if I could impress my own personality onto him, I could live *through* him—I could be young again. I was with him in all of his waking moments, teaching him, helping him, aiding him, and for a few precious years, I felt peace." Thales sighed, tugged at his white toga, and continued.

"Yet when my nephew became a young man, wanting to strike out on his own, to leave me, I felt the cold touch of death again. Rather than letting Cybisthus go to live his own life, I clung harder to him. The poor youth, trying to please me and cater to his own instinct, found that he could not both please the man he loved as a father and become the man he wished to be. The light slowly left his eyes, and he began to resent me, hate the sight of me, and he didn't know why, which caused him to hate himself as well. He became listless and withdrawn, and I knew that all I had to do to help him, all he needed, was for me to allow him to grow on his own. Yet still I clung to him."

Brown eyes became glassy, and the visual pain of his guide made Simon tug at his own shirt, to look down at the damp rocks at his feet.

When Thales spoke again, his words were heavy with a sadness that threatened to drown him.

"This is lost to the winds of time, but my adopted son, my nephew, not knowing why he hated me so and hating himself for his feelings, felt so trapped that he took his own life. Finally, looking at his dead body, I saw what I had done, what my desperate fight against death had caused, and something snapped within me. I never fully reclaimed selfhood after that."

Simon scratched his head and tugged at his long hair. He wanted to comfort Thales, to hug him, but he found he could not move.

"When I finally accepted death's call and somehow awoke here in Dara, I was amazed and shocked. Frantically, I looked for my son, but to no avail. I hunted for him all over this land, praying that he had joined me here. I must have looked for centuries, living in different villages and towns, dying, and Returning again, only to pick a new town. Young men and women were drawn to me, as is the curse of my Journey, but I refused to have another pupil—to be a guide. I simply could not. I kept searching, until, all corners of this plane searched, I resigned myself to the fact that I would never be granted forgiveness. I deserved to live here, for eternity, to attempt to atone for my sin, for my selfish actions cutting short a young life." Here, Thales sighed again and returned to eating his apple, the crunching sound echoing off of the sharp slope behind him.

Simon listened quietly, and when Thales stopped talking, he waited in silence, waiting for Thales to continue. When the man did not, he cleared his throat. "Why me, then? Why did you choose to be my guide?"

Thales swallowed his morsel. "I did not choose. When I found you, trapped in the alley with the man who would have your honor, I barely thought at all. I intervened, and when I ended that man's life and returned you to Mary, I realized that I had entered into your destiny, and you into mine. You had not Returned before, had not managed to live multiple lives, so you did not know what to expect from the world where you now found yourself. Since I saved your life once, at such a pivotal time, you would seek me out again, with or without my permission and consent. I realized this and decided to accept my fate. Now, here we are, and, I can say that I feel thankful that I acted the way I did, and I thank you for it as well, young Simon." Thales looked at his young ward and smiled. Simon returned the expression, smiling despite himself. In truth, he did not know how to react.

It seems that if I talk to someone for more than five minutes, I am faced with more truth than I ever wanted to deal with, Simon thought. *But I am thankful that he told me. I wonder what his nephew was like. Who could hate Thales so much that they would want to kill themselves? I've hated people. I hated my boss, hated my neighbor two doors down, but not enough to kill them or myself. Maybe the kid had a mental illness. Better not ask, though; Thales would probably get upset.*

Keeping his thoughts to himself and deciding that no response was the best response, Simon finished his lunch in silence. The bread was a little staler than the day before, but the fruit was still delicious. Simon munched away, his mind and his belly full.

Once Thales and Simon had finished their repast, and what was left of their provisions was placed back into Simon's bindle ("You're young, you carry the rest," Thales had said with a chuckle), they began their ascent up the staircase hewn into the rocky hillside. The steps were made of a dark grey stone, slick with the mist that had sent foggy tendrils down the hillside, wetting their path. Simon carefully picked his way up the path, following Thales, who walked as though he was on the flattest path on the driest patch of earth, his sandals never slipping. Simon's feet were not as efficient, and he quickly found himself to be more wet than dry as he ascended the stone staircase, and fresh bruises could be felt blooming on his knees and shins. Grumbling, Simon trudged forward, having to again remind himself not to be angry at Thales because of his maddening grace and surefootedness.

The smell of moisture, of wet earth, filled Simon's nostrils as he climbed. The small roar in his ears became louder and louder, until it threatened to overwhelm Simon's eardrums. The higher he ascended, the thicker the mist became, until Simon felt as if he had walked directly into a rain cloud. Looking up, his body now drenched with the moisture of the fog, Simon could make out the summit, a jagged dark line outlined in the mist.

Thales, ahead of Simon by a significant margin now, disappeared over the top of the precipice, his toga giving a splash of white in a sea of grey. Simon hurried after him, his moccasins now drenched with dew and sliding as he moved. He slipped for what seemed to be the thousandth time, scraping his knee on a stone step, but kept on moving, ignoring the pain in his leg. His bindle nearly fell from his hands, threatening to slide down the slick stone steps, but at the last moment, Simon managed to snatch his belongings before they plummeted to the bottom of the hill. Muttering a silent curse, Simon made a tighter grip on his walking stick and continued to pick his way carefully up the stairs. Soon, he had reached the summit of the stairs and walked into a scene that seemed to have been ripped from the recesses of a lucid dream.

A giant waterfall, the cause of the deafening, overwhelming noise in his ears, filled Simon's vision. To call it enormous was an understatement, and Simon could not think of another word to describe the monstrous liquid beast cascading down a steep cliffside and disappearing into a sea of mist. Pale rainbows reflected off the water spray, lending a mystical air to the plateau.

As Simon stepped forward, he saw, through the mist, a dark wooden bridge protruding from the curtain of water droplets. The plateau became narrower, and to Simon's left, nothing but fog and emptiness resided. As he cautiously stepped alongside Thales, Simon looked down and watched the roaring water disappear into a sea of foam, the pale rainbows dancing among the dew drops. Not being able to see the bottom, Simon felt a touch of dizziness threaten to overwhelm his senses, but he forced it down and stepped onto the single wooden slab that formed the beginning of the bridge.

The other side was covered by fog, so Simon had no idea the length of the walkway. He knew only that he was to cross it, as shown by Thales striding forward, his white toga damp from the water and his curly hair stuck to his head, dripping down almost to his eyes. Using his staff as a walking stick, Simon stepped quickly until he strode shoulder to shoulder with his guide and friend.

As the pair walked across the wooden bridge, its bottom slick with moisture, an outline of a person began to take shape in the middle of the wall of fog. The being was moving from one side of the bridge to the other, pausing on occasion on the edge of the bridge that overlooked the descent into nothingness below, only to return to the other side of the floating structure. As Simon continued closer, he realized that the form was a man, his broad shoulders covered with a golden shirt and his brown skin slick with moisture and sweat. The man went to one side of the walkway to retrieve a wrapped bundle from a wooden cart, carried it over to the opposite railing, and threw it over the edge. He did not pause to look where it fell, or to stop for a breath between heaving the parcels off the edge, which appeared to be heavy and irregular in shape.

When Simon stepped closer, his heart began to race, as the bundles, long and tied at two places, began to take on a distinct, recognizable shape. With a gasp he could barely control, Simon jerked as he saw one of the bundles start to squirm and make a muffled moan. Seeing the two approach, the man stopped his methodical motion and turned to face the two travelers. As he turned, he set his stance wide, effectively blocking the way to the other end of the bridge.

He was tall, with dark skin, black hair, and eyes that looked almost black. Long mustachios drooped from his upper lip, and his golden shirt, open at the neck, cascaded down a powerful chest and stopped at blue sash and blue trousers. The trousers were pushed into soft leather boots, which narrowed to a point at the toe. The man did not smile, did not frown; he simply stood and watched Thales and Simon with those dark eyes, calculating and weighing them, checking their measure. This cold calculation left Simon unnerved.

"Good day to you, sir. May we pass?" The calmness in the eyes of Thales, the easy smile, was an expression and feeling that Simon tried to replicate, without much success.

"Now, why would I allow you to do that? You have interrupted my task, and I find that to be off-putting." The man spoke with a voice that told of dark depths and indecipherable history, of a time long past when men could still find communion with beasts. It was an ancient voice, a voice of power, whose words danced with an accent that called to the dawn of time.

Jesus, this guy makes my knees shake. Stay calm, stay relaxed. The voice in Simon's head did not seem to heed its own advice, and Simon had to focus furiously on keeping his knees from buckling.

"Sir, we do not mean to interrupt your ... *task*," Thales gestured to the wagon of squirming forms, "but we really must be on our way. My young friend and I have traveled far, and we mean to reach our destination by nightfall."

Thales, with all the degree of casualness that such a motion could offer, lifted his spear from his shoulder and appeared to calmly wipe down the shaft with his hand. Simon barely noticed that the philosopher had shifted his feet so that his right was slightly behind his left, and he had dropped his weight slightly. A practiced eye would see that the man had readied himself for a quick thrust with the dangerous barbed metal point, should the need arise.

The dark-haired man's eyes flashed, if only for a moment, then returned to their calm calculation so quickly that Simon couldn't be entirely sure that he had seen anything at all. The man paused and turned his large frame slightly to point at his cart. His other hand came to rest casually on the curved blade that was shoved in the bright blue sash at his waist.

"Do you not wonder why I am here? Does it not cross your mind to wonder why I am sending my bundles ...?" He then touched the cart slowly, intimately sliding his hand down the wooden cart, and when his hand touched a tied bundle, it jerked. He continued, "...Over the edge of this beautiful bridge? Come now, you must at least be a little curious. A man, alone, throwing things off a bridge? That doesn't pique your interest, even a little?"

Thales, still the embodiment of calm, scratched his beard with his free hand and shrugged. "That is not our business, good sir. Now, if you will excuse us, my young companion and I—"

Quicker than thought, quicker than Simon's eyes could register, the man's hand flashed from his knife's hilt and flicked his wrist, sending the curved blade flying in a deadly arc, spinning until it buried itself to the hilt in Thales's abdomen. The philosopher, faster than Simon could realize, had managed to set his feet and fling his spear with deadly purpose just as the huge man threw his deadly missile, but the impact of the blade caused the bearded man's throw to go slightly wide of its mark, cutting into the man's golden tunic and leaving a gash that bloomed red on the man's shoulder. After taking a bite out of its target, the spear hurtled into the mist on the other side of the bridge and disappeared. Thales, grunting, gripped the golden hilt and sagged heavily to the ground, no word escaping his lips.

Simon was frozen, fear and disbelief overwhelming his mind. His brain became nothing more than a scramble of images, sensations, and half-forgotten words. Nothing seemed to make sense, and his mind, confused and terrified, tried to deny what his eyes could not deny as a terrible truth. Thales couldn't be dead. He couldn't have left him alone, in a foreign place, with no aid to speak of. Such a tragedy was so unlikely that it made Simon believe it to be impossible.

"You must be wondering why I decided to kill your companion." The large man's rich voice cascaded with the sound of the falling water, breaking into Simon's terrified heart. "Oh, I could say that he was threatening me, that he seemed quite capable with that spear of his," here the man touched his shoulder, "but, that would be a lie."

Walking over casually, the man bent over Thales, and with a quick jerk, dislodged his blade from his stomach, causing a ribbon of red to cascade from the elevated blade and down onto the spotless white toga of the ancient philosopher. Simon became fascinated by the red marring the always spotless white garment. *He never gets anything on his clothes. No stains, nothing,* Simon thought numbly. Thales's assailant wiped his blade on that immaculate white toga and placed it back in his blue sash at his waist. Simon's feet were still rooted to the ground, but his eyes followed the dark man's every move.

"If I am honest with myself—and why should I not be? —I do not believe anyone should ever, ever, be able to hold a position above me, and this man here had a bearing that was lofty, to say the least. My brothers, in my first life, were the same. They tried to claim my birthright as their own, simply because they were *older* than me." The man chuckled, shaking his head. "And this lovely group of people that I have *detained*"—long fingers gestured toward the cart— "believed that they could refuse my desire to live at their home. Now, they must live their last moments, trapped together in agony, until they feel the stomach-lurching drop from this beautiful bridge."

The man strode back to the wagon and stroked the human parcels. With each touch, the bundle would jerk feebly, a sad attempt at escape, which caused the large man to smile, a dark grin that danced in the blood of innocents.

"Did you know that there is a creature with a sting so powerful that it makes the skin feel as though it has been pierced by a racing missile? Some call it the *hormiga veinticuatro,* though I've often heard it called the bullet ant. This remarkable insect's sting lasts for a full day, and with enough bites, can drive a man mad." Dark mustachios tilted upward as the man smiled. "I do not think my *guests* particularly enjoyed discovering the strength of this sting as I stuffed them into their respective pouches."

Simon looked over at the covered forms—just two remaining in the cart—and looked back at the man, his feet still refusing to move.

"Who ... who are you?" Simon worked his tongue, trying to find moisture in a mouth that had gone as dry as the Sahara. His body revolted against him at every turn, and the words that escaped his mouth were little more than a dry croak.

"Who am I? Oh, you poor innocent fool. I am demise, I am the fell swoop, I am the decider of fates. My name is Sumadra, and my purpose is death."

The man strode over to his cart, hefting another of his bundles over his shoulder and walking it to the railing of the bridge. The waterfall's thunder had diminished in Simon's ears. The package barely moved, and the man, Sumadra, carried his burden as if it were made of little more than feathers. *Jesus Christ, he's strong. I've got to make a run for it. I have to. He's blocking the way to the other side! Maybe I can run back the way we came, come back after he has left. He's only got one body left, right? Shit, what am I saying? Should I help the last person escape? I can't fight this guy; he's a giant! Jesus Christ.* His mind racing, attempting to decide whether to turn and flee or try to rescue the last remaining person in the bundle, Simon remained rooted until Sumadra, with a chilling nonchalance, chucked the feebly writhing mummy off the edge of the bridge and turned again to face him.

"What is to happen next, you must wonder? What is to become of you? Will I kill you as I did your friend here?" A huge brown finger

240

waved in the general direction of Thales's prostrate form. "Or, will I let you go? I see you are terrified of me, that you realize you cannot defeat me, which gives me pleasure, but I also see a hint of defiance within your eyes, which gives me pause."

Sumadra began stroking his mustache, presumably thinking of what to do to Simon, while pacing to the cart and back to the edge of the cliff. This occurred for several moments, and Simon was again thinking of making a run for it, of doing something to help the poor trapped soul, when Sumadra spoke up again, his finger thrust up into the air and his eyes burning into Simon's.

"I have it! I will have you complete my work for me. If you are willing to kill this poor trapped human being, I will let you live. If you do not, I will kill you as I did your friend over there. This will prove that you are willing to do what is necessary to preserve yourself, even kill, and that I can understand. If, however, you choose to defy me, then I cannot trust you, and you must die." Sumadra spread his meaty arms wide, wide palms facing upward. "The choice is yours."

Simon stood there, eyes flitting from the cart to Sumadra, who had taken a stance of nonchalance, arms folded at his chest and eyes hooded. *Jesus Christ, what do I do? What am I supposed to do with that? If I kill the person, then they will just Return, right? But if I don't, and he kills me, then I also Return. Goddamn it, that knife looks like it hurts. What was that about bullet ants? The person wrapped up like a damn mummy probably wants to die if what that guy says is true. Jesus Christ, I don't want to die again! Thales, why did you have to go and die on me? What do I do? I'm a good person, right? Right?*

The last thought seemed to flood through Simon's mind, unlocking visceral images of times in which he acted less than admirably. Times when drunkenness, stubbornness, or plain selfishness caused him to become the man he hoped his mother never saw and never would. Moments when pain drove him to near madness and the resulting chaos that followed as he lashed out violently at those around him or near his heart. The belief that he was, in fact, even a shadow of a good person began to slip away. He looked to Thales, hoping that the man, his guide, could help him in some way, but the philosopher remained motionless, hands now clutching his open wound, his breathing ragged and shallow. Thales could not help him. Simon's chest tightened as he looked at the man who had guided him, aided him. Hopelessness and rage warred inside his heart.

Slowly, Simon forced his feet to move. Sumadra's dark eyes burned like coals recently plucked from a fire. Simon felt the heat of the gaze as he turned his terrified, damp form toward the cart. His mind slowly felt the grip of icy numbness as he reached down and hefted the tied-up frame of a body onto his shoulder. The bundle felt surprisingly light. *Please don't be a child,* he begged silently, *please don't let it be a child.* Yet even that horrifying possibility did not stop his slow shuffle toward the bridge railing.

The water thundered in his ears, matching the thumping of his heart as it hammered against his rib cage. Sumadra followed, a sickening smile peeking out of his dark brown mustache. Simon could see the large man's golden outline to his right as he came to the railing. Looking down, he saw the white, foaming, turbulent water crashing down many feet below, causing mist to rise up, obscuring the end of the waterfall. The small parcel kicked feebly on his shoulder, which brought tears, hot and angry, to his eyes. Simon hesitated, grappling with himself one more time, the unhappy arbiter of life and death.

"What are you waiting for, my new young friend? Simply toss the bundle off the bridge and be on your way. A simple movement for freedom. Relieve your burden, quite literally."

Sumadra took a step closer to Simon, coming near his right shoulder. The curved dagger flashed wickedly as he fingered the hilt.

"Don't you want to continue? Why should you die, so someone you do not even know can, well, still die?" Sumadra chuckled, gravel in a cement mixer. "It is inevitable. There is nothing that will deter my purpose, and the only choice you have, a single move, is whether you wish to die with this stranger. Toss it over the side and be done with it!"

Sumadra's breathing had quickened, and his golden shirt billowed as his chest moved. The fire in his eyes had become feverish, and his grip on the curved blade tucked in his blue sash turned his knuckles white. The red on his shoulder provided sharp contrast to the grey world.

Simon looked down at the mist and crash of water. His hands gripped the bundle on his left shoulder, and he set his feet. Tears fell down his face as he pushed his hands under the burlap and began to heave.

"I'm sorry," he whispered to the bundle. "I'm so sorry. Please forgive me. I bid you safe Return." Simon's heart dropped as he lifted the tied form off of his shoulder.

What happened next occurred so quickly that Simon could not be entirely sure that it happened. A flash of white streaked by, exploding into the gold and blue form of Sumadra. The big man, taken completely by surprise, was shoved violently toward and over the bridge's water-soaked railing, arms grappling with the white shape. Simon, staring open-mouthed, watched as Thales, impossibly, threw himself onto Sumadra, white toga flapping and dark eyes set to deadly purpose. Gold and yellow flashed in the mist, then they were gone, disappearing into the foam below.

Simon unceremoniously dropped his burden onto the slick floor of the bridge and rushed to where the two grapplers had disappeared, still locked in a deadly embrace. Only foam and a small rainbow of reflected light greeted his eyes, and the only sound was the roaring of water, yet still he desperately searched, hoping for a glimpse of white, a hint of curly hair.

He's gone. Thales is gone. These words inside his head seemed to be spoken by a voice not his own, and Simon felt all of the remaining energy leave him, turning his arms to jelly and his legs to wet sand. He sank down to the bridge floor, the slick wood soaking his leggings and the damp railing dampening the back of his shirt. He barely noticed his skin growing cold or the contrast of hot tears on his icy face. His whole body had become numb, his mind a slug covered in salt. He wept for Thales, wept for himself, wept for all that had befallen him.

Completely and utterly alone, Simon allowed hopelessness to swallow him up. He did not know how long he sat, head in his hands, but when sleep came to claim him, he welcomed the blackness and prayed that it would never again allow him entry back into this world of madness.

Simon was awoken by a strange pressure, repeated at odd intervals, on his right calf. Half groggy from sleep, he thought it must be Scout, the family dog, telling him he needed to be let out to the backyard to do his business. "Five minutes, buddy. Go bother Anna." The thumping continued, and Simon's hand reached out, intending to find a wet nose and furry head, and he was shocked awake by the distinct feel of coarse burlap and knotted rope. Eyes shooting open, Simon looked down and around him, surprised to find a waterfall in his bedroom, no dog to speak of, and a tied-up form pathetically kicking his calf.

Everything came rushing back, ending again with the death of his companion and guide, of the horrible loss he felt, of the growing hollow emptiness in his chest. He felt tears well in his eyes, and the only reason that they did not fall freely was the continued interruption of the steady kicking of the captive person at his side. *How did you get over here? Jesus Christ, how long was I asleep?* Simon looked about at the grey mist surrounding him and decided that it was darkening, and night would fall soon. *I've got to get out of here before anyone else shows up. If they are anything like Sumadra, I won't stand a chance.*

Fear gave rise to locomotion, and soon Simon was on his feet. He retrieved his bindle and, with a silent farewell to Thales, began to walk back the way he had come, toward the crystal hills and the little amount of peace that he had known while he lived in Dara. Yet, inexplicably, something stopped his walk. He turned and looked down at the feebly kicking figure tied and squirming on the bridge floor. *I can't just leave it lying there. I can't.*

Slowly, Simon laid his bindle down and retrieved his familiar blade from its sheath. He felt a stab of self-hatred at the fact that he didn't even draw it when Sumadra murdered his companion, but he forced it down. Kneeling, he cut the ropes that bound the captive and gently pulled the burlap up and away. Tears welled in his eyes again as he looked down at the captive, at the person he almost killed to save his own skin.

Purple welts covered her entire body, and almond-shaped doe eyes ringed with jet black hair darted about, terrified of the world, reborn out of a nightmare. She was dressed in what was once a simple white dress, with a green ribbon sewn at the waist, but the fabric had long ago turned to a stained grey, like a storm cloud streaked with blood and grime. She tried to rise, tried to run, but her knees buckled, and she fell into an emaciated heap, a newborn fawn who could not yet master the art of standing. Simon watched as sobs racked her tiny body, and as her tiny frame heaved, he felt his heart break. *I am so sorry, kid. I am so sorry for what I almost did.*

Slowly, he put his hand out to touch her shoulder, and she flinched as if he had struck her.

"It's okay, I'm a friend. He's gone. He can't hurt you anymore." Simon again placed his hand on her shoulder, and this time, she turned and buried herself in his chest, clutching him like a piece of driftwood to a capsized sailor. She clung to him, and he held her, letting her cry. Before long, her ragged breathing became more regular and deeper, and Simon rocked her, letting her sleep, thanking whatever god there was that he had not murdered this innocent child.

It was an hour before the girl awoke, and when she did, she jerked away from Simon, pushing herself against the bridge railing and bringing her knees up to her chest. Her eyes never left Simon as he rose, hands outstretched toward her.

"It's all right. I am a friend, remember? I cut you out of that sack. He, Sumadra, is gone. He went over the side of the bridge, so you're safe."

The girl did not move, did not react, and those eyes stared into Simon. He felt his heart break again.

"I ... I'm sorry, but your family is gone, too. We didn't arrive until, well, until he was almost done with what he was doing." Simon felt stupid. *I don't know what to say. What am I supposed to say? "Sorry your whole family died and that I almost killed you earlier? You're okay now, though, sort of." Jesus Christ, what am I supposed to say to this person?*

"My name's Simon. I was with someone, too, but he died. He saved my life, and now he's gone. His name, his name was Thales. I miss him already." Simon fought back tears and tried to swallow the lump in his throat. "What's your name? Do you have a name?"

The girl continued to look at him, not moving, not talking, just staring. Simon felt himself shrink under that gaze. Suddenly, an idea came to him, and he moved quickly toward his bindle. The girl shrank even more into herself, trying to squeeze her tiny body into the railing.

Simon's hands came up again. "I'm sorry, I didn't mean to scare you. I just, well, are you hungry?" Simon opened his bindle and removed an apple and some cheese. He placed the food on the ground in front of the little girl and stepped back.

The girl hesitated, but only for a moment, before she darted out and grabbed the food. She devoured the cheese so fast that Simon would have thought that she dropped it over the edge, if not for the smear of white on her cheeks. She ate the apple with the same amount of ravenous speed, pausing only briefly before she decided to ingest everything, core and all. Licking her fingers and wiping her face to retrieve that last vestige of food, she looked at Simon hopefully. He stepped back, showing her what remained of his provisions, and she hesitated only briefly before diving into the remaining bread, cheese, and a remaining small red apple. Simon smiled despite himself, worried that he didn't have any more food, but happy to be of some help. *Jesus, I wonder when the last time she ate.* Within moments, all the food was gone, and the girl began picking crumbs off of her ruined dress and shoving them into her mouth.

"What's your name?"

The girl straightened quickly, having forgotten that Simon existed as she devoured all of his food. The food seemed to have done wonders for her, for she stood, a bit wobbly at first, and turned to face Simon. The purple welts on her face and arms made a sharp contrast to her pale skin. Her large eyes, still coated with fear, began to crackle with a look of anger and pain as she took in her rescuer.

"Are they... are they all gone? The people I was with?" The little girl's voice was high and lilting, a singsong cascade of sound. It was a dialect meant for poetry and song, not the angry sadness that now impregnated it.

"Yes, I am sorry. I am sorry that I couldn't save them."

"You didn't save anyone. You didn't save anyone at all. The only person saved here was you." The little girl spoke with a finality, her small voice weighted with a sadness that people don't learn until much later in life.

"What? I don't understand." *She's in shock.* "You were just in a terrible ordeal. You almost died. Why don't you sit back down, and you can tell me your name?"

The girl, rather than answering, walked back to the railing, gripping the slick wooden barrier with her small hands. Simon suddenly felt fear, and he did not know why.

"Hey, let's get away from that ledge. I'm sorry I couldn't save your family. I'm sorry I couldn't help them. Let's take a step back and talk."

"Family? Save them? You are either stupid, or you haven't Returned many times before." The girl laughed, a mirthless chuckle. When she turned to face Simon, the smile had broken one of the purple welts, causing it to ooze a dark liquid. "That wasn't my family, and you didn't save me. Like I said, the only person to be saved here was you."

"I don't know what you're talking about. Please step away from that ledge."

"Your friend? Thales? He saved you. He saved you from killing me, which would have condemned your soul to Return and be born again. It seems to me that you are doing something important, and your friend destroyed himself so you could continue."

"How could you possibly know that?"

"Such an act—the killing of a child to preserve your own skin—cannot be a part of your Journey. You would have tainted yourself. Trust me, I know. That is why I'm going to start over." The girl turned, gripping the railing in her small hands. She looked over her shoulder at Simon as he yelled for her to stop.

"Why? There is nothing for me here. I am a young girl in the worst possible place in this world. If I am found by some of the other *residents* of this area, my fate will be worse than you can possibly imagine. No, I will Return to Elysium and start over. You, you must go on, or the sacrifice of your friend would be in vain. Do not let such a brave act fall upon blind eyes. I wish you well."

Simon lunged for the girl, but he was too late. Without so much as another moment's hesitation, the auburn-haired girl vaulted over the railing and slid into the grey mist below. Simon's outstretched hand managed to grab the ribbon tied to her waist, and with a rip, it came off in his hand. He stared down, hopeless, as the girl vanished. Simon looked numbly at the green ribbon and sat against the railing.

I hate this place. I hate it so much! Why did I have to wake up here? Why am I alive at all? Why can't I just die? Looking down at the ribbon, Simon contemplated joining the girl's descent. Perhaps he would end up in a new place, a new home. He could be a child again, start over. *No. Thales would still be gone. My memories wouldn't disappear. I would just add more pain and death to my mind until it cracked.* Simon sat, staring at the emerald ribbon, unsure of what to do. In truth, he did not want to do anything at all. He simply wanted the world to pass him by, and for death, true death, to claim him.

Moments ticked by, and soon, darkness slipped its shroud over the world. Icicles of fear punctured the numbness that encircled Simon, and he decided that, if nothing else, he did not want to be found on this bridge at night by whomever lived on the other side. Wrapping the ribbon around his wrist and hefting his walking stick, Simon strode to the closest end of the bridge, whose edge disappeared into a sea of fog. He moved quickly and carefully, hoping to find a quiet, hidden place to sleep and to decide what he was to do in the morning. The fog enveloped him, and he walked almost blindly, hands outstretched, hoping to not run into anything, or any*one*, if he could help it.

The hard planks under his feet soon gave way to gravel, and his soft shoes made a crunching sound over the stones. The fog seemed to insulate sound, causing the small shifting of tiny rocks to make a noise reminiscent of thunder in Simon's mind. The young man cursed inwardly and tried to walk on his tiptoes, though it did not do much good. Blindly, he moved about, stretching his eyes to their limit, hoping to make out some shape in front of him, something he could see.

Suddenly, his feet stopped their forward momentum, and Simon found himself hurtling face-first onto the rocky road. He yelped as he fell, and the jarring pain in his hands and knees made him curse inwardly as he took a sharp intake of breath. Angrily, he felt for the object that had hindered his movement, planning to commit some form of violence to it, when his hand grasped smooth, round wood.

Gripping the shaft, Simon quickly picked up Thales's spear, its barbed tip stained with the dark blood of his assailant. *A final present from a generous man. Thank you, Thales.* Simon pulled his wrapped belongings from his own staff and tied them just below the spear tip of Thales's old weapon. Relieved of its burden, Simon placed his old walking stick on the side of the path, thinking that maybe someone else might need it.

Simon continued walking forward, the barbed tip of the spear piercing the fog. He felt better somehow, felt as if Thales, or a piece of him, had been embedded in the spear and was walking with him as he strode through the murky world. Looking at the sharp iron, Simon felt as though he could speak to the philosopher, almost as if he was communicating with him with thought alone. The idea, as ludicrous as it seemed, comforted him, made the hollowness in his chest less dense.

Thank you, Thales. Thank you for saving me, for helping me even after you're gone. I'm going to continue on, to see this through, because I think that's how you would have wanted it. I am scared, terrified even, but I think I'm going anyway. What's the worst they could do? Kill me? Please do. I'm not sure if you can hear me or if I'm just going crazy, but I hope that, wherever you end up, wherever you Return, you will find some peace.

Rolling his shoulders back, eyes clear, Simon strode down the path. He was alone, hungry, and terrified, but he had a purpose. Sometimes, a purpose is more powerful than the richest clothes or the closest companion. A purpose can drive people to incredible things, light a fire in their breast in the coldest, darkest night. His heart thus lit, Simon walked into the unknown, hoping to fulfill his Journey and to honor his guide and companion.

The path led downward after a few paces, and the farther Simon stepped from the thunderous roar of the waterfall, the clearer the world became. Stars began to poke their way out of the fog, and bright orbs of an undetermined source flitted about, lighting the path and chasing away the tendrils of mist.

Before long, Simon was on dry earth, the night sky shining clear above him, and the path leveled out into a valley bristling with white flowers whose sweet smell seemed to cover the world in a canopy of scent. The plants themselves were the source of the orbs of light, ejaculating them as they blossomed and died. Simon watched, transfixed, as a single bushy plant produced flowers that shot the shining orbs into the sky, then wilted, only to bring new flowers to take its place. *It's like they are giving birth to stars.* Simon gave his head a shake, and continued walking. *I can't get distracted. I need to find a place to hide and plan my next move.*

To his right, through the dense undergrowth, Simon spotted a single, giant tree, its branches stretching to the heavens and cascading back down to the ground. Thinking he could hide there for the evening, Simon marched forward, pushing the dark green leaves of the bushes aside to clear a path. Lights exploded around him as he walked, causing the dim world to shine bright in tiny bursts, then descend back into darkness. *Might as well send up a goddamn flair.* Simon grimaced. *Oh well, just have to get to the tree. Got to hide out for the night.*

Shoulders forward, Simon strode on, hoping that no one had seen him. *Can't do anything about it now, anyway. Just got to get there. Got to make it.* Soon, the bushes gave way to a perfectly circular clearing, with the giant tree rising to the heavens in the middle. Huge branches came down to touch the earth as well as spread their leafy arms into the sky, and the shining orbs of the star flowers danced among its branches. Simon walked forward, feeling a sense of safety and security under the tree's canopy.

Leaning the spear of Thales against the tree, Simon rested his back against the giant trunk and closed his eyes. His stomach rumbled, but he ignored it, though he had to force down the desire to curse the little girl who ate all of his food and leapt off the bridge with all of his provisions in her tiny stomach. *Could've left me a damn apple, at least.* Luckily, sleep came quickly, and Simon drifted away to the sounds of his stomach gurgling and the ever-present wind dancing with green leaves and orbs of light.

CHAPTER XVI—AND HID HIS FACE

Simon found himself in the middle of a family camping trip, before everything went sour, before his world had been swallowed by madness. Anna was there, her beautiful, kind face reflected back at him by firelight. His children had already gone to sleep, and he and Anna were enjoying an *anejo* tequila he had stored in his old forest-green burlap hiking bag, taking nips from the squat brown bottle and laughing quietly, so as not to disturb the sleeping children in their little blue tent. The look in Anna's eyes suddenly glinted with mischievous purpose, and Simon smiled widely, thanking the gods of agave. *Damn, she's beautiful.* The fire burned brighter, making a perfect metaphor for his rising passion. The smoky smell of burning wood danced pleasantly in his nostrils.

Anna's eyes reflected the growing flame, and Simon walked over to her. The summer night had become very hot, and he could not wait to get out of his clothes. He bent to kiss her soft lips, cupping her face in his hands. Yet as he bent down, his hands became weightless, and he opened his eyes to see nothing but smoke where his wife once stood.

Looking frantically about, Simon tried to find his wife, find his children, but all he saw were angry flames and smoke burning his eyes. Opaque walls of ash and wind closed in on him, and his lungs erupted into a coughing fit. The grey walls became thicker, denser, and collapsed on Simon. His terrified mind tried to find his family, tried to run, but there was nowhere to go. Covering his mouth with his hand, Simon tried to make one last, final attempt to escape, but the smoke had become as solid as a grey tomb, and he screamed as he careened down into a bottomless depth of darkness.

Simon awoke with a start, hands flailing about, still searching for his family. His relief that the dark smoke that became as thick as concrete was only a dream was short-lived as he realized quickly that the tree in which he had found shelter was fast becoming a pillar of flame. Grabbing his blanket and spear, Simon leapt up and rushed away from the tree, back toward the relative safety of the road.

Dawn was breaking as he ran, bathing the world in a murky grey. The witching hour caused an already mystical place to somehow appear even more mysterious. The flowers from the night before had gone, replaced by simple shrubberies covering the world with dark green leaves. Simon thought, in passing, that the flowers must be nocturnal, but such a thought disappeared quickly as he stepped onto the road. Eyes still stinging, Simon quickly rubbed them with his palm and looked to the giant tree that had once been his shelter.

The limbs had been set ablaze, and thin grey tendrils reached into the sky, partially blocking the rising sun. Simon stood transfixed, as all humanity does when it really stares into an open flame in the natural world. It felt strange, finding comfort in such a deadly force, but Simon could not help himself. The fire raged upward, but it looked as though an invisible wall prevented it from moving horizontally, with sparks billowing toward the green ground cover and tracing a transparent line up into the breaking dawn. Soon, the tree itself was obscured by a cylinder of smoke and ash, pushing its way into the sky.

"Amazing really, watching nature's power at work."

Simon jumped back and landed in a crouch, spear forward and ready to stab at the sound. His eyes darted to where a man had appeared, gazing at the fiery scene, standing so close to Simon that he could smell his sweat. Long dark hair cascaded down to almost the middle of his back, framing deep set, intelligent eyes. He was stripped to the waist, a dark kilt the only stitch of clothing he had on. Seemingly unperturbed by the sharp spear pointed at his chest, Simon's new companion continued looking at the blazing torch that had once been a majestic tree. Shrugging, the man turned toward Simon, a crooked grin on his face.

"But if wood wasn't meant to burn, why is it so easily Changed to do so? Why would the universe tempt us, its creators and greatest creation, with the ability to light things on fire, and not expect us to do so?"

Simon's heart began to race as he crouched behind the sharp spear of Thales. *This son of a bitch tried to burn me alive!* A growl escaped his throat, and he wished Thales was there to help him.

The long-haired man, sweating from previous exertions, looked back at the flames for a moment longer, then turned his gaze on Simon. His face was young and smooth, with a jaw chiseled out of marble. He smiled, but the kind expression never touched his Quixotic eyes. "Take, for example, that beautiful spear of yours. A wonderful weapon, and by my guess, one that has seen a bit of use. However, it is made of steel and wood, and wood burns."

With a yelp, Simon jerked his hands back as if his fingers had been bit by a venomous snake. The spear, his barrier between himself and this lunatic, became engulfed in flames. The shaft exploded into a fiery blaze that stung his eyes and burned merrily for a moment on the ground where Simon stood, until nothing remained but the barbed tip. Terrified now, Simon took a step back, reaching toward the knife at his belt, praying that the man didn't light *it* on fire as well. The man smiled again, and, as if nothing had happened at all, returned to watching the tree continue its transformation to smoke and ash.

Moments passed, and Simon, not knowing what to do, not knowing whether to run, hide, or leap for the man, simply stood and watched him. *Jesus Christ, who is this guy now? Why did he try to light me on fire? Why do I never know what's going on?* The man's voice again broke the silence, scattering Simon's thoughts.

"You will be coming with me now. It's not every day that someone new makes it here, let alone someone who hasn't Returned many times before. I find this … interesting. Come on, daybreak is coming, and I am hungry."

The man, without another word, turned and began walking down the path, which wound around a hill and disappeared. Simon remained rooted to where he was, not knowing what to do, but knowing that he did *not* want to follow this madman. Realizing he wasn't being followed, the shirtless man turned to look at Simon, that smile still on his lips. He crossed his arms and looked levelly at the youth frozen in place.

"You *will* follow me, young one. I want to hear about your time, discover what you know, learn about where you come from. However, if you refuse to do as you're told," the man opened his arms, palms facing upward, "I will simply break your arms and legs and drag you where I want you to go. You do not need legs to talk. The choice is yours." The smile disappeared from the man's face, and he stared at Simon. "Decide wisely. I do not like when people keep me from my breakfast. Entire wars have been won or lost depending on a good morning meal."

Moments passed, and Simon's heart hammered in his chest. Slowly, against the screaming protests in his head, Simon's feet began to move toward the threatening presence on the road, shuffling slowly in the direction of whatever destiny had in store for him. The man, his false smile returning to his face, waited for the young man to catch up to him, then resumed walking down the path, bare shoulder grazing Simon. *Why is this guy so damn close to me?* Simon wondered, but he kept his mouth shut.

The smell of smoke and copper filled Simon's nostrils as he walked near his new traveling companion. The shirtless man had slipped into an easy silence, a quiet that was only earned through a deep confidence of self—an understanding that the world could be bent, just by the force of one's will alone. A mad confidence. Simon placed one hand on his knife at his waist and kept walking. The green ribbon fluttered as he walked, its ends slightly frayed from the fires of the morning.

The shrubbery that hedged the path Simon and the strange man walked gave way to a perfectly flat field with a spherical mound right in its center. Circular indentations in the emerald green grass that formed the mound's covering spiraled to the top, reminding Simon of a baked dessert—*Alaska something.* The path crunched under his feet as Simon walked, and the giant mound drew close, rising up to Simon's right.

His companion—or captor, Simon wasn't sure which—continued walking in silence. The sun came up, illuminating the top of the hill, and as the rays of light touched the green, the emerald grass reflected the pale light like shards of colored glass, making the hill a spiraling beacon that bathed everything in green. The world seemed to have been bathed in life, seemed to have been soaked in a vitality that Simon had missed before. The upside-down mountains loomed large above him, giant incisors coming to devour the world. If he wasn't terrified, enraged, and mourning the loss of his friend, Simon might have believed this place to be beautiful.

They continued walking around the green-beacon hill, and the wide road circled the mound, white gravel bathed in green crunching under sandals and moccasins. Simon walked, both watching the road in front of him and the odd man by his side, who still had not uttered a word. Before long, Simon felt the silence and thought to speak to the man, perhaps to better understand him, or at least to know the name of his captor. As he cleared his throat to speak, however, the kilted warrior suddenly stopped, and Simon, skidding to halt himself as well, nearly fell into an abyss. *Did this damn road just grow a mouth and try to swallow me?* Simon barely managed to keep his feet on the gravel path for a moment before his momentum carried him forward, and he slipped off the edge and into blackness.

Thump. The fall took no more than a moment, with the ground beneath the shadow hidden by a few feet of darkness. Simon fell hard on his backside, and the jarring pain traveled up his spine and made his teeth click together. A rich, thick laughter filled his ears, and when Simon regained his footing, he turned to see his captor hunched over, laughing merrily at the young man's plight.

"Better watch where you are going, young one. I would hate to have you break your neck before we could even have a conversation." Casually, the man hopped down. "What is your name? What is it?"

Simon spoke his name, rubbing his backside as he stood.

"Simon? Simon. Good name. I like it. You may call me Scipio." Here, the man made a bow. "I have been called many names, been given many titles, but I have always enjoyed Scipio. Master Scipio is also acceptable, but not necessary. In my experience, a man earns his titles."

Scipio smiled a malevolent smile, but Simon did not understand why. The evil that danced on the man's chiseled jaw disappeared as quickly as it appeared, replaced with benign placidity. "Now, let's continue forward. Well, downward, I should say."

The "mouth" that Simon had fallen into was a collection of stone steps leading into the mound, downward into darkness. The gravel path lay above him, and the green light was slowly beginning to fade as the dark storm clouds once again obscured the sun's golden rays.

Scipio briefly disappeared into the darkness to Simon's left, then returned carrying two torches that had somehow managed to appear in his hands. "Wood and flame are two lovers, destined to meet and destroy each other," he said with a smile as he outstretched his hand.

Simon didn't even react, being so used to the madness of the day that one more statement of insanity did not even reach the threshold of his capacity for the strange. He quietly grabbed the torch and began walking into the darkness, careful not to repeat his previous blunder.

Scipio followed, and, on his lips, a nameless tune hummed that bore a cadence fit for marching.

Together they walked. Deeper and deeper into the darkness they went. The steps beneath their feet were smooth stone, and the air became cooler the more they descended. Simon heard the dripping of water to his right and wondered just how big the cavern was. The light of the torches illuminated the stairs and his companion, but outside of a few precious feet, darkness reigned supreme, threatening to engulf the tiny light in his outstretched hand. It was an inky blackness, a dark that had a pressure to it, and Simon could feel it try to settle on his already-shaking shoulders.

Get it together, man. You've been in darkness before. Just relax and keep walking. What's the worst that can happen? Skippy kills you? Good. Start over again. Maybe go back to Elysium and stay for a while. Shoulders straightening, pushing back against the weight of bleak blackness, Simon trudged on.

Walking in silence, deep within his own thoughts, Simon almost missed the flicker of light ahead. A tiny golden speck had become barely visible, hundreds of feet down from where he stood. The tiny orb of light, in such contrast to the gloom all around the travelers, gave Simon hope. He did not know why. Perhaps it was a primal love of light kicking in, but he felt his pace quicken as he walked down the stone steps.

The curve of golden light expanded the more he made his descent, and soon, Simon could make out an arched opening, a doorway in solid rock at the end of the seemingly endless flight of stairs. Briefly, he wondered if Skippy, the nickname sticking in his head, had led him to meet Satan himself, but he quickly pushed the thought away. *Ol' Skippy here would probably scare the devil, anyway.* The flickering light had grown larger and larger, and soon Simon could almost make out figures on the other side of the doorway, shadowy shapes that flitted around the light like moths.

Simon's stride lengthened. The archway soon loomed large over him, and Simon saw, intricately carved in the stone, dancing figures of scantily dressed nymphs and dryads running slowly from reed pipe-playing satyrs. Occasionally, a satyr would catch a beautiful maiden, and the coupling that resulted made Simon quickly look away, his cheeks flaring. Looking down, Simon passed through the archway, hands fidgeting with the green ribbon tied at his wrist, and with the knife with the well-worn handle still stuck in his waistband.

As soon as he stepped through the archway, the world dilated wildly in scope, like the iris of an eye plunged into near darkness. A giant cavern opened before him, the ceiling of which Simon could not see. Giant mountains stood in the distance, stoic and snow-capped, rising into the shadows above and nestling a town of picturesque perfection below. Red-roofed cabins lay nuzzled in the protective nook of the mountain range, and a slow river wound through the middle of the village, sliding from the mountains, under a collection of stone bridges, and off into the darkness. For light, the same flowers that Simon had seen the night before spouted their phosphorescent orbs, creating a canopy of fireflies and stars, bathing the world in twilight.

This place feels old, *like an ancient dream.* Shaking his head, Simon continued walking with the long-haired fellow toward the pristine little village. *Jesus Christ, I've got to keep my head on a swivel. I bet this is the place Thales was taking me to. Full of psychopaths and nut jobs, just like Skippy over here.*

"I know what you are thinking." The sudden speech from Scipio made Simon jump. "You are thinking that this place is the root of all evil, the navel of corruption and wrong-doing. You, my new friend, could not be further from the truth. This place, called Nisadi, *not* Sanke or any of the other vulgar names used for it, is the place of freedom, the place where true humanity can blossom."

Simon did not reply, choosing instead to remain silent. *He sounds like a serial killer explaining why all the people had to die, why their deaths lead him to Nirvana. Freaking psychopath. Skippy the Psychopath—that's what his name should be.* Seeing that his fellow traveler wasn't going to respond, Scipio continued, picking up a stone and tossing it from one hand to the other.

"You see, Simian. *Simian?* That doesn't sound right."

"Simon."

"Right, Simon. You see, Simon, we are told how to live, how to act, how to speak, from the moment we draw our first breath. We are governed by instinct and by society that reinforces that instinct, and we are kept in line by civilization that rose from our primitive needs. We are supposed to be born, live according to these rules, die, and be done with it. Yet I ask you: How did we arrive here? How are we not dead?"

Simon didn't speak at first, but the words of Scipio tickled something in his mind. *He's right. He's a psychopath still, and I'm waiting for the other shoe to drop with this nutcase, but Skippy has a point.* Scipio stared at Simon, obviously waiting for a response, which he blurted out quickly.

"We aren't dead. We aren't dead because we transcended our instinctual self. We survived because we became something other than human."

"Exactly correct! We *transcended* ourselves, became more than we were meant to be, and, as such, became eternal." The tone of Scipio became more feverish, and he stopped, grabbing Simon's arm and turning him until he came face-to-face with the shirtless man. His bright eyes burned.

"So, why is it, why do we have to complete these so-called Journeys ..." Scipio spat on the ground and angrily threw the rock he was carrying, "... if the only way we made it here in the first place is because we did *not* cater to who we were? Does that make any sense? No! Why should we complete these Journeys, only to die like the rest of humanity? It's madness!"

Both of Scipio's hands clasped Simon's narrow shoulders. Simon was surprised to discover that the shorter man's grips were like iron.

"This is why we have come to Nisadi, why Nisadi exists at all. We who live here are the true seekers of immortality, the ones who desire to live forever, the ones who refuse to submit to the yoke of our own instinctual impulses! We are free, Simon, free of the tyranny of ourselves. How can anyone in their right mind argue with such truth?"

Simon stood, locked in the oppressive grip of Scipio, uncertain what to do. *Should I respond to him? Does he want me to talk to him at all? Why won't he let me go?* Slowly, Simon smiled as best as he could and nodded his head. Scipio, the feverish light disappearing from his eyes, released him, and, with a sigh, he turned back to the road and began walking toward the red-roofed houses before him.

"Sometimes, it is best if you are shown, rather than told. I still need my breakfast, and you still need to be convinced. Perhaps we can do both of these at once." Scipio brightened again and, leading Simon by the arm, began to walk more rapidly into the village. Simon quietly followed, resigned to his fate, whatever that might be.

The first home was slightly removed from the rest, its red roof reflecting dully in the firefly light. Beautiful roses of an amazing variety of hues blossomed from the ground in front of an intricately carved wooden door, and roses seemed to grow out of the polished wood and fuse with the logs that formed the cabin's walls. Simon could not help but feel awed by the craftsmanship and beauty of the entrance. He stood open-mouthed as the carved thorns and leaves of roses intertwined with the polished grain of the wood, growing and blooming into beautiful flowers. The walls were alive and writhing with a magical energy, and Simon felt his mind slip and fall into its hypnotic embrace.

Scipio, by contrast, did not even give the walls and wooden doorway a second glance and instead gripped the worn brass handle that poked out from the polished plank and pushed his way inside. Simon, snapped out of his reverie by the movement, followed the shirtless man into the interior of the expertly crafted cabin.

The cabin was a singular room, made cozy by a cheery fire in the far corner of the place. The flame, rather than being kept in a traditional fireplace, was instead free-floating, a luminous teardrop that crackled and produced a calming heat yet somehow managed to not expel any smoke. The light from the suspended flame cast shadows upon a well-worn, comfortable red lounge chair just near the edge of visibility, and a large, rectangular table grown from the middle of the floor and blossoming into a flat surface was full of food of every description. Simon's mouth watered, and his stomach grumbled as he gazed at the mountain of grapes, apples, and cheeses, and the mountain of what looked to be large slabs of bacon made an actual moan run from his lips.

His mind quickly did a backflip. *It's poison. This is some sick trick by Skippy the Psychopath so he can watch me die, rolling on the floor and choking on my own puke. He's lulling me into a false sense of security, I bet.* Simon gazed longingly at the table of splendid delicacies and forced his hands to remain at their sides.

Unconcerned with Simon's plight, Scipio sat down at the head of the giant table, plopping his backside on a perfectly smooth stump, and began to grab and devour whatever his hands could reach. Grapes and apples, boiled eggs and fresh apricots, all made the increasingly quick trip from his hands to his open mouth. Convinced that the food wasn't all poison, Simon sat down and began to eat as well, though he was careful to only eat the items that Scipio himself had indulged in.

"Did I tell you that you were allowed to eat?"

Mouth open and hand outstretched, Simon froze. His eyes turned to gaze at Scipio, whose face had turned to a mask of fury. Egg and cheese stuck to his chin, and his hand, covered with the juice of some fruit, fused into a fist with a single, accusatory finger jutting toward Simon.

"Did I say that you could take my food? Answer me!" The pitch of Scipio's voice rose, and his free hand gripped the table. To Simon, it almost appeared as though the shirtless man were preparing to spring from his chair and throttle the youth where he sat.

"Answer me now, young one, or I swear by the balls of Jupiter that I will rip your eyes out and use your skull as a goblet while you still breathe."

"No. I—I am sorry. I should have asked." Simon's hands shook as he slowly replaced the cheese to its original home, once again an adornment on a bright silver platter.

Uproarious laughter exploded from Scipio's large mouth, and perfect white teeth popped in the firelight as his lips peeled back in his merriment. Cheese and crumbs exploded out of his mouth as he roared, and his olive skin became purple with mirth. Simon, if he had been frozen before, could have made marble look as fluid as water, by comparison. He sat, still as a rocky outcrop, and waited for Scipio to stop his merry outburst. Soon, his laughter died down, replaced by the occasional giggle and cough.

"Of course you should not ask! Why would you ask? You saw something that you wanted, that you *needed,* and you took it. What is wrong with such a thing?"

Simon, still reeling from the belief that he was about to be unceremoniously murdered, remained still. Scipio, still chuckling, returned to devouring everything he could reach.

"Please, eat, eat, and enjoy it! It is yours."

Simon slowly reached out to a small loaf of bread to his left, pulled it apart, and began to chew. It was warm in the center with a flaky crust, and the soft middle seemed to melt in his mouth. He added a slice of white sharp cheese to the next piece, and the flavor of sweet cream and almonds encircled his taste buds. Simon's stomach growled, and, with his fear momentarily forgotten, he dug into the feast with relish. He barely cared that Scipio had begun to stare at him, a dangerous glint in his eyes. *Whatever. It's not poison, so at least I'll die with a full stomach.* Simon smiled back at the man and continued filling his hands and cheeks. The bacon was particularly delicious, and the wine that he found in a carafe to his left was dry and fresh, with a hint of melon. He ate until he could eat no more.

Satisfied, Simon stretched and tried to lean back, forgetting that there was no back to his chair. He nearly toppled over onto his head and only barely managed to catch himself by flailing his arms rapidly. His stomach tried to jump out of his mouth and help catch him before he fell, but instead of helping, it almost emptied its contents on Simon's shirt. Squawking and cursing until the small backless chair righted itself, Simon wasn't even remotely surprised to hear the laughter of Scipio emanating from the head of the table when the stool stopped its infuriating attempt to dump the youth off of its back.

"Well, my young friend, now that you have remembered how gravity works, let's talk. I know that your name is Simon, and I know that you haven't Returned many times, if at all. So, tell me: What have you learned of this world? What do you think of it? I wish to hear your story, and …" A large finger came up and pointed at Simon. "… don't leave anything out. Tell me absolutely every detail."

Elbows on the table, head cupped in his hands, Scipio leaned forward, looking for all the world like an attentive listener, a child waiting for a fascinating tale of wonder and intrigue to begin.

Simon, haltingly at first, began to tell the long-haired man of his life in Dara. In fact, he was surprised to discover just how easy it was to tell the shirtless man all he had endured since first arriving on the strange alternative plane of existence he now called home. Scipio would ask pointed questions at certain parts of the narrative and had an off-putting second sense about moments when Simon tried to leave details or people out of his story. Every time he thought he could hide a certain embarrassing fact or particular sad moment, Scipio's eyes would narrow, and he would threaten to torture or murder Simon if he did not tell the whole truth. Simon, eyes widening and heart quickening, would hasten to explain his misstep or his attempt at glossing over certain information, then would recount the moment in full.

When Simon came to the part about the amoral invader in the tree house who had killed his caretaker Mary, a strange cloud covered Scipio's vision. When Simon stopped to look again at the odd shirtless man's change in expression, Scipio had returned to his slightly amused, attentive self, and, if he was being honest, Simon couldn't be sure that he had seen anything at all. When he reached the point in his story when he had recently fallen asleep under the tree, Scipio interjected, "And that's where I came in!" and stood, signaling that the narrative was over—for Simon, at least.

Simon leaned forward, finding himself to be out of breath, and sat quietly, elbows on the exquisite table, waiting for what Scipio would say next. The shirtless man paced around the room, hands clasped behind his back. He began speaking to Simon as he moved, the kilt he was wearing swaying back and forth as he walked.

"You see, Simon, you have fallen into the great trap that so many have been victim to when they first enter this wonderful place. They believe these so-called *Journeys* must be complete in order to experience enlightenment, inner peace, or some other pile of goat dung. They see that when they don't follow along with their instinct—with what drives them—the world becomes tougher, more unbearable, and they give up!" Scipio snapped his fingers at the last, causing a jolt to ricochet up Simon's spine. *Jesus Christ, this guy has me on edge,* Simon thought.

"And what does that sound like to you?" Scipio asked. "Eh? To always move in a certain way? Always remain where you are intended to be?" Scipio stopped, staring at Simon, seemingly waiting for a reply. When he received none, he pointed at Simon again and continued. "How did you get here? By living exactly in accordance with your instinct and needs? No! You did something that placed you outside of the human condition. Something so terrible or so giving or so unique that it ripped your consciousness away from your flesh and made your soul separate from your human self. And now, you are here. You are immortal! You are in paradise!"

265

Scipio raised his arms, seemingly to embrace the world around him. His sharp nose and bright eyes made him appear to be a bird of prey in the midst of taking flight. "I tell you true: Journeys are only the universe attempting to return you, your consciousness, to the eternal ether, for you to simply cease to exist. This entire place was not *supposed* to have been created, and the universe is trying to right its wrong."

The words spoken by the man, seemingly rattled off from a script, tickled a memory in Simon, and he thought of a clearing in a forest, of a portly man doomed to wander for millennia. *Is Paracelsus one of them? Is he one of these psychopaths?* Yet despite himself, Simon felt some truth ring in Scipio's words. He hated himself for how much he was agreeing with the shirtless man parading around inside the small cabin. Scipio continued his speech, returning to pacing back and forth in the single room.

"However, Nisadi refuses to bend under the yoke of oppression, and instead stands tall, rigid in its decision to fight for freedom from the tyranny of finite existence!" Suddenly, Scipio stopped, eyes looking past Simon and through him, chest heaving as the impassioned words were expelled from his mouth. "Here, in this place, there is truth. Here, in Nisadi, there is freedom. And for that, we are shunned from other societies, pushed away by those who would, even after all they have experienced here, still search for death's embrace. It's madness, I tell you, madness!"

With the last, Scipio had become red in the face, and veins bulged out of his forehead. *Careful, Skippy, you might blow a blood vessel.* "I controlled thousands of men, led legions to their death, all for the glory to believe that my name would live on for eternity through the annals of history. Why should I, after achieving actual immortality, work consciously toward reversing my eternal presence? It makes no sense!"

With his eyes locked onto Simon, the now-sweating Scipio walked up and towered over the youth, who was still seated on his stool. Simon felt a stab of fear but forced it down. Sweat beaded on Scipio's forehead, and when he leaned in, he smelled of lemon and garlic.

"Well? Do you understand? Do you understand how crazy it is to accept and attempt to complete one's Journey? Well?"

Simon sat perfectly still, looking up at the looming Scipio, uncertain what to say. Moments passed, and Simon realized that Scipio was actually waiting for some sort of response. Simon cleared his throat.

"We might go somewhere else, though, right? If there is a place like this one, why can't there be another one like it?"

Scipio waved Simon's comments away like an annoying flying insect and stepped back. Simon heaved a sigh of relief as the sandals and kilt slid away from him. Scipio kept his back turned to Simon for a moment, shaking his head at the apparent ignorance of the younger man's comment. Eventually, he turned around, and his sharp nose and aquiline jaw were turned slightly downward, as if he were addressing a child who had managed to accomplish a task of unfathomable stupidity.

"Look around you, Simon. How many friends and family have you met? How many people are even here at all? Even in my own time, there were men and women of glorious renown who never came here, simply because they stayed within their instinctual drives. The warrior general that I managed to defeat, and in so doing save my country, did not even make it to Dara, and he almost brought the known world to its knees! So, my young friend, if the chances that we have made it *here* are as slim as they are, what do you think the chances are that you would end up at the *next* plane, if there is a world after this one? And I am still not convinced such a place exists at all. No, we are here, we are immortal, and that is enough. It should be enough!"

The last statement he made seemed to be to himself, and Scipio turned and looked down at the glossy wooden floorboards as he spoke the words.

Simon, against his better judgement, against the experiences of his past, felt himself beginning to agree, at least in part, with what this madman was saying. *There is no proof that a place after this one exists, so who's to say there even is a next phase? The next phase might just be death. Why can't we just be happy with the fact that we aren't dead now, we can simply Return every time we die? What is wrong with that?*

The more Simon thought about the words of Scipio, the more they began to make sense. Nihilistic and defeatist as they may have been, the words of Scipio began to worm their way into Simon's head, to become truth. Simon was soon nodding to the logic of Scipio, stepping to the beat of his drum, and he hated himself for it. *Mary, Thales, I'm sorry, but it makes sense. Too much sense.* Simon rubbed the ribbon on his wrist and felt his cheeks redden. *I'm sorry.*

Scipio, seeming to notice the acceptance growing on Simon's face, smiled and placed a hand on the young man's shoulder. "You are beginning to see. You are starting to understand the lie that you were told since you were born here. There is no after, there is no new plane. All we have is this life, all we have is this existence, and once you realize that to be true, you will discover you already have found paradise. Everything you wished for is yours: all your hopes, desires, and dreams. You simply have to reach out your hand and take it!"

Scipio gripped an invisible desire in his fist and brought his clenched hand to Simon's face to illustrate his point.

Simon sat still, letting all that Scipio said sink in. *I can do whatever I want, whenever I want, however I want? That sounds pretty goddamned wonderful. Why not give this a try? Why not see what this place has to offer? Why the hell not? What is the worst that could happen, really? I'm wrong, I die, and I come back to try again? Sounds good to me.*

Simon looked up at the shirtless man, who had not removed his hand from Simon's shoulder and was looking back at him intently, waiting for a reply. "I want to believe you. I really do. But it just *feels* wrong. I don't *want* to die; I want to live. But I can't shake the fact that I need—I need a *purpose* for living."

"Of course, of course! Now we come to the truth of it. So many of us human beings believe there is a lofty goal, a divine path, for us to follow. We must suffer, sacrifice, and die for the greater good? Jupiter's balls, boy. That is the biggest lie of them all. Did you know I was a general? A damn good one, too. I had thousands of men willing to fight for me and die for me, all for the greater good, for the glory of our country. Do you know how many of my men I met while here? Guess how many men I was convinced were going to live forever in the glorious afterlife of a soldier ended up walking eternity with me. Now guess how many I found in Dara."

The question hung unanswered between them, filling the room with its silence. After a few moments, Scipio spoke again.

"The truth is, the powerful few have always manipulated the masses to suit their own ends, even if that means eternal sleep for those who swore devotion to them. We do not need to believe that lie anymore, for here, we are free! Imagine all the things you have ever wanted to do, ever wanted to *feel,* and make it so." Scipio stepped away and walked toward the door.

"You must see the world as it should be; mere words will not do it justice. Come with me, see Nisadi for what it is, and you will see that I speak truth. Come, Simon, and see what Dara truly can be!" With a magnanimous flourish, Scipio threw the door open and stepped out.

I can see why men would follow this man, Simon thought as he started toward the door with barely a hesitation. *All right, Skippy, let's see what you mean. I hate that you make so much sense.* Simon walked out of the small cabin and back into twilight.

He found Scipio waiting outside the open door, standing on the path that wound toward the other idyllic red-roofed houses. Seeing Simon emerge, the man smiled and began walking shoulder-to-shoulder with him, occasionally pointing out houses and the names of the residents.

"See that house with the gilded lions out front? That's the home of Xerxes. See the place where the light seems to run from? That's the home of Crowley. He and I never seemed to get along. And see over here..."

Scipio rattled on, stating his personal views on one resident or another, the sound of his voice sliding in and out of the sound of the bubbling brook that rolled through the center of the twilight village.

Simon found himself hypnotized by the light, by the murmur of the water, and by the perfect watercolor landscape he found himself in. He watched as two people, an ancient man and a stout woman, stopped and began chatting near the worn path. She was in her middle years, with a handsome face and curly hair that was nearly white, and he was ancient, his head egg-shaped and full of veins and his skin wrinkled and liver-spotted. The woman placed her arms around his feeble shoulders, and he leaned into her in a familiar embrace, a small smile on his lips as he murmured something to his companion. They seemed at peace.

"And those two, that is Danu and Tiberius. If you ever have a moment, stop and listen to those two speak. It is fascinating, to say the least. I thought that Tiberius and I would get along when he first came here, but, if I am being honest, I can hardly stand him at all. So much complaining and backstabbing. Now, Danu, *she's* an absolute pleasure. Real old-religion, backed by some interesting philosophies. One night, we were chatting, and she…"

Scipio rattled on, but Simon had completely lost his ability to pay attention to what the general had to say, as Danu, still holding the embrace of Tiberius, had pulled a small knife out of the folds of her grey wool dress and thrust the blade up and under the chin of her companion. The old man gurgled, flailed feebly at the knife handle, then collapsed and lay still. Simon froze, his jaw hanging open.

"…which is why, to this day, I hate the taste of olives. What are you doing? Why have you stopped?" Scipio turned to look at Simon, then at the mature woman who unceremoniously placed her foot on the prone form of Tiberius and yanked her knife out of his still-bleeding skull. He heard a crack as old bones snapped under the weight of the woman's foot.

Scipio stopped and watched with Simon as Danu wiped the red-stained blade on the tunic of her fallen comrade and made the sharp tool disappear back into its grey woolen hiding place. Seeing that she was being watched, the stout woman came forward and greeted the pair, with a surprisingly warm smile for Simon and a hearty embrace for Scipio.

"Scipio, you handsome devil, how are you this morning? Well-fed, I hope? And who is this fine-looking young man?" Danu placed her hands on her hips as she looked at Scipio's companion. She really must have once been beautiful, and still would be, if it weren't for the blood staining her cheek and hands. *One day, just once, I will wake up and not be in a place that scares the holy hell out of me. Jesus Christ, why is everything so damn terrifying?*

"Scipio, why is your friend looking at me like I just killed his favorite dog? Is it because of old Tiberius here?" The concern remained on Danu's face, and she moved one blood-stained hand up, cupping the face of Simon. "He *asked* for me to do it, child. He wanted to be a babe again, wanted to feel the fire of youth. He was tired of living in his ancient, worn-down body. It was a mercy, I promise."

That kind smile stayed on her lips, and Simon found himself, surprisingly, smiling back. He remembered a hospital bed, an ancient body fighting for survival and failing. *I can't blame the man. Hell, if I knew I would come back, I would have pulled the plug myself when I was back on Earth. It would have been a damn mercy.* Simon felt a connection to this woman, to her kind face and smile, and he began to see her less as a murderer and more as a guardian angel, as an arbiter of peace.

Danu, seeing Simon's change of view marked upon his face, released him from her embrace and turned back to Scipio. "He's young and fresh, but I think he will be an excellent addition to our little community. Have you called a Gathering?"

"We have only just arrived. I was going to call one for the evening. Would you mind helping me spread the word, letting everyone know we have someone new for our little village?" Scipio smiled, again resting his hand on Simon's shoulder.

Simon felt as though he had missed something, that he had somehow agreed to be a part of this place and instantly forgot it. *I knew it. They are going to torture me in front of the entire village. I knew I was a hostage. I should have run!*

Fuming inwardly, Simon tried to retain a calm exterior, making sure to look Scipio in the face as he spoke. "A Gathering? What is that? And I don't recall agreeing to live here."

Scipio turned his face uncomfortably close to Simon's. His breath smelled of cheese and apricots. "Don't you see, Simon? Don't you understand yet? You have agreed to live here because you agree with *why* we live here. I can see it on your face, hear it in the stories you told me. I know because of your actions on the bridge. You are beginning to understand that this place, this plane after death, is paradise if we make it so. It is because of this that you will belong here in Nisadi."

Scipio turned away from Simon, facing Danu again. "However, you also need to be introduced to the community. We would hate to have anything ... *untoward* ... happen to you, and the best way for that not to happen is to introduce you to everyone en masse. That is what a Gathering is. Danu, would you mind terribly telling everyone of our new friend and finding someone appropriate to be Master of ceremonies?" A small smile that did not touch his eyes graced Scipio's lips. Danu, smiling back her kind, knowing smile, nodded, gave Simon a kiss on the cheek and Scipio another hug, and walked away.

Scipio, arm now draped over Simon's shoulders, led the youth back down the road, once again pointing out various residents, their histories, and his personal relationship to them. Simon barely heard him as he fell deep into thought, wondering what a Gathering truly was and why so many people had to meet him at once. He disappeared into his mind, and his feet kept pace with Scipio, like a soldier keeping time.

The village was spread evenly between the gurgling stream, with red-roofed homes dotting both sides of the riverbank. Stone bridges made of singular slabs of sparkling granite were dotted throughout the village, and the shining stone reflected the light of the phosphorus orbs that were emitted by the strange white flowers. Scipio had called them star flowers, and Simon felt that the name did the pale plants justice. They were dotted all over Nisadi, which was good, because it appeared as though they were the only source of light in this twilight town under a hill.

The dark stream wound around slick river rocks further upstream, and Simon was shocked and delighted when he noticed the large, smooth stones were in fact caricatures of men and women, of animals and plants, that flowed and danced to the rhythm of the water. The place was mystically beautiful, nestled perfectly between the darkness and the light, the day and the night, the majestic and the terrifying. Long shadows danced, and Simon kept his eyes moving.

The people of Nisadi were as varied as everywhere else in Dara, with clothing of all ages represented and all races, colors, and creeds milling about their homes and the road that Scipio and Simon walked. Simon noticed there were no shops, unlike in the other towns he had visited, and wondered in passing how the people of Nisadi acquired the goods they needed. Yet that thought was instantly stripped from his mind as a woman, tall and nimble, with the body of a deer and the eyes of a tiger, slid past him with a grace that matched a reed blowing slightly in the breeze. But it wasn't her grace that caused Simon to stop; it was the fact that she was without a stitch of clothing on her entire body.

Simon stared open-mouthed as she strode down the road to a bend in the stream and slid sinuously into the cold water. Simon's eyes darted about, looking for someone to confirm what he saw with their own expression of surprise and confusion. However, as he looked about him, Simon was surprised to see that no one seemed to have noticed the woman at all. Scipio kept talking, people continued walking, and

Simon was left feeling like a pervert who peeked in on someone taking a bath. Face red, he continued walking with Scipio, making a point to not look down at the slow-moving water or at the woman splashing there. *Calm down. This isn't even the weirdest thing you have seen today.* Simon shook his head, smiled slightly, and kept walking.

Scipio stopped suddenly in front of a dwelling with a roof that seemed a darker shade of red, deeper in hue than the others that surrounded it. "Well, I don't know about you, but I could use a drink. All this talking has made me quite parched. What do you say we go inside and have some wine?"

Simon nodded, and Scipio turned toward the entrance to the house. The small pathway was bordered by purple flowers, their tiny petals tipped with yellow. The door itself was solid polished oak, with a man's bearded face carved into its middle. The beard rustled in an invisible wind as it was pushed open, and Simon swore that the carving's eyes followed him as he and Scipio entered the sparsely lit abode.

The sounds of laughter and the tinkling of glasses filled the air. Candlelight flickered, and Simon could make out dark shapes sliding about as he stepped inside. The room became even darker as the door shut behind him, and it took a moment for the young man's eyes to adjust to the dimness.

Men and women moved about slowly, sliding in and out of shadows, filling pewter cups from a giant barrel that encompassed all of the room's back wall. Giant tables with log benches stretched the length of the single room, and wax candles were strewn about the entirety of the place, sending off an odor of beeswax and a floral note that Simon could not place. When a man, eyes glassy and grin cockeyed, splashed a little of his drink on the table near Simon's left hand, the smell of honey and the tang of alcohol filled the air.

Scipio, leaving Simon's side with a pat on the shoulder, grabbed an empty cup, filled it from the giant barrel's tap, and sat down at a table near a woman who nearly spilled out of her dress and onto his lap. She laughed, a hearty guffaw that matched the size of her chest, and she leaned her head against his bare shoulder. Scipio, seeming to barely notice his new companion, reached past her, grabbed another empty glass, and handed it to Simon, who took the cup and filled it to the brim with a golden liquid that came out slowly, almost like a syrup.

He sat down and tasted the beverage, and honey filled his mouth, coating his tongue with its sweet song. It was delicious and strong, and Simon could feel it warming his entire body from just that one sip. He smiled and had another. The knot of fear that had lived in his stomach since he first set foot in this strange land under the hill began to loosen.

Scipio had already downed his first glass, and as he stood for another, his bawdy female companion fell forward onto the table and, after a mumbled curse, fell soundly asleep. Simon, taking a sharp inhale, drank all of the contents of his glass as well, deciding it was an excellent time to become intoxicated, and to hell with everyone and everything else. He stood, filled his glass again, and emptied it in one gulp. This process continued over and over, and with each sip of the golden, viscous fluid, Simon's plight became less and less terrible. The words of Scipio became more reasonable, and the people in the dimly lit abode became friendlier—and, decidedly, more attractive. Simon smiled at a young woman across the table, and the expression was returned. *This place really isn't that bad. Maybe I can get used to it here.* Simon finished yet another cup and sighed as his entire body began to uncoil.

After the fifth cup of honey wine, when the world had become warm and bathed in a soft golden light, Simon stumbled over to the shirtless form of Scipio, who had taken up residence at another end of the dimly lit room. Simon poured himself onto the bench on the opposite side of the long table where his companion had seated himself. The man's skin had taken on a red hue, and a crooked grin seemed to have permanently affixed itself to his face. He sat sandwiched between two equally inebriated individuals—a man and a woman, him with dark skin and a severe face and her with flaming red hair and emerald eyes that seemed to devour everything she looked upon.

"Simon! Jupiter's balls, where have you been? I was just about to spread the word of your Gathering. Sit here with Maeve and Sunni, and … and I'm going to tell everyone."

Scipio's words had a slight slur, like his tongue had been dipped in honey. He flashed a crooked smile at Simon, then blatantly looked down the blouse of Maeve, who shook her shoulders at him and slapped him in the face with a long, pale hand. Scipio stood up with shocking speed, his eyes blazing at the woman with the flaming red hair. He raised his fist to his face, preparing to strike the woman. Without breaking eye contact, the green-eyed lady casually reached between Scipio's legs, giving a tender squeeze. A lilted voice, smoky and sweet, slipped from full lips as the woman spoke, her hand slowly massaging Scipio.

"Oh come now, you know I love ta play wit me food before I devour it." She stood, slowly kissed Scipio full on the mouth, and, without another word, slipped away like a spirit of wind and trees.

Scipio stood, slack-jawed, and stared at the crowd that the red hair and green eyes had disappeared into. After a moment, he shook his head, muttered something that Simon couldn't quite understand, and turned back to face him.

"Don't wander off, or I'll cut your balls off and give them to Maeve as earrings." With a chortle, Scipio wandered unsteadily away to tell everyone his news, leaving Simon alone with his new compatriot, the dark-skinned man with the intense gaze. Simon smiled and lifted his pewter cup.

"Nice to you meet me. I'm me, ugh, Simon." Simon worriedly mumbled then nervously giggled. Sunni gazed into Simon, dark eyes unreadable as the candlelight flickered off nearly black pupils. Silence stretched for an uncomfortable amount of time, and the grin on Simon's face withered. Suddenly, the dark-skinned man smiled, the smile of a predator looking at a small animal trapped in a snare. The expression change was so swift that it almost felt as though Simon had been struck.

"It is nice to meet you, my new friend. Scipio tells me that you are from the most recent time and that you only just arrived here in Dara. I would love to know about your time, how the world has changed." Those dark eyes were unfathomable pools of history. *This is a man I would follow into the lion's den. Lions? Jesus Christ, I must be drunk.*

"Tell me of your time. What are the people like? Do they look like you or me? How is my empire? How is the kingdom of the Songhai?" Those eyes flickered, but only for a moment, before they returned to their unreadable pools.

Simon said he did not know what a Songhai was, or of any empire by that name. He tried to explain how his government had worked, how democracy ruled his old country, but Sunni simply shook his head, disbelief marking his features. He simply could not accept that "the rabble" could rule themselves. He did not believe for a moment that the world wouldn't descend into chaos without the strong hand of a capable ruler to guide it.

Soon, Simon gave up and resigned himself to simply telling his new drinking buddy about his old home, his old profession, and the various adventures his career landed him in. The wine had loosened his tongue, and he was happy to speak about a time when he felt at least a semblance of control. In the middle of his explanation of microwaves, Maeve returned, squeezing next to Sunni, and seemed to be enraptured by Simon's tale. Simon loved the attention the beautiful woman was giving his story, so he couldn't help but embellish some of his own exploits as he spoke.

"So there I was, alone, no bullets—*bullets,* they are like little metal arrows that go real, real fast into people. Boom! Anyway, I'm surrounded by these guys selling this drug called cocaine. Well, you guys don't really care about drugs, but we did—to stop crime. Crime would be much lower if drugs weren't criminalized and instead were just regulated," Simon coughed, not wanting to overthink what he just said.

"So, here they come, and they are *mad,* and I didn't know what to do. Back-up wasn't there yet, and I had only been on the job a few years, so I decided to take a chance. I jumped in my car, punched the gas, and drove it right toward them. A car—it's like a horse with wheels and no horses. So, I jumped out of the car right before it hit this warehouse they were all in, and *boom!* Explosions. How was I supposed to know there were explosives in there? But you know what? Took almost a million dollars of coke off the street that day. Lots of paperwork, but man, it felt good to blow something up. And not die. Didn't want to die." Simon laughed at that, spilling more of his drink on the floor.

Maeve, emerald eyes flashing, spoke when Simon had finally stopped talking long enough to take a breath.

"You were a warrior, like us. That is why you understand this place. That is why you can embrace Nisadi. You understand what it is like to risk all, not knowing that there is another side waiting for you when you die. So now, when you have a chance to live forever and never truly feel that fear again, why wouldn't you?"

Maeve's voice felt like smoke rolling over a bog, earthy and mysterious and not quite human. Sunni nodded and leaned back as he drained the rest of his cup. Haltingly, he stood and stumbled toward the barrel, leaving Simon and Maeve alone. The red-haired woman leaned against Simon, the smell of alcohol on her lips and her body warm underneath her green dress.

"Here, we take what we want, do what we want, live how we want, and if we do not like where we are…" Slowly, with effort, Maeve snapped her fingers. "…we start over. There is no limit to the joys, to

278

the ecstasy of the world in which you now live. We are in paradise, and we rule as gods."

Before Simon could reply, Maeve's lips covered his, and with a strength that surprised him, she pushed him to the ground and straddled him, her green dress pushed up to her waist. Simon's breath became ragged as he disappeared into her embrace, and soon, all was ice and fire, prolonged pain and sweet heat. Simon was happily devoured by it.

CHAPTER XVII–AMID A CROWD

"Simon. Simon! Get up. It's time." A blurred shape dominated his vision, and Simon felt a blunt object prodding his rib. Rubbing his eyes with his palms, Simon's eyesight sharpened, and the form of Scipio came into focus, his sandaled foot gently kicking the young man's rib cage.

"Come on, you can't miss the Gathering." Scipio smiled and unceremoniously dumped ice-cold water on Simon's face.

Spluttering and coughing, Simon clambered to his feet. The room spun a few times, and Simon nearly emptied his stomach before the world regained its balance. Rubbing his eyes again, Simon pushed his now-wet hair out of his eyes. Scipio, seeing that his young ward had arisen, walked out of the door.

Quickly looking about him for Maeve, Simon was struck with embarrassment as he realized that his pants, so hastily pushed down, never made it back to their original position around his waist. As he glanced about him, Simon stood and jerked his leggings back up, tying them at the waist. *Where's my knife? Where is my damn knife?*

Simon looked around, checking the floor and under the tables, but all he found was dirt, disregarded cups, a single moccasin, and solid wood floors. Fear that had been muted by the mead came rushing back, as Simon's only weapon, his last connection to Mary and Thales, seemed to have disappeared. Bent double, Simon frantically searched for his knife among the cups, husks, and bits of food that had found their way to the floor.

"Simon, I will not tell you again. Come with me. Everyone is waiting." Scipio had popped his head back inside the dimly lit room, twilight creeping inside the dark hall. With another quick look around, the youth joined Scipio at the door and stepped outside. *God, I hope I don't need that knife at this Gathering thing.* Peering back at the dimly lit hall one last time, Simon realized that it was empty. He sent a silent prayer of thanks to whatever deity was in charge of embarrassment, and another pleading for safety to whomever was in charge of the well-being of reincarnated teenagers, and he slipped out the door and back into the wide world outside.

The light of the star flowers remained the same, but the air was cooler than when Simon and Scipio first stepped inside the dark-roofed building. It appeared as though the world under the mound had descended into night, or as close to night as an underground city could become.

As Scipio led him onto the beaten road, Simon looked about him and saw that the entire town had become completely depleted of its occupants, lending an unsettling air to an already mystical world. The red roofs of the houses reflected dully, and the large mountain range seemed to have inched closer than when last seen. Even the burbling stream seemed to laugh acidly as it danced among the smooth river stones. Simon felt the slosh of the honey wine in his stomach become spiked with fear, threatening to bubble to the surface.

"Quickly now, we don't want to keep them waiting."

Scipio's tone, in stark contrast to the day before, was grave and serious as he led Simon by the arm and marched toward the tall, dark mountains. The silence was almost overbearing, and the sound of stones crunching under Simon's feet became deafening. Simon's heart began to race, and he quickly wiped sweat from his palms. His stomach was doing backflips, and his heart was in his mouth. He tugged at the green ribbon on his wrist and kept walking.

The path continued winding toward the dark mountain range, and as the houses faded away, the road became illuminated by torches that had been plunged into the ground, their pale light dancing among the shadows. The small bursts of fiery illumination made the surrounding

281

darkness a deeper shade of black, and Simon's feet began to move more quickly. Scipio, still solemn, matched Simon's pace, his face a block of granite cut at sharp angles. *Jesus Christ, I wish he wouldn't look so serious.* The constant sound of the stream disappeared after they had walked for a few minutes, and soon, the only sounds were the crackle of burning wood and the crunch of stones underfoot.

In the darkness, a large orb of light began to take shape, and dread filled Simon's heart, though he didn't know why. As he and Scipio walked, the circle became larger and larger, until Simon could see that it was a circular stone slab, about fifty feet across, its surface reflecting dully in the light of the dozens of torches that surrounded it. Figures of all shapes and sizes encircled the slab, firelight flickering in eyes that followed Scipio and Simon as they approached.

Simon, fear nearly overwhelming his faculties, felt his legs deaden underneath him. He stopped walking and began to turn around, trying to head back down the road, away from the fire and stone. *I can't deal with this. I don't even know what* this *is, but I know that I can't deal with it. I'm going to make a run for it—make for the darkness. Maybe they won't catch me.* A sharp sting pricked the small of his back, and when he turned to look, he saw the familiar glint of his knife with the well-worn handle protruding from Scipio's clenched fist.

"Walk forward, Simon. There is no choice here." The shirtless man's face was stone. The jovial nature of the long-haired man was gone, replaced by grim purpose. Simon stepped back.

"What is going on, Scipio? Why are you threatening me all of a sudden? I thought we were getting along." Simon took another step back.

"You and I were getting along, and can get along again, once this is done." Scipio stepped toward Simon, the menacing blade inching closer to the youth's stomach.

"I thought this was just to introduce me to the village. I didn't expect … all of this. I think I want to leave."

"As I said, there is no choice here. This is how you are to be introduced. There is nothing to fear, if you do as I say. Walk forward and become a part of this place. Or ..." Scipio brought the blade up to within inches of Simon's nose. "... I will leave you to the more *eccentric* residents of Nisadi. You will die, but only after every drop of suffering has been wrung from your writhing frame." Scipio spread his arms wide and shrugged. "As I said, there is no choice."

Damn him. Damn this place. Damn everything! Simon fumed silently. *I wish I could have that knife for just a few seconds. I would stick it in Skippy's eye socket.* Looking about, seeing the hopelessness of his plight, Simon begrudgingly forced his feet to move and walked to the center of the stone circle. Scipio followed, knife blade still pointed at Simon's back. As they reached the center, Scipio turned, bringing his hands up as if to embrace the world around him.

"Brothers and sisters of Nisadi, I welcome you to our Gathering of Souls. I call you here to bring another into our midst, so that he too may live the life of everlasting bliss." Scipio pointed at Simon with the knife. "I present to you: Simon, a freshly Returned soul, a warrior of his time, who wishes to shirk the yoke of Journeys, and instead live forever!"

The crowd rustled, and Simon felt the eyes of a hundred souls levelling their gaze at him, weighing him, measuring him, gauging his worth. Simon felt the fear of a child who was asked to answer a question in front of the class that he did not know the answer to—if the incorrect answer would lead to death. Simon tried to keep his breathing regular as Scipio moved about the stone circle, addressing the crowd.

"He stands before you, this youth, to tell you how he came to be, how he made it here, and what his Journey was to be. Only through truth can he be accepted into Nisadi, and only through the rejection of his Journey can he find his place among us."

Simon was struck dumb. *What the hell is he talking about? He never said I would have to do any of this. Jesus Christ, Skippy, what are you*

283

trying to make me do? As Simon stood, motionless and afraid, the crowd surrounding him became still, and Scipio's eyes, dark embers, burned into his skull. Simon, standing on this strange stage, was completely at a loss for words. Scipio stared at him, mouth screwed into a frown, then, after a few moments, addressed the crowd once again.

"We all know the truth of Nisadi. We all know that it is only through the removal of our Journeys that we can truly begin to live." Scipio came to stand behind Simon and laid the knife edge casually onto the young man's skin. "It can be difficult, this initiation, and some of us need to be convinced more than others. There are a few of you here who would like to place their hands on this young gentleman. Isn't that right, LaLaurie?"

"Too pale for my taste," a woman's voice answered, to which the crowd chuckled. Simon felt a chill run all the way down to his toes.

"Yes, but there are others who would like to use this young man, am I right?"

Murmurs of assent rippled through the crowd.

"Very well. If Simon does not speak of his Journey, of his Moment of Ascension, then he will be used for other ... *pursuits.*" The knife pushed into Simon's neck, and the warm trickle of blood slid down his chest, staining his shirt. Scipio, after leaving his mark, released the young man and stepped back, mouth closed and eyes digging deep into the back of Simon's mind. The crowd once again became silent. Simon took a deep breath.

"Everyone I have become close to, everyone who has helped me, cared for me, has died in front of my eyes. Ever since I was born into this horrible place, I have found three people to connect to—three people who have shown me true kindness—and all three have died in front of me, have died *because* of me."

Simon felt hot tears threatening to fall down his cheeks, and he took a breath, fighting to force them down. When he saw that he could not, he continued, letting the salty liquid run down his cheeks.

"A woman named Mary protected and raised me, only to be killed by someone just like *you*." Anger flared as he spoke. "As did Thales, the man who took me in when Mary was murdered. The third—the third completed his Journey because of me, which means, if I am to believe what you say, that I killed him—permanently ended his life. His not being able to Return is my fault."

Simon took another deep breath, looking around him. The crowd remained silent, and Scipio simply stared at him, a small mirthless smile on his lips. "So, I do not know what my Journey entails, how it is to end, but I know that it involves this place, and the loss of those I loved, and for those who cared for me."

Slow, sad realization began to dawn on Simon. He saw bright lights dancing in the rain, heard the horrible screech of tires. Phantom pains in his neck throbbed. "I, I know how my Journey started, how my soul became trapped here. I know."

Silence from the crowd. Simon did not want to speak, but it was the fear, the fear of death, or whatever was worse than death, that kept him speaking. *If I knew that I could run and escape, I would, but I wouldn't make it ten feet.* Haltingly, Simon continued.

"They didn't know, couldn't know, that I was in no position to drive. It was late, and Dad had had one too many again. We knew that if he didn't come home by a certain time on Fridays, that we were supposed to go get him." Images of a middle-aged man, dark stubble covering his square jaw and the smell of cheap beer and vomit on his breath, falling over himself in dimly lit rooms, filled Simon's mind.

"You see, my father, he would say that he never really made it out, that the war had 'followed him home,' and that the only way to keep the demons at bay was the sweet sadness of whiskey and beer. So, after work on Fridays and every Saturday and Sunday, my dear old dad would find the nearest watering hole and attempt to drink everything in sight. My mother, and later, my mother and I, when I was old enough, would go find him at whatever hole he crawled into and bring him home." Simon chuckled a little inwardly.

"He never drank during the week, to his credit, and the lights were always on, but my mom and I both knew that the weekends were for him and him alone. So, when 11:00 rolled around, my mother put on her raincoat and boots and grabbed the keys. She told me to drive and said, 'I hate driving in the rain, dear. You go ahead and drive.' I should have said no."

Simon could not hold back his heartbreak anymore. Tears fell, unhindered, down his cheeks and onto the ground, and the rest of the tale, like a torrent held back by a small dam, broke and flooded out of him.

"I just wanted to know what it was like! I wanted to know why my dad loved it so much, why he would leave his family every weekend for it. I knew that there was a bottle of Kentucky bourbon under the sink, behind the bleach, that my mom would take a nip of every now and then if life became a little too much.

"So, after school, I took the bottle and hid it in my room. After dinner, I went upstairs, telling my mom I needed to do homework, and grabbed the bottle from its hiding spot. I remember being nervous about it, about how the first taste burned like fire, and the second and third were like … were a warmth that covered my entire body. Before I knew it, I had drunk half of what was left, which would have just been a few drinks at a bar, and was about to finish the second half, when my mom called me down to go pick up my father."

Tears came freely down his face, and Simon did not attempt to hide them.

"I just didn't want to get caught! How stupid is that? I drove us there, picked up my comatose dad, and was driving home. I was feeling good. I was feeling like, like I was going to get away with it. I was getting cocky. I remember taking one hand off the wheel, relaxing back into the old leather seat, and even turning the radio up. 'Good Vibrations' was playing, and it was one of the few hit songs that my mom actually liked. When I looked up and saw the curve, it was too late."

Simon's head became heavy, and his heart fell to his feet. The torches crackled, and Simon's tears reflected off the orange light as they fell to the stone floor.

"My father and I survived, with barely a scratch on either of us. My mom, she wasn't so lucky. The doctors, they said … they said that it was quick."

Sobs wracked Simon, and he fell to his knees. He cried, and the town stared, emotionless eyes drinking in his grief. Simon didn't care who saw him anymore, couldn't remember why he ever cared about anything. All that filled his heart, all that consumed his mind, were grief and regret. He saw his father's eyes, blurry and red, suddenly become clear when he focused on his son. He saw how, after a fleeting touch of concern, the eyes of Simon's father became overwhelmed with grief, then hardened by hatred. He saw those hard eyes in his dreams. The hatred never left the gaze of his father until he died ten years later. *There were only five people at that funeral, including the pastor. My dad looked so small in that box.* Simon cried, and the crowd remained silent.

"I, I never got to say goodbye, never got to show my mother her grandchildren, never got to show her that I had become a man, that I had dedicated my life to helping people. Everything I did seemed like a way to make up for one mistake. A debt I tried to pay with a life of service." Simon's head hung lower, almost touching the tear stained ground.

"My father never forgave me. His hate followed me every day until he finally died a decade later. I couldn't wait to leave my house, to escape the way he looked at me. That is why those close to me keep dying."

Simon suddenly became angry—angry at the world, angry at Scipio, at the people who watched him with an amazing degree of impassivity. *How can they just watch me like that? Watch me, then. To hell with all of you!* A growl escaped his lips. Slowly, he rose back to his feet. His eyes flashed with defiance.

"What are you all staring at? How can you just stare at someone's pain, and do nothing? Have you truly forgotten your humanity?" The crowd remained silent, but their eyes seemed to flash, to absorb Simon's pain.

"To hell with Journeys, with facing my past, with trying to fix something that cannot be fixed. My parents died because of me! Is that what you want to hear? Do you want to hear me admit that my mom's death was my fault, and that my father died with her, and it just took some time for his body to catch up? My father died hating me, and I can't even blame him for it."

Simon's voice rose higher and higher, until he was shouting. "To hell with everyone. Jesus Christ, stop staring at me!"

Simon stopped, his chest heaving, beads of sweat blooming on his forehead. The crowd remained silent and staring. The world seemed frozen in place. The only sound was the torches crackling and popping as they burned.

"You see, Simon? Now you know what your Journey is, what you are called to, why people will be called to you. And now, you can avoid it, escape it, and live forever!"

Scipio had stepped forward again, his hand coming to rest on Simon's shoulder. He lifted the blade, stained with red, and spun it in his hands so the handle faced Simon. "Take this back and join us. Become one with us, and never face the fear of death, of true death, again."

Simon mechanically reached out and gripped the well-worn handle. *That's it? I'm a part of this place now? They're not going to kill me or do whatever else these sick bastards are into?*

Simon rose, the knife in his hand, and wondered why relief did not come, why he did not feel anything at all. His tears still stained his face, his heart still hammered in his chest, but instead of sickening pain or numbing fear, he felt hollow, swallowed by a great emptiness that was born out of where his heart used to be. His mind danced about, throwing pictures and half-remembered words onto the walls of his consciousness.

Images of his mother flitted through his mind, splicing together moments of joy and peace with the moment when she stared at him, eyes wide in terror, as life slid through her grasp and disappeared forever. He saw his father, his stoic, quiet father, with a face that seemed to become weighed down over the years with hatred and loathing, until his tired body simply gave up. Simon remembered the moment his father passed away, about how the old man seemed *relieved* to be free of life. Simon had envied him in that moment, and he did not know why.

I'm sorry, Dad. I'm sorry, Mom. I'm sorry. Why did you have to leave me? Why did you have to hate me? I didn't know it would end that way! Please, please forgive me. I wish I could have made it right, could have somehow atoned for my mistakes.

It was with shocking revelation that Simon truly saw just how much the single event in his life had redirected his course. Like an inky darkness, it had seeped into his marriage, how he spoke to his children, how he treated the men and women at work. It drove him to join the force, to try to find a way to ease the hole in his heart. A single decision dictated so much. *How could I have not seen it?*

Simon looked out at the quiet crowd, his hand on his knife, his heart in his throat. The crowd had remained motionless, yet their eyes had become more eager, and Simon sensed that the group was waiting for him to do *something,* yet he did not know what.

A rustle occurred to Simon's right, and a section of the crowd moved aside so that a large man, blond beard nearly touching his chest, could step onto the stone circle. Corded muscles flexed in arms as large as Simon's legs as they carried a small human form, its head covered with a sack. The huge man dumped his burden on the ground and forced his captive to its knees. Whipping the hood away, corded muscles and beard stepped back, eyes on Simon as he crossed his gargantuan arms. The fire made his eyes take on the color of obsidian.

An older woman, her hair white and dashed about by the sudden movement of the sack, blinked her eyes in the torchlight. Liver-spotted hands with long, bony fingers reached out from her long robe, pleading for aid with their movement.

"Please, take my life," she begged. "It is not right. It is not right! They have done nothing wrong!" Still on her knees, the old woman's eyes darted about, looking for a kind face in the crowd. Her robe, once white but now stained with dirt and refuse, swung about as she moved. Finding no one to help her, she turned her gaze upon Simon, eyes going wide when she saw the knife in his hand.

"You! Kill me, please. They said that if you were to kill me, they would let them go—let them live. Please, they are just children! Who can do this to children, even here? They won't even let them die! They are alone in the dark, suffering. Please, help them. Please!"

Simon, terrified and confused, remained still, his eyes first focusing on the now-prostrate woman and then slowly moving to look at Scipio, whose hand was still on his shoulder. The shirtless man's smile made Simon's stomach flip.

"We always love giving newcomers a chance to choose wisely, because, as I am sure you have guessed, only so many people make it to Dara. Newness is precious, especially to those of us who wish to stay here, unlike the fools who simply wish to die, or disappear." Scipio's mouth twitched. "So, we want to give you a choice, now that we have you all to ourselves." Scipio's hands opened wide, palms facing upwards. The woman on the ground whimpered, so he gave her a sharp kick until she fell on her hands and knees at Simon's feet.

"We always *procure* a few options when we discover that someone has recently come to Dara. This woman represents your commitment to your new life, your willingness to go against your Journey to survive and continue here forever." Scipio's eyes flashed. "She is a Nurturer, a caregiver to many. She wishes to live long so that she can see her 'offspring' live long and prosperous lives, as that is what she believes her life was lacking in the old world. In response, Rix and I" Scipio jerked a thumb toward the large bearded man "stole her children and placed them in the darkest, largest hole we could find. Kill her and we will let them go free." Scipio reached forward and placed his hand on Simon's shoulder.

The hand gave a squeeze that might have been meant to be reassuring, but to the youth, it felt like the mouth of a predator testing to see how easy it would be to snap the bones of its prey. *Jesus Christ, who else did they procure for me?* Simon shuddered.

"Oh, and one more thing," Scipio continued, "If you do not kill her, then we will torture and kill her children in front of her. One of our number has a weird fascination with keeping people alive and removing their appendages, and he is *dying* for some new playmates. There really is nothing stronger than a mother's love."

A man in the depths of the crowd fidgeted, then stepped back quickly. Simon saw a splash of black hair and broad shoulders before the man slid away.

"Now choose, though it is no choice." Hand still on Simon's shoulder, Scipio fell silent, waiting for Simon's reply.

Simon looked at the old woman kneeling before him and felt his hand grip the knife handle so hard that his knuckles turned white. His heart was a bird trying to jump out of his rib cage, and sweat flowed with his tears. His legs had deadened beneath him.

Think of the kids; think of the kids. If I don't do this, I will be sentencing them to die a death I can't even imagine. Yet when he tried to move, Simon's legs felt as though his feet had become encased in lead, and the bones of his legs transformed into wet spaghetti. He was surprised that he was even standing. *Jesus Christ, what am I to do? What do I do? I'm sorry. I'm sorry. Someone, please help!*

Slowly, woodenly, Simon finally forced his feet to move, and soon he stood over the woman, whose eyes lifted up to his. Scipio's hand felt heavy on his shoulder, and Simon realized that the shirtless man must have followed his movement. *Psycho wants a front-row seat,* Simon thought as he looked down. The woman's eyes were kind and dark—the eyes of a mother, of a woman who loves. Simon took a deep breath and prepared to perform the unthinkable.

As he loomed over the old woman, towering above her so that she had to crane her neck to look at him with large, pleading eyes, Simon experienced the overwhelming sensation that he had been forced into a gelatinous bubble. Time seemed to slow as he stood over her, and the air around him became heavy. The knife in his hand was a stone dragging him to the depths of the ocean, and he had to strain to lift the blade over his head. Flashes of green caught his peripheral vision, and he glanced at his wrist and then found himself staring at the singed emerald cloth that fluttered in the ever-present breeze.

"Please. End it. Let the children live, please." The woman's voice had become a whisper, fear choking her words as she spoke, yet Simon barely heard her. Fixated on the ribbon on his wrist, Simon heard another voice, the voice of a child on a bridge, telling him of the purpose of Thales's sacrifice. He looked back down at the woman and took a deep breath.

An idea had blossomed within Simon's mind. He did not know where it came from, yet it felt *right.* Its beautiful simplicity, the majestic ease of its truth, dried Simon's eyes and straightened his spine. His legs were relieved of their leaden weight and were replaced by the soft touch of clouds. He locked eyes with someone directly across from him—a woman, her hair dark as a starless night and eyes beady and murderous.

"You are all cowards. Horrible, *despicable* cowards," he said, staring at the dark-haired woman but speaking to the gathered crowd. The woman's gaze, harsh and full of malice, narrowed slightly, and a small ripple cascaded through the crowd. Scipio removed his hand from Simon's shoulder and stepped back, laughing a mirthless laugh.

"Scared of death? Of course we are! Why would we not be scared of true death?" Scipio's retort sent small ripples of subdued laughter through the throng of people.

"Not just death, of *yourselves*. You aren't scared to die; you are scared to *live*—scared to face the truths of the world, of the memories that haunt you. Like rats you hide here, literally under a hill, away from the light, away from the reality of the world. You can't face the truth, so you hide from it with your pleasures and your horrible acts, and you lie to yourselves, saying that it is a way to create *paradise!* Ha!" It was now Simon's turn to laugh bitterly.

"And I, I was no better. I hid from the fact that I never got over my mother's death, or my father's hatred. It ruined my marriage, messed up the way I dealt with the world, and hurt those I cared for the most. All because I couldn't come to terms with my loss, with my horrible mistake. I did not *grow* from my life's errors and mistakes; I allowed myself to be *stuck* by them.

"And now ..." Simon's hands swept wide, enveloping the now-churning crowd. "... you wish me to continue doing the things that ruined my life in the first place. You want me to join you by sticking my head in the sand. I will not. I accept my fate and the fate of this woman. I accept the truth of the world, of my faults. I understand, and I am not afraid!"

Scipio stepped forward again, and Simon's wrist twitched. Almost without thought, the blade lashed out, and its biting edge opened Scipio's throat. Blood spurted from the wound as the man, eyes wide in shock, brought his hands up to his neck in a vain attempt to close the hole that had been unzipped by the knife's edge. Simon and the crowd stared as red liquid covered Scipio's chest and arms with an unbelievable speed and dripped onto the stone circle at their feet. Skin, fabric, and sandals flailed about as the flow of life leaked from

Scipio's throat. With a final gurgle, the kilted man stumbled and fell to the stone floor, his limp body making a hard thud as it crumpled to the ground. The crowd encircling the stone slab seemed to inhale all at once, sucking the air out of the world.

Simon, turning to look at the kneeling woman, was surprised to find her standing, eyes still locked onto his face, hands outstretched. "Why would you do this? You have doomed the children to a fate worse than death!"

Simon swept his free arm to encompass the crowd. The other was sticky with the quickly drying blood of Scipio. "Do you think they would actually let them go free? Do you think that there was any chance for them not to suffer? To be in their hands *is* to suffer, and they would not allow one of their own to not be given a chance to play their twisted little games. They would just kill you as well, and probably make me watch, make it a point of showing me that they are only interested in their own wants." Simon took a breath. The woman continued to stare at him.

"But, as my father left me to my fate, refusing to shield me or guide me from the world, when I needed him most, I cannot possibly do the same for these children. So, ma'am, I have only one question: have you ever heard of glass?" When the woman dumbly shook her head, Simon smiled, and closed his eyes

He thought of Mary and Thales, and their lessons. He remembered that he must keep in mind the rules of the object he was to change. He reached deep into the very molecular structure of the sand surrounding him, and forced the building blocks of each grain to speed up exponentially. Soon the surface outside a small circle that was populated by the old woman, himself, and the corpse of Scipio, was a shimmering, clear floor. The people had cried out first in pain at the heat, then in amazement at the beautiful glass. Simon, seeing the crowd looking downward, seized upon his chance and forced out a singular word to the floor of glass.

Shatter.

Screams erupted into the twilight as hundreds of feet became impaled by razor sharp shards. The screaming and wailing became a din as Simon released the shattering glass and turned his attention to the ever present wind of Dara, gripping it tightly with his mind. He felt beads of sweat slide down his forehead as he grabbed as much of the wind as he could, enveloping all of the spectators with it, muffling their screams. He opened his palms, mimicking a separation. *Like the red sea* he thought dully, but he could not remember why. Then, with force, he clapped his hands together and willed the wind, now a storm of razor sharp glass, to cut through the people of Nisadi with incredible speed and force. What was once a cacophony of wails and screams became a deafening silence.

Without another word, desperately fighting exhaustion, Simon grabbed the old woman, leapt over the writhing bodies surrounding him, and landed on the path from which he came. He took off at a sprint, his cargo still draped over his shoulder.

"Quickly, do you know where the children are?"

"No, but I can guess. There is a pit. Take a left here, and run. *Run.*"

Simon sprinted, and was amazed at how light he felt. He had exposed the darkest secrets of his life to a crowd of strangers, had admitted his greatest weakness, yet somehow felt so, *light.* He ran harder and harder, until it seemed as though his feet barely touched the ground.

"Stop here."

Simon abruptly ceased his locomotion and placed the old woman gently to her feet and looked around. He was surrounded by the strange flowers that gave off the pale glow of Nisadi, and as his eyes adjusted to the change in lighting, Simon saw that they were spiraling inward, stopping at a hole that was darker than the inkiest blackness Simon had ever experienced.

"They are down there. I know it." The woman was by Simon's side, staring down into the abyss with him. Her high cheekbones and tear drop eyes stood out starkly because of the pale light. "Please, please save them."

Simon called down, but heard nothing. The wailing behind him seemed to have abated somewhat, which made him nervous. *I have a feeling that my stunt won't hold them off forever.* Simon looked back down into the darkness.

"You are sure they are down there?"

"No, I am not, but if they are down there, you must save them. Please."

"Where would they be if not down here?"

"I do not know, but I will find them. You have killed almost the entire village of Nisadi, which will give me time. That is all I require." The woman drew herself up, "but we must see if they are in this darkness first."

Simon looked down, and fear threatened to envelop his senses. He called down, and heard nothing yet again. Moments passed, and Simon soon found himself laughing.

"What is funny? Please, we must find them." Fear was soaking the woman's eyes, an emotion that Simon no longer felt.

"I am laughing because it is a leap of faith. I have to save these children, though I don't know if they are even down there. I must be the man that my father never could be. I must."

Simon, unsure where that realization even came from but realizing it was true nonetheless, stood even straighter. His arms and chest had taken on the lightness of his legs. He felt as if his bones were replaced by air. The woman, hearing the truth of Simon's words, nodded. Simon, taking a deep breath, leapt into the abyss.

I should be scared right now. I should be terrified. Why am I not scared? Why am I so ... light?

The world seemed to slow to a crawl as Simon floated downward, looking for the children but knowing that they were not to be found there. *I know that she will find them. I know they will be alright. I have done what I could.* His falling seemed to slow, and before long, Simon felt as though he was no longer falling, but floating in a sea of darkness.

Nothingness can sometimes be felt with more effect and power than the most exquisite ecstasy or the most horrendous agony. The complete *lack* of feeling can overwhelm the senses just as much as any other actual sensation the world can invoke. Simon felt the lightness overtake what was left of his physical self, felt the darkness form a kind of impenetrable, safe cocoon around him.

Simon, his body slowly becoming less and less permanent, felt himself, the essence of who he was, also begin to disappear. *It's like dying over again, but peaceful. I want to go. I feel right.* Suddenly, Simon's thoughts turned to Anna, turned to his mother and father, turned to the people he loved. *I hope they went like this. I hope that most people go like this. Just, peace.* Simon smiled again and closed his eyes. Soon, who he was, who he had become, simply ceased to be.

CHAPTER XVIII-OF STARS

This time, there was no life flashing before the mind's eye. This time, there was no fear of finality. This time, Simon, or what was once Simon, simply was somewhere else. There was no body, no attachment to gender, race, or age; there was only Thought. The Thought that was once Simon simply evaporated from one realm and appeared in another, more fluid space. The Thought that was Simon slid into the current of eternity and traveled into a realm outside of all things. It could observe, but it was separate.

The Thought traveled the length and breadth of the universe. Life across all of space danced before it, and it slid between eons as easily as breathing. The Thought reveled in this new power, in the eternal scope of its movement.

Time did not exist in this realm, not as most life understood it, but change did. The Thought that was Simon, after skirting through space and time at the speed of its imagination, realized that it wasn't alone. There was another presence, another force, that resided with it. The Thought felt the power of the Being and understood it to be there. To feel fear or awe was too base an emotion for the Thought to possess, but it realized that the Being was of immense power and importance. The Thought that was Simon allowed its awareness to stretch to the Being, waited for it to communicate. Soon, the Being spoke, and the words became matter. Truth poured out of the Being and flooded the Thought.

"I am Choice. I am born of the consciousness of all sentience from all planes. Ever since the first entity became aware of itself, I was born. Once beings became aware and could understand, Choice came into existence.

No longer ruled by the instinctual drive of their genetic coding, one could truly Choose how to live, how to die. That is when I came to be."

The universe moved around Choice, and the Thought that was Simon knew its words to be true.

"Now that you have lived, have died, have Ascended, and completed your Journey, you have come to the Choice. Listen well and Choose."

The words were not spoken, but were simply fundamental truth. The Thought saw its life, the life of an organic, finite being, drawn out from the depths of its memory. The Thought saw its first birth and knew that it had once been male. That infant's mind was nothing more than impulse and survival. The Thought was amused at just how basic and simple its mind once was. The Thought saw the mind grow and change, ingesting new stimuli and interpreting it to form the bedrock of personality. It saw the mind develop its own motivations and desires, its own myths and deep truths. The years moved as fast as moments and as slow as millennia as the Thought watched.

The Thought, now a boy, began to see the world around and was able to make judgment, to understand, and to love. The boy loved his parents, loved his family, and from that love grew hope and faith. But this love was also sharp, and the Thought watched as the love was used to hurt and manipulate the boy. The Thought watched through the eyes of a terrified child as a drunken father shook him and slapped him in the face, yelling that he never really wanted children. The Thought felt the pain and felt the love of the boy retreat, but not disappear. It felt the love come back when the father embraced the boy the next day, sobbing a thousand apologies into the boy's blue shirt.

The years passed, and the boy became a youth who became a man. His love spread to those around him, to friends and mentors and lovers, and his heart was at peace. Stubble sprang out of his chin, and shoulders broadened. The Thought felt the young man change into someone who no longer simply understood the world around him, but could influence and change it. Then, the Thought saw the Moment of Ascension, and the Moment of Definition, loom bright in the young man's life: one bright and powerful as a diadem, the other dark and destructive as a black hole. Slowly, The Moment of Definition spread its inky tendrils into every moment of the young man's life.

Every memory, every encounter, every change in the man's life was now tainted with this singular moment. Relationships, love, family— it all carried the ghost of the man's mother. He had become stuck, and his spirit could not continue its growth. The Thought watched a stunted life unfold, marred by grief, until cancer came and ate the vessel from within. The Thought watched, and it understood. It understood that this Journey could only become complete with a second chance, with a second mother and a second father, and a choice to become someone that the young man never had. It understood that all of humanity cannot find its peace without the help of others, and that Thales and Mary had helped what was once Simon Floyd to complete his Journey. The Thought understood, and relished in its peace.

Images of the world that had once been Simon's home, of the plane called Earth, flitted around the infinite consciousness called Choice. It spoke, and as it did, pictures of humanity from across the planet danced near it.

"Sadly, so few of your species have managed to Ascend past the pull of their base instincts, to reach beyond the control of their primal selves. They live, and they die, and that is all. Without the drive to Ascend, to reach above, planes such as Dara will disappear and die, and there will only be true death for all."

The being paused, and the Thought that was Simon felt the rush of sadness from it, a sorrow the size of a sentient star understanding its demise.

"You may, if you wish, Return to the world of the humans, and try to guide them to the next plane, direct them to the place after death. Or, you may join the current around you and simply be a part of the fabric of the universe. You may visit an untold number of worlds, see the edges of what is, and find peace. Choose."

The being ceased speaking, and it was the Thoughts turn to speak, though it had no mouth. The words simply became manifest, and Choice answered.

"No, there is no guarantee that people will believe you. Many have tried and have been killed, banished, or deemed simply insane. You will not come back as yourself; you will be in a completely new body. Gender and physicality mean little when you know the secrets of the universe. Choose."

The Thought felt the life it had lived before Dara, of the world it had left behind. It had died, alone in a hospital bed, with no one around to watch it go, to ease its pain. It wondered why it should Return to such a place. Its imagination wandered to all the wonders the universe had to offer. If it simply let go and allowed himself to flow into it, everything and anything could be explored.

Yet, just as it was about to choose to wander the universe forever, about to disappear into the tapestry of time and space, it thought of Thales, of Mary, of those who had loved and sacrificed for it. It thought of Anna, of children and grandchildren. How wonderful would it have been if there were someone who could have told those it loved that there was a chance to live past the moment of death? How amazing would it have been if its mother understood that life wasn't the only chance humanity had to grow? Its family's faces made a glowing halo around it, and the current that it and Choice rested in seemed to brighten and explode into the stars of a billion souls. For some reason, that still did not feel enough.

"Think of your Journey. Think of why you are here." Choice's words pierced the Thought.

Images of the Thought's father bled into the space it resided, a current of images, sounds, and feelings. How those moments of unrequited love had broken its spirit over and over again. What if it could alter that for someone else, to show that there is love and peace from a creature greater than oneself, just as Thales and Mary did? What if it could help fill that void in a dozen people? A thousand? A million? The light around the Thought began to glow bright, and a choice was made.

"It is done. You will be given gifts to help those around you, if you can discover how to use them. You will be granted the joys and pains of humanity once again and must live with everything that entails. You have chosen, and I bid you safe Return."

Searing white light enveloped all that was, and the Thought that was Simon felt the current move once again. To a beginning once more.

End of Book One

CPSIA information can be obtained
at www.ICGtesting.com
Printed in the USA
LVHW091809080421
683893LV00022B/536/J